From
Something
Old

ALSO BY NICK ALEXANDER

From Something Old

nick alexander

LAKE UNION
PUBLISHING

Text copyright © 2021 by Nick Alexander
All rights reserved.

Published by Lake Union Publishing, Seattle

www.apub.com

Amazon, the Amazon logo, and Lake Union Publishing are trademarks of Amazon.com, Inc., or its affiliates.

ISBN-13: 9781542026840
ISBN-10: 1542026849

Cover design by @blacksheep-uk.com

Cover illustration by Jelly London

Printed in the United States of America

From
Something
Old

One

Heather

Do you believe in ghosts? I don't. Or at least, I don't think I do.

Perhaps that means that I believe in premonitory dreams, or just freakily unlikely coincidences, because this, I swear, is true: a few days after her death, my mother spoke to me. Whether she appeared inside a dream or in what we like to call 'real life' remains unclear to me. I suppose we'll never know which of those it was, so you'll have to choose what you want to believe, or, like me, *not* choose and just wonder about it for ever more.

Whatever the explanation, the experience felt shockingly real. I saw her in front of me – she was semi-transparent as if made not of atoms but of light, and she was smiling. She walked towards me and paused before continuing until we were taking up the same physical space. I could sense her presence glowing and swelling within me as she expanded outwards into my fingers and toes.

I felt shocked, I remember, but the overriding feeling was one of being ecstatic to the point of tears to discover that she still existed, that despite the fact we had buried her in the cold hard earth a few days earlier, she could still visit me, be with me, be *within* me, even. It felt as if she was using my eyes to take one last look at the world she had recently left, and she was loving it.

As my body throbbed with the warm glow of her presence, I discovered that she could speak to me too, much as you might speak to yourself when debating what to do about some difficult situation. 'Don't worry,' her voice said within the confines of my head. 'Things will get worse, but then they'll get better because you'll go with the . . . and be happy.'

By the time I woke up the next morning, Mum was gone for good, and as I said before, I couldn't tell if she'd really been there or if I'd dreamed her up. More importantly, nor could I remember that missing word, the one that would supposedly lead to my happiness.

It turned out, much later, that there was a perfectly good reason why I couldn't remember that word: it was a term I never used. In fact, I don't think I had ever come across it until that day, which is perhaps the strongest indication that this wasn't a dream manufactured by my own mind but something that came from an external source. Another sign was that the thing she was referring to hadn't happened yet, which would seem to reinforce the other-worldly origin of the message. But when I finally did understand what she'd said, it would make more sense to me than anything else in my life ever had.

I tried many times to plug that gap, made hundreds of attempts at understanding Mum's message. But nothing that I could think of – go with *the flow*, for example, or go with *your feelings* – seemed to work. Go with *the postman* . . . go with *grace*, none of it made any sense. In fact, as time went by, Mum's message became more and more incomprehensible, because the final part of her revelation, the *be happy* bit, seemed to be getting not closer, but further away.

But I'm getting ahead of myself, aren't I? Because for me to explain how complicated being happy was, I need to tell you the whole story. And to do that, I need to dig deep and admit that I wasn't always unhappy with my lot. In fact, for a while back there, I thought I'd struck lucky.

I'll start my story, then, in 2009 – the year I met Anthony.

My mother was still in perfect health, or at any rate we thought she was. The beginnings of her illness must have been present, I suppose, already pushing out roots and dropping deadly seeds that would float around her body before settling and pushing out roots of their own, but we certainly didn't know that back then.

My father had died three years earlier and Mum was enjoying a brief renaissance, having been liberated from his toxic presence by the very thing that had made him toxic in the first place: he'd died, you see, of alcohol poisoning. Is the fact that the thing which made him so hateful is also the thing that took him from us ironic, or simply logical? I'm still not sure.

Anyway, Mum – a gentle soul who had mistakenly devoted her life to a man who loved vodka more than he loved her – surprised my sister and me with an unexpected capacity to adapt to an alcoholic-husband-free life. Within a month of his death she had signed up for gym sessions and fine-art evening classes. And within six, she was taking her first ever overseas holidays with the new friends she had made.

Dad's illness hadn't only polluted Mum's life, of course.

When I was five, he'd left my sister and me alone in the Dorchester Arms. He'd told us he was nipping to the cashpoint, but never returned. At closing time the barman had phoned Mum so that she could come and pick us up in a taxi. She'd been incandescently angry, and she and Dad had screamed at each other until the sun came up the next day.

When I was seven, Mrs Wilson had caused a scandal by refusing to hand us over at the school gates because Dad couldn't walk without zigzagging, and by age eighteen, I was repeatedly picking him up from the police station after he'd spent a night in the cells, or settling his debts at various pubs to avoid them calling the police in the first place. And these, my friends, are just highlights – simply

3

the first awful memories that come to mind, to give you a taste, so to speak. Because the drama, the *trauma*, was incessant. Dad's alcoholism had been the dominant, most reliable constant of our day-to-day lives for as long as any of us could remember.

It will sound awful to anyone who hasn't lived through that kind of chaos, but as frequently as I have thought of Dad and missed him, I've remembered the fact that he's dead and sensed the fear I'd got used to slipping blissfully from my shoulders, like a well-worn cloak. Until he died, we'd lived in constant dread of answering the phone, you see. We never knew quite what form the next episode of drama would take, nor when it would occur. And to realise that was over was a source of sadness but also great relief.

By 2009 Dad had been gone for three years, so I too was in full flow, finally enjoying my all-new drama-free life. I was nursing at Canterbury Hospital, and had moved to a cute flat above a trendy record shop in Castle Street.

I believed, back then, that the bad times were over. I thought that all the anguish and misery in our lives had vanished the moment Dad downed his final half-bottle of vodka. But his shadow – or, more precisely, the shadow of our upbringing – was just snoozing, as it turned out. It was just having a kip beneath a tree while it dreamed up new ways to ruin my life.

I first laid eyes on Anthony in a DIY superstore, of all places. I'd been living in Castle Street for almost a year and had finally decided to install a toilet roll holder. Though leaving the roll on the floor hadn't much bothered me, my sister had given me a kitten – Dandy – for Christmas. Because Dandy's main joy in life seemed to be ripping the toilet paper to shreds, getting it out of his reach had become essential.

In B&Q's bathroom aisle there were a surprising – some would say *unreasonable* – number of different options to choose from, running from a £1.49 pink plastic affair to a 'deluxe' chrome-plated model at £14.99. Disappointingly, none of them was reduced in the January sale.

The problem I faced was that they all required screwing to the wall, and as drilling into tiles, using Rawlplugs and all the other kerfuffle that went with it had been Dad's exclusive domain, I was at a bit of a loss to know how to proceed. As I studied the instructions on the back of each blister pack, I began to think about how much I missed him. After what I said previously, that may sound contradictory, but my feelings about Dad would come and go in waves: relief that he was gone, then sadness at his absence, and occasionally a specific kind of overwhelming grief, not so much for who he had been, or for what our relationship had held, but for who he *might* have been, the kind of relationship we *could* have had, if only things had been different. By things being different, I suppose I mean if Dad had been an entirely different person.

Anyway, amid these conflicting thoughts and feelings actual tears were welling up, there in the bathroom fittings section of B&Q, prompting the man beside me to ask if I was all right.

'I'm sorry?' I asked, turning, only to realise that my vision was too blurry to actually see.

'You just look a bit . . .' he said, sounding hesitant, '. . . overwrought . . . maybe?'

I wiped away the tears with my sleeve and studied the man. He was tall, athletic, red-headed and elegantly dressed. He smiled at me kindly, confusedly, and the skin around his blue eyes wrinkled a little. He was five or six years older than me, I guessed, and he had a hint of what sounded like a Liverpudlian accent.

I forced a smile. 'Oh! My eyes . . . ?' I asked, embarrassedly faking a laugh. 'It's just an allergy. I'm fine. Really.'

'What are you allergic to?' he asked. 'Toilet roll holders?'

'Oh . . . no . . .' I spluttered, before realising that this had been a joke. I've always been a bit slow on the uptake, joke-wise. 'Allergic to the idea of fixing one to the wall, maybe?' I offered, attempting a joke of my own.

The man smiled more broadly and held out a big hand with long fingers and manicured fingernails. I remember thinking that his nails were in a better state than my own. 'Anthony,' he said, 'but everyone calls me Ant.'

'Heather,' I replied, shaking his hand loosely and blushing.

'Some of them just stick on,' he explained, nodding towards the wall of toilet roll dispensers. 'They come with double-sided tape. So you could avoid the whole drilling thing that way if you want.'

'Yeah?' I said. 'I haven't found a stick-on one yet.' And so Anthony helped me look until we had confirmed that there was in fact no such option, at least not today, not here, not in B&Q.

'You no good with a drill, then?' he asked finally. 'Cos I think it's going to be your only option.'

I shook my head. 'I'm more likely to drill the cat than the wall.'

'I could give you a hand, maybe,' he offered. 'I'm quite good at that stuff. If you live around here?'

'Oh, um, thanks,' I said. I could feel myself blushing again, and my awareness of it only made me blush even more. 'That's really nice of you, but . . . I'm sure I'll be fine.'

Anthony shrugged and smiled again, but I was desperate to escape the moment, so I dropped the package I was currently holding into my basket – it was, unfortunately, the deluxe model – and ran for the tills. 'You, um, have a good day!' I offered over my shoulder as I escaped. I did not look back. I was hating myself for running away even before I had realised that was what I was doing.

I was still single, after all. Being normally constituted, I was also gagging for my romantic life to begin and, at thirty-three years old, this was indisputably overdue. But Dad's illness had punched a hole in all our lives. For the longest time, everything had been put on hold and, in my case, this included being able to cope with the complication of a man in my life or indeed developing any sense of self-confidence that would enable me to chat one up. Sometimes I even feared that my childhood had somehow left me broken, and that I'd never be able to have a meaningful relationship. Anyway, the moment had begun to feel excruciating and I had run. It was pathetic, I knew it, but it hadn't felt like a choice.

Once outside, I began to chide myself, muttering, 'Stupid, stupid woman!' as I marched through the drizzle towards the bus stop, yet by the time I got home with my pointless purchase – even if I'd known how to drill holes in the wall tiles, I didn't have a drill – objectivity was setting in. Anthony had been out of my league anyway. There was no way that an athletic, red-headed alpha male in an expensive suit would be interested in little old me, so why worry about it? Oh, he'd *flirted* with me all right, but men like that will flirt with anything in a skirt, just to prove that they can. I knew from experience that the story would have ended at the precise moment Anthony felt he'd succeeded, at the exact moment I'd succumbed to his indisputable charm.

I don't think I'm being falsely modest here, either. I'm just being honest and objective by stating that I'm a very ordinary woman. I know that's an unfashionable thing to say these days; I know we're supposed to big up just how unique and fabulous we all are, but I'm not ashamed or embarrassed to admit that I'm nothing special.

I'm a small woman, a smidgin under five feet tall, and of average intellect. I did neither well nor particularly badly at school and my parents were neither rich nor poor. My hair isn't bombshell blonde nor sultry black but brown ('mousy' is the technical term,

I believe), and it's neither straight nor frizzy but a special kind of wavy that looks unkempt in virtually all circumstances. My eyes are a not unpleasant aqueous colour that can look blue, or green, or grey, depending on the weather and what I'm wearing. Anyway, you get the picture: I'm pretty unexceptional and I've known that for as long as I can remember.

Viking descendants like Anthony, on the other hand, *are* exceptional, so it didn't seem to take a genius to work out that he was not destined for me.

The tall, square-shouldered, beautifully dressed men might *eye up* women like me occasionally – for kicks, or out of habit. But the women they date – even more so the women they *marry* – are, and always have been, those same girls we both envied and *hated* at school: the ones with the tiny waists and the perfectly aligned teeth; the ones whose fathers bought them cars for their eighteenth birthdays. In short, men like Anthony choose the same girls, the ones who always got picked first for netball practice back in the day. And there's no point complaining about it because that's just how life is.

The next time I saw Anthony was outside the cinema ten days later.

I was queuing with my friend Sheena, a cheeky nurse from work who I got on really well with. We were waiting to see a film with Nicole Kidman and Hugh Jackman. It was an icy-cold January day, but for the time being the forecast rain remained thankfully absent.

'How's the bog roll holder?' a voice asked, and I turned to see Anthony standing on the pavement beside me. He was wearing pointy, shiny shoes and a full-length woollen overcoat, the kind of thing American lawyers wear in films.

'Oh, hello!' I said, flushing with my habitual embarrassment.

'Well?' he prompted. 'Did you get it done?'

'It's, um, still in the box,' I admitted.

Sheena was looking at me questioningly, silently waiting to be introduced, so I sent her a complex stare that was supposed to communicate the fact that I'd explain everything later.

But Sheena had no intention of being left out. 'Hello, I'm Sheena,' she said, fluttering her lashes, despite the fact that she'd been in a relationship with her partner for almost a decade.

Anthony dragged his attention from me and shook her hand briefly, then glanced in my direction again. 'You should have let me fix it for you,' he said. 'I did offer.'

'Are you coming to see *Australia* with us?' Sheena asked, pouting slightly and subtly pushing one hip out. Her flirting was starting to annoy me.

'Um?' Anthony said. 'Oh, no! No, I was just walking past and I spotted Heather here.' I was shocked that he'd remembered my name.

'You could come anyway,' Sheena said. 'It's supposed to be really good.'

Anthony glanced up at the poster above our heads, momentarily considering it, I think. But then he said, 'Nah. Not really my sort of film.'

The queue suddenly shuffled forward and, as ever, desperate to end the embarrassment of talking to a man, I faked a laugh and said, 'Well, it was good to see you,' before staring at my feet, then at Sheena, and finally turning resolutely towards the front of the queue.

'Call me sometime,' Anthony said. He was holding out a business card. 'Let me give you some DIY tips.'

'You get my vote, honey,' Sheena said, taking the card. I snatched it from her and slipped it into my coat pocket. 'Thanks,' I told Anthony, hoping it would get rid of him, 'I will.' At that moment the queue moved forward again, and as we'd reached the glass door into the lobby I gave him a fingertip wave and stepped inside.

I stared at my feet for a moment longer until I saw from the corner of my vision that he had swooshed away in his long coat.

When I looked up, Sheena was frowning at me. 'Was that the bloke from Homebase you told me about?' she asked. 'The one who wanted to put up your bog roll holder?'

'B&Q,' I said, 'not Homebase.'

'Don't just do it, B&Q it,' she said salaciously. 'He's *hot*.'

'He's a property developer,' I commented. I'd pulled the card from my pocket and was studying it. His surname was Doyle. 'Anthony Doyle,' I murmured out loud. And then, rather pathetically, I couldn't resist trying out another combination in my mind. *Heather Doyle*. It didn't sound so bad.

'He's *smoking* hot,' Sheena said. 'You should get in there. I bloody would.'

'I know *you* would, even though you're married!' I said. She was reaching out for the card, so I slipped it back into my pocket.

'I'm not actually *married* . . .' she said, winking. 'You are going to call him, aren't you?'

I shrugged again.

'God! The way you go on about being single . . .' she said. 'It's all day, every day. It's all you talk about most of the time. How there are no decent men around, or they're all gay, or blah blah blah. And then something like this happens . . . I mean, a good-looking bloke . . . a *very* good-looking bloke, actually. Virtually lapping at your feet and—'

'Please stop,' I said. I'd had these conversations with my nursing friends many times, but they didn't help. My incapacity to find a man always remained as much a mystery to myself as it was to them.

'Get a grip,' Sheena continued. 'Stop acting like an adolescent and just, you know, grab life by the balls. Grab *Anthony* by the balls, for Christ's sake.'

'Just . . . stop!' I said again, more forcefully than I'd intended. 'I know, all right? It's just . . .'

'Just *what*?'

'I'm not convinced, that's all.'

'Something's wrong with you,' Sheena said.

'You think?' I asked, trying to sound sassy.

'You know who you're going to end up like?' she continued. 'Bridget Jones! A hundred years old in a room full of cats. You do realise that, don't you?'

'*Actually*, Bridget ends up with Colin Firth,' I pointed out. But we had reached the ticket booth, so I didn't have to listen to Sheena's depressing view of my future any longer.

The film was a bit of a waste, really. I was too busy thinking about Anthony, about the card in my coat pocket and getting old in a room full of cats. I was too busy thinking about the fact that I was thirty-three, that I'd always imagined having children but was running out of time; about the fact that I'd had sex on only a handful of occasions, and had only ever dated for the sum total of three weeks during nursing college (he'd turned out to be a heavy drinker, which had been a definite no-no). But Sheena was right, something was wrong with me, I had known it for years, and so I spent the rest of the film wondering, not for the first time, if there was some special kind of shrink or dating coach I could consult to get over my fear of talking to men. Because otherwise I really was going to be single *for ever*.

What happened next was entirely Sheena's fault.

We went for coffee after the film and, while I was in the loo, she fished, unbeknown to me, my phone and Anthony's card from my pocket.

I noticed how strangely buoyant she seemed during the half an hour we were together, but I didn't guess why until I got home.

I fed Dandy and sat down on the sofa, and as I reached for the TV remote, my indestructible Nokia buzzed with an incoming SMS.

'Wow. Now there's a programme!' the message read. 'Happy to help. Let me know when you are free.'

I frowned at the screen and, thinking that it was a wrong number, was about to delete the message when it occurred to me to check my own sent message list.

'LOVELY TO SEE U TODAY,' the outgoing text read. 'IF THE OFFERS STILL ON ID LOVE YOU TO TEACH ME HOW TO DRILL. AND SCREW.'

'Oh Christ!' I said out loud, a sickening feeling rising. 'Oh, the cow!' And then I reread the message Sheena had sent and noticed the full stop she had inserted between DRILL. AND SCREW. Typing text messages on a Nokia back then was no mean feat, requiring multiple presses for each letter. Punctuation did not happen by accident. I felt so embarrassed I had to fight back tears.

Anthony, it turned out, really was 'into me', though. Now he had my number, the text messages didn't stop.

His enthusiasm still made no sense to me – I honestly couldn't understand what the attraction was. But after a few days, encouraged, nay *pushed*, by Sheena, I started to go along with it, just to see what would happen. I'd been lonely for too long, I suppose.

Our first official date was in a pretentious restaurant that was basically a pizzeria with candles, though I've nothing against pizza and admit that I rather liked the romantic feel the candles brought to the whole thing.

Anthony was looking good in a dark blue suit with an open-necked shirt. He was polite, chivalrous even, standing behind me to take my coat and then lingering long enough to slide my chair in for me as I sat down. I had never seen anyone actually do that before – well, not outside of a black-and-white film, at any rate. He talked about himself quite a lot, I remember. He told me about growing up in Warrington, and how he was 'making a killing' in property development, which seemed a bit of a brash, bragging thing to say on a date, but being so shy I was basically just happy that he was doing all the talking.

Our second date was in The Millers Arms, and we sat in front of the flickering open fire. Once again, Ant was chatty and animated. Because he was driving back home afterwards, he refused to drink alcohol and that certainly ticked a few boxes as far as I was concerned.

The third date was in Alberrys wine bar, and this time I watched him drink (reasonably) and, understanding the implication that he *wasn't* intending to drive home afterwards, allowed him to ply me with slightly less reasonable quantities of Chardonnay. I watched him walk me home, then invite himself in for coffee. I noticed the gentle presence of his hand on my back as I boiled the kettle to make it.

I was so nervous that I felt as if I had stepped out of my body and was watching what was happening from the outside – watching myself being seduced.

I was surprised, shortly after the coffee, to find myself lying down beneath his tall, slender body; shocked, too, as he entered me, then relieved, I remember, when I grasped that he had managed to fit his not insignificant-looking organ inside me. I'd feared that I was too out of practice to manage it. I thought about asking him to use a condom, but couldn't summon the strength to interrupt something that was, by then, already very much a work in progress.

If something happened as a result, I'd just have to deal with it afterwards.

It was all a little faster than I would have preferred, and just as I was beginning to relax into the moment, I understood that it was over. But I couldn't honestly say I had a problem with any aspect of it. In fact, I liked the sensation of his body, enjoyed the way his vastness so inevitably dominated my tiny frame.

From that point on, we were a couple, and that surprised me as well.

I'm not quite sure what I expected, but I suppose I thought there would be a moment when we'd have to decide whether we were going to go out together or not. I thought there would at least be a moment of conscious decision, a question asked, a reply given, whereas, in fact, our relationship just seemed to happen, like a snowball gathering size as it rolls downhill. It turned out that it was questioning, refusing, or trying to change direction that required effort, and I remember thinking, *It's that easy, huh? Who knew?*

I finally managed to pronounce the word *condom* one evening, but when Ant claimed he couldn't hold an erection while wearing one, I found myself too embarrassed to pursue the subject any further.

I decided I should probably go to the doctor and get a prescription for the pill, but continually forgot to book the appointment in that special way you forget to do things that make you feel uneasy. Each time we had sex, I'd reassure myself by thinking about Sheena, who'd been trying, and failing, to get pregnant for the best part of a decade. It wasn't, it seemed, something that necessarily happened that easily.

A second toothbrush appeared in my bathroom mug. I stared at it as I sat on the loo one morning and wondered if Anthony should have asked me first. Leaving a toothbrush seemed like a definitive marking of territory, like a dog peeing against a lamp post just to show you that it can. But I reminded myself that I was seriously unpractised at this whole dating lark and so I said nothing when a spare shirt appeared in my wardrobe, as socks and underpants and then a tie materialised in the bottom drawer.

About three weeks into what I was finally accepting might be what people call 'a relationship', I woke up to the sound of moving furniture.

'It's better like this,' Ant declared as I entered my lounge. He'd moved the TV to the opposite wall and turned the sofa through ninety degrees. 'You don't get the reflection on the TV screen any more.'

I considered the new layout and decided that I didn't like it at all. But just as I opened my mouth to say so, Ant said, 'I thought we could go out to mine later on. It's about time you saw the place. What d'you think?'

'Oh?' I said. 'Oh, all right then.'

'Yes?' Ant asked, and I realised I'd sounded uncertain. In truth, I'd been beginning to doubt the existence of Ant's 'little cottage' in Sturry, but here it was, an official invitation to visit. I decided I could probably cope with the new furniture configuration for the moment, at least.

'Yes, I'd love to!' I said, correcting my tone of voice. 'That would be great!'

Anthony's car – a spotless grey BMW convertible that looked as if it had never been sat in, let alone driven anywhere – was a shock, but this was as nothing compared to his house. In fact, when he pulled up on the driveway, I assumed we were visiting someone else en route.

'So? What do you think?' he asked, indicating the view of the garage door through the windscreen.

'Is this . . . Oh! This is it?' I asked. 'We're here?'

15

'Of course this is it,' he said, sounding annoyed for the first time since I had met him. 'What were you expecting? Buckingham bloody Palace?'

'Oh, no . . . just . . . nothing so posh,' I lied. 'It looks brand new.'

'It is, pretty much. I bought it on spec. Got a good deal because the developer was going bust.'

I'd expected his 'cottage' in Sturry to look, well, like a cottage. I'd had visions of thatched roofs and low beams, of open fireplaces and those ancient panes of glass that make the world outside look wrinkly. Instead, Ant lived in what could only be described as a new-build bungalow.

Once inside the PVC front door, the surprises kept coming: perfect beige walls, pretty pastel vases, generic art and built-in mood lighting that changed colour at the press of a button. The furniture was modern and looked as if it came from Ikea but was, Ant informed me, Italian. 'It's a damn sight more expensive, of course,' he said, 'but much better quality, too. I like to have the best of everything. It's my philosophy in life.'

I padded on after him (he'd made me leave my shoes in the shoe rack in the hallway) over carpets so thick that walking on them made me feel seasick. In the lounge he proudly showed me enough hi-fi to fill the shelves of a small electrical store, even pressing a button to reveal a cinema screen that dropped from the ceiling.

I pretended to be impressed, but a wave of anxiety was rippling through me. As far as I could see, other than wanting to own the most expensive model of everything, Anthony didn't have any taste at all.

He showed me the bedrooms – they were hotel-like and immaculately tidy (the bed had an electric sitty-uppy device, which he proudly demonstrated) – then the fully equipped kitchen (the fridge was empty – I checked), and then out on to the patio to view his fake plastic lawn.

'I don't have time for gardening,' he explained, 'so this is ideal for me.'

'It's quite realistic,' I said.

In theory, we'd stayed at mine because it was easier for me to get to work, but now I was beginning to question if that was the real reason. The place looked so much like a show home that I was wondering if it was even his.

Anthony slid the window closed behind us – it was freezing out there – and led me back to the front door, where he handed me my shoes from the rack. 'Are we leaving?' I asked.

'Yeah, sorry, I need to see Mum this afternoon,' he said. 'Did I not mention that?' The answer was that, no, he hadn't mentioned it, and I was pretty sure that he knew it.

'You're not upset with me or something, are you?' I asked.

'Nope,' he said, stepping back outside and jangling his keys. 'Why? Should I be?'

Those early days, I tried to put my fears into words, but it was hard, as they weren't that clearly defined even to me. I tried to talk to Mum, to my sister Kerry and to Sheena about it all. But context, I have discovered, is everything, and identical words carry entirely different weights depending on who exactly is speaking them.

So if you're known to have been single *for years*, for example, or to have run away from multiple encounters with the opposite sex, it's hard to sound sane when complaining about your new boyfriend, whatever the cause.

'He's too *tidy*, you say?' Mum said, and in her echoing of my words down the phone line, I could hear exactly how delusional I sounded. 'He has too much hi-fi . . . *right*,' Kerry would say flatly,

17

valiantly struggling to understand, and prompting me to drop the subject immediately.

These days, things have changed, and I seem to have earned the right to have a judgement on such matters. So when I tell the story, instead of frowning at me, people repeat my words in horror. 'His CDs were in *alphabetical order*?' they gasp. 'His books were organised by *colour*? That should have set alarm bells ringing – didn't it?' But back then, it really wasn't the case.

'You're having doubts because he has two soap dishes?' I remember Sheena saying mockingly. And though she was missing the point of how utterly, freakily terrifying it was for a thirty-eight-year-old man to have two soap dishes so that he, or rather his cleaner, could cycle them twice-weekly through the dishwasher, I'd replied, 'You're right, I'm being silly.' And faced with so much doubt, I did my best to convince myself that this was true.

'But is he nice to you?' Mum had asked me, interrupting me during one of my rambling whinges. And the only honest answer I'd been able to give at that point was, 'Yes, he's nice to me.'

'Well, then!' she had said. 'Think yourself lucky. A kind, sober man is a rare find. And if anyone knows that, it's me.'

Ant's niceness towards me continued for a while, and everything he had said turned out to be true. He did work in property development, the bungalow was his, and he did visit his mother on Sundays. For a while, my doubts eased and I started to luxuriate in the entirely novel sensation of being in a relationship.

I started staying over at his place on Friday and Saturday nights. Most times he'd drive me back and forth between Sturry and Canterbury, adjusting his working hours to fit my own without complaint. When he couldn't, I'd catch the train.

Though he did seem to have a surprising number of rules about things: the soap dishes, for example; putting plates in the dishwasher straight after eating; and squeegeeing the glass shower partition immediately after use . . . He also began paying me lots of compliments, telling me how pretty I was, or how turned on he was by my 'cute little bod'. I suspected there was something wrong with his eyesight, but I'd be lying if I said that I didn't also feel a massive sense of relief that at least one person on the planet saw me that way.

On my fourth Sunday at 'the cottage', as he preferred to call it, he surprised me by not rushing me home as usual, but instead asking me if I'd mind putting on a 'nice dress' for the day.

I had a few clothes at Ant's place by then, including a summer dress. I peered out at the garden – it was a wet, blustery March morning and, although it was nearly eleven, almost dark. So, I explained that the weather was a bit cold for dresses.

'Wear one anyway,' he said. 'You'll be fine.'

I looked out at the garden again and despite the fact that I found it quite sexy when he got all masterful like that, I replied, 'Ant, I'm not wearing a dress today. Anyway, aren't you going to take me home? What do you care what I wear?'

'I wanted to take you to see Mum,' he said. 'I thought you might like a trip to the seaside.'

'Oh,' I said, thinking, *Wow, this is serious. Meeting the in-laws!* 'Sure, that would be lovely, Ant. But unless the weather down there is better than here, which I doubt, I still don't think I'm wearing a dress.'

'Oh, just wear what the fuck you want,' Ant said. 'I don't know why I *give* a shit.'

I was so shocked that my mouth fell open.

The drive to Broadstairs took about forty minutes, and the rain didn't let up for one instant. Ant's mood remained as dark and brooding as the weather, and I couldn't help but think I would rather have gone back to my flat, my dressing gown and my lonely little kitten.

I suspected Ant's silence was to do with my failure to wear the dress, but as I was quite certain he was being unreasonable and was scared of getting into an argument about it, I said nothing. Instead, I sat with my palms in my lap and watched the windscreen wipers sloshing the rain back and forth.

As we drove past a road sign to Broadstairs, I momentarily forgot that I was supposed to be sulking. 'What's she like?' I asked, wincing when I realised that I had spoken first.

'Who?' he asked obtusely.

'Your mum,' I replied. 'You've never told me much about her.'

'Well, she's my mother,' he said, wrinkling his nose as he glanced at me and shrugging.

I tried for a moment to work out whether the fact of her being his mother was supposed to explain why he couldn't describe her, or whether it was supposed to be description enough, then tried a different tack. 'What did she do?' I asked. 'When she worked, I mean.'

'She didn't work,' he said. 'She was *way* too busy to work.'

'Oh?' I said. 'Busy doing what?'

'Busy being my mother,' he replied.

I turned to the side window, discreetly pulled a face, and went back to being silent.

His mother's place was in a generic nineties build of what would best be described as 'retirement flats'. It was only about a mile from the sea, but faced the wrong way, looking out instead over a supermarket car park.

Anthony had bought flowers from the corner shop and when we reached her shiny blue door he held them out in front of him so that they would be the first thing she saw.

Marjory, a tallish white-haired woman, was unimpressed by the flowers, which she pushed unceremoniously to one side. She looked about seventy, I thought, and had a lot of crow's feet around the edges of her mouth, which seemed to have been caused by her permanent thin-lipped sneer. To say that she was not instantly likeable would be a pretty severe understatement.

'So you're 'evvah, are ya?' she asked, looking down at me from her dominant position on the step. 'A real 'alf-pint model, ain't ya?'

I felt as if I'd been slapped, but when I looked back at Anthony for reassurance, he simply gestured with his chin for me to follow her into the flat.

'Sit darn, then!' she said, sounding as if I'd been standing in the middle of the room for minutes, rather than seconds. 'I'll make tea.'

I swallowed with difficulty and perched on the edge of the floral sofa, glancing around at all the knick-knacks on the surfaces – she seemed to have a penchant for china cows. The room was severely overheated, so much so that it seemed difficult to breathe. I patted the space beside me, hoping that Ant's proximity would provide a feeling of support, but instead he sighed and followed his mother to the kitchen.

'They're from the garage,' I heard her say, presumably referring to the flowers. 'I dunno why you bovvah. They don't last more than a day.'

'They're not from the garage,' Anthony replied. 'They're from the shop on the corner.'

'Hmm,' she said. 'Same difference. And that's 'er, is it? That's the one you've been on about?'

'Yes, Mum. I thought it was time you met.'

'If you'd found yourself a smaller model,' she said, making no effort to be discreet, 'you could have kept 'er in yer pocket.'

'*Mum*,' Ant said, sounding part plaintive, part amused. 'Be nice.'

'And why's she dressed like a boy?' Marjory asked.

'It's cold,' Ant said. 'It's not exactly dress weather out there, is it?'

'Cold?' she said. 'You kids don't know what cold is. In my day the boys looked like boys and the girls looked like girls, no matter what the wevvah.'

'Mum,' Ant pleaded. 'Give it a break, OK?'

We only stayed an hour, but honestly it felt like four.

At first, I did my best to break through Marjory's icy force field by doing everything I could to charm her. But as it was clearly an impossible task – she only ever replied to my comments with at best lazy sarcasm, at worst silence and a sneer – I quickly gave up.

Instead, I sat listening to her talking at her son. I choose the word *at* rather than *with*, or even *to*, intentionally, for it was far more a monologue than any kind of conversation.

In essence, Marjory complained. She complained about the pain in her hip and her noisy neighbour. She complained about the useless idiots at the town hall and joyriders in the car park; about someone called Trish who hadn't returned her Tupperware box and 'the immigrants' who were the reason she couldn't get an appointment at the clinic. Finally, she complained about the doctor (implying that she *had* got an appointment), who didn't even speak what Marjory called 'propah' English.

By one, we were back outside and as the rain had stopped we wandered down to the seafront in search of food. The sky out to sea was dramatic-looking, with dark clouds to the left and pretty patches of sunlight over the waves to the right.

'I love the sea,' I said, thanking the gods that Marjory's dodgy hip had kept her at home.

'Mum does too,' Ant said. 'That's why she came back here.'

'From Warrington?' I asked. 'That's where you grew up, right?'

Ant paused outside a fish and chip restaurant and held the door open for me. 'Yeah. She moved back here when Dad left,' he said, once he'd followed me in. 'She grew up in Botany Bay. It's just along the coast.'

I almost asked when and why his father had left, but decided it would be tactless to do so. Plus, the 'why' part of the equation seemed fairly obvious, for who could possibly put up with Marjory? 'Was she always like that?' I asked instead as we slid into a booth, that thought leading to this one.

'Like what?' Ant asked, sounding genuinely confused. He picked up the menu and began to study it.

'I don't know,' I said, treading carefully. 'She doesn't seem very happy.'

'Happy?' Ant repeated, looking up at me and frowning.

'No. I mean, she seems a bit angry, really, doesn't she?'

'Angry? Wow,' Ant said, raising an eyebrow. 'And what brings you to that conclusion, Little Miss Psychology?'

'Well, she wasn't very nice to me,' I pointed out.

'No?'

'No. Calling me half-pint . . . Telling you that you couldn't have found a smaller model. It wasn't exactly tactful, was it?'

Ant laughed at this, and it was genuine laughter that erupted from within.

'Sorry, I think I missed the joke,' I said, bitterness creeping into my voice.

'Don't tell me you didn't know?' Ant laughed, and there was something in his thin-lipped sneer that reminded me of his mother. I hadn't known before where that came from, but now I did, it scared me.

'Know what?'

'That you're small,' he said.

'No, I know that,' I replied. I was starting to reach the borderline between anger and tears, and I didn't really want to lapse into either, not now, not here, in the middle of a fish restaurant. 'I know I'm not huge, but . . .'

'So she was merely stating the obvious,' Ant said.

'Yes, but why?'

Ant shrugged. 'How should I know?' he said. 'We can pop in on the way back and you can ask her if you want. Anyway, what are you having? I think I'll just go for cod and chips.'

'So his mother's horrible,' Mum said when I phoned her that evening. 'Not everyone can be as lucky as you, sweetheart.'

'Yeah, but she's *really* horrible,' I insisted. 'And he didn't even stick up for me.'

'I thought you said he did,' Mum replied. 'I thought he asked her to be nice.'

'Yeah, he did ask her to be nice. And she wasn't. She wasn't nice at all.'

'Look, honey,' Mum said. 'Do you want my advice?'

'Sure,' I said. 'Go for it.'

'Don't go to war with his mother. Because that's a battle you can never win.'

'But she's . . .'

'Just see as little of her as you can, and ignore her when you do. It's not her you're dating, after all. And whatever you do, don't try to make him choose, because blood runs thicker than water and all that. If you force him to choose between the two of you, you'll just end up single all over again, and none of us wants that, do we? The only way you can get a mummy's boy away from his mother is to wait.'

'Wait?' I repeated. 'Wait for what?'

'Eventually she'll either come around, or she'll drop dead,' Mum said.

'Right,' I said, sighing deeply.

'Actually, I need to see you,' Mum added. 'Can you come up next weekend?'

I couldn't. I had to work the following weekend, covering for Sheena, who was on leave.

'The one after, then,' Mum said.

'I might get Ant to drive me,' I told her. 'Maybe it's time you met him too. Make up your own mind.'

'No, don't,' Mum said, surprising me. 'I want you all to myself.'

I didn't see that much of Anthony over the following two weeks. He had to work a few evenings, wining and dining some developer he was trying to do business with, and when he wasn't working he claimed to be tired. As I myself had to work right through the weekend, I was shattered in the evenings as well.

So I spent my time with Dandy, staring at but not really watching the reflection-free TV screen. It turned out that the way Ant had positioned the sofa *was* better after all.

I didn't actually mind being alone, because the only time I'd met Ant – for lunch on the Wednesday – he hadn't been that nice anyway. He'd seemed different, somehow – harsher, harder, more like his mother, perhaps. I wondered if it was just a phase or whether something had broken between us. Perhaps meeting his mother had changed the way I saw him for ever. Whatever the explanation, I found myself feeling relieved when he said he couldn't see me.

By the end of the second week, I sensed that I was reaching a decision. The time had come to end the relationship, I suspected. I just had to find the courage to tell my friends and family, to face down their judgements about the fact that I'd failed at my shot at a relationship. Kerry would probably ask me again if I wanted to admit that I was lesbian, and Mum would be worried and disappointed. But it wasn't working out and I realised that, deep down, I'd always known that it wouldn't.

Mum lived in the same semi-detached house we'd moved to just before Dad died, and it was an absolute nightmare to get to.

It was in a tiny hamlet called Oxen End, about ten miles from Braintree in Essex. Her last-ditch plan, her final attempt at saving him, had been to get him away from the pubs. As he'd simply driven – drunk – to Great Bardfield, or even as far as Braintree, and then home again, his smuggled bottles of vodka hidden beneath the spare wheel, it hadn't made a blind bit of difference. If anything, it was a miracle he'd hadn't killed anyone.

As Mum didn't drive, it was she who'd ended up stranded in the middle of nowhere. Luckily, since his death, she'd made friends with people who had cars.

The lack of regular public transport, combined with my inability to pass the driving test – I'd failed three times before giving up – was the main reason I'd taken the job in well-connected Canterbury, but also the reason I hadn't visited Mum since Christmas.

The journey, which generally took about five hours door to door, involved a train to Stratford, then another to Braintree, followed by a bus to Great Bardfield, and then either a lift from a friend, a taxi (if I could find one) or an extremely long walk along dark country lanes with no footpaths. Which is why I was studying the various timetables on Friday evening when Kerry called.

'Hi,' she said. 'I was wondering if you wanted me to pick you up at Braintree tomorrow?'

'You're coming too?' I asked in surprise.

'Apparently so,' she said. 'Any idea what it's about?'

'None. I thought it was just me.'

'Mum asked me not to bring Agata, which seems weird,' Kerry said.

'She told me not to bring Anthony, either,' I said. 'Not that I particularly wanted to.'

But it was unusual that Mum didn't want Agata there. Kerry often complained that Mum loved her Polish girlfriend more than she loved her own daughter. 'Is something going down?' I asked. 'Is it something serious, do you think?'

'Maybe she's selling that bloody house.'

'Gosh, that would be great,' I said. 'The roof was leaking at Christmas, and the garden's totally out of control.'

'I guess we'll find out tomorrow,' Kerry said. 'Maybe she met some bearded guy in Morocco and wants to emigrate.'

'God, don't,' I laughed.

'I'm gutted I'm not gonna get to see the famous Anthony, though,' Kerry said.

Though I doubted very much that uptight Anthony would get on with my vegan, dub-loving sister, I said, 'Yeah, it's a shame. But to answer your question, yes, please *do* pick me up. I'm looking at trains now, and it's bad enough just getting to Braintree.'

On Saturday morning I woke up shockingly tired. I felt unreasonably sleepy and vaguely nauseous, almost as if I hadn't slept at all, yet by seven I'd forced myself out of bed and into the shower. I cleaned Dandy's litter tray (yuck), put out enough food and water for the weekend and rushed out the door.

By eight, I'd made it to the train station, and by nine I was at Ashford International, peering enviously out of the window at all the lucky sods travelling to Paris rather than Oxen End. Their journeys would be faster than mine, too.

As the Kent countryside rolled by, I thought about my tiredness and nausea and realised that I was feeling bloated too. Kerry, who was something of a supplement addict, would almost certainly have something to help with water retention, I reckoned. It was then that it dawned on me: I'd missed my period. I was almost two weeks late.

I watched the countryside spinning past, and when the sun came out I closed my eyes and let it flicker against my eyelids. I started cataloguing the sensations in my body over the past two weeks: my tender breasts, the tiredness, my mood swings, and the more I did so, the more convinced I became. I tried, for a bit, to get in touch with how shocked and scared I was, simply because that's how I'd always assumed I would feel. But I'd wanted children for as long as I could remember. Actually, 'wanted' doesn't really cover it – I'd simply never been able to *imagine* that I wouldn't have kids. It took a while before I was able to admit that my dominant feeling was joy.

We had taken no precautions, so I could hardly claim to be surprised. Would Ant be shocked if it was true? I wondered. Had he assumed I'd gone on the pill? Or did he see our relationship as long term and potentially fertile? My suspicion was that he simply didn't see my capacity to get pregnant as in any way his responsibility, and perhaps he was right. After all, *I'd* known I wasn't on the pill. All I would have had to do was say *no*. But I hadn't, had I? I'd not said *no* and I'd refused to think about what might happen.

Would I stay with him if I turned out to be pregnant? I surprised myself by thinking that it was unlikely, and shocked myself even more by realising that I didn't find the idea of being a single mother particularly scary. So perhaps my inability to organise contraception had been driven by my unconscious desire for a child.

Then again, maybe pregnancy would change our relationship for the better. Perhaps it would even change Ant himself. Had thin-lipped Marjory always dreamed of grandchildren? And if she had, and I provided one, would she too change her attitude?

I suspect that this was hormone-driven, but I began to list Ant's good points: his generosity, his professionalism in his work, his capacity and desire to provide. I daydreamed, imagining us as a perfect little cliché family in our luxurious future home. I imagined myself serving up a tasty nourishing meal to my hard-working husband while our cute, precociously clever son told his daddy about his day at school, and felt shamed by the fact that I found the vision so seductive.

I had so much to think about that for once the journey seemed to be over almost before it had started. The sign outside the window suddenly read 'Braintree' and I had to rush to get off the train before it moved on.

In the car park, I found Kerry sitting in her ancient green Volvo. The baseline of the reggae she was listening to was making the side window rattle. She was rolling a joint in full view, and the first thing she said when I yanked open the door and slid in beside her was, 'Shit, you look well! Is this the Anthony effect?'

'I don't think so,' I told her, reaching out to turn the music down. Then, in spite of myself, I added, 'No, I think I might be pregnant, actually. I've only just worked it out.' Apparently it was a secret that I just couldn't bear to keep to myself.

'Fuck!' Kerry said, turning the music back up a bit. 'No way!'

'I'm not *sure*,' I informed her. 'But I am definitely late, and I'm feeling bloated and a bit vommy, so . . .'

'That'll get the old dear off my back,' she said, licking the seal of the joint and raising it to her lips. 'D'you want to go to a chemist's and get a test?'

'No,' I said definitively. There was no way I was doing that in my mother's house. I wanted to be all alone with my emotions for that particular life event.

'Really?' Kerry insisted. 'There's one just—'

'No!' I said, more forcefully. 'And please don't smoke that stuff while you're driving. It scares me. Plus, like I said, I'm feeling a bit sick.'

'It's only a weak one,' she protested. 'It's nearly all tobacco. It's just to take the edge off.'

'And you're not to tell Mum, OK?' I said, as she ignored my request and lit up.

'Why not?' she replied, speaking in smoke as she started the engine, engaged reverse gear and lurched out of the parking space. 'She'll be thrilled. She's been banging on at *me* to have a baby.'

'You?'

'Yes, me! I told her it's not happening, but she wasn't happy about it. This'll take the pressure off me big time.'

'At least open the fucking window, Kes,' I said, waving my hand at the clouds of smoke she was producing.

'Oops,' Kerry said, reaching for the window winder. The smoke swirled around as the cold air rushed in. 'Sorry. I forgot we had a baby on board. God, I can't wait to see Mum's face!'

'Stop it. Look, I just want to wait till I'm sure,' I told her. 'Then I'll tell her. In the meantime, not a word, you hear?'

'Sure, whatever. It's your call,' she said. Then, 'Fuck, though . . . A baby!'

When we got to the house, Kerry used her key to let us in, so we surprised Mum snoozing on the sofa in front of the television. She looked shocking when she woke up, and it was one of those moments when I suddenly noticed she had aged.

'Oh! Girls!' Mum said, standing and rubbing her face with her hands until the colour returned to her cheeks. 'Gosh, I fell sound asleep.'

'Hi, Mum,' Kerry said, leaning in to embrace her, an annoying dope-induced smile on her lips.

Mum sniffed at her, prompting Kerry to pre-empt any criticism by moaning, '*And yes*, Mum, I'm *still* smoking.'

Kerry stepped aside and I took my turn to hug our mother. 'Gosh, you look well,' Mum told me, prompting Kerry to snigger. I suspected the joint had been stronger than she'd admitted and shot her a glare, warning her not to say anything.

Growing up, hiding anything from Mum had been impossible. It had always felt as if she had invisible nerves running through the house, and it didn't matter if you were stealing a bit of cooking chocolate or merely *thinking* about maybe staying out late . . . whatever it was, Mum already knew.

It was the same, even now. She'd noted Kerry's snigger and had sensed my glare even though her back was turned. 'You're not pregnant, are you?' she asked, now piercing me with her blue eyes. I was stunned. No matter how many times it's demonstrated, you can never get used to that kind of prescience.

Kerry laughed out loud. 'Amazing!' she said, forming a gun with two fingers and pointing at Mum, gangster-style. 'Our mother is *amazing*.'

By now, there was no point even trying to lie, so I admitted it. 'I might be,' I said. 'I don't know yet.'

Mum started to cry then. 'Oh, you *are!*' she said, through tears. 'Oh, you are! I can tell! Oh, I'm so happy for you, sweetheart!'

It took half an hour before we could have anything that resembled a reasoned discussion about the fact that I might or might not be pregnant.

Over drinks – orange juice for 'pregnant' me – I tried to convince them that even if I did turn out to be pregnant, I might choose not to keep it. But I don't think I convinced anyone. I couldn't really convince myself.

Once lunch had been served, an unusually lazy vegan lasagne from the freezer, I tried to change the subject by asking Mum about Morocco.

'I'll tell you once we've eaten,' she replied mysteriously.

'Why?' Kerry asked, her fork suspended in mid-air. 'What happened?'

I frowned at Mum, then glanced at Kerry and back at Mum again. 'You're pale,' I said, noticing it as I said it. 'If you'd been to Morocco, you'd have a suntan. But you're as white as a sheet.'

'I know,' Mum said. 'I didn't go.'

'But the postcard,' Kerry said. 'You sent me a postcard.'

'Me too,' I agreed. 'It *said* you were on a beach.'

'Ada sent them for me,' Mum said. 'I had to cancel. I wasn't able to go and I didn't want to worry you.'

'You weren't able to go *because* . . . ?' I asked.

'I was in Broomfield Hospital,' Mum said. 'I had to go in for some tests.'

From that point on, I don't remember much. I suspect that our minds protect us from reliving the pain of such moments by erasing, or at least blurring, our memories. Suffice to say that lots of tears were shed and many hours were spent having heart-to-hearts while holding hands.

Kerry smoked even more than usual and much of the time she was only half there. I envied her emotional opt-out, but it struck me that at least one of us needed to be fully present to share Mum's pain.

'I'm so happy you've found yourself a lovely man,' Mum told me on the doorstep as we were leaving on Sunday afternoon, and I wondered where she'd magicked that titbit up from. With hindsight, I think that, what with everything else she was facing, it was just something she needed to believe and so she'd decided that it was true. 'And if you're going to have a baby, then that's the best news you could possibly have given me,' she said. 'It'll give me an extra reason to stick around.'

No pressure, then! I remember thinking.

I didn't bother repeating that I might not be having a baby at all. Because the subject had suddenly become so vast and complex and loaded, involving as it did not only myself and Ant but my mother as well, that I no longer seemed to have space in my brain to sort through it all.

Instead, all I could think as I trundled homeward, blinking back tears, was, *She's got cancer. She's got cancer. She's got cancer. My wonderful mother has got cancer.*

Ant called in to see me on the Monday. When I opened the door to greet him, he looked as grave as I was feeling. Was he preparing to leave me? I still wonder to this day.

'We need to talk,' he said, once he'd sat on the couch.

'I know,' I said, trying to think about all the things we indeed needed to talk about: about the fact that I might, or might not, be pregnant. About the fact that if I was pregnant I might, or might not, decide to keep the baby, and that if I *were* to decide to keep it, then I might, or might not, decide to stay with Ant. But there were too many conditionals in there for me to even begin to know where to start untangling them, let alone *explain* the whole process to Ant. Plus, in truth, the only subject I could really concentrate on was my poor mother. So instead I began to cry.

Ant held me in his arms as I wept, and that was the start of what I think of as his 'nice' period. In the end it was Mum's illness, not the baby, that changed him, albeit temporarily. Being so close to his mother, it was maybe something he could relate to. Then again, another part of me has always suspected him of being a scheming monster, so perhaps he simply saw a door opening as I collapsed, heartbroken and needy, into his arms.

Whatever the reason, he was lovely for the duration of Mum's illness, far nicer than he ever was before or afterwards, driving me back and forth to Oxen End, and then, later, to the hospital in Braintree; cooking meals for me when I got home exhausted from a stint at Mum's, and even taking in Dandy – who he hated – when I had to stay over towards the end. OK, Ant didn't *hate* Dandy, but he did get very upset when he sharpened his claws on Ant's Italian furniture, and the cat hair that clung to his suits could send him into such a tizzy that it would have been funny to watch had his raging not been so scary.

Mum kept things quiet for a month or so by telling us she was having tests or waiting for appointments, and as this was perfectly possible, we believed her. In truth, she'd known from the start that the cancer had metastasised all over, and she had already decided not to bother with chemo – it could only give her a few extra weeks anyway. She was simply sparing us the pain of it all for as long as she possibly could.

I could fill a book with details of Mum's illness, but it would be a miserable book that no one would want to read, and it's a story that was horrific to live through once, without having to go through it all again. Plus, if I'm honest, a lot of my memories are blurred, recorded, as they were, through tears.

I coped better with it all than Kerry, and though this was a surprise, because I'd always thought of Kerry as the tough one, it shouldn't have been, I suppose. Though nothing can truly prepare you for that kind of thing – not when it's your own mother – as a nurse, unlike Kerry, at least I'd seen it all before. I knew how fast these things could move, whereas Kerry was totally blindsided.

Mum never did get to meet her first grandchild, and that's a fact that brings tears to my eyes even now. But she did at least get to break the news to Anthony.

I'd been struggling to breathe at her hospital bedside, on the verge of emotional collapse, I feared. And I'd thought that some fresh air might help me be brave again, so had gone for a walk around Braintree. It was sunny, I remember, but cold.

Mum called for me while I was out, and it was Anthony who sat and took her frail hand in his own. I like to imagine that Mum knew what she was doing, that she was enjoying fiddling around with my destiny, but I suspect that she was simply delirious from all the morphine she was on.

'Have you thought about names?' she asked, apparently, and Anthony twigged immediately what she meant.

'I like Luke,' he said, after a pause. It was the first name that popped into his mind.

'Is it a boy then?' Mum asked him.

'We don't know,' Ant told her. 'If it's a girl, we're thinking maybe . . . um . . . Lucy.'

'Oh yes!' Mum said, 'Lucy! Lucy's a lovely name.'

When I got back from my walk, Anthony seemed strange, avoiding eye contact and fleeing the room. As I sat down to take his place, the seat was still warm.

'Yes, Lucy's a lovely name,' Mum said.

'I'm sorry?' I said, shrugging my way out of my coat.

'He says you're going to call her Lucy,' Mum said. 'If it's a girl.'

'Oh,' I said, swallowing with difficulty. 'Did he?'

'Or Luke,' Mum said, 'if it's a boy.'

'Yeah.' I coughed. 'Do you, erm, approve?'

'Completely,' Mum said. 'They're lovely names.'

I apologised in the car as we were leaving. 'I didn't want you to find out like that,' I explained. 'I was going to tell you, but there's just never been a right moment.' I couldn't find words to explain that I hadn't wanted to taint this news with that news, but that when one event so strongly influenced the other, it seemed hard to avoid putting them within the same set of brackets.

'It's OK,' Ant said, surprising me. 'I get it. There's been a lot going on.'

After driving in total silence to Mum's house, where we were staying, he asked me if I wanted to get married.

'Married,' I repeated flatly. My mind felt too numb to properly consider the concept.

'Yes, I thought you might want to get married before . . .'

'Oh, before the baby's born?' I said, trying to use logic to fill the void left by my inability to actually feel anything about his suggestion. It seemed, indeed, to be something we should consider.

'Yeah . . . No . . .' Ant spluttered. 'I mean, before . . . um . . . While your mum can still make it to the wedding.'

'Oh,' I said, turning to look out of the side window and fighting back tears. I think it was only at that moment the inevitability of her death finally dawned on me.

'I think it would make her happy, don't you? To know that you're all safe and sound.'

'Maybe,' I said, barely able to breathe. 'Maybe it would.'

We booked a mid-May wedding, but had to cancel a week before. We dealt with both cancelling the wedding and registering Mum's death during a single trip to the register office, something that would forever link those two concepts in my brain.

After the funeral, I went to Ant's place. I couldn't face being alone, and my beloved cat was there, after all. Other than to pick up my stuff, clean the flat and hand over the keys, I never went back to my own place again.

In June, we drove down to Broadstairs to give Marjory the news. She guessed as soon as she opened the door – I was, after all, starting to show.

'I know it's a sad time for you, darlin',' she said, 'but try to let yerself be 'appy.'

I'm sure that she was right and, perhaps, for once, what she said was intended kindly. But my hand balled into a fist and it was as much as I could do not to punch her.

Have you ever looked at a couple and thought, simply, *how?* How on earth did *he* manage to snag her? How on earth does she put up with him? What could they possibly have in common? I certainly have, which is something I suppose you might describe as 'ironic'.

But the thing about other people's relationships is that you only ever see the tip of the iceberg. So you never get to understand that your dumpy friend's drop-dead-gorgeous boyfriend is broke, or lazy, or impotent – or all three. You don't get to see quite how nice Brian's horrible girlfriend was when they met way back when. Or how much trauma he was dealing with. Or how needy, or depressed, or suicidal he was before she helped him. You never get to understand quite how big the debt he's paying off might be.

In my case there were plenty of warning signs, I'll admit it. Anthony *was* too tidy, he *did* have too much hi-fi; he did make too many rules and was far too subservient to his really-not-very-nice mother.

But I was lonely and needy and quite probably a little traumatised too. And when I was at my neediest, Anthony was at his nicest. He genuinely helped me through the worst period of my life, and by the time I came out the other side of what felt like a very dark cloud, we were living as a family with our daughter, Lucy, with another one on the way as well.

Did I think about leaving him as things soured over the years? Constantly. But did I ever make a plan to escape? Inexplicably, no, I didn't.

I want to explain to you how he made me dependent on him, but I'm struggling with that word: *made*. It seems like such a black hole of a word – a black hole into which personal responsibility vanishes. He *made* me. Because, did he? Can someone *make* you do something? Does anyone really have that power? And yet that's honestly how it feels, looking back.

Anthony dug away at my sense of worth in such a sustained, methodical way that it's hard for me to see it as an accident. It's almost impossible for me to imagine that he wasn't following some nasty plan of his own.

Slowly but surely, he chiselled away at my confidence in the things that I was good at, while obtusely complimenting me on attributes I knew that I didn't have.

Thus I came, over time, to believe that I'd never been much good at my job (and so there was no point going back), that my cooking was terrible, that I was lazy around the home, inept at social interaction, and that my friends didn't really like me that much.

On the other hand, he'd intersperse this grinding undermining of my ego with compliments about my body, my beauty (!) and how 'hot' I was 'in the sack'.

Understand that these aspects of our relationship crept in over a long, long period of time. Anthony never actually said, 'Have you ever suspected that your friends don't really like you?' – because to do so would have given the game away. Instead, if Sheena cancelled on me, he'd say, 'Hmm, I wonder why she did that? I suppose she must have just had a better offer or something. Still, you've got me. At least *I'd* rather spend the night with you.' So I thought I was receiving a compliment.

When I spoke about going back to work, he'd say, 'Has anyone actually asked you to go back? Or don't they really care that much either way?' And when I admitted that no one had shown a great deal of interest in my return, he'd say, 'Lucky me! Getting you all to myself.'

The process being so stealthy, it's a tough one to explain to an outsider, but I hope you're at least getting a glimpse of how I came to depend on Anthony, and Anthony alone, for any remaining sense of worth.

By the time our second child, Sarah, was born, my life had changed completely. I'd given up any idea of returning to work, become so uncomfortable in social situations that I avoided them like the plague, and believed myself to be at my best – or let's say at my least worst – when mothering or trying to please my man, either domestically or sexually.

I kept a spotless house, constantly mopping and dusting and bleaching as I tried to prove the erroneous nature of the 'lazy' label Ant had given me.

On the sexual side of things, I'll spare you the gruesome details; suffice to say that Anthony had quite specific tastes. And he used the births of our daughters – claiming they had made me 'loose' – to justify pursuing those, let's say *tighter* interests, with vigour. Heaven help me, I managed to pretend, even, to enjoy that. And that really took some doing.

So *did* he *make* me do anything? *Can* someone *make* you do something? I ask the question again, and the only honest answer I can give you is *yes*. A determined, calculating person can override the will of a weak, insecure, eager-to-please one.

The progression was so subtle that I rarely noticed it was happening. In fact, the only moments his hostility burst into plain view were in the presence of his mother.

During Marge's visits, I would field a barrage of snide digs and smoothly delivered insults – it was truly horrific. But I put up and shut up and turned the other cheek.

What little confidence I'd once had – and let's face it, I'd never been exactly cocky – was long gone, so I sat and smiled placidly as they delivered their alternate blows. I mopped and dusted and looked after my gorgeous daughters, and at night I rolled over, spread my legs and cried out just loud enough that Marge – in the spare room next door – might hear, because I'd finally understood that this was what my husband required of me and that he would go at it with increasing vigour until that happened.

Marge would die soon anyway, I told myself, and any gasps or groans she'd heard would be buried along with her body. Does that make me a terrible person, do you think?

My mother once told me that the only way to deal with Ant's difficult mother was to wait until she either 'came around' or died, but Marjorie refused to do either. She was younger than she looked, it transpired. And she was in far better health than I would have guessed, too.

All the same, for a few years her influence waned. Because it was clear that she didn't like me, and because Ant and I had children who she didn't seem that keen on either, my presence was no longer required during his now fortnightly visits to Broadstairs.

Looking after Lucy and Sarah was the perfect alibi, and one I exploited to the max.

Once we'd moved Sarah to what had been the spare room, Marge's regular visits to Sturry stopped as well.

Ant's desire to hear me squeal ceased around the same time. I suspected that he was having affairs – he'd come home very late from work and jump straight in the shower – but I convinced myself that I didn't care. My evenings alone with Lucy, Sarah and Walt Disney were pretty much perfect, and as far as lack of sex was concerned, my primary sensation was one of relief.

In 2014 Ant surprised me by announcing he'd bought a bigger house – a five-bedroom red-brick monster in nearby Chislet – and as soon as we had a spare bed installed, Marge's visits resumed. She was still in perfect health – thriving, as I saw it, on negativity – and was more than able to drive out to us for visits. Her character hadn't improved with age, either, and if anything, she'd become even more obnoxious.

My relationship with my sister had become so complicated by then that we only ever spoke on the phone. As for Sheena, even phone conversations had become challenging to the point where I'd pretend to miss her calls. The problem in both cases was the same: my own inconsistency. Due to my litany of complaints about Ant's behaviour, they'd individually come to realise that he wasn't the nicest person. But as they'd ceased, one after the other, telling me to stop whingeing and begun, instead, to encourage me to leave him, I'd found myself rather perversely defending him. A point had been reached where no matter *how* Kerry or Sheena reacted to whatever I'd just told them about Ant, good or bad, I'd find myself telling them they were wrong.

So yes, it was entirely a function of my own neurotic attitude that I'd ended up so alone. All the same, within that context, Marge's renewed presence in my life felt quite overwhelming.

The moving process had been horrendous, but worst of all, Dandy had gone missing on only our second day in the new house. I'd spent my evenings for the first two weeks wandering around the gardens and fields calling for him, but to no avail. Though neither Ant nor the girls seemed devastated about his disappearance, coming home to an empty house had really made me feel quite desolate.

Kerry had moved to Rome and my other friends had drifted away. Actually, by then, I no longer even thought of them as friends. Ant had been working on me for years, relentlessly encouraging me to spot their faults – and Lord knows, we all have plenty of those – while subtly suggesting that I'd overestimated their qualities. So without really noticing that it was an ongoing process, I'd ceased, one by one, to pursue them, and they'd all but vanished from my life.

Of course, I made acquaintances. There were women I came to know well enough to chat to at the school gates, and there were even some who'd pop round for a cup of tea, though it honestly didn't happen that often. But the conversation was always superficial and invariably child-centric, and I came to believe that this suited me. Actually, I'd go further and say I came to believe that, what with human nature being so disappointing and all, 'real' friendships only led to pain and disillusionment. I thought that I was in control. I really believed that it was I who had *decided* to keep all that dangerous intimacy at bay.

What kept me going was the joyful existence of my daughters. Lucy and Sarah were clever, funny, and (most of the time) great fun to be with. In a nutshell, I loved them to bits.

Anthony wasn't the world's worst father to them, either. I suppose, looking back, I'd have to say that he used them to feel good about himself, and that perhaps isn't the healthiest of ways for a father to behave. But I honestly don't think that they were harmed by it.

'Who's the best daddy in the world?' he would ask them as he swung them around the garden by their arms.

'You are!' they'd cry, their Pavlovian brainwashing complete.

'And who loves you most in the whole wide world?'

'You do!' they'd shout, grinning from ear to ear.

If you're going to manipulate your kids in order to massage your own ego, I suppose there are worse ways to do it.

Anthony met all our other needs, too, whether physical or financial. He was a good DIY buff around the house and a patient Lego builder with the girls. His business had done well, and though I never knew how much he earned, I could tell we weren't short of a bob or two. I had a gold credit card that his bank account paid off every month – encouraged by Ant, I'd closed my own some years earlier – and this I used to buy pretty much anything we needed. As long as the stuff we ordered matched Ant's tastes – dresses and heels for me (no trousers or flats), and trousers or long dresses for the girls (other than school uniform, no skirts) – he pretty much gave me free rein. The fridge was stacked, the house was warm and comfortable, and Lucy and Sarah were thriving.

There were frustrations, too; of course there were.

Being unable to drive, I was isolated living out in Chislet and sometimes I felt lonely. But the only time I ever suggested taking fresh lessons, Ant's response – a burst of authentic laughter – convinced me more than words ever could what a silly idea that was.

On sunny days I'd take long walks around the edges of the furrowed fields – always half hoping to spot Dandy – and sometimes I'd even push as far as Herne Bay, where, at the sight of the sea, I could feel almost happy. On rainy ones I'd sit beside the range, losing myself in fictional worlds. Whether it was discovering a sunnier existence than my own, or reminding myself that there were far worse ones, reading invariably made me feel better.

Occasionally, none of this was enough. I'd set out on my walk and be overcome by a terrible desire to just keep on walking, to never turn back. I'd think of my mother and the dream. Go with the . . . *what?!* I'd wonder angrily. Maybe it had been *your.* Go with your *desire?* How far would I get before I collapsed? I wondered. How far can a person walk? Of course, I could walk to Herne Bay and get a train – silly me. Go with the *train?* Could her message have been that simple? But how far could I travel before the credit card got stopped? And would that be far enough to escape Anthony for ever?

And then the sun would dip behind a copse of trees and I'd remember it was time to pick the girls up pretty soon. I'd imagine them asking Ant where Mummy had gone or, if I took them with me, why we were poor now and living in a council flat with a pay-as-you-go meter.

And would they even choose me? If push came to shove, I seriously suspected they would not, that they'd choose, instead, the 'best dad in the whole wide world', the one who 'loved them the most', and the one with the six-figure income to pay for their every whim.

Our home life continued to grow more and more comfortable. A conservatory appeared at the rear of the house, so I'd sit and read in the warm afternoon sun. A new kitchen was fitted one summer, and our refrigerator was swapped for one that dispensed ice cubes. A kitchen robot whizzed and whirred and made unspectacular but lazy soup. Things kept getting more luxurious and I'd be lying if I said that sense of ease wasn't seductive.

In fact, the only aspect of our lives that didn't follow this upwardly mobile trajectory was the type of holiday we booked.

Anthony simply wouldn't consider travelling overseas, you see. He had a deeply ingrained distrust of foreigners, based on a selective view of history that included, for instance, the French collaborating with the Germans, but excluded the Resistance; that included the Blitz, but excluded Queen Victoria's German mother. Foreigners were by nature incomprehensible but, more importantly, they were untrustworthy.

Our holidays, therefore, took place in Cornwall, Devon or Scotland. If I'm being honest, being full of Scots as it is, even Scotland was seen as something of a challenge.

That's not to say that these trips were unpleasant. With the exception of the few occasions when Marge came along, they were actually pretty enjoyable.

We'd rent a flat somewhere, or, in the later years, a cottage, and by day we'd take the kids to theme parks or the beach, and by night we'd eat in the most expensive (but not too foreign) restaurants we could find.

Funnily enough, both our best and worst holidays ever were taken in exactly the same place: Blackpool Sands, down in Devon. We even stayed in the same cottage both times.

The first trip – the good one – took place in August 2016.

Ant had been working all hours on a huge housing project out in Whitfield. He never wanted to talk much about his job, and I think it pleased him to imagine that what he did was beyond the capabilities of my tiny woman-brain to understand. But he did work hard, I could see that, and whatever it was that he was up to, it involved a lot of late-night wining and dining of various members of the planning committee, and even taking them away on lush weekend breaks.

The deal had been signed mid-June, and he'd been paid his commission in July, so, to celebrate, he booked a luxury holiday home for our August holiday – Beach Cottage, in Blackpool Sands.

The drive from Canterbury to Devon took almost six hours, and we did the entire journey non-stop.

One of Ant's many rules was that he didn't like to stop during a drive. No matter how far we were travelling, any request for food, or to wee, or simply to stretch my legs was met with stony-faced refusal. The only exceptions were if the car needed fuel (this, I'd pray for) or, during one of the rare trips when Marge was with us, if it was she who'd requested the stop. Even then, the break would last less than ten minutes, the strict minimum required to dash in, go to the loo, buy a sandwich, and sprint back out to the car.

These non-stop journeys had become more difficult since the girls had graduated from nappies, and in the early days I'd tried protesting that Ant was being unreasonable. As this made him so furious that he drove even faster, it turned out to be entirely counterproductive. Instead, I developed a technique of clambering over into the back to stick a potty beneath one or other of our children as Ant continued to thunder down the motorway. I always hoped that he'd be pulled over and told off for putting our lives in danger – hoped that a policeman could make him change his ways – but though we got some strange looks from the occupants of nearby vehicles, it sadly never happened.

By 2016 I'd perfected a far safer technique of denying the girls anything to drink for five hours before the journey, thus dehydrating them to the point where they wouldn't even ask to use the toilet.

It was dark by the time we reached Devon and, as the moon wasn't up yet either, you couldn't see much. The only clue as to the presence of the sea nearby was a gorgeous iodine smell hanging in the air.

I woke up extra early the next morning and crept from the bed to check on the girls. Ant was still snoring, and I hoped that he'd sleep in until lunchtime.

I'd never much enjoyed Ant's morning moods, but lately I suppose you could say that I'd shifted to a strategy of minimising contact at pretty much any time of the day. So holidays were, in that aspect at least, more challenging than the rest of the year.

The girls, too, were fast asleep, stretched blissfully over the covers, so I slipped out on to the patio. The air was fresh and the sun was just rising. Through the trees I could make out a swathe of blue horizon.

I padded barefoot across the lush lawn – it felt as soft underfoot as a carpet – to a gap in the bushes, where I gasped at my first glimpse of the beach down below, a vast, golden crescent sandwiched between the grey-blue of the sea and vibrant green fields. I sighed and smiled to myself. I just knew that this holiday was going to be a good one.

And it was! The sun shone every day for two whole weeks and we basically lived on the beach, eating burgers and chips from the beach café at lunchtime and straying no further than nearby Stoke Fleming in the evening.

Ant would spend the day wandering back and forth between the beach and the cottage, as if he couldn't quite decide where he wanted to be. He never could sit still for more than half an hour. But other than his habitual irritation if any of 'my' responsibilities – the four Cs of childcare, cooking, clothing and cleaning – were perceived as unfulfilled, he was as relaxed as I'd ever seen him. In fact, the only time he shouted during the entire two-week holiday was when I inadvertently got sand in the bed, and even I could see how annoying that was.

The girls, for their part, were in beach heaven, spending the days digging dams and rivers, and burying each other; splashing in and out of the waves, and slurping dribbling ice creams from soggy cones. My rapport with my daughters was magical, and there was even a moment when Ant slipped into the mood.

He and I had gone swimming with the girls on our backs and we'd swum all the way out to a buoy. Ant joked that he'd felt an octopus touch his leg, and this set the girls squealing and squirming deliciously.

'You're strangling me!' I gasped back at Sarah, whose tiny arms were clasped around my neck.

'This one's deafening *me*,' Ant replied, smiling broadly at me.

And for a moment, I understood how a 'normal' relationship might feel: the comfortable friendship, the confidence that this moment might continue; the knowledge that it wouldn't inevitably morph into something dark and disagreeable. How *nice* that must feel, I remember thinking.

Surrounded by fluorescent buoys and sparkly waves, we swam, side by side, in the sunshine, and then headed back to the shore, where we followed the girls to our towels.

'Your hair looks like shite now,' Ant said unexpectedly. And boom! Our magic moment was over.

'Don't worry,' I replied with fake joviality, 'it's washable. I'll sort it when we get back.'

'Women!' Ant said dismissively.

As I tried to work out whether I was being berated for being too careless or too vain, or perhaps both simultaneously, Ant threw himself on his towel, reached for his phone, and started jabbing quite aggressively at the screen.

As Beach Cottage was a rare and much-in-demand property, Ant rebooked almost as soon as we got home. It had been the most successful holiday we'd ever had, after all.

I looked forward to the repeat trip for the whole year. As I raked autumn leaves or lit fires to get through the dark January days, as the first buds sprouted on the trees, I thought almost daily about Blackpool Sands. Whenever Ant was particularly antsy, which was often, or when Marge came to stay and started haranguing me, I'd slip into a reverie and daydream about that beach and our upcoming trip back to paradise. I even imagined we might move there one day.

It wasn't until the third week of July – just a week before our departure – that Ant revealed that there was to be one significant change this year: he'd invited his mother to join us. That was the first thing to go wrong.

The second was the weather. It started to rain mere seconds after Marge climbed aboard, stealing my comfortable seat up front. 'Oh, don't say it's bloody rainin'!' she said, as Ant programmed the GPS with the address in Devon. 'I tell you, I've got my own personal rain cloud following me around.'

'Is that true, Mummy?' Lucy asked me.

'If Marge says it is, then it must be,' I told her as I hunted for the middle seat belt, which seemed to have got lost somewhere beneath Sarah's child seat. Contradicting Marge was rarely worth the trouble, I'd discovered, even when she was being facetious.

'It's Gran to the girls,' Marge corrected me. 'And of course it ain't true. Fillin' 'er 'ead with nonsense like that! Honestly!'

Reflected in the rear-view mirror, I caught Ant's eye, and realised that he'd seen me pulling a face. He shook his head in a way that implied we were both equally responsible for the tone of the conversation, and I wondered, as ever, how he could be so blind to his mother's rudeness.

As we pulled away, he asked her how she'd been, and so began a fresh litany of complaint. As she started banging on about her headaches, I closed my eyes and prayed for sleep.

It rained all the way down to Devon, and due to an accident on the A303 the journey took seven hours, not six, meaning that despite having set off earlier, it was dark again by the time we arrived. As we'd eaten sandwiches during the drive, we carried the girls in and tucked them straight into their beds. What with the excitement of being back in the holiday house, they weren't going to get to sleep for a while, but as Ant had declared it was past their bedtime – and he was not in a mood to be argued with – I just warned them not to make too much noise and closed the door to avoid complaints.

'It's damp in 'ere,' Marge said, when I got back to the lounge.

'It's only because of the rain,' I offered, feeling as if I'd be lacking loyalty if I failed to defend Beach Cottage.

'*No!* You don't say!' Marge said acidly.

'So what do you think, Mum?' Ant asked, zipping around the room switching on lights, the better to show off our comfortable lounge.

''s all right,' Marge replied, looking around, her nose almost, but not quite, scrunched up. 'I expected it to be bigger if I'm honest, especially the way that one's been banging on about it all year. But it's fine. For a holiday let, yes, it's fine.'

'It's the beach that's amazing,' I said, doing my best to cling to the positives.

'Yeah, the beach is really nice,' Ant agreed. 'You'll see in the morning, Mum.'

'If it ever stops raining, I will,' Marge said. 'If we can even get down there to see it.'

But it hadn't stopped raining by morning. Even before I got up, I could hear it pitter-pattering in the pauses between Ant's thundering snores.

Hoping to make the most of some quiet time in the empty house, and perhaps even walk down to the beach despite the rain, I slipped from beneath the covers and pulled a dressing gown on before creeping through to the kitchen.

Marge was already up, peering disconsolately into the empty refrigerator. 'There's nothing for breakfast,' she said. 'There's not even enough milk for tea.'

'Oh, we've got stuff in the car, don't worry,' I said. 'I'll get it.'

'Fat lot of good it is out there,' Marge replied as I turned to head off in search of Ant's keys.

Her comment caused me to pause in the doorway, but I took a deep breath, and succeeded in controlling my anger. I'd managed to keep my calm around Marge for years, but I sensed that something was changing. A fury was rising within me and I was seriously concerned that this holiday might be the thing to send me over the edge.

I lifted the keys from the pocket of Ant's jacket and headed out into the drizzle. We'd only brought the basics: bread, butter, Marmite, tea, coffee and milk, but it was enough to last until we could get to the shop in Stoke Fleming.

When I returned, Marge was in the lounge, staring out through the rain-splattered window at the dingy garden. She made no sign of noticing my return, so I carried the bags into the kitchen, distributed the items between cupboards and the fridge, and then, as a peace offering, I made two mugs of tea. I'd decided that 'losing it' would provoke a maelstrom that I might not be able to control. I couldn't face that prospect, and I specifically didn't want it happening at the beginning of my holiday, here in my perfect place.

51

When I carried the mugs of tea into the lounge, I found Marge in the same spot as before, still staring out at the wet garden. She looked as if she'd been deactivated by the use of some magical remote control. 'Here,' I said, holding out one of the mugs.

She turned her head so slowly and in such a smooth manner that she truly looked like a robot. As her face was devoid of emotion, there was something creepy, something deeply menacing, about her that I couldn't quite put my finger on.

She looked at me as if she had no idea who I was, and I remember wondering if she'd perhaps had a stroke, or whether this was the beginning of Alzheimer's. If I'm being honest, I have to admit that by that point, neither possibility exactly filled me with horror. My God, how quickly abuse can destroy what was once a basically charitable nature.

But then Marge blinked, forced a rictus of a smile revealing stained dentures, and reached for the mug. 'Thanks, you're a sweetheart,' she said, reinforcing the impression that she'd momentarily forgotten who I was, or who she was, or perhaps both.

She sipped at her drink, pulled a face, and said, 'Oh, this ain't tea, love. This is cat's pee.'

I think my mouth fell open. I was certainly lost for words.

Muttering, 'Jesus! How the hell anyone can get to your age without knowing how to make a decent cuppa . . . !', she left the room.

In a weird, dreamlike mood – perhaps a *nightmare* mood would be more accurate – I followed her through to the kitchen and watched from the doorway as she tipped the tea I had made down the sink, and filled the kettle to start again from scratch.

'You don't like the tea,' I heard myself say without emotion.

'No, I don't,' Marge replied.

'You don't like *me* very much, do you?' I added. *Wow!* I thought. *Daring!*

She glanced at me, frowned, and worked her wrinkled lips silently for a moment before returning her attention to the kettle. 'Like you,' she repeated flatly.

'Yes . . . you don't. You really don't, do you?' I repeated.

'Well, I don't *dis*like you,' she said, surprising me.

'You don't?'

'No, not really,' she said, still addressing the kettle.

'Well, let's say that you don't think much of me, then,' I said. 'And I really don't know why that is.'

'I don't think much of you,' she repeated, sounding thoughtful. Then, 'No, I wouldn't say that's true either, dear.'

Surprised at this, and thinking that maybe we were actually making progress here, that perhaps all that had been needed all along was for me to challenge her, I asked, 'So what would you say about it, Marge? What *would* you say is true?'

She shrugged again. 'I dunno really,' she said.

'Really? You don't know? Or you won't say?'

'I suppose,' she said, 'if pushed . . . I mean, if you really *pushed* me to say something, I'd have to admit that I don't really think about you at all.'

I took a sharp intake of breath and felt myself flush red from the verbal slap.

'I mean, you did ask,' Marge said. 'You sort of insisted, didn't you?'

'Yes,' I whispered.

'And the thing is, well, it's just that there's not much *to* think about, is there, love? There's so little to you. So, I suppose, if I was forced, like, to think about it, I'd say that the only real problem I have with you is that.'

Because her comment contained a shadow of truth, because so much of my personality *had* vanished over the years, it cut me to the bone. So, I didn't say a word. I simply put my mug of tea down on the counter and turned and went back to the bedroom, where I lay, drowning silently in a mixture of shame and rage. When Lucy came in half an hour later, I feigned sleep until, thankfully, Ant climbed from the bed.

The rain continued and because, when I occasionally did get up for the bathroom or for a drink, the atmosphere in the house felt quite suffocating, I pretended to be ill and basically hid in the bedroom all day.

Finally, at about five, Ant came and sat on the edge of the bed. 'Do we need a doctor?' he asked, laying the back of his hand across my forehead. 'Or are you going to get up?' The message was clear enough: I'd reached the end of my permitted downtime.

That evening we ate in the Green Dragon in Stoke Fleming. The food was basic pub grub, but it was well cooked and tasty: burgers for Ant and his mother, a huge cheese ploughman's plus some sides for me and the girls.

Their behaviour was angelic, but still Marge managed to find fault, telling Lucy off for not holding the huge knife properly and mocking little Sarah for asking if someone could remove the 'slimy bit' from the inside of the onion ring.

'It's an onion ring,' Marge told her. 'And if you take out the onion, it won't be a bloody onion ring, will it? So stop being daft and just eat, will you?'

'She's fine,' I told her, as I proceeded to extract the onion from the batter.

'You need to get these kids eating properly,' Marge said. 'Stop catering to all their silly whims and wants, because they'll drive you insane if—'

'She's fine!' I said again, shooting Ant a glare.

I think he must have sensed just how close to the edge I was, because, unusually, he backed me up. 'She's only six, Mum,' he said. 'Give her a break, OK?'

Marge snorted. 'Because what could *I* possibly know about child rearing?' she muttered.

It was still drizzling when we stepped back outside, and though I was starting to enjoy a certain sense of satisfaction that the weather was ruining Marge's holiday, I wasn't so caught up in it that I didn't notice it was spoiling ours as well. So it was with relief (plus a smidgin of perverse disappointment) that I received news that tomorrow would be sunny.

That evening we watched a couple of films, which everyone except Marge enjoyed.

Having declared them 'pointless spearmint for the mind', she dozed off in her armchair, so by shifting sideways in my seat, I was able to pretend she wasn't there.

About three in the morning, Ant woke me up, purportedly to ask how I was feeling.

Such concern was rare enough, but actually waking me up to ask me seemed plain weird.

'I'm fine,' I told him, frowning, yawning and glancing at the alarm clock simultaneously. 'Why? Is something wrong with one of the girls?'

'I just wanted to check you're OK,' he said.

'I'm *fine*,' I told him again, feeling annoyed that he'd woken me for nothing. 'I just need to sl—'

'I know *exactly* what you need,' he said, pulling at my shoulder in an attempt to get me to roll on to my stomach.

'No, Ant,' I said, pushing back. 'I'm sleepy. In fact, I *am* asleep.'

'I think I might know how to wake you up,' he said, in what I guessed was supposed to be his sexy voice.

'Ant, no,' I said again, but he was pulling so hard that I had no choice but to give way.

'I'm horny,' he said, lowering his weight on to my back. I could tell from the hard sensation against my buttocks that what he was saying was the truth.

'That's as maybe, but I'm *not*, Ant,' I whined. 'I'm sleepy.'

'You don't have to do anything,' he said. 'Just let me—'

'No!' I said, squeezing my legs together.

'It's been ages,' he said, starting to sound angry. 'It's been fucking for ever.'

I thought about pointing out that it was he who had ceased asking for sex, but as that absence of sex had suited me, it felt like it would be a strategic error to do so.

'All right then,' I finally sighed, thinking that the choice here was between an argument or sex, and that the sex option almost certainly took less effort. 'Just not . . . you know.'

'Not here?' he asked, running a finger down between my butt cheeks.

'No, not there,' I said, in the most definitive tone of voice I could manage. 'I'm sore.'

'Not from me, you're not,' Ant said. 'Who's been making you sore, then?'

'No, not from you, Ant,' I told him. 'From pooing.' And that seemed to do the trick. I'd managed to make his preferred option seem suddenly far less sexy. I only wished I'd thought of it before.

'Oh, OK then,' he said, rolling me over on to my back and lowering himself on top of me instead. 'Let's play missionaries.'

Would I have chosen to have sex with him at that precise moment? No, of course not. In fact, had it been up to me, I'm not sure we would ever have had sex again.

But my body responded and about five minutes in I forgot to be annoyed with him about it and started to enjoy the sensations of him over me, within me – that long-forgotten feeling of being consumed.

As ever, Ant seemed to be going for gold, and I was pretty sure that his aim was to force me to get noisy. He had always seemed to need witnesses for everything, as if, without someone watching, he couldn't know what was real. I suspect his ego was so fragile that he needed external proof that he was good, that he was successful, that he *existed*, perhaps. But with the girls in the room to the left, and Marge in the room to the right, I simply couldn't allow myself to fulfil that need tonight.

'Ant,' I said, through my breath. 'Quiet. The girls.'

It was then that I noticed a thin strip of light across the ceiling and, as Ant ignored my request for calm and went at it with ever more vigour, I twisted sideways in an attempt at looking across the room. But I couldn't see. The room was too dark and Ant's big body was obscuring the view.

'A— A— Ant . . .' I panted, managing to point to the wall behind him. 'The door.'

'What?' he asked, straining to look over his shoulder.

Only when he froze did I finally get to see why the door was half open. I thought for a moment I was going to throw up.

'Mum . . .' Ant said. 'Close the door.'

But Marge didn't move. She looked, once again, as if she'd been switched off.

'Mum!' Ant repeated, more loudly. 'Close the fucking door!'

He started to roll off me then, but aware that if he did so, it was me who Marge would see naked rather than her son, I pulled him close. 'No,' I said, gesturing. 'Grab that sheet.'

By the time Ant had reeled in the covers and pulled them over us, the door had silently closed.

Saying, 'Well, that was strange,' Ant centred himself on top of me and started grinding his hips against mine once again.

'You are joking, right?' I told him. When he continued, I said, 'No, Ant. Stop!' And when *still* he continued, I whacked the side of his head.

He froze. Time stood still.

It hadn't been a hard slap by any means, but it was the first time I'd ever hit him, so I wondered if, for the first time ever, he would now hit me back.

Thanks be, he simply rolled off me. 'Fuck you then,' he said. And promptly started to masturbate.

In the morning, I was woken by the sound of Sarah crying. Telling Ant, who was also stirring, to sleep on, I pulled my dressing gown around me and went next door to the girls' room.

'What's the matter?' I asked, quickly closing the door behind me.

Sarah was red-faced and snotty. 'She stole Piggy,' she told me, pointing at Lucy in the bed across the room. Piggy was Sarah's once-fluffy, now-bald piglet that she'd slept with almost since birth.

'She *gave* him to me,' Lucy said, which, though most unlikely, was not entirely impossible.

'Give it to me,' I said, sweeping Sarah up in my arms, then crouching down and extending the other hand to receive the stolen piglet.

Lucy shrugged and produced the toy from beneath the covers. 'I don't want her stupid pig anyway,' she said.

But as the toy changed hands, Sarah, emboldened by my presence, took a swipe at her sister, managing to just about make contact. Lucy, of course, started crying.

'Oh, stop it, both of you!' I said. 'You've got your piglet back, and she didn't hurt *you* at all.' That didn't calm either of them down.

'Hey, hey, HEY!' I said, jiggling Sarah, while attempting to stroke Lucy's head. 'Hey, how about . . . we go to the beach?'

'The beach?' Lucy asked. Sarah's sobbing had ceased, too.

'Why not? The rain's stopped. If you're really, really quiet and you don't wake Grandma up, we could have breakfast down on the beach.'

'What, like a picnic?' Lucy asked, bright-eyed.

'Exactly like a picnic,' I said. 'A breakfast picnic.'

The girls, motivated by the idea of a picnic on the beach, were as good as gold, creeping around the house and whispering excitedly. I managed to pull everything together before either Marge or Anthony woke up.

Beneath the surface, the sand was still soaked from the previous day's rain, but the sun was shining and the sea was calm, and we were finally alone on our beach. All was well.

We ate jam sandwiches and drank milk straight from the bottle, and then I stretched out on the already damp towel as the girls ran into the waves.

Blackpool Sands had suddenly become paradise again. I closed my eyes for a moment and let the sunshine warm my face.

About ten, Anthony joined us briefly. 'I wondered where you'd all gone,' he said. 'It was weird waking up in an empty house.'

'We're just here,' I said, thinking about last night and feeling relieved that he seemed to be in a reasonable mood despite it.

'Where's Mum?' he asked, scanning the beach.

I told him I didn't know and that I'd assumed she was at the house.

'She must have gone for a wander,' he said. 'I hope she doesn't get lost.'

'Indeed,' I replied. It was as much as I could do not to raise an eyebrow.

He wandered off in search of Marge, leaving me alone with the girls once again.

'Can you help us make a dam?' Lucy asked.

'Sure,' I said. 'Of course I can!'

At midday, Ant returned. He hadn't found Marge and was starting to sound concerned.

'She's fine,' I told him.

'You don't know that,' he said. 'Anything could have happened.'

I asked if he'd tried calling her, but it seemed she'd left her phone in the bedroom.

'Well, maybe she wants some time alone,' I said. 'It happens.'

He started to leave again, so I asked him if he'd nip up to the café first for sandwiches. When he pulled a face, I offered to do it instead. 'Just keep an eye on the girls for me. It'll only take five minutes.'

I picked up my handbag and started to cross to the beach café. But the sand was surprisingly hot, so I returned for my flip-flops and, as an afterthought, pulled on a T-shirt and shorts. I'd have to cross the restaurant, after all.

With it being Saturday and the first sunny day for a week, the beach café was busy, so it wasn't until I'd almost reached the counter that I spotted Marge. She was seated at a table playing cards with two elderly gentlemen, and she looked like she was having fun. I remember being surprised, because I'd honestly never imagined that she had any capacity for actual enjoyment.

It took a moment before she saw me watching, but when she did, she nodded in my direction and then leaned in to discreetly tell the men some scurrilous snippet.

I didn't know what she'd said but I could see their reaction clearly enough: one of the men, the one with what was obviously a toupee, laughed, while the bald one sniggered and looked away.

When the man in front of me finished paying and moved away, I stepped forward so that the cashier could ring up my purchases: three sandwiches and a bottle of juice – items I squashed into my handbag.

When I turned to leave, they were still glancing at me, still laughing, and something within me snapped. I marched over to their table to confront them. 'Morning, Marge. Is something funny?' I asked.

Marge pulled an expression of fake innocence and shook her head. 'Not at all, dear,' she said.

'Hello,' wig man said, extending a hand. 'I'm Billy.'

'You looked like you were laughing at me,' I said, ignoring him. I was hearing my own words as I spoke and feeling embarrassed at how childish they sounded. I was also becoming hyperconscious of the fact that people at nearby tables were turning to look. 'I thought you might like to share the joke, that's all,' I added quietly. 'I could do with a laugh.'

'Oh, there's no joke!' Marge said, sounding entirely disingenuous. 'No joke at all. And no laughter 'ere, dear. We wouldn't dare, would we?'

I rolled my eyes at the ceiling and turned to leave. But as I started to slalom between the tables, I heard her mutter, 'Anyways, after last night, I'm all laughed out, ain't I?' and as I glanced back at them, Billy cracked up once again.

I span on one foot and returned. I hitched my handbag higher on my shoulder and gripped the edge of the table. 'What did you just say?' I asked.

'Nothing,' Marge said, looking with barely disguised mirth between her two companions.

61

'Yeah, c'mon, Madge,' said the man who wasn't Billy, glancing at me apologetically before lowering his gaze to his hands. 'That's a bit under the belt.'

'It's Marge,' she said. 'Get it right.'

It was then that I understood definitively that she had told them. She hadn't been sleepwalking, she remembered everything. And worst of all, she'd been joking with strangers about it.

I lifted the sandwiches from my handbag and placed them on the edge of the table.

'You can take those out to your grandchildren,' I said coldly. 'They're just out the front there.'

And then, without looking back, I crossed to the other side of the restaurant, where I left by the street-side door.

I was so embarrassed and angry that I couldn't work out if I needed to scream or cry, and the confusion between those different emotions left me feeling a bit numb. So I simply walked as fast as I could along the seafront and then hesitated before changing direction and walking the other way, back to the house.

Once indoors, I stared out of that same window I'd caught Marge looking from and I suspect that to an onlooker I would have appeared just as lifeless.

After a certain time, perhaps a few minutes, perhaps much longer, I snapped out of it. Anthony, I realised, would be back soon. And if I didn't leave now, I'd have to explain, and then deal with whatever reaction my explanation produced.

I trotted to the bedroom, changed my clothes, pulled on a pair of espadrilles, and added knickers, a T-shirt, a jumper and my toothbrush to the contents of my handbag. I had no coherent idea what I was doing or where I was going – I was simply aware that I needed to be anywhere but here.

It took me fifteen minutes to walk to Stoke Fleming and, for no other reason than that it was familiar, I headed to the Green Dragon, where I bought a large white wine at the bar.

'Are you OK?' the barman asked me. I think he was concerned at the speed with which I'd gulped down my vase of wine.

'Yes, I'm fine,' I said. 'But do you rent rooms?'

He shook his head. 'You could try Fords House, up that way,' he suggested, pointing. 'Or if not, Leonards Cove. They're much bigger, more capacity . . . But, honestly?'

I nodded for him to continue.

'A Saturday? In July? It's unlikely.'

I walked in the direction he'd indicated and by the time I reached Fords House the alcohol was starting to take effect. I was feeling quite seriously tipsy.

The guest house was a large, pretty building with Georgian leaded windows, baby-blue stucco walls and ivy climbing up the drainpipes.

When a sullen teenager informed me that they were full, I almost cried, but before I'd reached the end of the street, a woman tapped me on the shoulder.

'Sorry,' she said breathlessly, 'but we've had a cancellation. Would you like to see the room?' And so I followed her back to the house.

The room was clean and pretty, with a view out over the garden.

Because the owner seemed concerned about my lack of luggage, I told her I'd be fetching it later from the car. I'd parked on the wrong side of town, I lied.

I've never been a very good liar, and she seemed doubtful, but then she caught sight of the golden tint of my credit card, and suddenly all was well.

I took a shower and dried myself on fluffy towels before laying myself across the cool cotton sheets.

I stared at the ceiling for a while, and when my phone rang with an incoming call from Anthony, I reached over and switched it to silent.

It was only then that I took a normal, full breath of air. It was, I realised, the first time I'd managed to do so in days.

I must have fallen asleep for a bit because when I next glanced at my phone it was almost three. The screen also informed me that I'd missed five calls from Anthony, and that I had three voicemails and four text messages waiting.

I listened to the voicemails first. They started off by informing me that he'd found Marge and that I could return. Had he actually imagined I was looking for her? He then went on to ask where I was, and if I was OK, and then, with an increasing sense of urgency and irritation, when I was coming home.

The most recent text message read, 'The girls are crying for their mummy. What the fuck do I tell them?'

I knew this had been purpose designed as a heat-seeking missile aimed at my heart, but knowing this didn't seem to offer any protection. I needed to know that my girls were OK.

Anthony answered immediately. 'Jesus, where *are* you?' he asked. 'We've been looking all over.'

'I'm fine,' I told him. 'I'm in a hotel.'

There was a pause then, before he repeated, 'In a hotel?'

'Yes, I'm in a hotel for the night. I needed a break. I'll be back in the morning.'

'No, you're coming back right now,' he said.

'I'm not. I—'

'You're to come home now. You're needed.'

'Oh, you can cope without me for one night,' I said.

'For fuck's sake,' Ant said, getting angry. 'The girls need you. And a break from *what*, anyway?'

'I'll explain tomorrow,' I said.

'No, you'll tell me now. You're to come home and we can talk about whatever it is right now.'

'No. Sorry. Um, good night, Ant,' I said, as lightly as I could manage. And then I ended the call.

My phone rang again immediately, and as not answering it made me feel sick, I switched it off, only to discover that made me feel even worse.

So I switched it back on and no sooner had I typed the code to unlock it than it began to ring all over again.

'Ant!' I said, on answering. 'Can't you just . . . chill . . . or something? Can't I just have—'

'Chill?' he spat. 'You're telling *me* to chill?'

'I just need a few hours on my own. I just . . .'

'What?' he said. 'You just *what*?'

'I can't be under the same roof as that woman. Not this evening.'

'If by *that woman* you mean my mother,' Ant said, 'she doesn't want to be here either. In fact, she wants to go home.'

'Home?' I said. 'What do you mean, home?'

'Apparently it's going to piss down all week, anyway. Starting tomorrow, so . . .'

'Look, we can talk about it in the morning,' I said. 'We can look at the weather and decide what to do.'

'I'm not angry or anything,' Ant said. 'I promise. Just come back.'

'Tomorrow,' I said. 'I've paid anyway, so . . .'

'The girls need you,' he said. 'They're worried.'

'Then reassure them,' I told him. 'You know they don't need to be worried, so reassure them.'

'Only I don't know anything, do I?' Ant said. 'Not with you behaving like a lunatic.'

'Ant,' I said. 'Just give me a break, OK?' It was one of his favourite phrases. 'One night alone. Is that really too much to ask?'

'Yes,' he said. 'Yes, it's too much to ask.'

'Well, tough. I'll see you in the morning.'

'I'm not OK with this,' he said.

'I can hear that.'

'This is bullshit, Heather, and you know it. This is absolute bullshit, and if you don't—'

That's when I hung up on him again. And it's when I switched my phone off for good.

I stayed there for another hour, staring at the ceiling, trying to catch my breath again. But I felt stressed and nauseous and miserable. Whatever I'd hoped for, it wasn't this.

I was just wondering if it wouldn't be better to return and face the music when there was a timid knock on the door.

'That's it,' I heard a woman's voice say. 'Knock harder.'

I opened the door to find Sarah beaming up at me from the hallway. Behind her stood the adolescent I'd seen earlier.

'She wanted to surprise you,' she explained.

'Daddy says to tell you to come down,' Sarah said with precision. 'He says the car's all packed and we're ready to go. And he's on *yellow double* lines.'

'Gosh,' I said, crouching down and forcing a reassuring smile for my daughter. 'Is he here?'

She nodded. 'Gran and Lucy are in the car. Gran says we have to go home now, but Lucy wants to go to the beach.'

'OK . . .' I said.

'Do we *have* to go home?'

I sighed and mentally sieved through all the possibilities, working out various knock-on scenarios. And then I scooped her up in my arms and wrinkled my nose as I said, 'Yeah, I'm afraid we do, honey. But we'll do something nice at home instead, OK?'

She nodded reluctantly. 'Will we be able to go to a funfair?' she asked.

'Yeah, maybe,' I said. 'Maybe we can.'

'OK then,' she conceded. 'Is that where you've been all day?' she asked, pointing over my shoulder.

'Yes,' I said, 'I came here for a snooze.'

'Can I see?' she asked.

'Sure,' I said. 'You can help me gather my things.'

No one spoke for the first half an hour of the drive, and eventually Ant switched on the radio, which was a relief. Marge sat up front, stony-faced, though perhaps no more so than usual, while the girls slept either side of me. To avoid interaction, I pretended to have fallen asleep, and a few hours into the journey my anger cooled enough for it to really happen.

When I woke up, we were already in Broadstairs, and Ant was lifting Marge's bag from the back of the car. Cool night air was rushing in.

'God, what time is it?' I asked, over my shoulder.

'It's half eleven,' he replied. 'Go back to sleep. We'll be home soon.'

He never did ask me what had happened that lunchtime, and by the next morning I didn't want to think about it, let alone talk about it, ever again.

But I suspected Marge had told Ant something, or he'd pieced his own version together from clues, because he certainly seemed more tolerant than usual of my aversion to his mother.

According to the TV, the weather was indeed far worse down in Devon than in Kent, so we felt blessed whenever the sun came out, and managed to make the most of our holiday-at-home, taking the girls, as promised, to Dreamland, and even managing two full days on the beach.

The only oblique reference to the whole drama came the following spring when Ant asked me if I thought he should reserve Beach Cottage again, 'or not'.

'Not,' I replied, with conviction. It was unusual that he should even seek my opinion, so I assumed he'd been expecting my reply. He certainly didn't seem surprised.

'Mum thought maybe Cornwall . . .' he started, but seeing my expression, his voice faded. 'OK. Where then?' he asked.

'Here's just fine,' I told him. 'As long as it's just the four of us.'

'Oh . . . OK,' he said. Again, it wasn't the reaction I would have expected.

By May, I was regretting my decision. I spent all day, every day, in Chislet, after all, and the idea of spending the two weeks of Ant's holidays cooped up with him there was even less attractive than my normal day-to-day solitude.

But Devon had left a nasty taste in my mouth – actually, more of a physical aversion – and I was terrified that Marge would worm her way into any trip that we could plan within driving distance.

What I secretly wanted was to discover somewhere further afield – maybe even a new country with a different language – somewhere with different coins and foods and customs.

But how on earth could I make that happen? As I say, as far as Ant was concerned, trips to foreign parts, even to visit my sister – still living in Rome, but now single – were out of the question. He would have liked the idea of me travelling without him even less.

At the beginning of June, Lucy surprised us at the dinner table by asking if we could go to Spain.

'Spain?' I laughed. I glanced at Ant, who shrugged in a *search me* kind of way. 'Why do you want to go to Spain?'

'Ben wants us to go,' she said.

'What?' I asked, frowning at my daughter. Though I knew that Ben was her current sweetheart, her statement made no sense to me.

'He *wants* us to go to *Spain*,' Lucy repeated, as if I was stupid for not understanding.

'I'm sorry, darling,' I said, shooting an amused glance at Ant, 'but you're not making any sense to me. Where did this idea come from?'

Lucy rolled her eyes. 'We had to write a story. A holiday story,' Lucy told me. 'I said I haven't got one, cos we're staying at home. And Ben said we should go to Spain.'

'Because Ben's going to Spain?' I said.

'Yes!' Lucy replied.

'Ah, I see,' I said. 'Well, I'm afraid it's a bit more complicated than that. We'd have to book flights and find a house to stay in. We don't even have passp—'

'No, stupid!' Lucy said. 'We can stay in—'

'*Don't* call your mother stupid,' Ant interjected, raising one finger.

Lucy tutted and rolled her eyes again. My angelic child was starting to become a proper little madam. 'Ben's got a house to stay in,' she said. 'A big house with lots of rooms.'

'Right,' I said. 'But I'm sure Ben's parents aren't expecting to share that house with us. It's like the house we rented in Dorset. That was just for us, remember? So the house they've rented is for them. Do you understand, honey?'

'It was Devon,' Ant corrected me, 'not Dorset.'

'OK, Devon,' I said. 'But the point is—'

'His mum says it's OK,' Lucy said with a shrug.

'You've asked his *mum* about this?'

'It's a special gnome house,' Lucy said, nodding as she warmed to her subject. 'It's made out of caves the gnomes used to live in and Ben's grandad can't go with them any more and Ben's sad cos he really likes him even though sometimes he's a bit strict, and they've got loads of rooms for everyone. It's got a *jamuzzi* or something, and a swimming pool with water that goes the wrong way so you have to swim and swim but you don't get anywhere, but Ben's mum doesn't like that because she says it feels like being in a bad dream.'

'Honey, you know that you can't just go away with strangers,' Ant said.

'But Ben's not a stranger,' Lucy said.

'No, but his parents are,' I explained. 'I've seen his mother maybe once or twice in my whole life. And I'm not sure I've *ever* laid eyes on his father.' The truth was that I was struggling to picture either of them.

'Oh, he's really nice,' Lucy said. 'Isn't Ben's dad nice?' she asked, turning to Sarah, who nodded her agreement.

'He gave me a lollipop,' Sarah said.

'Well, that's as maybe, but we still can't go on holiday with strangers. Now eat up your tea,' Ant told her.

Lucy pushed her bottom lip out and picked up her fork. 'A stranger's, like, a *bad* person,' she said. 'A stranger is someone you mustn't get in a car with. But Ben's not a stranger. He's my friend.'

Two

Joe

My parents were basically brilliant. I know people are surprised when I say that because so many bad-mouth their mums and dads these days, but it's true. They were ace.

Actually, I wonder sometimes if all the horror stories you hear are even true – if there isn't a bit of exaggeration going on, do you know what I mean? Because it does sometimes seem like everyone wants to be a victim these days.

Anyway, no victim status here – no excuses for whatever I'm supposed to be but am not. My childhood was great, so it's all on me.

My dad, Reg, is retired now, but for most of my childhood he was a plumber. A lot of middle-class people assume that because he was a tradesman he must be a bit thick, but they're wrong. There are actually plenty of clever plumbers out there, and the majority of them earn more than most teachers. If you've ever had the misfortune to call out an emergency plumber at midnight, you'll know that they don't come cheap.

Mum always worked, too. When I was little, she was a cashier in one of those little local shops that try to sell everything but never really have what you want, bang in the middle of Whitby. And yes, you've guessed it: that's how the two of them met. If chatting up your sweetheart in front of a selection of plastic buckets might not be everyone's idea of romance, it certainly worked for Mum and Dad. No one ever doubted how much they loved each other.

Willis Bargains went bust the year that I went to secondary school, put out of business by the arrival of various out-of-town superstores, so Mum and Dad ploughed their savings into a Regency terrace on the seafront, which they'd decided to run as a guest house.

Everyone said it was a mistake, that it couldn't possibly work, and I suppose those weren't the best years to be opening a bed and breakfast in Whitby. But Mum – who had a flair for shabby chic long before anyone had thought of calling it that – made a go of it, and with Dad's DIY skills, plus a little cash from occasional plumbing jobs, they made it look brilliant. Though nothing we ever had was brand new, we honestly never lacked for anything.

Mum and Dad were both big readers, so the house was always stuffed full of books. Dad, who I suppose you could say was on a spiritual quest, favoured biographies and hefty volumes about philosophy or religion, while Mum was more into fiction and would plough her way through the Booker longlist every year, titles she would request at the local library.

For a while, in the nineties, Dad was a Buddhist – he even used to chant, which always gave Mum the giggles. But then his reading led him to Christian Science, then TM and deism and the rambling writings of Walt Whitman, and at that point the chanting stopped. In the end I think he slotted together everything he'd read – plumber-style – to build his own hybrid belief system. Whatever it was he came up with, it certainly worked for him: he was pretty much always smiling.

So yes, my childhood was good. I felt loved and cherished by two calm, centred people who clearly loved one another. And I grew up with a healthy attitude to life, specifically to the money and material issues that everyone else seems to struggle so much with.

Just occasionally I'd get jealous – what kid doesn't? So, sure, a friend's Raleigh racer would catch my eye, or the school bully's All Star boots, and I'd wonder why I couldn't have stuff like that. But then I'd go round to friends' houses and hear the lifeless discussions about *EastEnders*; I'd see the empty bookcases, the lack of hi-fi (our Marantz was ancient but sounded amazing); I'd sit on their brand-new mock-leather sofa, bought on tick, and understand on a subconscious level – these thoughts were never actually words or phrases – that my parents were unusual, were special, and I was lucky to be growing up the way I was.

Mum died unexpectedly when she was fifty-two, and the shock of it almost killed Dad. He was older than her and a smoker and a drinker, whereas Mum was a healthy-eating, teetotal hillwalker. I don't think any of us ever imagined that she might go first. But hearts are unpredictable, it would seem. No one can tell when a heart is going to stop.

For six months Dad barely left his bed, and I thought he'd decided to die. With effort, I even understood how logical willing his own death would be. They'd been everything to each other, after all. How could life without the other be imagined?

But then about nine months after the funeral he started reading again, and at the one-year anniversary he tidied the house. I can only assume that something in one of his books enabled him to make sense of it all.

We never spoke about what had changed, but one weekend I went to visit and there he was, looking spritely, painting walls. I have never felt so relieved.

The only person I ever met who raved about her parents as much as I do was Amy, but in the end that all turned out to be lies.

Perhaps I went overboard telling her about my own amazing parents, so she felt she needed to get competitive about it. She was always pretty driven about most things.

I met her at a yoga retreat, which might sound weird from a bloke like me. Yoga isn't necessarily something that you expect a kitchen fitter to be doing, I guess.

But all that humping flat-pack kitchen units around – all the squeezing myself beneath countertops – was doing terrible things to my vertebrae, and one of Dad's Buddhist mates suggested yoga might help.

As by then I was on painkillers 24/7, and because they were playing havoc with my guts, I was ready to try anything. I'd reached the end of the road with the local NHS; acupuncture hadn't worked, and nor had my sessions with the osteopath. I'd recently split up with my girlfriend, Gemma, as well, so was at a loss to know what to do with my summer holiday. So I booked myself on to a yoga course down near Malaga. I'd combine beach, sunshine and fixing my back; or at least, that's what I hoped.

Amy was the first person I spoke to. In fact, she greeted me as I walked up the dusty path from where the taxi had dropped me off. She had a great figure and perfect poise – she walked like a ballerina, if you know what I mean – and because she greeted me and led me to my room, I assumed that she was the organiser.

It wasn't until next morning at breakfast that I understood she was just another punter. I was even more surprised when it dawned that she was chatting me up.

Now, I don't have any kind of downer on myself – I don't think I'm a monster or anything. But I knew I was no James Dean either, and Amy seemed out of my league from the start. I never quite got over my surprise that she wanted me in her bed. Then again, every person present: the other students, the teachers, the cooks and cleaners . . . every single one was female. So maybe, at the beginning, that's all it was.

The yoga retreat turned out to be a great holiday, and though it didn't provide an instant solution to my back problems, it did set me on a long road to recovery. By the end of my ten-day stay I was tanned, relaxed and, through eating their ultra-healthy vegan fare, I'd lost a few pounds as well.

On top of this – mega bonus – I came home from the trip with a new girlfriend. And not any old girlfriend, either: a witty, stunningly sexy, surprisingly bendy girlfriend. And that was totally unexpected.

Until the final morning, when she asked, 'So can I come with you?', I truly hadn't believed that Amy was anything more than a holiday romance.

She had dual nationality, it transpired. She was both Canadian and English, and had alternated, since her parents' divorce many years before, between Toronto and Kent. She had a boyfriend back in Toronto too, though I suppose 'she'd had' would be the correct tense. Because other than to collect some things during her single trip back to Canada, she never saw him again.

Amy was so bright and funny and sexy that none of my mates could believe she was mine. Even Dad was under her spell. 'Well done, son,' he told me. 'You've surpassed yourself this time.'

But no matter how much everyone liked Amy, Amy didn't seem to like Whitby at all.

'Do you have to live here?' she asked me, halfway through our second week of living as a couple. 'Or would you consider moving down south?'

'Why? Don't you like it?' I asked her, feeling quite shocked.

She shrugged and pulled a face. 'It's a bit . . . you know . . . gritty.'

'Gritty?' I said.

'It's a bit like living in a documentary.'

'Well, my dad's here,' I pointed out, doing my best to ignore the slur on my home town. 'And he's not getting any younger. My mates are here, too. My business is here . . .'

'Yeah, and *my* mum's in Kent,' Amy said, 'and she's even older. *My* friends are all in Canterbury.'

'I thought they were all in Toronto,' I said.

'Not really,' Amy replied. 'Not my real friends.'

And I was in love with her, wasn't I? It wasn't the calm, deep, meaningful kind of love that my parents had either. It was the hormonal, raised-heartbeat kind of love, where you struggle to work out where sex ends and love begins, where *you* end and the loved one begins . . . And there's not much you can do to fight that kind of love. It makes everything seem possible. It makes nothing seem unreasonable.

So we moved south. What else was I going to do?

We rented a flat in the north of Canterbury, and Amy introduced me to her friends. They were all crystals-and-homeopathy kind of people, and I didn't feel I had a huge amount in common with them. If I'm honest, I struggled to convince myself that they were particularly good friends to Amy, either, but I never would have said that out loud.

I found work easily, and putting up kitchens in Kent rather than Yorkshire made little difference; if anything, I was simply better paid. There was more money down south, that much was clear.

I made some new drinking buddies through work, and though these weren't the deep friendships I'd left behind, they were enough to stop me feeling lonely. Amy found work teaching Pilates and jazz dance at the local gym, so between us we started to live quite well. For a while, everything seemed fine.

But Amy wasn't happy in Canterbury, either, it transpired. The people were superficial, she said. City life was too aggressive. She wanted to get closer to nature.

We started visiting villages around Canterbury, but none of them really suited Amy.

They were too small, so she'd never be able to earn a living. Or they were too big and didn't feel like the country at all. It was the same with the houses we looked at: too big, too small, too draughty, too new . . . The hormones that had fired up our relationship for two years were finally wearing off as well, so I was starting to be able to see Amy more clearly. I was beginning to understand she had a problem. Nothing was ever enough.

Amy had skeletons in the closet, too. Something about her fabulous family wasn't quite right.

Her mother lived in nearby Ashford, and Amy would visit her most weeks. But me? Though Amy would tell me often how kind or clever or funny she was, I didn't seem to be allowed even to glimpse the woman, nor did I ever speak to her on the phone. I began to wonder if she existed; wondered if Amy wasn't seeing another man.

The day I challenged her about it was the day we had the biggest row we'd ever had. But though there was lots of shouting, it was an argument that provided no answers.

'She's my mother!' was all Amy would tell me. 'She's not *your* mother.'

'You've met my dad,' I pointed out reasonably. 'And he loves you to bits.'

'So what?' Amy asked, her voice trembling. 'I mean, for fuck's sake, Joe. It's up to me, isn't it?'

Eventually, I scratched my head and conceded. It *was* up to her, wasn't it? And if she didn't want me to meet her amazing mother, then who was I to complain? 'Think yourself lucky,' a joiner I worked with told me one day. '*My* mother-in-law's an absolute bloody nightmare.'

The next time Amy returned from Ashford she showed me a photo she'd taken on her Blackberry. It pictured her wearing the clothes she'd left the house in that morning, next to a grey-haired woman. They had the same shape of nose, the same distinguished jawline . . . It was obvious they were mother and daughter.

'Happy?' Amy asked. 'Convinced?'

'Sure,' I said. 'Fine. Whatever.' My business had really taken off by then, and there was far more work than I could manage. So Amy's mother wasn't that high on my list of priorities anyway.

I took on a twenty-year-old apprentice, who, amusingly, was also called Joe. Our clients began referring to us as 'the Joes', and eventually that's what we painted on the side of the van.

In 2008 we bought a house, a red-brick doer-upper out in Chislet. Actually, though I did all the work on the place, it was always more Amy's than it was mine. Her dad, in Toronto, had retired and sold his business, sending her a chunk of money in the process.

It had been Amy's idea to buy the place, too. What with the financial crisis and everything, she didn't trust the banks, she said, so buying a house was the logical choice. In theory, she was going to grow organic vegetables in the huge garden. We were going to be self-sufficient – as if that was ever going to happen. Like most things, digging didn't turn out to be as much fun as Amy had hoped.

It was about then that she read *The Power of Now*. I mention that book specifically because it was a turning point in Amy's life, and I don't mean that in a good way. I never read it myself – after seeing how it affected Amy, I was a bit scared, I suppose. But Dad skimmed it and told me it all seemed quite reasonable, so it remains something of a mystery as to why it messed so badly with Amy's head.

Amy had always been a woman who *wanted things*, and I'd come to see that this was a big part of why she was never happy. Being happy, it seems to me, requires wanting what you have, whereas being unhappy requires wanting something different. So, yes, she'd always been a dissatisfied sort of person, and these days, looking back, I can see much of our story as little more than an expression of that dissatisfaction. Amy had wanted to bed the only guy on the yoga course, then she'd wanted to see if she could make him her new boyfriend. She'd wanted to change countries; change towns; change houses . . . It was all part of an ongoing process.

But when she read *The Power of Now* the whole thing went into overdrive. 'Everything is possible,' Amy started insisting, something she'd 'learned' from the book. 'Anything' could be achieved, as long as you believed it was possible. And if anything was truly possible, how could anything ever be enough?

She started ploughing her way through the self-help section of Waterstones. She bought so many self-help books I had to put up new shelves just to hold them all. There were books on mindfulness and meditation; there were tomes on *manifesting happiness* and *overcoming limitations*.

Dad, who in an attempt at making sense of his life had read some similar ideas, albeit in somewhat heftier, more traditional volumes, convinced me for a while that this was healthy. But like everything else in Amy's life, nothing was ever enough. In fact, I started to see her obsession with mindfulness, with living in the now, with manifesting success, as obtuse escape routes to avoid ever being present. Because whenever she was talking about her latest craze, or reading about a new one, whether she was following an online course or listening to a guru on the Internet, she was always anywhere but here.

'I want a baby,' she announced, one January day, looking up from the book she'd just finished reading. It was *The Secret*, and the fact that the book was still on her lap made me doubt the profundity of this revelation about what, after all, was not an insignificant matter.

'OK . . .' I said dubiously, reluctantly dragging my attention from the chilling Scandi crime novel I'd been enjoying and trying to recentre myself in the here and now of our overheated lounge.

'Don't be like that!' she whined. 'I want a baby.'

'Right,' I said, trying to find a way to frame the question: was this real? Or was this just the latest thing Amy 'needed' to be happy?

'Don't look at me like that,' she laughed. 'I'm not crazy, you know. I've been delving into the depths of my psyche for weeks here, and I've finally worked out what's missing from my life.'

'And that would be?' I prompted.

'Dependence,' she said.

'Dependence,' I repeated.

'Yes, someone I can depend on, and someone who depends on me.'

'You can depend on me,' I said, feeling a little affronted.

'Yeah, but if we were married, with a child, then I'd really *know* that, yeah? Deep down. In my soul.'

'If you say so,' I said.

'And I need someone who depends *on me*,' Amy continued. 'I need to feel that unconditional love in order to feel whole. It's the point of all existence.'

'Are you sure that's healthy?' I asked. 'Using a child to feel whole about yourself?'

'I'm not *using* anyone,' Amy said. 'Jesus, Joe!'

'No,' I said. 'It's just, well, a *kid* . . . It's a biggie. Maybe we can think about it for a bit?'

'I already have,' Amy announced. 'I stopped taking the pill three weeks ago.'

We got married on the twenty-eighth of February. It was a simple service: half an hour in the register office, a new suit from Moss Bros for me, a plain white dress from French Connection for Amy. A few mates came from Whitby on my side, and some yoga girls from Canterbury primped and puffed Amy to perfection. My dad came too, obviously. And so did Amy's mum.

Valerie's appearance was by far the biggest surprise of the day. She was a tall thin woman with wild grey hair and mad blue eyes, and whenever I tried to speak to her, she replied as if she was answering someone else's question.

So when I told her it was nice to finally meet her, her reply was, 'Rain, probably, dear.'

When Dad commented how beautiful Amy looked, she said, 'Almost certainly, but with rose petals.'

'She's barking mad, that one,' was Dad's verdict, and I couldn't really find grounds to disagree.

At the reception in our local pub, afterwards, I asked Amy if her mother was OK.

'What do you mean?' she asked, sounding annoyed. 'Why wouldn't she be?'

'Um, well, the conversation with her seems a bit strange,' I explained. 'A bit off-key, that's all. I was just wondering if she's always like that?'

'Well, she's a very original woman,' Amy said. 'A poet, if you must know.' When she saw that this hadn't entirely convinced me, she added, 'Plus, she's drunk and on Valium. It's just nerves, don't worry.'

An hour into the reception, a car arrived to sweep the poetess back to Ashford.

'She didn't stay long,' I said, as we waved at the departing black Prius.

'It's better that way, trust me,' Amy said. 'Especially when there's a free bar.'

For our honeymoon we went to Madrid, where we alternated between museums, eating tapas, and shagging. So by the time we got home Amy was pregnant. And being pregnant transformed her. It made her into somebody totally different.

From the edgy, nervous bombshell of a girl she'd always been, she suddenly oozed calm femininity. She seemed more powerful somehow, and for a while at least, more centred. It was as if conception had infused her body with some ancient Mother Earth magic, and my love for her, which had all, I now saw, been about sex, became transformed into a deeply felt respect for her womanhood, the power of which was demonstrated by the fact that she was carrying our child. In a way, I suppose you could say that I fell in awe of her.

She gave birth to Ben on the eighth of December, and almost immediately I began to worry something was wrong. It will sound as if I'm criticising her, and that's totally not my intention – I really am just trying to describe how things felt . . . But she seemed *uncomfortable* in her role as a mother. She looked awkward when she held him, as if he didn't fit properly in her arms. Breastfeeding, she said, was too painful, and so she expressed her milk into bottles instead. And when he cried, sometimes she didn't seem to notice. She'd be staring into the middle distance, looking sad, while he was screaming in his cot beside her. And not one of her features would move in reaction to our son's obvious distress – it was truly as if she couldn't hear him. When prompted, she'd appear to wake up, as if from a trance, and snatch him from the cot.

She did the best she could, don't get me wrong. She fed him, changed him, cradled him, and if anyone was watching she'd mutter sweet nothings in his ear. But it always looked a bit as if she was acting. She always seemed to be playing a part.

I tried endlessly to get her to talk about how she felt, but all I ever got was more of the same. She was fine, she insisted. She was enjoying being a mother. She was happy.

Only once, because I caught her actually crying – her tears dropping on to Ben's forehead – did she ever admit anything was wrong. But even then she didn't give much away.

'I didn't think it would feel like this,' she told me, through sniffs.

'Like what?' I asked.

'I don't know,' she said, with a shrug. 'I suppose I didn't think it would feel so ordinary.'

Six months in, I'd convinced myself she was suffering from postnatal depression, but as Amy wouldn't even discuss that possibility with me, I eventually phoned one of her mates to ask if she'd intervene.

Wanda turned up the following Sunday and, while I nursed the baby downstairs, she lay next to Amy and chatted quietly. They were together all afternoon.

'It's her sister,' Wanda told me, as she was leaving.

I was flummoxed. Amy had never once mentioned the existence of a sister.

'She died when they were kids,' Wanda continued. 'And Ben's birth has dredged up painful memories.'

'Shit,' I said. 'So what do we need to do to help her get better? I'm assuming she needs some kind of thera—'

'It's all agreed,' Wanda said, laying one hand on my shoulder to interrupt me. 'She's going to start counselling this week.'

The problem – and I do blame myself for this – was that Wanda was the wrong person to have called. And the therapist Wanda advised – a devotee of an online guru called Benito Mungaro – was the worst possible kind of therapist for Amy to consult.

She became less unhappy almost instantly – that much, even I would admit. And she got up and started doing stuff again to prove it: joining me for yoga, cooking, cleaning, running . . . within three months, she was back teaching Pilates.

She was, as Dad would say, *bright-eyed and bushy-tailed*; she was enthusiastic and optimistic about everything. And that's precisely what made it so hard to name the problem. For how can you tell your previously miserable partner that she's *too* happy? How can you explain that being optimistic, nay, having utter faith that *all* life's situations are going to work out for the best isn't natural? That a smidgin of misery is part of being sane?

She saw Melissa, her 'Pure Being' therapist, twice a week, and on 'off' days she'd spend at least an hour watching Mungaro.

I took a peek at one of his videos while she was out, one time. He was Italian and younger and better-looking than I'd imagined. He gave off a vibe of enlightenment that was indisputable, but I found his mock-revelation delivery of what I knew were age-old platitudes more irritating than inspiring. At least now I knew where all the tripe Amy was spouting – her moments of 'pure God-like being' or the need to 'cease thinking in order to exist' – was coming from.

To check I wasn't overreacting, I chatted to Dad about it at length on the phone. But even he agreed that this Mungaro guy sounded dodgy. 'There are plenty of ancient philosophies around if she needs more sense in her life,' he said. 'I'm not sure why anyone would want to pay money to listen to some youngster winging it.'

'Do you think you could give your Mungaro guy a break for a bit?' I asked her that evening. 'I'm not sure putting all your eggs in his spiritual basket is . . . well . . . healthy, really . . .'

'I'm thinking of *giving up* eggs, actually,' she said, smiling at me beatifically. 'I think we need to go properly vegan.'

'Um, OK,' I said. 'Maybe. But all this Benito Mussolini stuff. It's not healthy. What d'you say we give it a break?'

'What do I say?'

'Yeah. What do you say?'

'I say you're suffering from the classic jealousy of an unenlightened heathen!' Amy exclaimed. 'That's what I say, *honey.*' And then she stood and, more floating than walking, left the room.

The Benito Mungaro phase lasted almost three years, and it was pretty damn irritating to live through. Amy spent most of that time with a weird half-smile on her lips, as if she knew some big secret that I didn't, which is almost certainly what she believed.

She went vegan, which was fine. She's a great cook, and I had no problem eating the Thai tofu curries and colourful Buddha bowls she came up with. Officially, we were all vegan, but when I was out and about with Ben, I'd feed him fish and eggs and dairy. I'd read up a bit on how to balance a vegan diet properly for growing children, and it seemed easier to me just to cheat.

Amy stopped drinking coffee, then tea and then alcohol. These were apparently destructive to her 'spirit soul'. That's what the guru had told her, anyway.

She found other adepts to hang out with as well. Whether she'd converted them or just bumped into them – implying they were perhaps less elusive than I'd imagined – I couldn't tell, but I would come home to find five or six people sitting at the kitchen table drinking juiced kale. They'd all smile at me at once, revealing matching sets of juice-green teeth, and I'd make my excuses and head through to the lounge. Sometimes I'd put on a really noisy action movie with lots of shooting just to piss them all off, but I never saw any sign they cared.

If Amy had ever tried to convert me, I think that our marriage might have been in trouble, but she never did. So perhaps, deep down, she knew that was the choice facing her: live with the heathen, or live alone.

On the few occasions when she did try to share her wisdom with me, I knocked her back with a heavy dose of sarcasm, at which she'd smile serenely and walk away. I think she managed to frame it so that my incapacity to understand actually made her feel better about herself. Her secret knowledge giving her the edge, as she saw it.

As you probably remember from the news, Mungaro's empire crashed and burned at the end of 2013. First he was arrested for tax evasion, and then within days he'd been accused of rape as well.

'It's all fake news,' Amy told me, when the first reports appeared on TV. 'They're going to crucify him exactly like they did Jesus.'

But then the horror stories became more specific. Women, more girls actually, with sad eyes and real tears, began appearing and describing in detail how they'd been abused. The Italian authorities were seizing Mungaro's millions and exploring his links with the Cosa Nostra mafia. There were even rumours of drug running.

'How else could he have managed to make seventy million?' I asked Amy. 'Unless his followers were actually giving him money?'

'I don't know,' Amy said, looking uncomfortable.

'They weren't, were they?' I asked. 'You didn't give him money, did you?'

'No,' she said. 'Of course not. Not at all.'

'Not at all,' I repeated. There was something wrong about her choice of words.

'OK, hardly any,' Amy said. 'I mean, I bought the books, obviously. I paid for the tutorials. There was, like, a membership fee, you know? For access. To all the courses.'

'Was that expensive?' I asked.

'Not really,' she said. 'And I don't regret a penny of it.'

But it was over, that was the main thing. The meetings had dried up. The books had moved to the bookcase, where they were sandwiched between *The Power of Now* and *The Secret*. Later on, I noticed they'd completely vanished. I think having been a fan of Mungaro became something to be ashamed of once everyone knew he was in jail.

The stupid smile had faded as well, to be replaced once again by the complex facial expressions of the woman I loved.

Ben started school the following year, and so Amy went back to working as close to full-time as she could manage. She ran yoga classes from our conservatory, taught jazz dance back in Canterbury, and ran senior stretching sessions in Herne Bay. Desperate to get rid of the last traces of her baby bump, she started bodybuilding, too. As her body became ever more ripped, I couldn't help but notice how much she was starting to look like Madonna.

She began spending money again, too, her dissatisfaction with life gradually returning and expressing itself through a need to constantly change our surroundings.

So we knocked out the wall between the kitchen and the dining room, replaced the bathtub with an Italian wet room and added an en suite to our bedroom.

The constant upheaval was exhausting and, of course, because of my job, I frequently got roped in to help with whatever transformation was in progress. But I still preferred it to the Mungaro years. Materialism was an enemy that at least I felt equipped to understand – and fight.

Little Ben floated through all of this effortlessly.

In fact, if there was a spiritual lesson to be learned, it was our Ben we needed to pay attention to, not Benito. Because everything seemed to make little Ben happy.

A pile of rubble in the kitchen? Happy. A new shower to stand under? *Very* happy. An old bathtub full of rainwater in the back garden? Ecstatic!

I'm guessing this is how most parents feel, but I honestly felt that he was the happiest child who'd ever lived. He'd come through his mum's various phases unscathed. Perhaps her fake spiritual contentment had even contributed to making him so easy-going, who knows?

My business was going from strength to strength and I'd even had to take on a second employee. Having learned his trade in Romania – where flat-pack was considered a luxury – fifty-year-old Marius was a master craftsman in the true sense of the word. He could make stunning kitchen cabinets from scratch and in not much more time than it took me to go to Ikea, bring them back and screw them together. So we started offering made-to-measure kitchens, built from solid oak. Our prices, and my turnover, went through the roof.

With Amy earning as well, we were on almost a hundred thousand a year, and even though we had no rent or mortgage to pay, she still managed to spend it all.

We had a pool installed in the garden. We had a sofa made to measure in Italy and new windows and an attic conversion and solar panels. We got new cars – an MX-5 for Amy and a massive Toyota pickup for me. We had a dressing room added to the bedroom, which Amy filled with expensive clothes for her and Hugo Boss suits for me. Other than for a very occasional trip to a posh restaurant, I could never work out when to wear the damn things.

By the time Ben was six, Amy started running out of projects, and I could see that her unhappiness was starting, once again, to leak out.

'Can't you just sit back and enjoy it all?' I suggested. 'Isn't that supposed to be the point?'

Amy sighed and shook her head. 'How would you feel about moving?' she asked.

We went to Whitby for the bank-holiday weekend, and while I took Ben for long windy walks along the seafront, I hoped that Dad would manage to talk some sense into Amy. He had, I suspected, the kind of philosophical vocabulary that could reach her.

But though he tried his best, it didn't seem to make any difference. Amy was already looking at houses on her iPhone during the drive back home.

Having spent massive amounts of blood, sweat and money turning our house into her personal version of paradise, I was loath to even enter into a conversation about starting from scratch somewhere else.

Amy started buying jewellery, including actual diamonds. She bought so many shoes I had to build her a shoe cupboard. For my birthday she gave me a Philippe Patek watch that was worth so much money (yes, I googled it) that I never dared take it out of the house. I took a sneaky look at her bank account shortly afterwards, and she was starting to go seriously overdrawn.

Her forty-fifth birthday came around and suddenly everything changed once again – one book was all it took. It seemed innocent enough, as gifts go, and Dad was so sure of his choice that he winked at me as he handed her the package. It was called 'Money as the root of well-being'.

'Don't worry,' he reassured me in the kitchen. 'I've read it and it's all perfectly sound. My Buddhist friend Emma swears by it.'

A week later we were on a beach in Faro, Portugal, and while I made sandcastles at the water's edge with Ben, Amy read the book.

'How's it going?' I asked her, not without apprehension.

'Oh, it's good,' she said, smiling up at me. 'It's really clever, actually.'

'Great,' I said. 'What do you want to do for food tonight?'

'I thought we could buy some veg and cook it back at the flat,' she said. 'I'm getting bored, I think, with restaurants.'

'Good,' I said, disguising my surprise. 'That would be nice.'

'You seem relaxed,' I told her towards the end of the flight home. What I meant was that she hadn't purchased anything from the TAP SkyShop. 'Was it that book you read? Was it useful?'

'Yeah,' Amy said, nodding thoughtfully. 'Yeah, I realised a lot of stuff, actually.'

'Such as?' I prompted.

'Oh, pretty basic stuff,' she said. 'Stuff that everyone else already knows, no doubt. You'd hate it.'

'Try me,' I said.

'I think I've been trying to buy happiness,' Amy said. 'And it hasn't really been working for me.'

'You think?' I said.

'Yeah.'

'That's cool,' I told her, managing to sound low-key even though within the privacy of my head I was screaming, *Hallelujah!*

So began The Year of Spending Nowt.

For a while, my wife's inner turmoil remained visible, so as she did her best to adjust to these new self-imposed rules, she'd pipe up, 'I was wondering if maybe we could . . .'

I'd look up from whatever I was doing and prompt her to continue, but she'd say, 'Forget it. I've changed my mind,' and I'd be left wondering what she'd wanted to spend money on and whether it was something that I would have enjoyed.

Within a few weeks she'd adjusted, though, and other than food she bought virtually nothing for a year. Our break from constant consumerism felt restful. It felt good.

Halfway through the year, she started selling things as well, putting spare furniture we'd had in the garage on eBay, selling old books on Amazon, and even getting rid of some of the flashier suits I'd never worn. But then my favourite armchair vanished. It was the one I sat in every evening to read. 'I *liked* that chair,' I protested. 'It's my reading chair.'

'You can sit somewhere else, can't you?' she asked, looking confused. 'I'm only trying to reduce all the clutter, honey. And I have to buy stuff for Ben – he's growing so fast. It seems healthier to finance that by getting rid of shit we don't want any more, you know?'

'Sure, but that wasn't *shit*,' I said. 'It was my *favourite chair*.'

'I'll get it back, then,' Amy promised. 'Or if I can't, if it's too late, then I'll get you another one exactly the same.'

'OK,' I said. 'Thank you. And maybe just ask, next time?'

Neither the old chair nor a similar chair ever appeared, but in the end Amy was right after all. I *could* just sit somewhere else.

After The Year of Spending Nowt came The Year of Helping Others, whereby Amy threw herself into just about any charitable opportunity that presented itself. She joined the parents' association at Ben's school, donated yoga lessons to a local old people's home and did a 'fun run' to raise money for Red Nose Day.

For once, this seemed like a sensible strategy for feeling better, so I encouraged her and even, when work constraints allowed, joined in with it all. We had fun together. Our relationship began to feel healthy again.

When March arrived, and the summer-holiday adverts began appearing on TV, I started pining for a proper holiday. We hadn't been abroad since Faro, and having seen the state of Amy's bank account and not having wanted to be the one to break the economy drive, I'd managed to restrain myself from mentioning holidays all year.

But winter had been cold and miserable, and spring was looking to be more of the same. I was physically exhausted from a series of huge kitchen renovations I'd been working on and a bit down in the dumps about the sense of pre-apocalyptic Brexit misery in the country – there was a feeling I was struggling to shake that the sun might never shine again. So one night, as a blue-sky-filled advert for Costa Cruises flickered on the TV screen, I asked if we were still allowed to have holidays.

'What do you mean, *allowed*?' Amy asked.

'I just mean, what with the economy drive and everything, can we still have holidays?'

'It's not an economy drive,' Amy said. 'Why would you say that?'

'Um, OK, sorry,' I said. 'But you know what I mean.'

'Stopping throwing money away on pointless consumerism isn't an *economy drive*,' Amy said, wiggling her fingers to make visual quotes to surround the final two words.

'No,' I said. 'So, let me rephrase that. Are holidays also considered pointless consumerism? Or are experiences, specifically sunny ones, all right?'

'They're all right,' Amy said. 'They're totally all right.'

'Oh,' I said. 'Um, good.'

'Actually, I was thinking it would be nice to take your dad somewhere,' Amy said, surprising me.

'Dad?' I repeated.

Amy shrugged. 'Why not?'

'Well, for one, he's not the world's greatest traveller,' I said.

'Last time we saw him, he was telling me all about Thailand,' Amy reminded me.

I laughed. 'That was in, like, 1970 or something. It was before he even met Mum.'

'Ask him,' Amy said. 'I bet you he'd say *yes*.'

'Really?' I asked. Perhaps it was my own lack of imagination, but I was struggling to picture Amy on holiday with my dad.

'He's not getting any younger, Joe,' Amy said seriously. 'And I just think it might be nice for Ben to have to proper memories of spending time with his grandad, you know?'

'Oh, OK . . .' I said. 'Yeah, maybe.'

'Ask him,' Amy said again.

'OK, I'll sound him out,' I agreed. 'Are we thinking of anywhere particular?'

'Oh, just local,' Amy said. 'Just Europe: France or Italy or something.'

'OK, I'll ask him,' I told her. 'If you're sure.'

Amy booked a weird-looking house in the countryside a few hours north-east of Granada. It was owned by a Spanish friend of Wanda's and comprised a series of seven rooms carved into the rock. It fulfilled Amy's criteria of being both affordable and quirky, plus it had the added bonus of being, according to Wanda, 'incredibly centring' and a great place for 'getting in contact with the earth mother'. It was two hours from the coast, which was a bummer, but had both a pool and a jacuzzi, which made up for the lack of beach just enough that I gave in. The weather would be furnace-like every day, which I hoped would be great for my back.

About two months before our departure date, Dad phoned me. It was mid-afternoon on a Wednesday, so I was at work and too busy to talk for long.

He couldn't come with us, he explained sadly. He'd sprained his ankle.

'A sprained ankle?' I repeated, wedging the phone beneath my chin as I continued to screw the cabinet to the wall. 'It'll be fine by August, then, won't it?'

'Unfortunately not,' Dad said. 'It's quite a *bad* sprain.'

'How d'you do that, then?' I asked.

'Oh, I slipped on the step or something,' Dad said.

'Or something?' I repeated, frowning and interrupting what I was doing. 'You haven't broken it, have you?'

'No,' Dad said. 'No, it's just a little sprain. Don't worry.'

'A little sprain that's going to stop you coming on holiday in well over two months' time.'

'Yes, I'll just rest up and read,' Dad said. 'Don't worry about me, I'll be fine.'

I exhaled sharply at the realisation I needed to visit him. Because there was something he wasn't telling me.

As Amy was teaching all weekend, I took Ben with me to see 'poor Grandad'. And he *was* limping badly when we arrived. Only, by that I don't mean that he had an impressive or worrying injury. I mean he was limping *badly.*

'Why are you walking like that?' I asked, squinting at him as we followed him down the hallway to the kitchen.

'I told you, I've—'

'But you're walking on the side of your foot,' I said.

'Yes, it hurts,' Dad said.

'Can I go out back?' Ben asked, standing on tiptoes and peering out at the garden. 'Is that big fat cat still here?'

'Yes, go see if you can find Boris,' Dad said, opening the door to let him out.

'So, come on. What's going on?' I asked, once Ben had left.

'I don't know what you mean,' Dad said.

'You're a terrible liar, Dad, and you know it,' I laughed.

'Oh,' Dad said, glancing down at his foot. He sighed deeply. 'I'm sorry, son,' he said. 'But I just don't think I want to go.'

'And your foot?'

'It's mostly fine.'

'*Mostly* fine?'

'It *is* fine, in fact,' Dad said, shrugging sheepishly.

'So why the change of heart?' I asked.

'Oh, it's too hot for me,' Dad said. 'I don't like those kinds of temperatures, you know I don't.'

'The house is cool, apparently,' I said. 'It'll be great. Come on. And there's a pool, and—'

'It's not just that,' Dad said. 'I've other reasons.'

'OK . . .' I said doubtfully. 'Go on.'

'I . . .' He turned to face the sink, looking out of the kitchen window at Ben, who was now sitting on the rusty swing. 'I'm not sure how you'll react,' he added, and I saw his neck change colour as he flushed red.

'Dad?' I said, stepping forward and placing one hand on his shoulder. 'Tell me. Has Amy said something? Have I said—'

'It's Emma,' Dad interrupted. 'My friend from the meditation centre.'

'Emma,' I said. 'What about her?'

'There's a bit of a thing,' Dad said.

'A thing?'

'A developing thing, I suppose you could say.'

I started to grin and had to restrain myself. 'A *romantic* kind of thing?' I asked.

'Yes,' Dad said, still staring out of the window. 'Potentially.'

'Do you want to bring her?' I asked. 'Is that it? Because—'

'No, I couldn't possibly,' Dad said. 'We're . . . not . . . you know . . .'

I squeezed his shoulder.

'We're not there, yet,' he said.

'Oh,' I said, still stifling a smile. 'And what? You don't want to interrupt a work in progress by vanishing to Spain for three weeks?'

'Yes, something like that,' Dad said, finally turning to look at me but quickly averting his gaze again by staring at his hands instead. 'There's another chap hanging around, so . . .'

I nodded and pushed my tongue into my cheek as I struggled not to smirk. Dad glanced at me and misinterpreted the resulting facial expression. 'You're angry, aren't you?' he said.

'*Angry?*'

'It's a perfectly normal reaction,' he said. 'But you need to understand that I'm not trying to replace your mother. That's not what this is about at all. Your mother—'

Finally I couldn't hold it in any longer, so I let my laughter break free. 'I'm *so* not angry, Dad,' I told him, tears in my eyes. 'I just . . . I suppose I didn't . . . Well . . . I didn't think you had it in you, I guess. You naughty old sod.'

'I'm only sixty-nine!' Dad said. 'Jesus, I'm not *dead*, boy.' And then he pushed me to one side, shook his head, and started to shuffle ridiculously from the room. Only as he reached the doorway did he remember that he no longer needed to limp.

96

That Sunday night, over dairy-free cauliflower 'cheese', Amy expressed her irritation.

'I've spent a lot of money on this, Joe,' she said. 'It was supposed to be a treat for him, for Christ's sake, not something for him to worm his way out of.'

'He's not worming out of it, honey,' I told her. 'And it's only a treat if he actually wants to go. You can't *make* someone want the treat you've chosen.'

'But he *did* want to go. I booked the flight for him and everything.'

'And now he doesn't want to go,' I explained reasonably. 'He's an adult. He's changed his mind.'

'Oh, can you convince him, Joe?' Amy asked, putting down her fork to raise her hands in prayer. 'Please?'

I shook my head and laughed. 'I don't even want him to change his mind. He's almost seventy, hon. And he's got a chance, this totally unexpected last chance, to not spend the rest of his life alone. I can't believe that you'd want him to give that up either – not if you really think about it.'

'But that can wait three weeks, can't it? I mean, she's not going to run off with someone else the second his back's turned, is she? Not at that age.'

'Well, apparently there is some other guy sniffing around, so . . .'

'What does *sniffing around* mean?' Ben asked.

'Daddy didn't mean that.'

'No, bad choice of words,' I agreed.

'Anyway, he could bring her,' Amy said. 'The more the merrier.'

'I suggested that. I told you already. But it's a no.'

Amy sighed and forked a lump of cauliflower from her plate, then, waving it at me, continued, 'Well, the place is too big for just the three of us. It's got five bedrooms, for God's sake.'

'I don't think there's a rule that you have to use them all,' I said. 'They're not going to apply the bedroom tax or anything.'

'I already paid the damn bedroom tax when I booked it. It was almost a thousand pounds.'

'It doesn't matter,' I said. 'Relax.'

'It's just a bit obscene,' Amy said, speaking through food now. 'His flight will go to waste, too.'

'It was fifty quid,' I protested. 'Who cares?'

'I was thinking more about the carbon footprint of that empty seat,' Amy explained. 'Maybe we could change the name on the ticket and invite someone else. Maybe I'll invite Wanda to join us. She knows the area—'

'No,' I interrupted, raising one finger and wiggling it in what I hoped was a comic manner.

Amy leaned forward and stared at me. 'No?' she said.

'Um, yeah. That's an absolute *no* to that one from me.'

'No to Wanda? Or no to anyone?'

'No to anyone. And a definite total absolute no to Wanda.'

'What's wrong with Wanda? She's my friend.'

'Yeah. Wanda's great. But I'm not going on holiday with her,' I said. 'Ever.'

'You . . .' Amy said, shaking her head. 'Joe, then? What about Joe?'

'He's twenty-five. He has a girlfriend. He has far better things to do than go on holiday with his boss.'

'Or Marius,' Amy said. 'I bet Marius can't afford many posh holidays.'

'Hey, Marius is doing fine, thank you very much. You make it sound like I don't pay the guy.'

'He always looks pretty broke to me.'

'Only because he sends all his money back to Romania,' I said. 'And actually, Romania's where he's going for his hols, so . . .'

'Mum?' Ben said.

'It just seems a waste, that's all,' Amy said, before turning to Ben and asking, 'Yes, dear?'

'Can't we invite Lucy?'

'Lucy?' I said. 'Who's Lucy?'

'Lucy's that little girl he hangs around with,' Amy informed me with a wink. 'His best friend.'

'She's not got a holiday this year,' Ben said. 'So maybe she could come with us. To Spain.'

I laughed and started to reply, 'You can't just invite—' But Amy was speaking too.

'She's the one who lives up the road, right? The one you play with sometimes at school?'

Ben nodded. 'At least I'd have someone to play with,' he said, looking plaintive.

'That's true, actually,' Amy told him, turning to me.

'Amy . . .' I told her in a special *listen to me* tone of voice.

She raised an eyebrow at me questioningly.

I shook my head definitively. 'Don't get his hopes up,' I said. 'It's not happening.'

'OK, let's talk about this another time,' Amy said, addressing Ben. 'Anyway, what else did you get up to at Grandad's?'

That night in bed, as she undressed, Amy asked me what I thought.

'What do I think about what?' I said. I'd assumed that the subject was closed.

'About Ben bringing his friend on holiday.'

'Amy,' I said, 'you're being crazy.'

'It's not easy for him, being an only child,' she said.

'I'm an only child,' I pointed out, with a shrug.

'So you *know* it's not always easy. I remember going on holiday with—'

'It's impossible, Amy,' I interrupted her. 'I mean, just, you know, legally speaking . . . Passports and parental rights and all that. It's totally impossible.'

'Oh yeah,' Amy said, lifting the covers and slipping in beside me. 'I didn't think about that. Do you think it is? Impossible, I mean.'

'Totally,' I said. 'Anyway, it'll be nice. Just the three of us.'

'I guess,' Amy said.

'God, don't be *too* enthusiastic about spending three weeks in Spain with your husband and son, will you?'

'OK,' Amy said. 'Sure, fine.'

'So that's settled?'

'Sure,' Amy said again, snuggling against me. 'Sure. OK.'

Three

Heather

A few days after the 'Spain' conversation, I got home from the school to find a little red sports car parked on our drive. 'It's Ben!' Lucy exclaimed, running up to tap on the passenger window.

The driver's side window slid down and an elegant blonde woman smiled up at me. She reminded me of someone famous, and I finally remembered her from parents' evening and realised that I'd been picturing Ben's mum as someone else entirely.

'Hey, I was wondering if I could talk to you,' she said. She sounded vaguely American and the accent brought the face of the famous person I was trying to find almost within reach. This made the fact that I still couldn't quite work out who that was even more annoying.

'Um, yes . . . Of course,' I said, thinking, *Lady Gaga? – No. Madonna? – Almost but not quite.* 'What's it about?'

'Um, it's about Lucy,' she replied.

'Oh, really? Has she done something?' I asked.

'Not at all,' the woman said. 'I, er . . .' And then she slid the window closed and climbed from the car. We shook hands.

'I'm Amy,' she said. Then, turning towards the car and leaning down to peer in and beckon to her son, she added, 'I'm Ben's mum.'

'Yes, I think we met once,' I said. 'Well, we were in the same room anyway. At Red Nose Day?'

'Yeah, that's right,' Amy said, reaching out to scoop Ben, who had joined us but was lingering a few feet away, to her side. 'Ben can be a bit shy, can't you?' she said.

'*No*,' Ben replied grumpily, half hiding behind her leg.

'Can I show Ben my room?' Lucy asked.

'Um, sure,' I said. Addressing Amy, I asked, 'If you have time?'

'I have,' Amy said, 'as it happens.'

'I'm coming too,' Sarah announced.

'Oh, we don't want *her*,' Lucy said, tugging at Ben's sleeve. 'We're not playing baby games.'

Amy smiled at me and raised an eyebrow.

'Let me rephrase that, then, Lucy,' I said. 'You can take Ben and show him your room *if* you let Sarah come too.'

Lucy sighed dramatically. 'Oh, come on then,' she said, leading the way. 'But you won't like it, silly Sarah.'

'They actually get on pretty well,' I said, as we entered the hallway. 'Lucy's just showing off because Ben's here.'

'Oh, I'm sure,' Amy said. 'They seem sweet.'

I made tea for us both in the kitchen and apologised for the mess as I handed Amy her mug. She looked around the room and commented, 'But it's spotless. It's, like, hospital clean.'

I glanced around the room again with fresh eyes and wondered what I was apologising for. But I could see the finger smudges on the oven door, even if Amy couldn't. I could see the dirty tea towel on the chair back and the soup bowl sitting in the sink. 'So, Amy,' I said, once we'd moved through to the conservatory. 'What's up?'

'Really, nothing's up as such,' Amy said, raising her tea to her lips, but not, I noticed, actually drinking. 'I'm not sure if Lucy said anything to you, but we're going to Spain in August.'

I smiled, and for no reason I could identify felt myself blush. 'Actually, she did,' I said. 'I think she's a bit jealous of Ben's holiday plans.'

'The thing is – and I hope you don't think I'm being . . . I don't know what the word is, really . . . *inappropriate*? I hope you don't think *this* is inappropriate. But Lucy said you're not able to go away this year and—'

'It's not that we're not *able*,' I corrected her. 'It's that we've decided not to.'

'Of course,' Amy said. 'God, I'm so bad at this. I really didn't mean . . .'

'No, go on,' I said. 'It's fine. Really.'

'So we've got this crazy goddam house booked down in Spain. It's a real monster, with living areas and five bedrooms and a pool and a jacuzzi, and there are only the three of us going now.'

'*OK*,' I said, sounding and probably looking a bit confused.

'Reg, that's Joe's dad – Joe's my husband, yeah? Anyway, he was supposed to come with us too.'

'Joe was? Oh, sorry, *Reg* was.'

'Yes. Yes, Joe's coming, obviously. But his dad was supposed to come too. I was even thinking about inviting my mum, though Joe doesn't know that, so not a word. But now neither of them are coming, so we have all this empty space.'

'Sure,' I said, frowning as I tried to work out where Amy was going with all of this.

'And it just seems such a waste, you know?'

'Yes, I'm sure.'

'And I know this is going to sound crazy, but . . . well . . . I mean, Ben's an only child, you know? And he gets on so well with Lucy and all . . .'

'So you wanted to invite Lucy to join you?' I offered, trying to help stammering Amy out a little.

'Yeah, kind of . . . Well, no, not really. I mean, that was my original idea. But Joe pointed out all the reasons that wouldn't fly. I mean, what with passports and parental guardianship and all. And so then I got to thinking that maybe we could all go together. Like a shared family holiday? It could be fun.' She leaned towards me and looked into my eyes, searching, I think, for a reaction. But I was struggling to decide what to think.

'That sounds crazy, right?' Amy continued, straightening. 'I'm sounding totally bat-shit crazy. It's just I get these ideas, you know? About how we're all on this planet in our separate little bubbles and it could all be so much nicer if we shared stuff. And . . .' She shrugged. 'Anyway.'

I sipped my tea and swallowed with difficulty. Something in her words, something about the *separate bubbles* had reached me, but I couldn't think of a sensible way to respond.

'Look, even I can hear how crazy I sound,' Amy said. 'So don't worry. I am aware.'

'Look, it doesn't sound crazy,' I said. 'Well, not completely. And I know what you mean, in a way. But, well, it's not going to . . . to *fly*, as you say.'

'It's not, is it?' Amy said, wrinkling her nose. 'And now I feel a bit dumb, so . . .'

'Please, don't,' I said. 'It's a sweet idea. And I'd love to go to Spain some day. But . . .'

'Maybe you'd like to discuss it with your husband?' Amy suggested. 'Just in case?'

'With Ant?' I laughed. 'No, look . . . I don't want to be rude, Amy . . .'

Amy raised her palms and made a quiet 'Ouch!' noise, which made me laugh.

'But the thing is, well, we don't know you, do we? We don't really know you at all.'

'God, that British reserve,' Amy said. 'I mean, I'm half British, but I never quite get used to it.'

'I don't think that's really what this is,' I said. 'I think this is more—'

'That the idea's just insane?' Amy said.

'Not insane, but, well . . . It is a bit *unusual*,' I offered, squinting at her in a kindly manner.

'OK,' Amy said. 'I just thought, you know . . . But OK.'

'It's really nice of you,' I said. 'But . . .' I shrugged.

'No worries,' Amy said, standing. 'I should probably go.'

'Please don't rush off,' I said. Despite her madcap idea, there was something I rather liked about her. Plus, it was so rare to have someone to talk to in the house. 'At least drink your tea,' I added.

Amy glanced at the mug of tea, still untouched. 'Um, this is gonna sound even crazier,' she said. 'But I don't actually drink tea.'

'You don't?'

'No. I gave up coffee and alcohol too, but I have to admit to caving in on the alcohol front.'

I laughed. 'Would you rather have a glass of wine or something?'

'Oh no,' Amy said. 'No, I didn't mean that. It's just that I don't drink tea.'

'Why didn't you say, though?' I asked her. 'I could have made you something else.'

Amy shrugged. 'I don't know,' she said. 'I was trying not to be rude, I guess.'

If there was one feeling I knew well, it was that of not saying what you want in order to avoid conflict. Strangely, it made me like her even more. 'Please have something else,' I said. 'I have juice. Or beer. Or wine. Or—'

'No. Thank you. Really,' Amy interrupted. 'I just want to go home and lick my wounds, I think.'

I followed her to the base of the stairs, where she shouted Ben's name in an impressively loud voice. He appeared, running down the stairs, seconds later. 'Are we going already?' he asked breathlessly.

'I'm afraid so,' Amy said as Lucy appeared on the landing above. 'But maybe you two can play together again some other time.'

'And Spain?' Ben asked.

'Sorry,' Amy said, ruffling his hair, and then pushing him towards the front door. 'But your dad was right. It's not going to work.'

'But why?' Ben asked.

'I'll explain later,' Amy said.

Just as I reached out for the latch, a shadow appeared on the other side of the window. I opened the door to find Anthony on the doorstep, key in hand.

'Oh, hello!' he said, raising his eyebrows in surprise. 'What are *you* doing here?'

'Ah, so *you're* Lucy's dad,' Amy said.

'And I'm guessing you're Ben's mum?' Ant replied.

'You two know each other?' I asked hesitantly.

'Yeah,' Ant said slowly, without dragging his eyes from Amy's face. 'Yeah, um, Joe, Amy's partner? Husband?'

'Husband,' Amy replied.

'He did the kitchens out at Powell's flats. Did a good job, too.'

'Oh,' I said, glancing between the two of them. 'Right.'

'Um, I should go,' Amy said, sounding a bit flustered as she glanced over Ant's shoulder towards her car.

'Sure, yeah,' Ant said, stepping aside so that they could shuffle around each other on the doorstep. 'Bye then. And, um, give my regards to Joe.'

'Yes, I'll do that,' Amy said.

'Bye, Ben,' Lucy, now glued to my leg, called out.

Once Ant had closed the front door and walked through to the kitchen, I went into the lounge. Through the bay window, I watched as the little sports car turned around and then pulled away down the drive. And I wondered what had just happened. Because *something* had. Of that much I was sure.

I watched the car vanish and then joined Ant in the kitchen. He had hung his jacket on the back of a chair and was crouching down to listen to Lucy's chatter.

'Where's Sarah?' I asked. '*Lucy*, where's Sarah?'

Lucy shrugged. The shrugging was a new thing and she did it awkwardly, as if she hadn't quite mastered the gesture yet.

'Then go and find her, please. Make sure she's OK.'

She huffed and then ran from the kitchen, shrieking 'Sarah, Saraaah! Are you OK?' as she climbed the stairs.

Ant moved to the sink, where he stared at the soup bowl and mugs. 'Dishwasher broken?' he asked.

Because I knew that this wasn't an actual question, merely a reproach about the dirty items sitting in the sink, I ignored it and began emptying the dishwasher. As I did so, I considered the fact that Ant hadn't initiated a conversation about Amy being here and how strange that seemed.

'So how do you know Amy?' I asked casually.

Ant had sat down at the table and was studying a wodge of paperwork. 'Um?' he said. 'Oh, I told you. Her husband did the kitchens out at Powell's.'

'Yes,' I said, pausing with three clean mugs in my hands. 'That explains how you know *him*. But how do you know her?'

'I went to their place once or twice,' Ant said, without looking up from his documents. 'To sign contracts and pay him and what-have-you.'

'He works from home then, does he?'

'No, they've got a workshop out in Hoath. But his office is at home, so . . .'

'And Amy was there, when you visited?'

Ant sighed and rolled his head around, stretching his neck. 'Apparently so, seeing as I'm telling you that's how I know her.'

'Where do they live?' I asked.

'What is this?' he asked. '*University Challenge*? A thousand questions about Amy?'

'Not at all,' I said, keeping my intonation as unchallenging as possible. 'No, I just wondered where they live. I gather it's not that far away, but I've never seen her around.'

'It's the house near the stables,' Ant said. 'The one just after the bend. They've got a massive Buddha in the window.'

'Oh, right,' I said. 'The house with the big truck outside?'

'That's the one,' Ant said.

'Are they Buddhists, then?'

'Not that I know of. But I don't actually ask people their religion when I sign contracts with them.'

'No,' I said. 'No, of course. Is it nice?'

'Is what nice?'

'Their house.'

Ant shrugged. 'It's . . . you know . . . normal.'

'Normal,' I said.

'Like here, I suppose,' he said. 'It's got a similar floor plan, but they've got a double garage out back. They've got a fuck-off pool in the garden, too.'

'You mean a big one?'

'Yeah, one of those lap pools that everyone's into now.'

'Gosh, a pool!' I said, as I straightened with a fresh batch of plates. 'That's nice. Maybe we should befriend them.'

'Since when did you want a pool?' Ant asked.

'I don't *want* a pool,' I said. 'But it would be nice for the girls, I mean, in summer, when it's hot. If they could go and splash in Ben's pool, that would be great. Lucy seems to be friends with him anyway.'

'Just . . .' Ant said, waving a hand as if to distance a fly. 'Give it a break, OK?'

Give what a break? I thought. But I didn't say a word. It wasn't worth trying to go any further when he was in that sort of mood.

I finished emptying the dishwasher and then loaded it with the offending soup bowl and mugs before swishing some bleach around the sink. 'She . . .' I started, but then stopped myself. I'd forgotten momentarily that I was *giving it a break.*

'She what?' Ant asked, sounding irritated.

'Nothing,' I said.

'No, go on,' he insisted. He put down his papers and folded his arms, then shifted in his chair to face me, giving me his full attention. 'I'm assuming this is about Amy again.'

'Really, Ant,' I said. 'It's nothing. I was just making conversation.'

'Why was she here, anyway?' he asked. 'Are you two best mates now or something?'

'Not at all,' I said. 'But that's what I was going to say. What I was about to tell you . . . Why she came.'

'And?'

'She came to . . . You remember Lucy going on about Spain the other night?'

'Spain?' Ant said. Then, 'Oh, *Spain.* Yeah, sure.'

'Well, she came to invite us, believe it or not. Officially, like.'

'Amy came to invite us to *Spain?*'

'Yes, they've rented some huge villa in Spain apparently, and she feels like it's a waste to have all those rooms empty or something.

109

Their parents were supposed to go with them, I think, but they can't make it. So . . .'

'So?'

'So that's it. She came to invite us to join them. On their holiday.'

'To Spain!' Ant said, laughing and shaking his head in disbelief.

'I know!' I agreed. 'It's a bit mad, really. I mean, we don't even know them.'

'It's totally mad,' Ant said.

'But well meant, I think.'

'Huh!' Ant said. 'I wonder if Joe knows about that. Because that doesn't sound like him.'

'Oh, don't tell him, maybe?' I suggested. 'Not if it's going to get her into trouble.'

Anthony laughed again, then, gathering his papers, he stood. 'Oh, I'll tell him all right,' he said. 'I need to read these, so I'm going upstairs for half an hour,' he added. 'Call me when tea's ready, yeah?'

No further mention was made of Amy, or Joe, or even Spain for the rest of the week.

But on Friday morning Ant left for work as normal, closing the front door behind him, only to return and surprise me in the kitchen.

'Did you forget something?' I asked, looking up from the kettle, which I was filling.

'No,' he said. 'Well, yeah, actually. Have we got a decent bottle of wine in the house?'

'A decent bottle of wine?' I repeated. 'Um, yes. Almost definitely.'

'Good,' he said. 'Because we're eating out tonight. At Joe's place. I forgot to tell you last night.'

'We're eating out?' I said, struggling to understand exactly what he meant.

'*Yes*,' Ant said slowly, as if I was being a bit thick. 'At . . . Joe's . . . place.'

'Is this Joe-and-Amy Joe?'

'Do we know any other Joes?'

'Um, no,' I said. It was just that it seemed so unlikely we'd be eating with them that I'd been wondering if *Joe's Place* wasn't perhaps the name of a restaurant. Not that the bottle of wine would have made much sense if that were the case, but . . . 'Really?' I said. 'We're going to dinner at their house?'

'Apparently so,' Ant said. Then in a softer tone, he added, 'That's OK, isn't it?'

'I suppose,' I said. 'Do we need a babysitter? Because it's a bit—'

'He said to bring the girls,' Ant said. 'He said he's going to order in pizza or something. He asked if vegan pizza was OK. I didn't even know they did vegan pizza.'

'Oh, yeah,' I said vaguely, because I was already worrying about what to wear. 'Yes, Kerry gets vegan pizza sometimes. She's quite chic, isn't she? Amy, I mean. So are we dressing up?'

Ant glanced down at himself. 'I'll be going straight from work, so . . .' He was wearing a dark blue suit and a deep-blue open-necked shirt. Clothes are so easy for men, aren't they?

'Just wear that blue dress,' Ant said. 'You look great in that.'

'Oh, OK,' I said, grasping at this rare compliment as a lifeline in what was, after all, an unusual and destabilising situation. 'OK, the blue one. Yes, that'll be fine, won't it? And what time?'

'He said eight,' Ant said.

'Eight!' I exclaimed. 'Gosh, that's late. Especially for Sarah.'

'Some of us have to work,' Ant said. 'But they'll be fine. They'll be excited. And you can give them a snack before you go, can't you?'

'Can you come home first?' I asked. I was imagining how excruciating it would be if I got there before Ant and had to wait for him to arrive. Alternatively, I was imagining sitting at home trying to work out if it was late enough to be sure he was already there. 'So we can go together,' I said. 'I don't want to go alone.'

'It's just down the road,' Ant said. 'It's, like, a hundred yards.'

'I know,' I said. 'So come home first, and we can walk down together, OK?'

'You!' Ant said. Then, 'Sure, whatever. I'll come home first.'

It will give you some idea just how isolated and isolating my life had become if I tell you that I was so stressed and so utterly excited about the invitation that I couldn't think of anything else all day.

Other than the restaurants we visited during our holiday trips, Ant and I hardly ever ate out, and as for dinner at someone's house, that's simple: it hadn't happened since I'd met him. And I mean, really, not once.

I spent most of the day preening myself. I waxed my legs and plucked my eyebrows. I dyed my roots, ran an iron over my blue dress and polished my blue ankle boots. I tried on the outfit I'd envisaged – the blue dress with a grey cardigan and the boots – and then tried on a few other permutations as well. But in the end the best result, or the least ugly one, was definitely the blue dress Ant had suggested.

Finally, I changed back into my day-to-day clothes and walked down to meet the girls.

I passed Amy's house on the way, and did my best to look inside. But the sunlit leaves of a tree were reflected in the window, and other than the vague outline of the Buddha, I couldn't see a thing.

As I walked home with the girls, Ant phoned me to tell me the dinner was now at seven. Joe, apparently, thought he could get off work earlier and Amy, like myself, thought that eight was too late.

Ant arrived home just after six and I couldn't help but wonder if he too was feeling nervous. He showered, shaved, and even trimmed his nose hair, I noticed, before putting on a clean shirt and a more relaxed, tan-coloured suit.

I dressed the girls prettily in Victorian-style velvet dresses and, looking like the Waltons on their way to Sunday Mass, we tripped off down the lane.

It was Amy who opened the front door, with Ben, once again, clinging to her legs. She was wearing a black jumpsuit with a subtle white polka-dot design and a black cashmere wrap-around cardigan. The result looked casual but somehow *expensive*.

'Joe's not in yet,' she said. 'But he should be here any minute.' And exactly at the moment she said this, his truck pulled up behind us.

Joe climbed out and I realised that I'd never seen him before. Then again, perhaps I had, and I hadn't noticed him. In his blue jeans and mustard builders' boots, he was somehow a very everyday-looking sort of man. 'Hi,' he said, slamming the door to the pickup and crossing the gravel to join us. 'Am I late?'

'Not at all,' I said.

'Only just,' Amy corrected, checking her watch. 'Two minutes late, to be precise.'

'She's got an atomic watch, that one,' he joked, holding out his hand. 'I'm Joe.'

I introduced myself and then we followed Amy into the house.

'Gosh!' I said, looking around. I was just blown away by the decor. In fact, I was so surprised that Ant had described it as 'normal' that I glanced at him to see if it had changed since he'd last been here. But he didn't look surprised, so I could only assume that he was impervious to how beautiful it was. Everything was white, that was the thing. I don't think I have ever seen so much white and light and sparkle in a house.

The floors were bleached wooden boards with natural-colour vintage rugs strewn around. The white walls were dotted with plank-like shelves holding books and pastel-tinted pots with plants. Amy led us through to the lounge, and it was more of the same, but with stripped antique bits of unmatched furniture, which gave the whole thing a kind of natural hippy-chic look that I hadn't really come across before. It was perhaps how I'd imagine Gwyneth Paltrow's place might look, only refreshingly jumbled and relaxed.

As the girls headed off upstairs with Ben, I started gliding around the room inspecting various objects as they caught my eye. There was a weathered builder's trestle with a sheepskin rug thrown across it, on which a cat was sleeping.

I walked over to stroke the cat and then crouched down to look more closely. 'He looks just like Dandy. *Isn't* this Dandy?' I asked, addressing Ant.

'God, I hope not,' Ant said.

Amy laughed. 'No, that's Riley,' she said. 'Who's Dandy?'

'Dandy was our cat,' Ant explained. 'We lost him when we moved here. He did look a bit like yours, actually.'

'No, this is definitely *our* cat,' Amy said, crossing to tickle his chin. 'You're Riley, aren't you?' she said, and the cat did seem to react to his name, or at least to Amy, more than to me calling him Dandy.

I moved to look the cat in the eye. 'He does look a *lot* like Dandy. The likeness is pretty striking.'

'Maybe he's Dandy's brother,' Ant said. 'Even if it was Dandy, we don't want him back. Living in a cloud of cat hair was *not* my thing.'

'Ant!' I protested.

'Well, it's true,' he said. 'Used to drive me crazy.'

'Oh, I know what you mean,' Amy said. 'The fur is annoying, but we love him, don't we? And these tabbies do all look the same. But we've had Riley since he was a kitten, haven't we, Joe?'

'Um,' Joe said, nodding, I thought, unconvincingly.

I stroked Riley one more time and, making an effort to tell myself that he looked happy, whoever's cat he was, I crossed to the bay window.

There was a huge bowl made of gobstopper marbles invisibly stuck together and an enormous teardrop planter suspended from the ceiling. Both were glinting in the sunlight next to the hefty jade Buddha. 'I love this,' I said, caressing the dish. 'And the Buddha's gorgeous.'

'A gift from Joe's dad,' Amy said. 'It's from Thailand, apparently. It's supposed to bring good luck.'

Joe made his excuses then and slipped upstairs to change while Amy led the way through to the kitchen, which was even prettier. It had white tongue-and-groove walls, and cupboards with grey slatted doors that looked like French shutters; a vast white marble-topped island in the middle, and more unvarnished plank shelves on the walls. The whole place seemed to shimmer, which was something to do with the halogen lighting and all the glassware Amy had dotted around the place. We'd had our own kitchen replaced when we moved in and I couldn't help but think that the ultra-safe gloss grey units we'd chosen said more about our lack of imagination than words ever could. I looked down at my blue dress, mentally comparing it with Amy's outfit, and decided it demonstrated a similar failure of imagination.

Three covered saucepans were simmering on the range and a perfume of coconut and curry floated in the air. 'Something smells good,' I said. Ant, who didn't much like spicy food, raised an eyebrow by way of reply.

We sat on vintage iron bar stools at the central island and Amy asked us what we wanted to drink. It was then that I realised I'd forgotten the wine. 'I'm so, so, sorry,' I said, 'but I left it chilling in the fridge.'

'Fat lot of good it is there,' Ant said. 'I can't believe that you forgot it.'

'Um, we both forgot it,' I said gently. 'But I'm happy to nip back.'

'It's fine!' Amy said. 'Don't be silly. We've got plenty of wine. Is that what you'd like? Wine, or beer, or I can do gin and tonics. I've got Prosecco in the fridge as well, and I've even got some of that weird . . .' She peered into a cupboard and produced a bottle of some fluorescent red mixer. 'I can do spritz, if you want.'

Ant caught my eye then and shook his head and rolled his eyes, silently berating me about the wine again. 'I've offered to go and get it,' I pointed out.

'Really!' Amy said. 'Just stop before I get offended.'

'Sorry,' I said, though I wasn't quite sure what I was apologising for.

'So, wine, beer, Prosecco, spritz? I might have a spritz myself,' Amy said.

'Um, I'll have a beer, if that's OK,' Ant said.

Joe appeared in the doorway. He was in jeans and a plaid shirt and was barefoot. His hair was still wet and he had a towel draped around his shoulders.

'Jeans?' Amy said. 'Really?'

'This is OK, isn't it?' Joe asked, for some reason addressing the question to me.

I nodded. 'Totally fine with me,' I said.

'Honey,' Amy said. 'Make an effort, huh? We have guests.'

'You don't care, do you?' Joe asked, now looking to Ant for reassurance.

'Not at all, mate,' Ant said.

'*I* care,' Amy said. 'We're all dressed up. Anthony's put on a lovely suit, Heather – *Heather?*'

I nodded.

'Sorry, I had a doubt there for a moment,' Amy continued. 'Yes, *Heather's* wearing a lovely evening dress . . . It's called being polite.'

'A suit?' Joe asked. 'Really?'

Amy gestured at Anthony as if to demonstrate that there was nothing ridiculous at all about wearing a suit.

'He's come from work, haven't you?' Joe said.

'Um, yeah,' Anthony lied. 'Totally true.'

'Just change,' Amy said. 'Humour me.'

'Christ,' Joe said. 'Whatever.'

'Honestly,' Amy said, once he'd left. 'He has all these lovely clothes, but all he ever wants to wear is jeans.'

'I've never much liked jeans, myself,' Ant said. Then, turning to me, he asked, 'Have I?'

'No,' I agreed, feeling a bit sorry for poor Joe and a bit shocked at the way Amy bossed him around.

Amy poured some of the red mixer into her glass and then started to uncork the Prosecco. 'Can I do that for you?' Ant asked.

'Thanks,' Amy said, handing over the bottle and going to the refrigerator for Ant's beer.

'And you? What would you like?' Amy asked me.

'She'll have Prosecco, won't you?' Ant said, and though I probably would have said that anyway, I hated him in that moment for replying for me.

Joe reappeared, looking a bit uncomfortable in a sleek navy suit over the top of the same plaid shirt as before. 'Better?' he asked, as he crossed to the stairs to pull a pair of white trainers from the cupboard.

'Shoes might be good,' Amy said, at which Joe raised the trainers and gave them a wiggle.

'I said *shoes*,' Amy said.

'No one cares,' Joe said, pulling the trainers on to his bare feet.

Amy stared at him for a moment. She froze, the beer bottle in her hand, and blinked very slowly, and for a minute I thought she was going to lose it. But then, as if what she'd actually done was press a reset button in her brain, she smiled instead, and asked Joe if he wanted Prosecco.

To ease the tension in the room, I said, 'I just love what you've done with your kitchen. I think it's one of the prettiest kitchens I've ever seen.'

'The guy *is* a kitchen fitter, sweetheart,' Ant said, with a hint of a sneer.

'Oh, of course,' I said. 'Well, I wish we'd got him to do ours.'

'Do you, now?' Ant said.

'Yes, I do,' I said, smiling at Joe and feeling brave.

'Maybe next time,' Joe said, smiling.

'Definitely!' I said.

'Oh, we're redoing the kitchen, are we?' Ant said. 'Women! Jesus, it just never stops.'

Despite the shaky start, the evening turned out to be a success.

Next door in the lounge, the kids ate pizza in front of a film, while we adults, to put it bluntly, got sozzled.

Amy opened two bottles of Prosecco just for the aperitif and she, Joe and I downed both bottles plus another of delicious Californian Chardonnay. Ant, for his part, drank four, perhaps even five bottles of Singha beer. And they weren't small bottles, either.

The food was excellent – though poor Ant ate more rice than he did Thai curry – and the conversation flowed easily, helped on, I think, by all the booze.

Ant's humour was a little prickly for my taste, and a lot of it seemed to be at my expense, but as Amy had a similar sense of humour directed at Joe, I didn't feel exclusively targeted, and if I'm honest, despite a lot of it being a little too close to the bone, I laughed more than I had in years.

The only truly difficult moment was when the subject of holidays came up and Ant explained that we weren't going away because I didn't want to go with his mother.

'Oh, now you see, I *did* want to go with Joe's father,' Amy said. 'It's Joe's father who doesn't want to come with *us*.'

'You see,' Ant said, nodding in my direction. 'Some people know how to appreciate their in-laws.'

I felt terribly trapped in that moment because it looked, to Amy and Joe, as if I was an awful person. But I could hardly explain that Ant's mother was a monster, could I? And my addled brain was unable to find any other way out.

'I . . .' I spluttered, trying to jump-start my brain into action.

'Yes?' Ant said, glancing at Amy and then nodding towards me in a *watch her get out of this* kind of way.

'I . . . I don't know . . .' I said.

'You can't stand her,' Ant said. 'Just say it.'

'Oh, really?' Amy said. 'How sad.'

It was then that Joe intervened. 'Well, not everyone can get on with everyone, eh?' he said forcefully. 'And things aren't that simple on our side, are they?'

Amy frowned at him. 'What do you mean?' she said. 'I get on with Reg just fine.'

'Yeah, but I've only met your mum once, for, like, an hour. And I've *never* met your dad.'

'Really?' Ant said. 'Why's that, then?'

I sighed with relief that the conversation had been moved on.

'Oh, I just don't think they'd get on,' Amy said. 'Mum and Joe, that is. So, I mean, what's the point?'

'We wouldn't get on?' Joe said, looking amused. 'Why is that, honey?'

'And your dad?' Ant asked.

'Oh, Dad lives in Toronto,' Amy said. 'So . . .'

'Toronto!' I exclaimed. 'So you're Canadian? Sorry, I thought . . .'

'American,' Amy said. 'You thought I was American.'

'I'm sorry,' I admitted, 'but yes, I think I did.'

'It happens all the time,' she said. 'But no. Nothing American about me. I'm half English, half Canadian.'

'And so you lived there?' Ant asked. 'I mean, if you have the accent and everything?'

'Till I was twelve,' Amy said. 'And then Mum and Dad split up . . . So I came home with Mum. And I've sort of flitted back and forth ever since. They're both so lovely, I could never decide which one I wanted to spend time with.'

'Though you haven't spent much time with your dad lately,' Joe commented.

'No,' Amy agreed. Was that a glare she sent his way? It was so fleeting it seemed hard to tell. I thought then how skilfully Joe had moved the conversation on, and as Ant was busy chatting to Amy, I sent him a hint of a smile by way of thanks. In return, he sent me the tiniest, quickest wink, and for some reason – and it probably had a great deal to do with all the alcohol I'd been drinking – that tiny gesture of complicity made me want to cry.

My plate moved then, and I snapped back into the moment to realise that Amy was trying to take it. 'Now for dessert,' she said.

'She's made her speciality,' Joe told me. 'It's bloody lovely, so I hope you're still hungry.'

As we tripped along the lane homeward, I commented on the amazing dessert. It had been a vegan banana and chocolate 'cheese' cake, and was probably the nicest cheesecake I'd ever eaten. 'She's a pretty impressive cook,' I added.

'The cheesecake was OK,' Ant agreed. 'Which is more than I can say for that banana curry.'

'It was banana blossom,' I said. 'And I thought it was delicious. It was just too spicy for you.'

'I didn't like the texture,' Ant said. 'It was weird.'

'It was like fish,' I said. 'The texture was like cod.'

'That's what you all kept saying,' Ant said. 'But it wasn't. It was weird and slimy, and other than the bloody spices, it tasted of nowt.'

'The pizza was weird, too,' Lucy chipped in, tugging at my hand for attention. Ant was carrying Sarah, who was sleeping.

'Why was it weird?' I asked, squeezing her fingers.

'The cheese was funny,' she said.

'Because it wasn't cheese,' Ant commented. 'And what's so wrong with cheese, anyway?'

'What do you mean, *what's wrong with cheese?*' I asked.

'I mean, why not just use bloody cheese,' Ant said. 'It's not like eating a cow, is it?'

'Well, they have to kill the calves so we can have the milk,' I explained. Kerry had explained the arguments in favour of veganism at great length to me over the years – in fact, so much so that I'd ended up agreeing with her, really. Had it not been for my uncanny ability to avoid thinking about anything that troubles me – the killing of baby cows, for instance – I would have been forced to go vegan myself.

'Do they?' Ant said. 'Oh, fair enough then, I suppose. If you're gonna get het up about that sort of thing . . .'

We walked past another house identical to our own and then Ant shocked me by saying, 'You know, we *could* go to Spain.'

I turned to study his features, and even though there wasn't a great deal of light, there was enough for me to see that he wasn't joking. 'Really?' I said.

'I'm not saying we should,' Ant continued. 'I'm not saying that at all. But . . .' He combined a shrug with hiking Sarah a bit higher. 'This one's getting heavy,' he said.

'I want to go to Spain,' Lucy commented, but without much enthusiasm. She was too tired to put any energy into it, I think.

'But *what*, Ant?' I prompted.

'What?' he said.

'You said, *you're not saying we should go, but . . .*'

'Oh, I don't know,' he said. 'It just doesn't seem as daft as it did when you explained it. Not now we know them.'

'I don't think you can really say we *know* them,' I pointed out. 'They seem nice enough, but that's not *knowing* them.'

'No,' Ant agreed. 'I suppose not. But I like her. She made me laugh. He's a bit of a nobody, though.'

'You just fancy her,' I teased. Saying it felt like poking my tongue into a bad tooth. It hurt, but I couldn't resist.

'Well, she's a good-looking woman,' Ant said. 'Who wouldn't?'

I immediately regretted my teasing. Life is better when certain things are left unsaid. Life is better when other, more attractive women and dead baby calves are not thought about.

'You know, she reminds me of someone,' I told him, to change the subject. 'I was trying to work out who all night.'

'Yeah?' he said, as we entered our driveway and the automatic light clicked on, blinding us. 'Who?'

'Some American actress or singer, I think.'

'Madonna,' he said. 'She looks like Madonna.'

'No,' I said, as we reached the front door and Ant slipped the key in the lock. 'No, I know what you mean, but that's not it.'

'Kylie?' he suggested.

I laughed. 'No!' I said. 'She's nothing like Kylie.'

'She's blonde,' Ant said. 'They've both got arms and legs and nice arses.'

'Yes, they're both women,' I said, hating him for mentioning Amy's nice arse. 'But that's about where it ends.'

'Anyway, she's nice,' Ant said. 'Lively. God knows what she sees in him, though.'

'I thought he was nice too,' I commented.

'Nice, yeah. But dull.'

'More quiet than dull,' I said.

'He's a good craftsman, but you're better getting him to fit your kitchen than tell you a joke. Still . . .'

'Still what?' I asked.

'Well, I mean, your jokes aren't exactly side-splitters, are they, and I'm with you.'

We'd reached the bottom of the stairs, so Ant pushed Lucy forward, and saying, 'I'm gonna put these two straight down,' he started to carry Sarah upstairs, behind her.

I watched them disappear from view and then walked to the lounge, where I stood in the dark, looking at the window. The tree outside was swaying in the breeze, casting orange patterns from the street light across the carpet. The room looked alien and, for some reason, a bit unfriendly. I realised I was unsteady on my feet from the alcohol and perched on the arm of the sofa to steady myself. It was because Amy's house looked so much more welcoming, I decided. It was in contrast that our own lounge looked so cold.

I'd spent the nicest evening I'd had with Ant in ages, I realised. If ever, in fact. Yet, I was feeling sad to find myself home alone with him. It was a strange feeling, almost as if I was *missing* Amy and Joe. I thought about Amy then, and despite my irritation that Ant had found her 'good-looking', I conceded to myself that he was right. She was, unarguably, good-looking. She was tall and slim and vivacious and funny and entertaining. In a nutshell, she was everything that I wasn't. But despite my jealousy, I'd liked her. A lot of what she said reminded me of the witty dialogues you get in American sitcoms. Everything she said had an edge of wit or sarcasm to it – nothing was ever delivered without some kind of linguistic spin. More than once, I'd missed something funny because I'd been laughing at the previous thing she'd said. She'd made me feel a bit frumpy, really – a bit slow, as if I'd been unable to quite keep up.

And then I thought of Joe, and though I'd liked him, though I'd found him to be kind and unusually attentive to everyone's moods and sensibilities, ultimately I agreed with Ant. He was nice, but 'nice' wasn't necessarily that much fun.

'Are you coming up?' Ant called from the top of the stairs. 'I'm gonna crash, I think. I'm bladdered.'

'Sure,' I replied. 'I'll be up in a minute.'

A gust of wind made the tree move again, and the patterns juddered across the floor. For some reason, I thought of my mother and her strange, indecipherable message. Had she said, 'Go to Spain?' I wondered. But no, that wasn't it either. I shivered and stood and with one last glance out of the window, turned to head upstairs to bed.

Neither Ant nor Lucy mentioned Amy, Joe or Ben again that week, but I thought about them almost constantly. The evening had been by far the most exciting thing to happen to me since we'd moved, after all. As for Spain, I couldn't help but feel I'd come close to getting something I'd wanted for ever – namely, a sunny holiday in a foreign country. Even though I still couldn't see any real way that we could have said *yes* to the proposition, I was fully aware of the irony in the fact that I was the person who had showed the least enthusiasm.

Early the following Saturday morning, Kerry called me on WhatsApp. I was in the conservatory with the girls, and Ant was still snoozing upstairs.

'Hello, stranger,' Kerry said. It was true that we hadn't spoken for months.

She'd just passed her Italian language test with flying colours, and was about to apply for Italian nationality, she explained excitedly. The whole Brexit business had made her self-employed status somewhat complicated in Italy, she said, and becoming Italian was the easiest solution.

'They make you jump through so many hoops,' she told me. 'I have to provide years and years of tax records, and I've got to get hold of Mum and Dad's birth and death certificates. You haven't got them, have you?'

I told her that I would ask Ant to look, as it was he who ran our filing system.

Kerry went on to babble about a new flat she'd found and how it had a spare room if ever I wanted to visit, but that she wasn't sure if she was going to take it because it was so expensive, and what if they refused her Italian citizenship . . .

She chattered on for a good twenty minutes about this and that before eventually saying, 'Anyway, enough of me. What's going on with you?'

'Oh, not much,' I said. 'Same old, same old. You know.'

'You always say that,' Kerry said. 'But I really can't believe your life is that boring. Have you got a secret lesbian lover or something?'

So I told her about our meal down the lane. And then I told her about Spain.

'That's totally *pazzo*, you know?' she said. This slipping Italian words into the conversation was a new thing.

'And *pazzo* means?'

'Crazy,' she said. 'Well, more *loony*, really. *Pazzesco* means sort of *absurd*, and it's that too. It's *pazzo e pazzesco*.'

'Italian always sounds like food to me,' I said. 'No matter what you're saying, it just sounds like a menu. But you're right, it's mad. I mean, as if we could just drop everything and whizz off on holiday with a couple of—'

'No, hang on,' Kerry said, interrupting me. 'You're misunderstanding me. What's crazy . . . what's totally crazy here, is you saying *no*.'

'Oh,' I said, a little taken aback. 'You think?'

'You've been wanting to go abroad for ages. That nightmare of a man you live with won't even let you visit your darling sister in Rome and—'

'Oh, it's not he won't *let* me,' I said. 'It's just complicated, with the kids and everything.'

'Um, *hello* . . . He'd go nuts and you know it,' Kerry insisted. Despite the fact that they had seen so little of each other, she understood Ant surprisingly well. 'And now you're turning down the opportunity to go to Spain with him.'

'I just don't see it as an actual opportunity, I suppose,' I explained. 'It's not really an option, is it?'

'Well, I say go,' Kerry said. 'If there's any possible way you can do it, then go. If he likes it, then that opens up the door to all kinds of new experiences for both of you. Hell, you could even come to Rome and visit little old me.'

'But he *wouldn't* like it,' I pointed out. 'It's full of *spics* and *dagos*, isn't it.'

'*Spics* and *dagos*?' Kerry said. 'You're kidding me, right?'

'It's not me, Kerry. That's what *Ant* calls them. Can you imagine how well that would go down? So no, I'm pretty sure he wouldn't like it.'

'And there you go,' Kerry said. 'It is him, isn't it? It's not *you* saying *no* at all.'

'Ant actually said it was a possibility,' I pointed out. 'It's just I don't really believe he'd do it.'

'Then call his bluff.'

'And I can't really convince myself it's a good idea anyway, Kes. Like I said, we just don't know them.'

'But they're nice, you said.'

'Yes,' I admitted. 'Yes, they're nice.'

'So it's a win-win,' Kerry said.

'Amy's a bit too good-looking for comfort, if you know what I mean.'

'Ah, so *that's* it,' Kerry laughed.

'She looks like someone . . .' And then it came to me. 'Actually, I'll tell you who she looks like. She looks exactly like that singer you used to have on your wall. The blonde one. What's her name?'

'No Doubt?' Kerry asked. 'Gwen Stefani?'

'That's it! God, it's been driving me mad trying to remember. But that's her. Gwen Stefani.'

'Wow,' Kerry said. 'Has she got the bod to go with it?'

'Well, she's a dance instructor and a Pilates teacher. So yes, she *totally* has the bod to go with it.'

'Jesus,' Kerry said. 'Can I come? I've had a crush on our Gwen for years.'

'I know,' I said. 'That's why I thought of her, I think: your posters.'

'But seriously. If you're saying *no* because you're worried Ant fancies her—'

'I'm not,' I interrupted. But even as I was saying it, I was thinking, *Or am I?* 'I'm saying *no* because people simply do not go on holiday with couples they met a week ago.'

'Oh, fuck *what people do*,' Kerry said. 'And if it *is* about how cute she is—'

'It isn't.'

'But if it *is*, remember she lives down the lane. That's what you said, right?'

'Yes.'

'So if he *was* going to fuck her, he would have fucked her already.'

'Oh, that's lovely, Kerry,' I said. 'Oh, yes, that's gorgeous. Thanks for that.'

'Morning!'

I turned to see Ant standing in the doorway.

'Who's that?' he asked.

'It's Kerry,' I said quietly.

Ant nodded unenthusiastically. 'Give her my love,' he said, through a yawn.

'I'd better go,' I told Kerry, once he'd returned to the kitchen.

'Of course,' Kerry said. 'Your lord and master has arisen.'

'Don't be like that. We've been talking for almost an hour.'

'Forty minutes,' she corrected.

'It's Saturday. I've got things to do. I have children.'

'Sure,' she said. 'Whatever. And send me a postcard this summer. From Chislet.'

I slipped the phone into my pocket, and it was only when I went to look at what the girls had been doing that I realised I hadn't passed the phone over so that they could say hello to their aunt. But they were engrossed in making flowers from coloured pipe cleaners and seemed to have forgotten about Kerry anyway.

'Those are lovely,' I told them. 'Are they for me?'

Sarah offered me her misshapen flower-in-progress immediately, while Lucy shook her head violently and said, 'No!' as if it was the silliest suggestion I could have made. At least with my daughters I always knew where I stood.

In the kitchen, Ant was reading the *Daily Mail* on his iPad.

'Look what Sarah made,' I said, showing him the flower.

'That's cool,' he replied, barely glancing up from the screen. 'Coffee?'

'Sure,' he said. 'Coffee would be good. So what did your big butch sister have to say for herself?'

'Oh, not much,' I told him. 'She wants to become Italian. That's the latest thing.'

'I'm sorry?'

'She's going to apply for Italian nationality,' I explained. 'Something to do with Brexit and her job.'

'Right,' Ant said disinterestedly. 'Fair enough.' He was clearly far more interested in the article he was reading than anything Kerry had had to say.

I crossed to the coffee maker and switched it on, then slipped in a capsule, and as I waited for the 'ready' light to come on, I licked my lips, turning the words over in my mind, trying them out for size.

It felt for some reason as if I'd reached a fork in the road. It seemed as if the slightest nudge could send me off down a different track, and that the repercussions on my destiny could be major. I was struck by a sense of foreboding that made me hesitate. I opened my mouth to speak and then closed it silently. I opened it to speak again, but then failed for the second time to make a sound.

'Kerry thinks—' I finally managed, but just at that moment, Ant's phone buzzed. He glanced at the screen and said, 'Christ! They're keen.'

'Who's keen?' I asked. I was assuming it was going to be about work.

'Joe,' Ant said.

'Oh? What does he say?'

'He's asking if we've had any more thoughts about Spain,' Ant said. 'Because otherwise Amy's going to invite someone else. Reading between the lines, I don't think Joe's that keen on whoever she's got in mind.'

'Ah, right,' I said, my finger hesitating over the coffee button. 'And have we? Had any thoughts, I mean?'

Ant shrugged. 'You gonna make that coffee or not?' he asked.

So I pressed the button and the machine lurched into action.

'I suppose it might be better than hanging around here,' he said, as the coffee maker buzzed and the brown liquid dripped into the cup.

'Really?' I said with consternation. 'Gosh. Then maybe we could, um . . . What would you think about us going on our own?'

'On our own?'

'Yes.'

'To Spain?'

'Yes,' I said. 'I mean, there's no reason we have to go with them, is there? And we could always go away with them later, when we know them better. I'd still like to go to Spain and get some sunshine, but just maybe not with them.'

'Speak Spanish, do you?' Ant asked.

'No,' I said. 'No, you know I don't, but I don't think we nec—'

'Amy does,' he said, interrupting me. 'She's fluent, apparently.'

'Does she?' I said. I had no recollection of any discussion about that subject.

'So it would make things easier, wouldn't it? Plus, they've got the house booked and everything's sorted. I mean, I wouldn't know where to start.'

'You're actually thinking of saying *yes*, then?' I said, so shocked I had frozen with Ant's coffee cup in my hand.

Ant shrugged again. 'Why not?' he said, reaching out for it. 'What have we got to lose?'

As things turned out, getting passports for the whole family was devilishly complicated, and as not one of us had ever had one before, and because we needed them all at the same time, the process required multiple trips up to London.

At the first meeting they'd warned Ant that it would take up to six weeks to complete the process, and though, in the end, it took five, we were unable to book the same flights as Joe and Amy, who were flying at the beginning of August.

But to be honest, leaving later suited me better. Though we'd seen them four more times before they'd left, even spending a pleasant afternoon around their pool, I was still feeling a bit nervous about the intimacy of sharing a house with them. Avoiding travelling with them on top of everything else seemed like a plus to me, despite the stress of having to deal with all the travel arrangements alone.

Flying for the first time was an amazing experience. I had butterflies in my stomach all morning, and when the plane finally left the tarmac I couldn't help but break out in a crazy grin. I almost cried, if I'm telling the truth. I was flying, like a bird! And we were on our way to Spain!

The girls took the whole thing in their stride, chattering and fidgeting excitedly throughout – kids are so adaptable at that age, nothing fazes them – while Ant looked pale and stared rigidly at the advert-covered headrest in front of him. As we'd got up at 1.30 a.m. to make our flight and as Ant had never been a morning person, I couldn't tell if he was scared or sick, or just tired. But as he would rather have died than ever admit to any of those, I simply left him to his own devices.

By the time we stepped off the plane, it was eleven in the morning, local time. The temperature, the pilot said, was thirty-six degrees.

Now, we'd had quite the heatwave back home just before we left, with temperatures reaching a sultry thirty-five. But this – this thirty-six degrees in Malaga – was a completely different kettle of fish. It felt like nothing I had ever experienced, and by the time I reached the bottom of the steps, I was soaked.

'Can this *really* be just thirty-six?' I asked Ant as we crossed the tarmac towards the bus.

'It's the humidity,' a stranger beside us said. 'It's a hundred per cent today.'

'It's like a bloody sauna,' Ant replied. 'I hope it's not gonna be like this the whole time.'

I found passport control unreasonably stressful and, despite the air conditioning, sweated so much that I feared they would think I looked guilty. Which, of course, only made me sweat even more.

For some reason, I'd got it into my head that one of the passports might not 'work' or something – I had visions of the Spanish police shaking their heads and taking our kids away. But in the end, the policeman barely glanced at them before waving us all through.

Finally, we trundled our suitcases out into the great unknown to face a wall of bearded men holding name tags.

'God, how are we supposed to find Joe among this rabble?' Ant asked, and it was exactly what I was thinking.

But then Lucy broke free from my grasp and ran straight under the barrier, pushed her way through the front row of men, and jumped into Joe's outstretched arms. 'I found him, Mum!' she shouted proudly. 'I found him!'

Four

Joe

The house was in a tiny hamlet called Fuente Nueva, and it was truly in the middle of nowhere – about two hours west of the coast and three north of Malaga airport. I had never realised just how big and empty Spain was until that first drive from Malaga through the rolling, sun-bleached landscape. Three hours barely moved us up the map.

Fuente Nueva consisted of twenty or thirty houses – actually, *dwellings* would be, I suppose, a better word, as they had all been dug out of the mountainside. The frontages overlooked a vast flat plain bordered in the distance by a mountain range, the Sierra Maria.

The landscape of the plain was bleak tundra interspersed with outcrops of rock, and to give you a better idea of how arid it was, if you'd filmed a drone attack on a couple of jeeps, everyone would have assumed it was Iraq. Only a patchwork of fluorescent green fields to the east, mainly comprised of heavily watered broccoli, gave the game away.

The house itself was extremely cool, in all senses of the word. It consisted of what looked, from the outside, like a tiny white stucco shed, but this was in fact merely the entrance to a series of caves cut deep into the hillside. These chambers were rounded and organic, with bumpy white-painted walls. They remained so cool that even at siesta time, when the outside temperature frequently hit forty, you still needed the thick quilts the owners had provided.

In front of the house, bordered by hewn rock face to the right and some unused outbuildings to the left, was an airless courtyard that shimmered in the heat, and in the middle was a blue-tiled pool with a so-called jacuzzi. I say *so-called* because, as the pump was out of order, it was really no more than a sit-down zone at one side of the pool – though that turned out, in the end, to be incredibly useful as a kiddy-pool.

There was quite literally *nothing* to do in Fuente Nueva. There were no shops, no cinemas; there was no beach. It was too hot to walk anywhere and there were no restaurants or bars to visit of an evening. Best or worst of all, depending on your perspective, we'd forgotten to ask about Internet, and not only was there no Wi-Fi, but our phones didn't pick up a signal either. Though she acted like it had been a conscious choice, saying how great it was to 'digitally detox' for a while, I could tell that Amy was gutted at the oversight.

With the exception of a brief drive to nearby Orce for food once or twice, we'd done nothing whatsoever for ten days.

Personally, other than the fact there was no beach, I thought the place was pretty amazing. My job, my *life*, was physically exhausting, and sitting in a super-heated pool reading, or taking long siestas in the deep, silent darkness of our cave-bedroom, was as close to paradise as I could imagine. But Amy and Ben were getting restless, and I was beginning to admit that perhaps it had been a good idea to invite the others after all, if only to take the pressure off me. Ben, particularly, was longing for the arrival of fresh blood.

All the same, my sense of unease remained and during the three-hour drive to the airport I tried to reason with myself that my nervousness was groundless. After all, what could go wrong?

But I'd once managed to fall out with a girlfriend in Italy, I remembered. And OK, I'd only been eighteen, but on another occasion I'd had a huge bust-up with one of my best friends in Amsterdam. So shit can happen, even on holiday. And I couldn't help but think that if something were to happen, that house, that constrained courtyard, our isolated village . . . well, it could all become a bit of a pressure cooker.

The fact that they'd decided not to rent their own car bugged me too. Of course, it meant that I had to drive back to Malaga to meet them, but that wasn't really the problem. I like driving, and it gave me some time to myself. It was more the fact that they'd be depending on us for everything the entire time that worried me. So even though I knew that the suggestion to rent a single seven-seater Kodiaq for all of us had been Amy's, I was unable to convince myself it had been one of her better ideas.

For the return trip from the airport, Ant sat up front, with Heather and the kids in the rear seats. As Ant fell asleep almost immediately, that was a bit of a shame, really. Heather was awake and seemed quite lively at first, and I would have enjoyed having someone to talk to for the drive home. But as it was all but impossible to hold a conversation with her in the rear, I quickly gave up and put on Spanish radio, and by the time we got home, they'd all been asleep for some time.

It was about 3 p.m. when we arrived, and Amy had laid out an impressive spread of food to welcome our new arrivals. Unfortunately, we'd all eaten sandwiches from a service station I'd stopped at, so it was food that nobody wanted. Amusingly, nobody mentioned the sandwiches – it seemed that even the girls understood that it was bad form to admit to having eaten. And so we sat and nibbled politely at Amy's vegan quiche, at her pasta and potato salads; at the kilo of hummus she'd whipped up.

'No one seems very hungry,' Amy said eventually.

'It's the heat, I think,' Heather said. 'But I'm sure we'll eat it later.'

'It was a mistake setting up outside,' Amy said, and she was right. Even in the shade of the olive tree the heat was unbearable. Sweat kept dripping off my chin on to my plate.

Once we'd cleared the table, they chose rooms. Heather went on so much about how lovely the place was that I thought she sounded a bit fake. Ant, on the other hand, seemed unimpressed and a bit edgy, but as the girls were unusually quiet too, I gave them all the benefit of the doubt and assumed they were just shell-shocked from the journey.

From four to six, we all slept. The cave-bedrooms were cool, silent and pitch black. I don't think I've ever slept better anywhere in my entire life than I did during those siestas in Spain.

After sleeping, as the temperature dropped, everyone seemed a little more relaxed. The kids splashed around in the pool; Amy sat nattering to Heather; and Ant wandered around holding his phone in the air, desperately trying to get reception. You could tell from the get-go that the lack of Internet was going to be a problem for him.

Around eight we ate the leftovers from lunch, and then while Heather and I cleared the table in amicable silence, Amy and Ant walked to the dirt track that ran in front of the courtyard.

From the kitchen, I heard a peal of Amy's laughter. The sound brought a smile to my face, and I decided, in that moment, that this would prove to have been a good idea after all. She'd laughed a lot when I'd first met her, but I was realising, only now, that laughter had become a rarity for both of us. In fact, the only time I could remember either of us laughing in recent times was the drunken meal we'd had with Ant and Heather.

When I returned outside for more plates, I saw them silhouetted against the flaming night sky. There was a rickety old wooden bench on the far side of the track and they were seated on it, looking out. The sky was so impressive that I decided to join them for a moment.

'What's so funny?' I asked when I got there, and they twisted in their seats to look up at me.

'Um?' Amy said.

'I heard you laughing at something,' I told her. 'I love to hear you laugh like that.'

'Oh, I asked her what you do around here for kicks,' Ant said. 'That's funny, apparently.'

'You look at that,' I said, nodding at the sky. It was turning purple along the tops of the mountains, and a deep red to the right above the fields.

'Amazing, huh?' Amy said.

'Yeah, it's pretty cool,' Ant said. 'But I'm not sure it's gonna keep me entertained all week.'

Despite an early night, I woke up late. A strip of sunshine was leaking through the gap beneath the door and I could hear children's shrieks coming from the pool.

I lay there for a moment in the darkness, slowly coming to, and then, realising that Amy was beside me, and concerned that I couldn't hear any adult voices outside, I got up.

The sunlight, when I opened the door, was blinding, and I had to hunt down my sunglasses before it was physically possible to step outside.

All three kids were in the jacuzzi and Heather was sitting on the side, dangling her feet in the water and reading a magazine. She was wearing a wide-brimmed straw hat and an off-the-shoulder T-shirt.

'Oh, good morning!' she exclaimed, looking up. 'I was worried you'd died in your sleep.'

I blinked, a little shocked by her off-key remark. 'Late, is it?' I asked.

'Ten thirty,' she said. 'We've been up since eight, haven't we, kids?'

'Where did that come from?' I asked, indicating the pink lilo the kids were playing on.

'Ant found it in the outhouse,' Heather explained. 'There were two, actually, but the green one had a puncture, so . . .'

'Is Ben being good?'

Heather nodded and smiled vaguely. 'As gold,' she said.

'And where *is* Ant?' I asked, looking around.

'Oh, he's around,' Heather said. Then, 'Look, have either of you *ever* managed to get phone reception? Because I think it's going to drive him insane pretty soon.'

'Amy did, briefly,' I said. 'Ben? Where was it Mum managed to get a phone signal?'

'Down the track,' Ben said, pointing. 'Where the trees are.'

'Only barely, though,' Amy said.

I turned to see her standing in the doorway, shading her eyes with her arm. 'It picked up for, like, a minute. But I couldn't even listen to my voicemail. Why, what's up? Does someone need to make a call?'

'It's just Ant,' Heather explained. 'He doesn't like to feel cut off.'

'Came to the wrong place then, didn't he?' Amy laughed. She started to turn towards the interior, then hesitated and asked, 'Coffee, anyone?'

Just as she returned with two mugs of coffee, Ant appeared as well, still waving his phone around in the air. '*Nada,*' he said.

'Wow!' Amy joked. 'Speaking the lingo already, are we?'

'I'm sorry?' Ant said.

'It's Spanish,' Heather explained. '*Nada*. It's Spanish for "nothing", right?' She glanced at me and I nodded.

'Oh,' Ant said. 'Right. And what's Spanish for "no bloody phone signal" then, clever clogs?' he asked her.

'*Sin señal de teléfono*,' Amy said. She put her mug down on the table and circled the pool to join Ant. 'Try over there,' she said, resting one hand in the small of his back and pointing down the track. 'I got a signal there yesterday, briefly.'

Once Ant had headed off, she returned to the table. 'If not, we could maybe take him into town later,' she suggested. 'I totally get how frustrating it is.'

'We probably need to get some bits anyway,' Heather said.

'You mean food, or . . . ?'

'Yeah, you know, just this and that,' Heather said.

'Oh, I think we're OK for food,' Amy said. 'I've got the next three meals planned, at least.'

'There's still a few bits I'd like to get,' Heather said again. 'There are things Ant likes, his little habits. You know how it is.'

'Non-vegan things,' I said, explaining it for Amy, who seemed to be missing the point.

'Oh,' she said. 'Oh, of course. Sorry.'

'Just some proper milk and some cheese and stuff. You know.'

'Sure,' Amy said again. 'No problem. There's a public pool apparently, too. So we could take the kids, maybe. Make an outing of it.'

They left just after lunch, and for the first time in ten days I found myself alone.

Initially, I went to lie down, but when sleep didn't come I got up again and sat beneath our olive tree. A dragonfly was flitting over the surface of the pool and the cicadas were making so much noise it was on the verge of annoying – something I would never have thought was possible.

I thought of Ant and his phone addiction, and I'll admit that in that instant I judged him for it. He'd been here less than twelve hours, after all. How urgent could it be?

But then I made an effort to understand him. I thought about the fact that, like me, he had his own business. Maybe he was waiting for important news. I remembered that his mother was elderly and lived alone. Perhaps he was worried about her.

I thought of Dad then, and wondered if there was any news of his romance.

Despite the heat, I decided to go for a walk. I felt pretty sure that I could find a sweet spot somewhere with a phone signal even if nobody else could. And if I could solve that, it would make things easier for Ant, too.

I packed the e-reader I'd bought for the trip and a bottle of water; I slipped on a T-shirt and a hat and set off.

I didn't have to walk far before my phone picked up – in fact, no further than the same group of trees Amy had mentioned. I sat down on the ground in the shade and called Dad, but there was no answer. He was out, and I wondered if that was a good sign.

The four trees were situated at the point where the track curved around the 'corner' of the hill our house had been carved into, and there was a gentle breeze coming from the north that felt good. I pulled my e-reader from my bag, but I'd forgotten to charge the damn thing. *Long live paper*, I thought, returning it to my little backpack.

I swigged at the bottle of water and fiddled with my phone instead. But though there were two bars of reception, there seemed to be no data connection. This meant no emails, no Facebook, no *Guardian* . . .

I wondered if there was anyone I needed to call, but the truth was that, other than Dad, I'd got out of the habit of speaking on the phone. Nearly all of my communications happened via text messages or emails these days. In fact, if I did get an incoming call, as likely as not I'd ignore it and wait for the follow-up text message to arrive instead. I wondered when actual calls had come to feel like an intrusion.

I remembered when phones had just been phones and felt a bit melancholic for the calmer, simpler times when you could be unaware for hours of everything that was happening in the world.

I slipped it back into my bag, took another swig of water, and wiped my brow on my sleeve.

I looked out over the plain – it was shimmering in the heat. A single, unreasonably cute cloud – like a cloud in an animated kid's film – was moving slowly towards the mountains, casting a shadow over the countryside as it wafted by.

A movement caught my eye – it was a beetle, dragging what looked like a rabbit dropping. It passed in front of me, right to left, pausing to rest or to change its grip from time to time. I wondered why it wanted that dropping so badly. It looked like bloody hard work.

I thought of my own life then, and how hard I worked, and wondered what I was striving for. I checked the time on my phone and wondered why I'd done so. It was 15.32, but so what? What possible meaning did 15.32 have here, today?

I thought about time, and how important it had become in my life. Every job I undertook seemed to take longer than I expected, and the available time was always slightly less than I hoped. I seemed to be living in a perpetual state of negotiation with myself, constantly checking the time, calculating how long whatever task I was doing was taking, and judging if that was acceptable or not, and whether I should be moving on to the next thing yet. Even just sitting here now, thinking, felt illicit, as if someone might come and 'catch me' doing nothing and tell me off.

And the weeks, the months, the years . . . Everyone tells you that time goes faster as you get older, but no amount of warning can prepare you for the reality. In my twenties I used to pray for Friday to come around. In my thirties I'd be surprised that the end of the month had already arrived. But nowadays it was the years. It was spring, summer, winter again, and I'd think, *Winter? Again? When the fuck did that happen?*

And Ben, above all Ben, that special time went by so fast. He'd stopped mispronouncing *marmalade* at some point, and I hadn't even noticed when that was. It had been so cute, as well . . . When had he first pulled on his own shoes? When had he told his first joke? When was the first time he'd failed to care that I was home from work?

A raggedy cat with bald, flea-bitten ears appeared. It sniffed around one of the trees and then came to sit right in front of me.

To start with, I thought it was after something – food, or caresses, or *something*. But it seemed just to want to sit beside me. Then again, perhaps it was nothing to do with me at all. Maybe it just wanted the same shade, view and gentle breeze that I was enjoying.

I stared at the back of the cat's head for a while and then looked out again at the scenery. A big bird – a buzzard or an eagle, I couldn't tell which – was circling. 'You want to watch yourself,' I told the cat. 'Or that bird will have you for breakfast.'

The cat turned then, and looked at me, and I swear it nodded before it turned back to look out at the bird.

I thought about the dog I'd had as a child. He'd been middle-aged when I was born, so by the time I'd got to Ben's age, he'd been ancient. An old, smelly bulldog called Butch. I'd loved that dog to bits – in fact, it would be no exaggeration to say that Butch had been my best friend. I'd always intended to get Ben a dog, but the years had slipped by and it hadn't happened and then suddenly we had a cat. And Ben seemed to love him just fine, so . . .

I remembered sitting with Butch in our back yard, and at other times on Whitby beach. Sometimes I'd put my arm around him and talk to him, and I was convinced that he understood everything I said. Sometimes, if I'd been told off, I used to bury my face in his fur and cry salty childish tears. But most of the time he was just there, beside me, a witness to whatever was happening, a witness who made the moment real, like this cat.

The strangest feeling rose up in me, a sort of flashback to being a child, to the long summer holidays, to the beach, to riding a bike aimlessly around, to poking at ants with a stick and just . . . Just what? Just *being*, perhaps?

I felt suddenly overcome by sadness, by a sort of grief for the loss of my childhood. It had slipped away unnoticed, and I'd failed to mark its passing; I'd failed to grieve for the loss. But now the moment was upon me.

When exactly *had* it gone? Had it been when Butch died, or when school ended? Was it when I started working for a living, or when Mum died? When had I lost the ability to just sit and be? When had I started counting the hours but letting the years slip by unnoticed? And how the hell had I got to forty without noticing?

My eyes were watery, blurring the landscape. 'Come here, will you?' I said to the cat, and though it turned and glanced at me again, though it blinked slowly at me, in what looked to me like an expression of compassion, it didn't move. It was too busy sitting there, looking out. It was too busy being present in the moment.

Altogether, I sat there almost two hours, until the cat walked off, and the feeling, like the cloud, drifted away. The moment became like any other and I started to feel hot and uncomfortable and bored, so I stood and started to walk back to the house.

But as I walked, another sensation rose within me, a strange sense of rage at the way my precious hours on this planet were being wasted. Something needed to change, I thought. And perhaps, even though I couldn't even begin to think what that meant, *everything* needed to change.

By the time they all returned, it was nine and the sun was setting.

The kids were babbling excitedly – something about a pig and a fish – but as they were all shouting at once, I couldn't really make head nor tail of it.

Ant was carrying four big pizza boxes and, for some reason, he handed them to me, as if he'd just arrived at my place for dinner.

'Thanks,' I said. 'I was wondering if I was meant to be cooking. Did you manage to get phone reception?'

'Oh yeah,' he said. 'Yeah, it works everywhere except here.'

Over pizza, which was a bit limp, but which having actual cheese on it tasted like a treat to my part-time vegan palate, they told me about their day out.

They'd explored Orce first, and it was there that they'd seen the piglet.

'It was just running around,' Lucy explained. 'It was really friendly.'

'Like a dog,' Ben said.

'It licked my hand,' Sarah said.

'I was worried it might bite her,' Heather told me. 'It did seem to have quite big teeth.'

'An old local guy told me it was safe,' Amy explained. 'He's a friendly pig, apparently. Tame.'

'And *why* is there a pig running around?'

'It's a tradition, I think,' Amy said. 'The whole town feeds it scraps. They let it run free.'

'How cute,' I said.

'And then at the end of August they have a party, and you know . . .'

I frowned at Amy.

'A spit roast,' she said, winking.

'Oh God, they *eat* the poor fucker?' Ant asked.

'Ant!' Heather said. 'Language!'

'Sorry,' he said.

'I was actually trying to avoid saying that in front of you know who,' Amy said, nodding at Sarah.

'Can we go?' Ben asked. 'Can we go to the pig party?' He'd clearly missed the point somewhere along the way.

'No, I'm afraid it's after we've left,' Amy said.

'How sad!' I said, with irony.

'I want a pig,' Ben said. 'Can I have a pig when we get home? It's way more fun than a cat. It could come to school with me and everything.'

'And there were fish in the pool, too,' Amy said.

'In the swimming pool?'

'Yeah, a lot of wildlife in Spain,' Ant commented. 'Pigs in the streets, fish in the pool. Goats on the road.'

'I was scared they were going to bite, too,' Heather said. 'They were all a bit deformed.'

'The goats?' I asked.

'No, the fish, silly,' she said.

'They *were* sort of Chernobyl fish,' Ant said.

'So, the pool is freshwater, right?' Amy explained. 'There's a hot spring that just, like, bubbles up at one end.'

'It's lovely and warm,' Heather said.

'But years and years ago, someone put some fish in it. And they've reproduced, so there are loads of them. But they're all a bit inbred. So they've got weird heads and lumps and things.'

146

'Ooh,' I said, pulling a face.

'But it's kind of fun, swimming with the fish.'

'And are we talking big fish, or little fish?'

Ben held up his hands to represent a fish of about four feet in length.

'Really?' I said.

'Yeah,' Ant laughed. 'That one was called Jaws, but only Ben saw it. No, they were the size of trout, maybe ten or twelve inches.'

'The biggest one was like this,' Ben insisted, waving his hands around again. 'You saw it, Lucy, right?'

'Yes,' Lucy said, nodding seriously. 'That looks about right, Ben.'

'But you had a nice time?' I asked. 'No one got mortally wounded by the pig or the fish?'

'It was lovely,' Amy said. 'We have to go back there together. The pool's pretty big, and free. The water's crystal clear and no chlorine or anything, obviously.'

'Just fish.'

'Exactly. Just fish. And all around it there's a lawn, so you can just lounge around in the shade of the trees.'

I glanced at Ant, who nodded. 'Yeah, it's cool,' he said. 'Phone picks up there, too.'

I looked at Heather then, and raised an eyebrow. 'Yes, it was nice,' she said, smiling falsely, and I wondered what had gone wrong.

Five

Heather

I had *not* had a particularly nice day in Orce, as it happens.

Amy had driven us into town. She'd parked in the centre, and I'd looked out at the deserted streets. It was 2.20 p.m. and the car thermometer, I noticed, read forty degrees. 'Here we are,' she said.

'Wouldn't it be better to go to the pool first?' I suggested. 'Then we could come back here when it's cooler. *And* when the shops are open.'

'Oh,' Amy said. 'But we're here now. The pool's on the other road, out of town.' She turned to Ant, who was in the passenger seat. 'What do you think?' she asked him.

'Ignore her,' he said. 'She's never happy, that one.'

'That's unfair!' I protested. 'It just makes more sense to do it the other way around because it's so hot, that's all I'm saying.'

'Yeah, well, you should have spoken up before,' Ant said, which was also unfair, as I couldn't possibly have known where Amy had decided to go first. He opened the door and the air that rushed in was so hot it was like someone had opened the oven in my kitchen back home.

Amy turned to me with a pained expression. 'I'm sorry,' she said. 'I mean, we *can* go now, if you really think it's better.'

But Ant was already unstrapping Sarah from the seat beside me and lifting her out into the death-ray sunshine. Luckily, I'd slathered us all with sunblock. 'It's fine,' I said, thinking, *It isn't fine, but Ant can own this one.* 'It was only a suggestion.'

'It was only a *suggestion*,' Ant repeated in a childish voice.

Amy wiggled a finger at him. 'He's naughty, that one,' she said, laughing.

No, he's a knob, I thought angrily.

As things turned out, I had been totally right, of course. It was fiendishly, unbearably hot – in fact, I can't really find words to describe to you just how hot it was in the centre of town that day. The paths shimmered, the sun beat down and even the walls of the buildings radiated heat . . . it came at you from every angle. The air was so hot it seemed to scorch your lungs when you breathed in. Every single shop was closed for lunch and those shops that had a sign indicated they'd be reopening at five, or sometimes even six. Despite glasses of Coke beneath parasols that were so hot they also seemed to act like radiators, within ten minutes Lucy and Ben were complaining and little Sarah was in tears. 'I want to go swimming like Mummy said,' she sniffled.

'Well, that's Mummy's fault for not saying so sooner, isn't it?' Ant told her, making her misery unexpectedly my responsibility.

'Come on, let's get out of here,' Amy said. 'It really *is* too hot for the kids.'

'It's too hot for me, let alone the kids,' I said. 'If we stay here any longer, I think I might faint.'

It was while we were walking back to the car that we came across the pig, scampering along the main street, clinging to the shadows.

An elderly man appeared in a doorway and crouched to give it some stale bread, and seeing us arriving, he began talking to Ben in Spanish.

'He says he's tame,' Amy translated. 'He says you can stroke him if you want to.'

Although he looked like a perfectly nice piglet, you could write everything I know about pigs on the back of a stamp, and from my position of total ignorance, I did not want my kids anywhere near it. Even from a distance, I'd caught a glimpse of his teeth as he'd gobbled up the bread, and they looked surprisingly pointy.

'Ant, keep them away,' I said, as I caught up.

'Don't worry, Mummy's just a bit scared, but it's fine,' Ant told Lucy, crouching down beside her. 'You're a lovely little fella, aren't you?' he added, addressing the pig as he scratched behind his ear.

Lucy started to stroke the pig's back at that point, and then Sarah pushed past Ant and the piglet started to lick her outstretched hand, looking, I suppose, for more bread.

I leaped in and swept her up into my arms. 'Ant!' I said. 'For Christ's sake. It's a pig. It's dirty.'

'It looks pretty clean to me,' Ant said.

'What if it's got rabies or something?'

Ant laughed. 'I don't think pigs even get rabies,' he said, and I betted mentally that he had no more idea about that than I did.

'Or swine fever,' I said. 'Pigs get that. Or hepatitis, or . . . anything. I don't know.'

'Jesus,' Ant said, standing. 'Take a chill pill, Heath. You're scaring the kids.'

'I *want* to scare the kids,' I told him solemnly. 'I want to scare them enough that they stop letting that pig lick their hands.'

Half an hour later, at the pool, I made a second mistake of being wary of the fish, and this unleashed a whole battery of mockery.

'Careful,' Ant said. 'You might catch fish fever. Or rainbow-trout rabies.'

'I'm not *scared* of them,' I said. 'I just think they look creepy.' But if I'm honest, I was a bit scared of the fish. For some reason I couldn't explain, I wouldn't have much liked the idea of brushing up against any kind of fish while swimming, but these fish had only one eye; these fish had deformed fins and twisted humpbacks. They really *did* look creepy.

'Well, I think it's fun,' Amy said, jumping into the pool right near where the fish were all gathered. 'It's a pool, but it's also nature.'

'Of course it's fun,' Ant said, addressing Lucy. 'Mummy's just scared of her own shadow, that's all.'

'There's one over there that's like Jaws,' Ben told me, giggling. 'He'll bite your toes off if you're not careful.'

'Thanks for that, Ben,' I said. 'That's really helpful.'

'Mummy's scared of fishes, Mummy's scared of fishes,' Lucy taunted.

Amy returned to collect Ben then, and while I remained in the shallows with Sarah, she and Ant swam back to the deep end where all the fish were, with Lucy and Ben clinging to their backs.

Once they'd reached the far side, Sarah looked up at me adoringly and I thought she was going to ask if we could join them. If she had done so, I would have done my best to overcome my fears for her sake, but instead, she said, 'Don't worry, I don't like the fishes either, Mummy.'

'Oh, you, you're gorgeous,' I told her, snuffling her neck with kisses. 'And I think the fish are all right really,' I told her. 'I just don't want them brushing against my leg, because it tickles.'

'Mummy's scared of fishes!' Lucy shouted again, this time from the far side of the pool. Some Spanish people glanced my way and I wondered if they understood what Lucy was saying.

'She's just showing off cos Ben's here,' Sarah said, making me laugh.

And then I thought about what she'd said, and thought that yes, she was right. Lucy was showing off because Ben was here. And

Ant was showing off because Amy was here. And I wondered what, if anything, that meant.

We stayed at the pool for over three hours.

The kids ended up playing with some Spanish children, one of whom had a withered arm that looked like it might be from polio. They couldn't say a single word to each other, but it didn't matter. Watching them, I thought about the fact that prejudice is learned – about how naturally accepting kids are of each other.

I thought about Ant and his dreadful remarks about *spics* and *dagos* and realised that he hadn't said either word since we'd arrived. Perhaps seeing that the Spaniards were people, 'just like us', had been enough to stop him thinking that way, or more likely he was simply watching his tongue. Whatever the explanation, it was a relief. I imagined Lucy and Sarah hearing those words from their peers at some point in the future and thought that, hopefully, they'd remember this day, this trip, and think, *No, I've been to Spain, and the people there are nice.*

I dozed under the tree for a while – knocked out, I think, by the heat – and when I woke up, Ant was chatting to Amy at the poolside, their legs dangling side by side in the water. In the gaps between the children's shrieks, I could just about hear what they were saying, and I was shocked to realise they were comparing notes on their partners. Annoyed and intrigued in equal measure, I pretended I was still asleep and listened on.

'Oh, that's just like Joe,' Amy was saying. 'He never wants to do anything, either. But you know, I think it's just normal stasis. It's just what happens when you're in a relationship for a long time.'

'It's people who've never moved,' Ant said. 'It's people who have always stayed in one town, that's the thing.'

'Oh, Joe's moved,' Amy said. 'He's from Whitby, up north.'

'Oh yeah, of course,' Ant said. 'Kind of like me.'

I almost sat up to point out that I too had moved – that I'd grown up in Essex – but I couldn't really see what it would achieve.

A couple walked past, talking loudly, but when I could hear again, Amy was saying, '. . . with Joe, it's not so much a geographical thing. It's just that he's contented with so little, you know?'

'Heather's the same,' Ant said, and I thought, *Huh! Luckily for you, I am.*

'It's like, if you sit Joe in an armchair with a book, then he's just happy for ever more,' Amy said. 'I got so bored with seeing him in that chair that I sold it on eBay, actually. But he just moved to the sofa instead.'

'Reading's so boring,' Ant said. 'I've never liked reading. I'd always rather be active, out and about, doing stuff.'

'Well, you need to nourish your spirit too,' Amy said. 'I mean, I like to read about other people's experiences, but it's not the only thing I want from my life, you know?'

'Heather's a reader,' Ant told her. 'She's got one of those e-book things – a Kindle. Just ploughs her way through books, she does. You should see the bill from Amazon on the card at the end of the month.'

'Oh, I prefer proper books,' Amy said. 'Books with a soul, printed on paper that's grown under the sun, you know?'

'Yeah, me too,' Ant said, and I felt suddenly embarrassed on his behalf. He was making a bit of a fool of himself and, obtusely, I felt a tiny wave of love for him, for the little lost child within, still trying to impress at forty-eight. So many of Ant's difficult aspects seemed to be caused by his insecurities, it seemed a shame, really.

To save him from digging himself an even deeper ditch, I yawned loudly and rolled on to my side, and they both turned their heads to look back at me.

'She's awake!' Amy said.

'Hey, sleepy head,' Ant said. 'You were snoring.'

'Hey,' I replied, stretching. 'Mmm, was I?'

'Like a trooper,' Ant said.

'And what are you two nattering about?' I asked.

'Oh, we were discussing the pros and cons of paper,' Amy said seamlessly.

'Paper?' I asked, pretending I hadn't heard their conversation.

'Yeah, books,' Ant said. 'Proper books versus your Kindle thing.'

'I like my books to have a soul,' Amy explained. 'I want my words to be printed on paper that's been grown, that's part of nature, you know?'

'Right,' I said. 'Well, I prefer to let the trees carry on growing in the sunshine. I prefer nature to owning physical books, I suppose. That's *my* problem.' To make my point I glanced at the tree above me, the one providing shade, and then added, 'But each to his own.'

I saw Amy wince as if she'd been slapped, and Ant raised an eyebrow in surprise that I'd momentarily outmanoeuvred Amy. Of course, he didn't know I'd had time to think about what they were saying.

I glanced beyond them at the shimmering pool, where the kids were still playing in the shallows. 'It's going to be hard to drag them away,' I said. 'They're loving it here.'

'We can always come back tomorrow,' Amy suggested. 'It's not like it's far.'

'God, it's still so *hot*, though!' I said, glancing at my watch – it was six – and then standing and heading towards the pool ladder. 'Did you put more cream on them?' I asked Ant.

'I did,' Amy said. 'Don't worry.'

'Careful of the fish,' Ant said, as I began to descend the ladder. 'Make sure they don't give you any diseases.'

'Um, I think we've done that joke already, Ant,' I said, casting the words over my shoulder as I launched myself into the velvety water.

On the way back, we stopped off once again in Orce. The temperature had dropped to a 'mere' thirty-seven degrees, and the few shops that existed were open. People were milling around carrying their shopping, or stopping to chat on the street corners.

We sat in the main square for another round of drinks and I noticed how many older people were present. Some were in groups, playing dominoes or cards, while others were with their families – three or even four generations at the same table.

How nice it must be to get old under the Spanish sun, I thought. How much easier on the soul it must be than sitting in a granny flat beneath a rainy British sky.

It wasn't until the waitress came to take our order that I noticed that Ant had the hump with me. He ordered a beer – luckily, the waitress spoke some English – and then Amy asked me and the kids what we wanted so that she could translate.

'I'm not sure,' I replied. 'What are you having?'

'God, I hate it when you do that,' Ant said.

'I'm sorry? When I do what?' I asked.

'Why do you need to know what Amy's having? Why can't you just make a decision on your own?' He was getting his own back because of the joke, I realised. Of course he was.

'I'm having a glass of white wine, I think,' Amy said, ignoring him.

'That sounds nice,' I said, glancing nervously at Ant. 'I'll have the same.'

'Of course you will,' Ant commented, sighing and then looking away across the square.

'Ant,' I pleaded. 'Please!'

'Please what?' he asked, glancing back at me briefly before turning his attention to his phone.

'That was gorgeous today,' Amy said, once the waitress had taken everyone's orders and moved to the next table.

'It was,' Ant said. 'Thanks, Amy. Thanks for *all* of this.'

'One of my better ideas,' Amy said.

'Definitely,' Ant said, nodding enthusiastically, and it was as much as I could do not to roll my eyes.

'What?' Ant asked me in a challenging tone of voice, which was strange because I felt certain I hadn't pulled a face or even sighed. Had I *actually* rolled my eyes without realising it, or had he picked up on my subconscious desire to do so?

'I didn't say a word!' I protested. 'Jesus, Ant, just relax, will you?'

He turned his attention to his phone again and I glanced around the square, hoping to spot the pig. I felt we needed a distraction here, but the pig was nowhere to be seen. 'There's a pizza place over there,' I said instead, pointing. 'Maybe we can get takeaway for dinner this evening.'

Ben and Lucy shrieked, 'Yes!' immediately, and after a few seconds, Sarah – who'd been lost to the world, fiddling with the buckle on her sandals – joined in too.

'I'm not sure,' Amy said. 'I'm pretty sure they don't have vegan options in Spain.'

'Oh, Mum!' Ben pleaded. 'Go on.'

'*We* can still have pizza, can't we, Dad?' Lucy asked.

'Of course we can,' Ant said. 'We're not vegans, are we?'

By accident, I'd thrown a spanner, albeit a tiny one, into the works of Ant and Amy's mutual appreciation society.

'*Mum!*' Ben said, raising his eyebrows almost to the top of his head. 'Come on! *They're* having pizza.'

'OK, OK!' Amy conceded. 'Just this once. Hopefully, they're not quite so mean to their cows in Spain, anyway.'

It was dark by the time we got back, and the sky was a deep purple all along the horizon.

Joe seemed a bit glum, or thoughtful, or just quiet – I couldn't really decide which – and Ant continued to be sullen and childish and rude. But the kids filled in all the gaps, telling Joe excitedly about the pig and the fish, and thankfully no one mentioned my fear of either.

I put the three kids to bed just before ten, but fell asleep on Sarah's bed while reading them a story. When I woke back up, the room was pitch black.

I fumbled around and understood that someone had thrown a cover over me, and the book was no longer in my grasp.

Whoever it was had forgotten to plug in the nightlight, but there was a sliver of light leaking beneath the door, so I stood and fumbled my way across the room towards that.

The rest of the house was silent, but when I checked our room, the bed was empty.

I pulled a cardigan around me and stepped out into the courtyard, but that too was empty and, with the exception of the cicadas, totally silent.

It was cool enough that I shivered as I walked to the track, from where I could look out over the plain. There was what looked like a full moon hanging in the sky, and some bats were circling around the single street lamp. I checked that the car was still parked behind the wall – it was – and then, with a shrug, I returned to the house, where I brushed my teeth and undressed for bed.

At some point during the night, Ant returned, sliding in beneath the covers beside me.

'Where were you?' I asked sleepily.

'We went for a walk,' he said, as he snuggled against my back. 'It's such a lovely night. The moon's amazing.'

'Yes,' I replied. 'I saw that.'

I noticed that he was no longer sulking. If anything, he sounded a bit wired, as if he'd perhaps drunk too much coffee. I wondered briefly if he was going to try to have sex, but sleep was already enveloping me, and I suppose he can't have, because the next thing I knew it was morning.

Those bedrooms were so dark and silent, it was impossible to know what time it was, and so easy to doze all morning, but I finally dragged myself from the bed to find everyone outside eating breakfast.

'What time is it?' I asked. The sun wasn't as high in the sky as I'd expected.

'About nine,' Joe said.

'Thirteen minutes past nine, to be precise,' Amy said, after checking her phone.

'You're up early,' I commented, addressing Ant. It was unusual for him to miss the chance of a lie-in.

'Not really,' Amy replied. She'd clearly thought I was talking to her. 'Anyway, I was just telling everyone, I met our neighbours earlier on.'

'We have neighbours?' I said, pouring some apple juice into a cup, because there were no spare glasses on the table.

'We do! Two guys. Hot, too.'

'Hey, hey!' Joe said. 'Calm down. Hubby's here.'

'I suspect they might be gay, though,' Amy added.

'Oh, well, that's OK then,' Joe said, smiling.

'Really?' Ant said. 'Gays? All the way out here?' And I wondered exactly what he meant by that.

'Just a feeling . . .' Amy said. 'I can't be sure, but, you know . . . They had matching shorts. Really nice shorts, too, so . . .'

I sipped my juice and watched Lucy buttering her toast. She was a bit manic about toast-buttering, and didn't like any corner to be spared.

'They're in the house down the end,' Amy continued. 'The one with the olive trees. They just arrived this morning. They're French, but they speak good English. And they want us to go to their place for a drink.'

'Oh?' Ant said, wrinkling his nose. 'Really? When?'

Amy shrugged. 'Sometime,' she said. 'Whenever. But in the meantime, they said there's a lake less than an hour away. And it sounds beautiful.'

By ten, we were all in the car, on our way to Lake Negratin. We'd only been in the house for two days, but it felt good to be on the road again, to watch the parched Spanish countryside rolling past the windows. With seven of us in the car, sitting in three rows, it felt like a proper holiday excursion.

Joe was driving, with Amy in the passenger seat. Ant was with Ben and Lucy in the middle row, while Sarah and I were in the back. At one point Joe switched on the radio, and the station it was tuned to was playing that awful 'Macarena' song. But when Joe changed stations, Lucy complained and begged him to put it back on. By the second chorus, Ben and Lucy were singing along, clapping and smiling, and by the third Sarah, Amy and Joe had joined in too.

Ant glanced back at me and pulled a face, but though I agree it's a pretty awful song, I refused to join him in his cynicism. The joy on the kids' faces was real, and it felt like a perfect holiday moment. I admired Joe and Amy's ability to be silly for the children's sake too, so, instead, I raised my hands and clapped along, grinning at Anthony manically.

It took about an hour to reach the lake, and when we got there the vista was quite breathtaking – a vast expanse of turquoise water surrounded by an arid landscape of cratered weather-worn sandstone.

We clambered down to the water's edge and immediately all stripped to our swimming costumes. There were a few other couples dotted across the vast expanse of rocky beach, but it was far less crowded than I would have expected. When I commented on this, Joe said, 'Probably too hot for the locals. Mad dogs and Englishmen, and all that.'

'Do you think there's fish?' Sarah asked nervously, as we waded into the shallows holding hands. Ben and Lucy were already in deeper, splashing around.

'You see?' Ant said, laughing. 'That's your fault, that is. That's how they end up paranoid.'

'No, I don't think there's any fish here,' I told Sarah to reassure her, because, in a way, Ant was right. 'And if there are, I'm sure they're tiny, friendly ones.'

'There's monsters, apparently,' Ben said. 'Like the Loch Ness monster. It'll probably eat us all alive.'

Sarah looked up at me with a worried expression on her face, but a simple wink and a shake of the head was enough to reassure her that he was joking.

The water was clear but surprisingly chilly, so we soon returned to the beach, whereupon Ben and Lucy ran off into the distance to 'find sticks'.

'Don't go too far!' I shouted out, but they ignored me completely, and quite soon had all but vanished from view.

I made to stand in order to follow them, but Amy jumped up. 'Don't worry,' she said. 'I'll go. I fancy a wander, anyway.'

Saying, 'I'll come too,' Ant then stood as well.

'Really?' Amy asked, glancing from Ant to me, worried, I think, that I might disapprove.

'He can *never* sit still on a beach,' I told her.

'Oh, right,' Amy said. 'Well, me neither.'

Joe started to read on his Kindle but paused when Sarah began piling up stones. He jumped up, collected some nice flat ones for her to play with, and then lay back down beside me. 'It's like being on the moon,' he said, looking out over the lake. 'Amazing landscape.'

'It is,' I agreed. 'It really could be a different planet.'

'Mummy!' Sarah said.

I leaned over and counted out loud the number of stones she'd piled up. 'Seven!' I said. 'I bet you can get at least one more on there before it falls over. Try that one.' I pointed to the flattest of her reserve stones.

'No water on the moon, though,' Joe said.

'Isn't there?' I asked. 'I thought they'd found some. I'm sure I read that somewhere.'

'I think they found ice,' Joe said. 'So that is water, I guess.'

I scanned the sky in case it was possible to see the moon, because sometimes you can; sometimes you can see it in broad daylight. 'It was a full moon last night, wasn't it?' I asked, that thought leading to this one.

'I think so,' Joe said.

'How far did you walk?' I asked.

'I'm sorry?' he asked distractedly. He was fiddling with his Kindle again.

'I thought you went for a walk last night – after I fell asleep.'

'Oh, no,' Joe said. 'Not me.'

'Oh,' I said. 'Ant did, and I just assumed . . .'

'Nope,' Joe said again. 'No, I threw a blanket over you and crashed pretty early. They were out there chatting and drinking till late, I think.'

'Fair enough,' I said. 'It must have just been Ant and Amy, then.'

'They were probably vampiring,' Joe said.

'Vampiring?'

He nodded. 'Yeah, you know . . .' He mimed having two pointy teeth and tipped his head sideways to bite an imaginary neck.

'Oh, *vampiring*!' I said. 'Yes, I expect that's exactly what they were up to. Those cute neighbours had better watch out.'

'We'll have to move soon,' Joe said, glancing around. 'There's no shade.'

I scanned the horizon, but the only tree that provided any real protection had been taken by a family with a dog. 'True,' I said. 'But I don't mind. These stones aren't that comfortable anyway. Plus, Ant can never sit still for long, so . . .'

'Yes, I noticed that,' Joe said. 'But is he having a good holiday all the same? Despite the place being so isolated, and no Internet and everything?'

'Yes,' I said. 'Yes, I think so.'

'And you?' Joe asked, with a strange intensity.

I nodded again. 'Yes,' I said. 'Yes, this is heaven. I've never been anywhere much, so this is all really exciting for me.'

'Good,' Joe said. 'I'm glad.'

'And you don't mind having us?' I asked. 'We're not getting on your nerves?'

'Nope,' Joe said. Then, with a cheeky grin, he added, 'Not yet, anyway. But I'll keep you posted.'

At the top of the hill, not far from where we'd left the car, was a hotel-restaurant called La Alcanacia, so when the heat got too much for us that's where we went, lured by the shady tables beneath their vines.

Initially, we were intending to have drinks, but when we got a glimpse of the next table's delicious-looking food order, this quickly morphed into lunch.

Amy ordered a selection of tapas dishes, which we all eagerly sampled. There was tortilla (such a big hit with the kids that we had to reorder it twice) and olives, cheese, calamari, aubergine caviar, mushroom croquettes and – a special request by Joe – octopus salad.

'It's naughty, I know,' he said. 'But I have this terrible weak spot for octopus.'

'Why's it naughty?' I asked, thinking he must be meaning that it was fattening or something.

'Well, it's quite a long way from being vegan,' Joe said, shooting an embarrassed glance at Amy.

'It's about as far from vegan as you can go,' Amy said. 'Octopi are some of the most intelligent animals on the planet.'

'Oh, of course!' I laughed. I'd actually forgotten that they were supposed to be vegan.

'Hardly any of this is vegan,' Amy said. 'Maybe the aubergines, but otherwise . . . I wanted you to taste the local food, though. It would be a shame to come to Spain and not eat Spanish once.'

'It would,' I agreed, biting into one of the mushroom croquettes. 'These have got to be vegan, haven't they?'

'They almost certainly have egg in them,' Amy said. 'Possibly a bit of cheese too.'

'You know, it's octopuses,' Joe told Amy. 'Everyone thinks it's octopi, but it isn't.'

'Is that true?' she said.

'It is.' Then, addressing me, he said, 'You should try some.'

I wrinkled my nose and refused politely. 'I've never much liked those sucker bits,' I admitted.

'I'll have a taste,' Ant said, shocking me by forking a lump of octopus.

'These onion rings are nice,' Lucy told me, and we all laughed.

'They're calamari rings,' Ant told her, 'not onion.'

'What's *carr-alari*?' she asked.

'It's . . . never mind . . .' Ant said. 'Just enjoy it. It's delicious. It's all delicious, Amy, so well done. Good ordering there.'

Now, this annoyed me. Ant had always been one of the fussiest eaters I'd ever known, but here he was, digging in to aubergine caviar and spicy octopus salad . . . Even now, when I try to think about it, I can't quite explain why the sudden change annoyed me so much, but it did. It really did.

'Maybe we can eat Spanish from time to time when we get home, then!' I said, being sassy. 'It would certainly make a change from steak and chips.'

'Ooh, you can't eat *steak*,' Ben said. 'Steak's *disgusting*.'

'Why's it disgusting?' Lucy asked. 'I like steak.'

'Steak's just dead cow,' Ben told her, pulling a face. 'It's like killing a little cow and then just eating the poor thing.'

Sarah, who was on my lap, turned to look at Ben in horror. 'That's not true, is it, Mummy?' she asked.

'Yes, it sort of is, I'm afraid,' I told her. 'Well, it's a bit of cow, anyway.'

'Eww,' she said, pulling a face.

We were home in time for the siesta, and we all slept quite soundly until four.

Lucy climbed on the bed and woke me up. 'Can we go in the pool?' she asked.

'Mmm? Of course,' I said, dragging myself from a rather pleasant dream.

'The door's locked,' she said. 'I can't find the key.'

Ant rolled on to his back. 'Joe took it,' he explained through a yawn. 'To stop them swimming without supervision.'

'You have to get up, Mummy,' Lucy said. 'It's too hot and I need to get in the pool right now!'

It *was* hotter than normal that afternoon – even the lounge felt stuffy. So everyone stayed indoors, merely nipping out to the pool from time to time in order to cool off: Amy, Ant and the kids playing snap, and Joe in his room, reading.

In spite of the heat, I wanted to be outside. I didn't feel as if I was on holiday indoors and I wanted to experience Spain, even if experiencing Spain meant feeling overly sweaty. So I lounged in the hammock that Ant had found in the outhouse and suspended beneath the olive tree, while Sarah ran back and forth all afternoon, alternating between disrupting the indoor card game and interrupting my reading instead.

Just as the sun began to set, a welcome breeze arrived, and the temperature dropped quite rapidly so that by the time it was dark we'd all had to put on sweaters.

We ate bits and bobs from the fridge and then sat drinking and chatting as insects buzzed around the light that hung over the table.

Our new neighbours walked past at one point. They stopped and waved at us across the courtyard but declined Amy's invitation to join us for a drink. 'We're going for a walk,' the tall dark one said, and he indeed sounded quite French. In fact, Amy had been right about everything. They were French, good-looking, and if I was pushed to guess, I'd have to agree they were almost certainly a couple.

Once the kids had fallen asleep, Joe got out a proper pack of cards, and after a brief refresher course given by Amy, we started to play gin rummy. Other than snap with the kids, I hadn't played cards for at least twenty years. It was far more fun than I remembered, though that may have had something to do with all the alcohol we were drinking. The problem was that everyone kept topping up my glass with white wine, and because it was warm and I was thirsty, and because there was no water on the table, I just kept drinking the damn stuff.

About eleven, I got up to go to the toilet, and realised that I could barely stand up. Though we were in the middle of a game, I decided to lie down for a bit, and from the moment my head hit the pillow I knew that I wasn't going to make it back. Though I could hear Joe and Ant calling drunkenly for me to return to the game, I simply couldn't move.

It was my body that woke me up initially. The wine had gone through me, and my bladder felt like it was about to explode. I was feeling thirsty, too, and had the beginnings of a headache.

The bedroom light was on and I was still fully clothed, which surprised me. But then I remembered the card game, the wine, my intention to rest and return to the game . . .

I listened for a moment, but the house was silent, so I stood, a little unstable still, and made my way through to the lounge, which was in darkness. Only the kitchen was lit, by the yellow bulb of the cooker hood.

I continued to the bathroom and then returned to the kitchen, where I gulped down three glasses of water, remembering belatedly that we weren't supposed to drink the tap water here. I peeped into the kids' room and saw that the nightlight was on and that all three beds were occupied, before returning to our bedroom, where I started to undress. But I got no further than removing my shoes and my jumper before Ant's absence began to bother me, so I returned to the kitchen, then stepped outside.

The moon seemed even bigger, so perhaps it hadn't been a full moon last night after all. The light outside was as bright as dawn, only cooler, giving a spooky bluish tinge to everything. Unusually, the table was still covered with the debris of the evening – numerous empty bottles, sparkling in the moonlight.

The air was quite cool now, almost cold in fact, but the paving slabs underfoot were still hot from all the sunshine they'd received during the day, so as I crossed the courtyard towards the track, I had the strange sensation of feeling chilly, with the exception of my feet. When I reached the track, I looked out at the plain. It appeared particularly strange in the moonlight, a bit like a dream sequence from a film.

Other than the non-stop cicadas and a dog barking wildly in the distance, all was quiet. I briefly considered walking to the end house to see if maybe everyone had gone to the neighbours' place for drinks. But as I didn't have my shoes on, and as it seemed unlikely, and mainly because I was simply feeling too sleepy, I sighed and turned back towards the house.

As I passed the pool, something caught my eye: a glint of orange light reflected at the spot where a jet of water created ripples, and that was strange because there were no sources of warm-coloured light outside at all. Everything looked chilly and blue.

I scanned the surroundings, trying to spot where the light was coming from, but I couldn't find it, and when I looked back at the pool the shimmer had vanished, so I started again towards the house, only for a noise to make me stop once more. I held my breath until I had located the origin. The sound was coming from the outhouse.

I approached the window and saw a tiny glint of light leaking out at the bottom of the blind – the same orange light I'd seen reflected in the pool. I was about to crouch down to peer in when I recognised the sound I was hearing, that regular thud, thud, thud . . .

Blushing, I returned to the house. *You idiot*, I thought. *Just because you don't have sex any more, you assume that nobody else does. But of course they do!*

Thinking that it was considerate of them at least to do it in the outhouse, I returned to the bedroom, but Ant's absence was still bothering me. My brain was working pretty slowly that evening, I'll admit, and I can only assume it was to do with all the alcohol I still had sloshing around my veins.

I went back to the kitchen and looked out at the unlit courtyard and tried to think. There was no way that Ant would have gone to the neighbours' place alone, of that much I was sure. I returned to the children's room and inspected the beds more closely, but other than the fact that Ben and Lucy had swapped places, all was as it should be.

I checked the two unused bedrooms, but they were both untouched and musty smelling. Finally, I hesitated outside Joe and Amy's room. I listened for a moment and heard the sound of snoring coming from within. It sounded a lot like Ant, so – smiling and thinking, *Lord, how drunk was he?* – I pushed the door open. The hinges creaked loudly but the occupant of the bed continued to snore.

I opened the door further until a little light from the kitchen fell across the bed, and then crept across the room to look. As I leaned over, I could smell wine and unfamiliar sweat – it was Joe lying there, smiling as he snored. I wondered what he was dreaming about.

I closed the creaky door once again and pinched the bridge of my nose as I tried to think. Perhaps the two neighbours were 'at it' in our shed? But I couldn't come up with any reason why it would be them. Perhaps it was some local kids, or maybe the owners?

I returned to the front door, let myself out and crossed the warm paving stones to the outhouse. The rhythmic thudding from within was still ongoing, and wasn't that a grunt I'd heard? I brushed the doorknob with my fingers, but then imagined bursting in on the boys from down the road or perhaps some strangers, so I walked to the window instead. Feeling like a peeping Tom, I crouched down to press my nose against the pane, but the chink of visibility was tiny and all I could see was a vague blur of flesh.

I straightened and returned to the door, where, after taking a deep breath, I reached for the handle. My heart was beating so fast and so hard that I could hear the blood surging through my veins as I pushed at the door. It was locked. Strangely, I hadn't imagined that possibility. I rattled the door handle, but the only thing that happened was that the noises stopped. A voice inside whispered something.

I needed to know, I realised. Whatever this was, I had to know. It was too late to walk away. So I rattled the handle again, and then with a croaky voice that surprised me, I called out, 'Who's in there, please?'

There was no answer, so I called out again, more assertively, 'Hello, who's in there, please?' The silence was absolute. Even the distant dog had stopped barking.

After thirty seconds or so, I heard a rustling noise, and then a voice said, 'Just open it.' There was a pause and the sound of the bolt sliding back before the door opened to reveal Ant, fully clothed, looking flushed. Behind him, Amy was sitting in a dusty old armchair, but even by the orange light of the old torch they were using I could see that her cheeks were red.

'*Heather*,' Ant said. Amazingly, he managed to sound irritated and perhaps even bored by the interruption.

'Christ,' I said, breathing the word more than saying it. 'It *is* you.' A batch of bile rose, and I had to swallow it back down to avoid being sick.

'It's, um, not what you think,' Ant said, sounding vague. He didn't seem to be able to find the energy to try to sound convincing. 'We were just . . .' He glanced over his shoulder at Amy and shrugged at her.

I laughed then, a sour, crazy, witchy sort of laugh that just erupted from nowhere. 'You were just what?' I asked, swiping at a couple of tears that were sliding down my cheeks. I couldn't tell you if they were tears of laughter, or tears of anger. Perhaps it's possible that they were both.

'We were just—' Anthony said again, but he still hadn't come up with a suitable alibi.

'Oh, for fuck's sake,' Amy said. 'She can see perfectly well what we were doing. She's not *stupid*, Ant.' And then she leaped from the seat, pushed past me quite brutally, and vanished into the house.

I covered my mouth with one hand and stared at Ant. He glanced over my shoulder towards the house and said, 'Fuck!', before grabbing my arm and pulling me inside. He closed the door behind me and turned so that he was blocking my exit.

'What the hell . . .' I murmured. But there were too many thoughts – too many phrases – swirling around my head, competing for airtime, and I couldn't seem to pin a specific one down.

'Listen,' Ant said, sounding serious, sounding businesslike. 'This doesn't have to be . . .'

I blinked at him numbly. I suspect I was in shock.

'What I mean is, you don't have to make this into a huge drama,' he said.

I snorted. 'No?' Once again, I felt stuck halfway between sour laughter and tears.

'No one has to know,' he said.

I frowned at him uncomprehendingly. His words made no sense to me.

'*Joe* doesn't need to know,' he said.

'Joe?' I repeated. 'But I know, Ant. *I* know!'

'Yeah, but you don't care, do you?' he said. 'You know I shag around. You've never cared.'

'I . . . You . . .' I tapped my forehead with two fingers as I tried to isolate a reasonable thought – any reasonable thought. I swallowed with difficulty. 'Are you insane?' I asked finally. 'Actually, are you still drunk? Is that it?'

'You know I am,' Ant said. 'That's why this doesn't mean—'

He paused. There was a noise outside, and it took us both a second or so to identify it as the sound of suitcase wheels on concrete. Ant's eyes opened wide, and then, telling me to wait, he spun, opened the door, and stepped outside.

'Wait?' I repeated, as I watched him leave.

I heard him ask, 'Where are you going?'

I stepped to the doorway and looked out. Amy was holding the handle of her suitcase with one hand and dangling the car key with the other. She had her jacket draped over her arm. She was efficient – I'll give her that.

'I'm getting away from this shitshow,' she said.

'What do you mean, you're getting away?' Ant asked.

'I can't stay here,' Amy said. 'Not now. I just can't.'

'She won't tell him,' Ant said, glancing back at me. 'We were just talking, and she won't tell him. I promise.'

Amy glanced at me questioningly. 'You're going to tell him,' she said, nodding sadly, and once again I laughed, quite madly. 'Aren't you?' she asked.

'You two . . .' I said. 'Jesus!' I was so angry that my anger had morphed into an almost amused state of disbelief.

Ant looked back at me. 'Just shut the fuck up, Heather,' he said. My mouth fell open in shock.

'No, I'm out of here,' Amy said, moving across the courtyard once again.

'Wait,' Ant told her, attempting to grab the handle of her suitcase. 'Wait for me,' he said. 'Just one minute.'

'I can't,' Amy replied.

'Ten seconds then,' he said, turning and jogging towards the house.

Amy paused and glared at me. 'What?!' she asked me aggressively.

I stared at her in mute astonishment for a few seconds, until Ant reappeared from the house. He had his jacket on and was patting his chest pocket, checking for the presence of his wallet, just as he did every morning when he left for work. 'Ant,' I said, as he passed by. 'You can't just leave!'

But Amy was on the move again, trundling her suitcase towards the track and then vanishing behind the wall to the left.

'We can talk about this tomorrow, OK?' Ant said, reaching out to touch my arm as he passed by, only to miss because I leaped instinctively away from his grasp. He froze for a second then, looking deep into my eyes, and I think he had an instant of regret or hesitation – a moment of lucidity, perhaps. But then the car beeped as Amy unlocked it and, patting his pocket once again, he lurched on after her, glancing back just once as he disappeared from view.

Feeling paralysed, I listened to the doors slamming and then the engine start. Finally, the tyres crunched off along the gravel of the track.

Once all was calm again, I sank to the ground so that I was sitting with my back against the warm wall of the outbuilding.

It took a while, perhaps twenty minutes, before I managed to feel anything, and the first sensation I had was feeling cold. I shivered a few times and gasped a juddering breath, and it was then that I started to cry.

The tears lasted for about half an hour, and by the time they ended I was numb and exhausted. I tried to think about what had just happened, but found myself unable to come up with any clear thoughts, unable to feel any emotion beyond anger.

It seemed like a nightmare, really, that was the thing. It seemed like this series of events was too awful to possibly be true.

Eventually, I stood and, driven by the cold, I went indoors. I sat, zombie-like, on the edge of my bed for a while, and then pulled my jumper back on and moved to the kitchen. After some hesitation, I gently pushed open the door to Joe's bedroom and stepped inside, but he was snoring loudly and it seemed unreasonable to disturb him to give him such news. And how could I tell him, anyway? I couldn't even imagine what words I might use.

I returned to the kitchen, where I quietly made a cup of tea, and then I sat on the doorstep, and as I stared out at the moonlit courtyard, nursing the warm mug, I imagined Ant reappearing around the corner and saying he was sorry and wondered what I'd say if he did.

I changed my mind twice about waking Joe, returning to his bedroom, even going as far as leaning over him and speaking his name on the final attempt. But he didn't stir, and I couldn't bring myself to shake him, so in the end I went back to my own room, where I lay staring at the ceiling, wishing for sleep that I knew would never come.

In the morning, the kids were up first: Ben just after eight, followed in short succession by both girls. None of them enquired about Amy or Ant during breakfast, so I decided to wait and speak to Joe first before saying anything. Without knowing what time

Ant and Amy would return, or what they might say when they did, it seemed impossible to think what to say anyway. What lie *would* best fit this situation?

Joe didn't surface until almost ten, and when he did he simply vanished into the bathroom.

Leaving the kids playing with a bucket in the jacuzzi, I moved to the kitchen in order to ambush him on his return, but when he finally did reappear, he had nothing more than a towel wrapped around his waist, and this, for some reason, embarrassed me. Inexplicably, a towel seemed far more intimate than the trunks he'd been wearing around the pool, so I turned and looked out of the window.

'Everything OK there, Heather?' he asked as he passed by.

'I need to talk to you,' I said without turning. 'But maybe you could get some clothes on, first?'

'Sure,' Joe said. 'I had that planned, as it happens, so . . .'

He returned wearing a pair of turquoise shorts and a faded Grateful Dead T-shirt. 'So, what's up?' he asked.

I was sitting at the kitchen table, biting my nails. I still didn't know how I was going to do this.

'God, you look even worse than I feel,' Joe said, leaning on the table and peering into my eyes. 'Bad night?'

'Thanks,' I told him sarcastically. 'It's always good to know when you look like shit. Can you, um, sit down, do you think?'

Joe made an amused but confused face, and after glancing at the kids, pulled out the chair and sat. 'Something's wrong, isn't it?' he said.

'I'm not sure really how to tell you this, Joe,' I said.

'Where's Amy?' he asked, suddenly noting her absence. 'And Ant? Is he still sleeping?'

I shook my head and swallowed with difficulty. I pinched the bridge of my nose. 'I caugh—' I started, but I couldn't get where I needed to go that way. It was too brutal. I coughed and then took a couple of gasps of air before starting again. 'They're not here,' I finally managed, my voice weak and brittle. 'That's the thing.'

'They're not?' Joe asked, looking pointlessly around the room as if perhaps they might be hiding in the corner. 'Um, where are they then?'

I lowered my face into my hands. 'This is so *hard*,' I murmured. 'And it's so unfair that I have to be the one to tell you.'

'Tell me what?' Joe asked, fidgeting in his seat and straightening. 'Are they OK? They haven't had an accident or something, have they?'

I shook my head and peeped out at him over my fingertips. 'I . . .' I said.

Ben appeared in the doorway then, dripping water all over the floor tiles. 'Dad!' he said. 'Can you come out? We want to go in the big pool.'

'Just go outside,' Joe said quietly. 'I'll be with you in a minute.'

'But if you just came and sat outside, we could—'

'Go!' Joe said again. 'I'll be with you in a minute.'

Ben tutted and said, '*Dad*,' in a whiny voice, but he turned and vanished from view.

'So what's happened?' Joe said. 'Tell me. Because you're scaring me now.'

'I caught them,' I said, momentarily standing and leaning over the table so that I could see out through the kitchen window. All three children were safely out of earshot, still playing in the jacuzzi. 'I caught them together in the outhouse,' I added, as I sat back down again.

'You caught them,' Joe repeated, frowning. 'Oh . . . You don't mean . . . you mean you *caught* them?'

I nodded sharply, dislodging a tear, which rolled down my cheek.

'Not . . . you know . . .' Joe said.

I nodded again.

'*Shagging?*' Joe said, more mouthing the word than speaking it. 'Or just . . .'

I bit my lip and managed another nod. 'I'm sorry,' I whispered.

'Christ!' Joe said, covering his mouth with one hand. 'And . . . ?' He shrugged and shook his head. 'What happened?'

'Um, there was a bit of an argument.'

'Yeah, I bet,' Joe said. 'And then?'

'And then they left.'

'They *left?*' Joe repeated.

'I'm sorry, Joe,' I said. 'But yes, they left. Together.'

Incongruously, Joe started to smile then. 'Oh, I get it,' he said. 'This is a wind-up, isn't it?' That was when the floodgates opened once again, and as quietly as I could manage, I began to sob.

Six

Joe

Until Heather started crying, I didn't really believe what she was telling me. After all, the scenario she was describing was so unlikely that a joke or a tasteless wind-up seemed as logical an explanation as any.

But when she began to cry, I believed her – or, at least, I understood that *she* believed what she was saying to be true. A different explanation came to mind then: that she was perhaps quite simply unhinged. We didn't really know either of them, I reminded myself. Strangers can do and say the strangest things.

'Heather,' I said, glancing out of the window at the kids. 'I'm sorry, but . . . well, they'll hear you.'

'Oh . . .' she breathed, screwing up her features to stifle her sobs and then standing. 'I'll, um . . . Of course. I'll be back. Just give me a minute.' And then she stumbled off into the bedroom, closing the door behind her.

I moved to the kitchen step and managed to fake a smile when Ben looked over my way. 'Can we go in the big pool, Dad?' he asked.

'In a bit,' I said. 'Stay there for now. I'll be back in a second to watch you.'

I ducked indoors for my phone, and when I returned I sat at the garden table, where I had a better view of the pool. 'OK,' I told them. 'Go for it. But only in the shallow end, mind.'

I watched them climb over, one by one, into the pool. Both Ben and Lucy could swim reasonably well, but little Sarah could barely keep her chin above the waterline. 'Are you OK, little one?' I asked her.

'Yes, I'm swimming!' she said, moving her arms in a breaststroke action as she walked on tiptoes across the width of the pool.

'You are!' I said, turning my attention to my phone, which had finally started up. But of course it was useless here. I'd hoped that its ability to find a signal would be proportional to my need for it to do so, but no matter what fiddling around I did with the settings, choosing the network manually, or switching on or off 4G, it stubbornly refused to work.

'Um, kids!' I called out, standing. 'You'll have to go back in the little pool for a bit. I need to go down the track to use my phone.'

Lucy and Ben protested, but then Heather's voice rang out from the doorway. 'I'll swim with them,' she said. 'Go, phone.'

I sat in the same spot as before, and it struck me as ironic to be feeling shaky and anxious where only yesterday I'd been centred and calm. I checked my voicemail first, but there were no messages, so, after a forced breath, I called Amy. Her phone rang for a while before switching to voicemail, which at least meant that wherever she was, she had coverage.

'Amy,' I said. 'It's me. Things are . . . a bit crazy here. I don't know what's going on. Just call me, OK?'

I stared at the phone for a few seconds, chewing my lip, then called back again. The fact that this time the call went straight to voicemail reassured me. It meant that she was almost certainly listening to my voicemail.

A text message appeared. 'I'll call you later,' it said. 'I can't talk right now.'

'And why might that be?' I asked.

'I need to think,' she replied.

'Think!' I said out loud, outraged. '*Think?* Think about what?'

'Call me now,' I texted. Then, 'Call me right NOW, please.'

'I'm sorry,' she replied.

I tried her number again then, but she didn't pick up, and I just about managed to refrain from leaving an incendiary voicemail.

'Heather says . . .' I started to type. But I couldn't think how to complete the sentence. 'Heather's saying some pretty . . .' I started over, only to delete what I'd written all over again. 'I just need to know if what Heather's saying is true,' I finally typed. My finger hesitated over the button for a moment before, with a shrug, I clicked *send.*

I waited for her reply. I decided I would make myself wait. I would not send anything else until she'd replied. But then I saw my fingers type, 'Did you do what she says you did? Are you with that wanker now?'

I chewed my lip and wiggled the phone so that it tapped between the fingers of my left hand while I waited for her reply. It vibrated to announce the arrival of another message.

'I'm sorry,' it read, again.

'Fuck it!' I mumbled, tapping the phone gently against my forehead. A wave of anger rolled through me and I whacked my head harder with the phone, until it hurt. *Why?* I thought. *The guy's such a loser anyway.* It was the first time I'd let any negative thoughts about Anthony crystallise, but now it had happened, I knew it to be true. The more I knew him, the less I liked him. I'd simply been trying not to acknowledge it.

I looked at the screen again, at Amy's minimalist messages. *I'm sorry*, I thought, repeating the words in my mind. Because what sort of reply was that? What did it even mean? *I'm sorry, but it's true?* Or *Yes, it's true, but I'm sorry it happened?*

'I'm sorry, I'm sorry, I'm so fucking sorry,' I muttered. Then, 'Yeah, I'm sorry too, baby.'

I clicked the screen in order to reply, but what did I want to say? If she was sorry, properly sorry, then there was hope, wasn't there? They'd been drunk. And now she'd woken with a hangover next to that dickhead, and she was sorry. I was sorry. We were all sorry. Couples get over that kind of stuff, don't they?

My phone buzzed again. 'I'm really sorry, Joe,' the new text message read.

I started to type my reply. 'Yes, I got that,' I wrote. 'Now come . . .' But before I could finish, the phone vibrated again with a new message: 'I won't be home tonight, so don't wait.' For a moment, I couldn't believe what I was reading.

My anger rising, I called her back immediately, but once again she didn't pick up. 'Amy,' I told her voicemail. 'You're losing it. I'm here with Ben, our son. Remember him? And we're waiting. So just . . . get it together. And get your arse back here.'

I sat for a few minutes waiting for a reply and then, with an angry gasp, I stood and slipped the phone back into my pocket.

I paced up and down the track a few times, repeatedly checking my phone each time I reached the olive trees until, finally accepting that she wasn't going to pick up or reply, I returned to the courtyard.

Heather, who had Sarah in her arms, climbed out of the pool immediately. She plopped Sarah down in the jacuzzi and circled the pool to join me.

'So?' she asked.

I shrugged and looked away.

'Did you speak to her? You did, didn't you?'

I shook my head ever so slightly and offered her the phone.

'Um, the screen,' she said, refusing to take it. 'It's locked. And my hands are wet.'

I unlocked my phone and swiped to the list of messages, before – telling her it was waterproof – I handed it back.

Ben appeared beside us, grasping the edge of the pool and looking up. 'Is something wrong?' he asked.

Yes, your mother's gone bat-shit crazy, I thought. 'No, champ,' I said. 'Everything's fine.'

I watched him swim to the far side.

'But this is . . .' Heather said quietly. '*Why* isn't she coming back?'

'I don't know.'

'Did you speak to her at all?'

'No, I told you,' I said, struggling to keep the anger from my voice. 'This is all I got.'

'God,' Heather said, handing back the phone and turning towards the house. 'I . . . Maybe I should phone Ant.'

I glanced at the screen again, as if to check that last message was still the same.

'Yeah, maybe you should call him,' I said, then, despite my best intentions, the next sentence slipped out. 'Does this a lot, does he?'

'I'm sorry?' Heather asked, pausing and frowning back at me.

'Does he make a habit of this? I mean, you don't seem overly shocked,' I said.

'Christ,' she said, and then she shook her head and continued on her way.

She returned a minute later, wearing a T-shirt and carrying her phone.

'Well? Does he?' I asked, as she approached. I was vaguely aware that my anger was misdirected, but I didn't seem to be able to help it.

'Does he *what*, Joe?' she asked, pausing in front of me.

181

'Does he make a habit of seducing other men's wives?' I said. 'Because if he does, you maybe could have warned us before we invited you on our holiday.'

She glanced at the kids and then leaned in towards my ear. 'Fuck you, Joe,' she said quietly.

I sat with the kids until, about fifteen minutes later, she returned. 'I'm sorry,' I said, as she passed by. 'That was out of order.'

'It was,' she said. 'But it's fine. Come inside for a minute. We need to talk.'

I glanced at the pool and she said, 'We can watch them from indoors. Come.'

I followed her into the house, where I found her holding on to the edge of the sink and looking out of the window. 'Ant said the same thing,' she said, without turning. 'That they're not coming back today.'

'*They're* not?' I said, wondering if this existence of a 'they' meant something.

'He says tomorrow,' she continued, in a weird, lifeless voice. 'He says he'll come and we can talk tomorrow. But he doesn't want to see you.'

I snorted bitterly.

'I think he's ashamed,' Heather continued. 'Or afraid. Maybe both.'

'Right,' I said, 'because I'm so scary and everything.'

'He says he thinks he should just fly home.'

'Home? Really?'

Heather half turned in my direction before she spoke. 'He thinks the atmosphere's gonna be awful if he stays.'

'No shit!' I said. 'Jesus, he's one clever dude, isn't he? He could maybe have thought of that before he . . .' But I couldn't bring myself to say it. Instead, I just shook my head.

'Anyway, we need to work out what to tell the kids,' Heather said. 'For today, I mean.'

I shrugged. My brain was refusing to even engage with the subject of what lies we needed to tell our children.

'I said I'd walk up to the main road to talk to him. Tomorrow . . . when he comes . . .'

'So I don't hit him?'

'Maybe,' she said. 'Do you think you might?'

I laughed sourly. 'If he was smaller,' I said, 'then perhaps.'

'Oh, Ant's no fighter,' Heather said. It almost sounded like she was egging me on. 'I thought we could tell the kids they've gone to Marbella.'

'Marbella? Why Marbella?'

'Well, they know it's a long drive. I thought we could say there's a problem with the tickets and they've had to go back to Marbella to sort them out.'

'D'you mean Malaga? Where we flew in to?'

'Sorry, yes, Malaga.'

'Sure,' I said. 'Whatever.'

'I don't know what to think about this, really, Joe,' she said, her voice beginning to wobble.

'I know,' I said quietly. I stepped forward and patted her hesitantly on the shoulder. 'Me neither. A great fucking holiday this is turning out to be.'

'It's awful,' Heather said. 'I'm sorry.'

'Yeah, everyone's sorry,' I said, a shudder of bitterness leaking out. 'It's just that sorry doesn't fix anything, does it?'

'But to answer your question,' Heather said.

'My question?'

'About Ant.'

'Oh, you don't have to. I was just—'

'The answer is maybe. Probably. Look, I'm not that sure, to be honest. I've had my suspicions, but it's never been quite this . . . It's never been as obvious as this, let's say.'

'Right,' I said.

'And you two?' Heather asked. 'I mean . . . you're . . .'

I frowned at her until she glanced my way. She licked her lips and swallowed. 'I'm assuming you're, you know . . . monogamous?'

'In theory?' I said. 'Yeah, we are. We're like totally, utterly monogamous, so make of that what you will.'

'Right,' she said. 'That's what I thought.'

'You know last night,' I said. 'I'm sorry, but I have to ask.'

'Go ahead.'

'Were they actually, you know . . . doing it? Or were they just messing around?'

'I'm not a hundred per cent sure,' Heather said. 'But I suspect . . . you know . . . that they were.'

We spent the morning alternating between misery time alone and lifeguard duty.

When it was Heather's turn to watch the kids, I'd walk to the tree and check for messages, but there never were any, and on the two occasions I tried to phone, the call went straight to voicemail. Amy had almost certainly switched her phone off, and as she'd left her charger in the kitchen, it was possible she'd had to do so in order to save the battery.

Other than to negotiate who was watching the kids and a couple of muttered phrases about lunch, neither Heather nor I spoke that afternoon.

Sarah asked at one point where her daddy was, and so Heather had the honour of telling the Malaga lie to all three. When she'd finished explaining about the tickets, Ben glanced at me for reassurance, so I think he suspected that something was up. But he quickly seemed to forget about his mum, concentrating instead on the utter misery of not having a car to take us to the fish-pool.

In the evening, while we were eating, one of the French neighbours dropped by to invite us again for drinks, but a simple 'Maybe another day' seemed enough to send him packing. I don't think either of us looked like we'd be much fun.

When I returned from reading the bedtime story, Heather had uncorked a bottle and served two massive glasses of wine.

'I think I need to get quite drunk,' she said flatly, handing me a glass and raising her own. 'Otherwise I'm not going to sleep a wink.'

I raised my glass and tapped it against hers. 'To the best holiday ever,' I said sourly.

'Indeed,' she replied, before taking a gulp. 'Do you think they're together?'

'Um?' I said as I tasted the wine. It was a slightly rough local Spanish one, but it was chilled and fruity – it would do fine.

'Ant and Amy,' she said. 'Do you think they're, you know, *together*?'

'Almost certainly,' I said. Then, 'Oh, you mean . . .'

Heather shrugged and squinted as if she was trying quite hard not to cry.

'No,' I said. 'No, I don't.'

'Really?' she said. 'That's not why they've decided to stay wherever they are? It's not so that they can—'

'No,' I said definitively. My brain didn't even want to explore the possibility. 'No, I think they're just dying of embarrassment, and they're too scared to face the music.'

'Yes,' Heather said, with an intensity that made me think she was trying to convince herself. 'Yes, that's exactly what I think, too. Good.'

Heather left the house at a quarter to ten the next morning, trundling Ant's suitcase behind her across the courtyard.

'You're taking him his suitcase?' I asked, catching up with her just beyond the pool.

'Yes,' she said. 'He asked for it. He's been in the same clothes for two days.'

'I'd make him come and get them himself,' I said, 'under the circumstances.'

Heather nodded. 'You're right,' she said. 'I should.'

'Don't you think we need to have some kind of discussion – I mean, before Ant goes home? It kind of involves all of us.'

'Yes,' Heather said. 'We probably should.' And then she continued towards the track, dragging the case behind her.

'Where's Mummy going?' Lucy asked, once she'd vanished from view.

'She's, um, taking some stuff up to the road,' I said.

'What stuff?'

'Just rubbish. For the dustbins.'

'In Daddy's suitcase?'

I smiled weakly. 'Sharp little cookie, aren't you?' I said. 'So . . . the rubbish was too heavy for her to carry, and she put it in a suitcase because it has wheels.'

'Why didn't you take it for her if it's heavy?'

'Because I have to stay here to look after you.'

Lucy furrowed her brow as she considered all of this, and then smiled. 'OK,' she said brightly.

It was ten minutes before Amy popped up, lingering at the entrance to the courtyard. She stood there, beckoning discreetly for me to join her.

'I can't,' I called out. 'I have to watch these three.'

'Mum!' Ben shouted, leaping from the jacuzzi and running across to hug Amy's legs. 'Can we go to the big pool now?' he asked. 'The one with the fish? And the pig. Can we go and see the pig again?'

Amy crouched down and hugged him. 'You're all wet!' she said. 'And now, so am I.'

'But can we?' Ben asked. 'We're fed up with this pool.'

'Maybe later,' she said, standing. 'First I need to talk to Dad, OK?'

She walked around the far side of the pool so that she was opposite me, but at a safe distance. 'So, how do we do this?' she asked.

'We can talk inside,' I told her.

'Go and play,' Amy said, giving Ben, who was still lingering, a gentle push.

'But we're *bored* with the little pool,' Ben protested.

'Just do it, champ,' I told him in my special no-nonsense voice. 'Your mum and I need to talk.'

'It's so *boring*,' he said, his parting shot, as I followed Amy into the house to find her already seated at the kitchen table.

'Has he been OK?' she asked, glancing up at me before returning her attention to her phone.

'Sure,' I said gruffly. 'He's fine.' We weren't here to talk about Ben, after all.

Amy swiped the screen of her iPhone back and forth.

'That doesn't pick up here,' I said.

'I know,' she said. 'It's just nerves.'

'Then put it away, please,' I told her. Her phone fiddling had always annoyed me, but at that moment it struck me as unbearable.

She slipped the phone into her bag. 'So,' she said, fiddling with her wedding ring instead. 'Are you going to sit?'

'I'm fine here,' I replied. I was resting against the cool porcelain of the kitchen sink.

'I'm not sure how to do this,' she said.

I coughed. I cleared my throat. 'Well, I guess that depends what you want to do.'

'I'm sorry,' she said. 'I am. I want you to know that. What happened . . . Well, it shouldn't have.'

'What *did* happen, Amy?'

'Oh, I think that you know what happened,' she said.

I laughed bitterly. 'So now you can't even say it?'

'Do I need to?'

I shrugged. 'I thought you placed so much onus on being honest. On naming things properly.'

'I slept with Ant,' she said. 'And I shouldn't have.'

'You *slept* with him?' I repeated.

Amy frowned.

'I thought you fucked him, that's all,' I said. 'I thought you went into that outhouse over there and you fucked him. When did the sleeping thing happen?'

'Joe,' she said. 'Please don't . . .'

'Don't?' I repeated. 'You're telling *me* don't?'

'There's no need to—'

'To be honest about what actually happened?' I said, completing her unfinished sentence.

'No,' she said. 'Not like that.'

'It might be good, though,' I said. 'To hear you say it, don't you think? It might be, what's the word? *Cathartic*.'

'OK!' Amy said angrily. 'I shouldn't have fucked Ant in the outhouse. Happy now?'

'Oh yeah,' I said. 'Yeah, I'm really thrilled.'

'So I'm sorry,' she said.

'Jesus, Ame,' I muttered. 'If you say that one more time then I swear . . .'

'But things haven't been right between us for years,' she continued. 'You need to admit that, too.'

I froze. I held my breath. She had stunned me into silence.

'They haven't, have they?' she insisted.

'I . . .' I croaked. But I couldn't think how to respond. I'd thought we were here to deal with a drunken incident in the outhouse. But this was morphing into something quite different.

'Joe?' Amy said.

'Is this . . . I don't know, Amy . . .' I finally spluttered. I looked out at the children for a moment and the vision of them playing, unaware, calmed me enough that I managed one coherent thought. 'Is that supposed to excuse it?' I asked, turning back. 'Is that it?'

'Excuse it?' Amy said.

'Yeah, is this, *things haven't been right with us so I perfectly justifiably fucked our friend's husband?*'

'No,' Amy said. 'No, that's not what I'm saying at all. And he's not . . .'

'Not what?'

'Nothing,' Amy said. 'Nothing. Forget it.'

We remained in silence for a moment and when she eventually looked up at me, she simply shrugged.

'I don't know what you want from me here, Amy,' I said.

'Nor do I,' she replied. 'That's the problem.'

'It seems to me that there are only two options really,' I said, trying to simplify things for her. She seemed so lost, the poor thing,

189

I was actually feeling sorry for her. 'Either you're sorry and you regret it. And in that case we try to—'

'I need more time, Joe,' she said, interrupting me. 'I'm sorry, but I do. I need more time.'

'OK,' I said slowly. 'I guess that's the third option I hadn't thought of. More time for what, though?'

'Look, I'm going to take Ant to the airport. He's changed his flight and he's flying home tonight.'

'What?'

'I'm taking Ant—'

'I *heard* you, Amy,' I said. 'But that doesn't make sense. His wife's here. His *kids* are here.'

'I know,' Amy said. 'But I can't decide what he does. That's between them, don't you think?'

'Um, I don't know,' I said, struggling to work through the ramifications. 'I am slightly involved in this whole equation too, you know. We are. I mean, we're going to be stuck here with Heather and the kids. And that's not exactly ideal, seeing as we have our own shit to work through.'

'I'll be back tomorrow,' Amy said, as if she hadn't been listening to me at all. 'Once I've sorted myself out.'

'Oh! You're going too, are you?' I asked, my anger rising. 'That's nice.'

'I told you. I have to take him to the airport. And I'll be back by tomorrow.'

'No,' I said.

'No?'

'No, I don't approve of this . . . this . . . plan. I'm not staying here with *her* while you two fuck off on a little trip together.'

'We're not going on a little trip,' Amy said. 'I'm taking him to the airport.'

'Well, I don't agree,' I said.

'I don't think you have much of a choice, actually.'

'Maybe we should all go home, then,' I said. 'Maybe we should pack our things, and all go home right now.'

'Well, you could,' Amy said. 'If that's what you want. But I'm going to stay on for a few days. I don't feel ready to go back home yet.'

'Christ, Amy,' I said. I couldn't believe that she'd torpedoed our holiday so thoroughly. 'Do you ever think of anyone but yourself?'

'But you'd have to leave right now,' she continued. 'If you did want to leave. Because Ant's flight is at four and I need to get moving.'

'I don't give a shit about Ant's flight.'

'Joe,' Amy said. 'Listen to me.'

'Oh, I'm listening,' I said. 'But I'm not *liking* what I'm hearing so much, you know?'

'Let me take him to the airport. That at least gets Ant out of the equation.'

'His wife, Amy,' I said. 'You're forgetting his wife and his daughters.'

'He's leaving her,' Amy said quietly. 'She doesn't know that yet, but he's leaving her. And they're not actually married anyway.'

'Oh Jesus . . .' I said. 'You two really are best mates, aren't you?'

'So let me get rid of Ant, have a day to clear my head, and then you and me can take it from there, OK?'

I frowned at her. A thought was manifesting with sudden clarity. 'You've discussed all this, haven't you?'

'Discussed what?'

'The state of Ant's marriage.'

'Of course,' Amy said. 'Otherwise how would I know?'

'Have you discussed ours, as well?'

'No,' she said. I didn't believe her.

'Are you leaving me, too? Is that it?'

'No,' she said again, and I managed for the first time in a minute or so to take a gulp of air. But then she continued, '*Maybe*. Look, I don't know, Joe. That's why I need some time alone.'

'Wow,' I said, whispering through my hand. 'Just wow.' Suddenly it was all too much for me. My rage was submerging every other emotion and I needed this exchange to be over, otherwise I was scared I might lose control completely. 'You know what, Amy?' I said. 'You're right.'

'Right about what?'

'You should go. You should definitely go.'

'Oh, OK,' she said. She looked disappointed, and I wondered what she'd hoped I would say.

'Because if you don't leave, right now, I . . . I'm not sure what might happen.'

'Listen, Joe,' she said.

'No,' I said. 'I've listened to enough of this shit.'

'No, seriously, listen,' she started.

'No, seriously. Stop talking!' I told her. 'And go.'

'OK, but . . .'

'GO!' I shouted. 'Just . . . GO, Amy! GO!'

It was after eleven by the time Heather returned. She was soaked in sweat and seemed changed, somehow. Her manner was surprisingly brusque.

'Well, that's done,' she said, on entering the courtyard. 'Where are the kids?'

I twisted in the hammock to face her. 'They're inside,' I said. 'Playing. I made them a tent out of sheets.'

'Right,' she said. 'Good.'

'Are you OK?' I asked.

She shrugged. 'Define OK,' she said, then started towards the house, so I rolled inelegantly from the hammock and called her back. 'You said it's done,' I said. 'What is? What's done?'

'Oh, I just mean he's gone,' she said. 'At least I don't have to look at him now.'

'And you?' I asked. 'What are you going to do?'

'I'm going to get a drink,' she said. 'I've been walking, and sweating, and I'm parched.'

I sat at the tiled garden table and listened to her talking playfully with the kids indoors, and then after a minute or two of silence, she returned with a jug and two glasses.

'Sorry I was so long,' she said. 'Coming back, I mean. But I had to go for a walk and collect my thoughts before I could face the girls.'

'Sure,' I said. 'It's fine.'

'I suppose you'll be wanting us to leave,' she said as she poured the lemonade. 'I've been thinking about it all, and that seems the most logical thing. We should never have come here anyway.'

I'd been thinking about it as well, and it seemed to me that though I had no great desire to hang out with Heather, and though I did feel a quite compelling desire to be alone with my own thoughts, her immediate departure wasn't perhaps ideal. Right now, for instance, neither Ben nor the girls had noticed anything was awry, and that was entirely due to the fact that they had each other to play with. If I suddenly found myself alone here with Ben, then not only would he be understandably upset about the loss of his play friends, but he'd immediately know that something was wrong. What's more, he'd focus all of his attention on me, and right now I desperately needed some downtime.

'Maybe once Amy comes back?' I said. 'If that works for you, maybe you could hang on until then.'

Heather nodded.

'Things might be a bit electric between you two, otherwise,' I said. 'I mean, that's why it's best you don't hang around too long once she's back.'

'Of course,' she replied, sipping her drink. 'Though if you could drive us to the airport, or wherever, when we get to that point, I'd be grateful. I'm not sure I want to spend three hours in the car with her.'

'Shit, the car,' I said. I'd momentarily forgotten about our lack of transport.

'I checked the fridge,' Heather said. 'We're OK for today, and maybe lunch tomorrow, if we're creative. But I think then we need to get to the shop, at the very least. Do you think there's maybe a taxi?'

'Around here?' I said, glancing around. 'I doubt it.'

'Those French lads have got a car. So maybe we could ask them.'

'Yeah,' I said. 'Yeah, that could work. Let's see what time Amy arrives tomorrow. See what she says . . . But yeah, if need be, we can get them to drive us, or I can rent something.'

Heather nodded. 'I'm not much help, I'm afraid. I can't even drive.'

'It's fine,' I said. 'Luckily, I can.'

She chewed her lip for a moment and then said, 'Look, you don't have to answer this. You really don't.'

'OK,' I said doubtfully.

'But, what did she say? What did Amy tell you? I mean, do you think you two are going to be OK?'

'I don't know,' I told her honestly. 'It's all a bit out of the blue. I wasn't even aware that we had a problem, so . . .'

'Right,' Heather said. 'OK.'

'And you?'

'What did Ant say?'

When I nodded, she surprised me with a little laugh. 'He said things haven't been right between us for ages.'

I nodded and sighed deeply. 'That's what Amy said. Her exact words, actually. It sounds like they've been comparing notes.'

'It does a bit,' Heather said. 'But it's true. Well, in our case it is, at any rate.'

'That things haven't been right?'

She nodded. 'They've not been right ever, really. Ant's, you know . . . a difficult character. And I'm a bit useless. That's sort of our deal, if you know what I mean? Those are our roles: me being useless, him being difficult. So it's been a strange set-up, really.'

'Oh,' I said. 'Gosh.'

'But you really had no idea?'

'No. Maybe I should have, but no.'

'You think you'll be OK, though, don't you? You think you can get through this.'

I shook my head and sighed. 'Shit, I don't know, Heather,' I said. 'Ask me tomorrow, OK?'

Seven

Heather

Because the majority of food items left in the cupboards were vegan, I struggled a bit to make lunch. Amy had brought tofu, egg replacer and 'seitan strips', whatever those might be, from England. There were cartons of hemp milk and packs of lentils and chickpeas. I thought Joe would be able to help, but it transpired he wasn't much of a cook. 'Amy makes a quiche with it, I think,' he said, when I asked him about the squidgy block of tofu. But he had absolutely no idea how she did this and in the absence of a recipe book and without Internet, I was pretty sure that was a mystery that would never be resolved – or not on my watch, anyway.

In the end, I made us a pasta salad and mixed in chunks of the harder tofu as a replacement for cheese. As everyone pushed these rubbery cubes to one side, that was clearly not one of my better ideas.

Joe was sullen during lunch, which was understandable but challenging, and though I did my best to put on a brave face for the kids, my turmoil must have been visible too, because afterwards Lucy and Sarah were unusually clingy, even insisting to the point of tears on sleeping in my bed at siesta time.

When I woke up just after four, it was a second or so before I could work out why I felt so strange – before I could remember what had actually happened.

I got up quietly and crept outside. Joe and Ben were still sleeping, so it was just me, the chirping cicadas and the gentle thrum of the pool pump.

I was glad. I needed this time to think. I needed time to try to feel something.

I sat beneath the olive tree and did my best to consciously reflect on it all, but it was like trying to grasp a handful of that toy slime we used to buy for the kids. The whole subject was an amorphous lump with no hard edges I could grasp it by.

I ran my conversation with Ant through my mind.

It had not been the angry screaming match I'd feared – in fact, it had been quite shockingly calm. Ant had made a series of statements and I'd listened almost entirely without intervening. He'd said that things had not been right for ages and that he'd been feeling, for a while, for years even, that something needed to change. He hadn't been happy and he didn't know why that was, but he felt that what had happened, no matter how unwelcome, had created an opportunity to rethink things.

I'd sat and listened and nodded, and during the silences, which were long, I'd simply waited. I hadn't said anything, partly because, as was typical, Ant hadn't asked me for my opinion anyway. But everything he'd said had struck me, for once, as true. It was rare that he spoke so honestly. Things *had* never been right between us. He *wasn't* really happy, anyone could see that. And things *would* have been horrifically awkward had he stayed on at the villa with Joe and Amy present.

The only question he'd asked was if I wanted to fly home with him that afternoon – *if* he could manage to change all our tickets – or if I wanted to stay on for a bit and make the most of the time alone 'to think about things'.

I'd said, 'Whatever you think is best,' and he'd replied, 'OK, then, we'll do that,' and I hadn't known which of the two options he meant until he was gone.

Right then, beneath the olive tree, despite the trauma of it all, and despite the difficulties of staying there with Joe, and even despite the fact that I was going to have to lie to the kids again, I found myself feeling relieved.

Travelling home with Ant right then would have been traumatic. But perhaps worst of all would have been finding ourselves back together in the middle of the life we'd built. The momentum of our lives, I was sure, would have taken over, carrying us beyond this crisis and on through middle age and retirement and ultimately to death. And neither of us would ever have had the courage to ever question anything again.

I was surprised to have had this thought – it wasn't, logically speaking, what I'd expected of myself. It reminded me a little of when I'd found out I was pregnant, how I'd been convinced that I would be horrified, then that I *should* feel horrified, only finally managing to accept that what I was really feeling was joy.

Of course, there was no joy to be found that day. But I *was* feeling a bit relieved – and what was that sensation deep down, that butterfly just behind my heart?

When life is awful, it's a terrible thing to live without hope. There's nothing worse than to believe that nothing will ever change – that every day will continue to be like every other.

And as scary as it might be to peer into the abyss of the unknown – and as a financially dependent mother with two children, it was truly terrifying – it's a very different kind of feeling to hopelessness, precisely because it *isn't* hopeless at all. It's fear, it's dread, it's terror, but sprinkled with the stardust of hope born of an infinite number of possible futures.

Half an hour later, Joe appeared in the doorway, blinking in the sunlight.

'You OK?' he asked.

I nodded vaguely.

'Drink?'

I raised my full glass by way of reply. I was so lost in my thoughts that speech seemed difficult.

A minute later, he returned with a can of Coke and sat opposite. 'So, how are you feeling?' he asked.

'Hot,' I said, to avoid the complexity of answering the question honestly.

'Huh,' Joe said. 'Me too. Ben's still fast asleep. I'm assuming your two are as well?'

I nodded. 'It took them ages to get off.'

'Ben too,' Joe said.

'They pick up on things.'

'They pick up on *everything*,' Joe said, sipping at his Coke. 'Have you thought what you're going to tell them? Because they're bound to ask what's going on.'

I shrugged and shook my head. 'Maybe the same as last time. Or something similar. Malaga. Tickets . . . something like that.'

'That will only work for so long. I mean, if Ant's gone home . . .'

'Maybe Daddy had to go home for work. They're used to him working all the time.'

'Will they mind about cutting the holiday short, do you think?' Joe asked. 'Will they give you hell?'

'I'm not sure,' I replied. 'I'm not sure they have that much understanding of how long we're supposed to be here, really. We had to cut our holiday short last year because of . . . stuff . . . the weather, mainly. And they didn't seem to mind much then.'

'Right,' Joe said. 'Good.'

'But I'm not sure I'm going to, actually.'

'You're not sure you're going to what?'

'Cut it short. I think I might just book us into a hotel if I can find one. I could do with the time alone. And I do love a bit of sunshine, so . . .'

'You're not, you know . . . having doubts, are you?' Joe asked.

'About my marriage?'

'Yeah.'

I laughed sourly. 'Honestly?' I said.

'Honestly.'

'I've been having doubts since the day we met.' I was shocked at the phrase I'd just uttered. I'd never let myself think it that clearly before, let alone express it out loud.

'Oh,' Joe said. 'Wow.'

I sighed. 'It is what it is,' I said. 'Actually, I hate it when people say that, don't you? It means nothing, does it?'

'Amy said you—' Joe started. But there was a sudden shriek of 'Dad!' from indoors. 'Sounds like someone's awake,' he said, standing.

We did our best to keep the kids entertained all afternoon and on into the evening, splashing around in the pool and involving them in the preparation of dinner – more pasta with some vegetables and a sauce made out of tasteless vegan 'cream'.

'It's a good job she's bringing the car back tomorrow,' Joe said, while we were stacking the dishwasher. 'I think they're going to get a bit stir-crazy otherwise.'

'Do you know what time she's arriving?' I asked. 'Because if you need us to leave right away, well, it might be complicated if she arrives late.'

'Don't worry,' Joe said. 'We'll just play it by ear. No one's kicking anyone out. And I can keep you two from each other's throats if necessary.'

'I really don't think it will come to that, Joe,' I said. 'Not from my side, anyway.'

'That was a joke, Heather,' Joe said. 'I was joking.'

'Oh,' I said. 'Good.'

After dinner we played snap with the kids, finally putting them to bed about ten thirty. These late siestas were playing havoc with their bedtime rhythms.

'I might go myself, I'm shattered,' Joe said, on returning from fetching me a fresh bottle of wine – I'd been getting through it at quite a rate.

'It's all the emotion,' I said, refilling my glass. I was feeling pretty tipsy, and it felt surprisingly good.

'Yeah, that's probably what it is,' Joe said. 'The emotion.'

'Is it tough?' I asked, emboldened by the wine. 'Are you having a hard time?'

Joe gripped the back of the chair and stared at me. 'Honestly?' he asked, mimicking my own reply at lunchtime.

'Honestly,' I said.

He glanced back at the house, visibly hesitating, and then pulled out his chair and sat back down. 'I had a weird moment the other day,' he said. 'You know, when you were all out at the pool?'

'A weird moment,' I repeated. 'Go on.'

'I had a flash of illumination.' He mimed a lightning bolt from on high with his hand.

'About your marriage?'

'Not really,' he said thoughtfully. 'Maybe a bit. It was more just a sensation, really. Like a feeling that everything needed to change.'

'Right,' I said.

'That sounds weird, I guess.'

'Not at all,' I reassured him. 'I think everyone feels like that all the time, don't they?'

'Do they?' Joe said. 'I wouldn't know.'

'I've been feeling like that since . . . well . . . for ever, really,' I told him honestly.

'For ever?'

'Pretty much.'

'Even before you got married?' Joe asked. Then, 'Oh, sorry, I, um, don't know if this is right, but Amy said you're . . . er . . .'

'No, we're not married,' I said, interrupting his stumbling. I wondered how Amy knew that. I could only assume Ant had told her.

'That surprised me,' Joe said. 'Was that, you know, a conscious decision or . . . ?'

So I told him how my mother's death had interrupted our marriage plans.

'I'm so sorry,' he said, once I'd finished.

'It's fine,' I told him. 'Well, it's not *fine*, obviously. I just mean that it was a while back, so . . .'

'So you've managed to get over it.'

'Yes, as much as you ever can with that sort of thing.'

'And you never wanted to get married since?'

'Not really,' I told him. 'The whole thing seemed sort of . . . I can't think of the word . . .'

'Tainted?' Joe asked.

'Yes, that's exactly it,' I said, surprised that he'd understood what I was trying to say so quickly. 'As if the two were somehow linked. And so it just never happened. Marriage had a bit of a bad smell about it after that.'

'I see,' Joe said. 'That's sad.'

'Is it?' I said. 'I suppose it must be.'

'Hmm,' Joe said, sipping at his drink. 'I wonder what she's going to say tomorrow.'

'Are you worried?' I asked. 'I mean, of course you're worried. But you're confident it will all work out, aren't you?'

'I don't know,' Joe said. 'I feel like . . . I guess . . . Look, I don't know. I think all I want is for her to be happy, if that makes any sense.'

'Gosh!' I said. 'That's a generous thing to say. Especially under the circumstances.'

'It's just that she's not, really,' Joe explained. 'And it's been quite hard work living with that – living with the fact that I'm never enough for her, that *nothing's* ever enough, you know?'

'Yes,' I told him. 'I know that feeling.'

'So I suppose I'd like her to be happy. One way or another. Either with me, or . . .' His voice broke a bit as he said that, and his eyes glistened in the moonlight. 'It's just Ben, isn't it? He's the one we need to worry about.'

'It sounds like you love them both a lot,' I said. 'Ben *and* Amy.'

'Oh, I do,' Joe said without hesitation. 'I love them both to bits. As far as Amy's concerned, I couldn't tell you why, but I do.'

'Well, that's got to help,' I reassured him. 'That's a good thing.'

'D'you think?' he said. 'We'll see.'

I sipped my wine and then turned to watch a bat that had caught my eye as it swooped at the insects gathered around the street lamp.

'And you?' Joe asked. 'Do you still love yours? And, um, don't feel you have to answer that one. I'm probably being insensitive.'

'It's fine,' I reassured him. 'I'm drunk. You can ask me anything.'

'So?' Joe asked. 'Do you?'

I shrugged sadly, exaggeratedly. 'The question isn't so much do I *still* love him,' I said. 'It's . . .'

'Whether you ever loved him at all,' Joe said, hesitantly finishing the phrase that I was unable to.

'That's the one,' I said, my voice wobbling as a tear welled up in the corner of my eye.

'I think I'm gonna leave you to your thoughts,' Joe said, looking embarrassed. He stood and leaned across the table to squeeze my shoulder gently.

'It's fine,' I told him. 'You've got your own stuff to deal with, haven't you?'

Once he'd gone, I downed the rest of the bottle of wine. It was only then that I let myself cry – at first a self-conscious whimper that seemed almost forced, but which soon morphed into an unstoppable flood of self-pitying tears.

Because I'd wasted my life, hadn't I? I could see that now. I'd spent my childhood and adolescence worrying about my father and as a result I'd found myself unable to have any kind of healthy relationship with a man. I'd accepted the first person to pursue me with any determination, and now here I was, as drunk as my father, miserable and alone.

The butterfly of excitement had vanished, the glimmer of alternative futures had faded, and now all I seemed to be left with was a series of bleak grey roads to choose from or, worse, to submit to, based on someone else's choices: a continuing life with Ant, who, in the light of his infidelity and with the help of lashings of rosé, I was momentarily able to admit I hated. Or a life alone as a single mother with no money, nowhere to live, no friends and no family . . .

I thought of Kerry then, and felt guilty. I was overdramatising, because the 'no family' bit simply wasn't true. *Kerry*. Suddenly, I desperately wanted to speak to my sister.

I wobblingly circled the swimming pool and did my best to enter the house silently for my phone. But I was drunk and it was dark, and someone had left a chair bang in the middle of the kitchen. I tumbled over it painfully and all but wrestled it to the floor.

Once upright again, I found my phone charging beside the sink and then weaved my way back across the courtyard and on down the track to the trees, where I sank to the ground, my back against a trunk. As I dialled Kerry's number, I tried to work out what time it was in Rome. There was a one-hour difference when I phoned her from England, and we had a one-hour difference with England from here too, but I couldn't for the life of me decide if that meant it was the same time in both places, or if it meant she was two hours in front, instead.

Whatever the time in Rome, she didn't pick up. I decided not to leave a message as to do so would achieve nothing other than worrying her.

I sat and stared out at the moonlit plain and the mountains and noticed again how beautiful it all was. A bird squawked somewhere in the distance, and there was an almost imperceptible thud of music coming from behind me.

I knew exactly what Kerry would say anyway, I realised. I could hear her voice so clearly it was as if she was right here beside me. How nice that would be, I thought, to have her here, looking at this view, her shoulder touching mine.

'Leave him,' she'd say. 'The guy's an arsehole.'

'But what will I do?' I'd ask. 'How will I live?'

'You can work,' she'd say. 'The girls go back to school in September, so you can work. You can go back to nursing again. You were happier back then anyway, weren't you?'

And it was true; my virtual sister was absolutely right. I had been happier back then.

I thought about my nights out with the girls in Canterbury and I remembered going to the pictures with Sheena. I thought of the friends I'd lost over the years, and I wondered why I'd let that happen, how it was possible I'd got to the stage where I didn't have a single person I could call.

The rhythm of the music changed and got a little louder and I realised it was coming from the house just behind me. It sounded like a very young person's kind of music – the rapid *thwak thwak thwak* of techno. I sniffed and wiped my eyes on my sleeve and then stood and, steadying myself by hanging on to the tree, I turned to look back at the house.

Like our own, it only had small windows, but beyond them I could see the tall guy's back silhouetted against the orange light of the interior as he bopped energetically from side to side.

I moved closer so that I could get a better view of their mini-party. The tall guy danced out of sight and the short one appeared instead, grooving in a more restrained manner, a can of beer in one hand and a cigarette in the other.

The tall guy shouted something and the man in the window laughed and then grinned as he span around on one foot, and that simple sight, of two friends dancing and laughing, struck me as so beautiful, and so simple, and so . . . what's the word? *quintessential*, perhaps . . . that I started to cry all over again. When was the last time I had danced? When was the last time I'd partied and been happy with friends? When was the last time I'd been truly happy at all?

In that moment this simple scene summed up, to my miserable drunken self, everything that was missing from my life.

In the morning, Sarah woke me up. It was too early and I had a hangover – in fact, I think I was probably still drunk. The ground seemed unsteady beneath my feet as I wobbled my way to the bathroom.

On returning, I snuggled with Sarah in my bed. I was hoping that she'd go back to sleep, but she was fidgety and chatty, and I knew from experience that it wasn't going to happen.

When I got back up for the second time, I found Joe in front of the stove, making coffee.

'Good morning,' I said.

'Is it?' he replied.

I pulled a face behind his back and took Sarah outside. Lucy and Ben were seated at the table eating bowls of cereal, so I served one for Sarah and returned indoors to speak to Joe.

'Thanks for fixing them up with breakfast,' I said. He grunted by way of reply, so I moved to his side and rested one hand on his back. 'Are you OK?' I asked.

'Not really,' he said, without looking up.

'That's what I thought.'

'I got a text,' he explained. 'She's not coming home today either. She now says she'll be in touch *tomorrow*.'

'Oh,' I said. 'Gosh.'

'I tried to phone her, but of course her phone's switched off.'

'I see,' I said. 'That must be upsetting.'

'Yeah, I'm a tiny bit pissed off,' Joe said. 'Did you get any news from Anthony?'

'I haven't looked. But I assume he's back home by now.'

'I'd be grateful if you could check,' Joe said.

I frowned at this for a moment, until I understood what he was implying. 'Oh,' I said. Then, 'Oh, I see. Yes, maybe I'll go and see if I have any messages.'

'Thanks,' Joe said. 'That would be good. Because my mind's going crazy here.'

I gulped down a few glasses of tap water. We were out of the bottled stuff, but it didn't seem to have done me any harm to drink it previously, so I assumed I'd probably survive.

Back beneath the group of trees, I sat on the ground and switched my phone on. I waited for a minute, but no messages appeared.

I thought about calling Ant, but I couldn't bring myself to do it. I started to send a text message asking if he'd got home all right, but, again, couldn't bring myself to give the impression I cared.

I tried to think of some neutral question I could ask about home. In the old days I might have reminded him to feed Dandy. I thought about asking what the weather was like, but that struck me as overly casual, considering the circumstances.

Finally, I had an idea. 'If you're home, can you look on Google for a taxi company in Orce?' I texted. 'Amy's not come back and we're stranded.'

I lowered my head to my hands as I waited for his reply. I was starting to feel quite awful.

A few minutes later my phone buzzed, but the message contained nothing more than a name and a number: Ramon Batista Alcazar: +34 67657 2042.

This was useful, but it wasn't going to help Joe.

'Is everything OK with the house?' I asked, hoping that this implied I cared about the house more than I did about my philandering absent partner.

'Yes, everything's fine,' he replied. Then, 'Talk soon.'

'Everything's fine!' I muttered, as I stood. The cheek of it!

'He's home,' I told Joe when I got back.

'Well, that's something at least,' he said. He was sitting in the shallow end of the pool, where the jet squirted out. If you sat in that exact spot it massaged your back rather nicely.

'I got a taxi number from him too,' I said. 'I thought that might come in useful.'

'Here?' Joe said, climbing from the pool. 'Can I have it?'

'In Orce,' I said. 'And yes, of course.'

He noted the number in his own phone, and then I returned to my bed to lie down.

At one, Lucy woke me to ask if I wanted lunch. She was excited because we were eating in the jacuzzi. I thought she'd probably got that wrong somehow, but when I got outside, I saw that Joe had set up a little plastic table in the middle and even positioned a parasol to provide shade. It was there, the water up to our waists, that we ate our hummus sandwiches.

Over lunch, he explained the plan: he was going to get the taxi to nearby Huéscar, where the taxi driver had said he could hire a car. On the way home he'd pick up supplies.

'We can probably get by until tomorrow, if you prefer to wait,' I told him.

'Actually, we can't,' he said. 'Why do you think we're eating chickpea sandwiches?'

Eight

Amy

I don't imagine for one instant that anyone wants to hear my point of view. I know how society judges women. It judges us all the time for everything, after all.

We're judged because our dresses are too long or too short, because our heels are too low or too high. We're labelled frigid, or weak, or sluts, whether we're following the 'rules' or not and whether the rules in question say we should be wearing a mini-skirt or a crinoline, or a burkini.

But the ones who cheat on their husbands? Well, everyone knows we're the worst of all.

Joe could sleep with another man's wife and his friends would say, 'Did you? You dirty so-and-so! Good on ya, mate.' But me? Well, you can answer that one for yourself. Because I'm pretty certain I know what you've decided.

But would it really be too much to ask that you take a second to know me first? The universe is big and messy – it's both beautiful and ugly. And part of its beauty is the very fact of our capacity to see that ugliness, and care.

So this is me. This is Amy. The temptress, the whore, the bitch. And these are the keystone events that made me.

I was born in Toronto, the daughter of a woman and a man who disliked each other pretty intensely. Why were they together in the first place? I guess we'll never know.

When I was twelve, my sister killed herself. She sat down in a bath full of warm, scented water and slit her wrists – she didn't make a sound. Downstairs, watching *Friends*, we were completely unaware. *Friends*! It sounds like the punchline to a joke. Only it isn't.

She didn't leave a suicide note, so officially no one knew why. Except we all knew. We all knew, without actually *knowing*, that it was my father's fault. And if there had been any proof, then we could have told the cops and prayed for him to go to prison for a very long time. Only we didn't have proof. My sister's death was the only hard fact, and without a suicide note it proved nothing at all. It didn't even really point a finger.

After the funeral, Mum told me she was going to leave him. We would move back to England together, she told me, whispering the words excitedly into my ear. I was so relieved that I wept. I didn't even want to be in a room with my father by then. I was terrified that, with my sister gone, I'd be next.

But instead of saving me, instead of protecting me, Mum slipped off the edge of reason. She'd been at the end of her tether for years, but when Jemma died Mum lost her grip entirely. And once she let go, she just fell and fell and fell.

Until she was well enough to return to England, I was left alone with him. And that process took almost two years.

To defend myself, I hid a kitchen knife under my pillow, and the only time he ever came into my room, about three months after Jem's death, I showed it to him. He never came near me again.

One evening, I got home from school to find him drunk and crying. The bastard was actually crying . . . I stood in the doorway staring at him coldly, and when he looked up and saw me, all he said was, 'I miss her.'

'I'll bet you do,' I said icily.

'It should have been you,' he said, through tears. 'It's not fair.'

'Fair . . .' I repeated. 'No, you're right, it isn't.'

'She was the clever one,' he told me. 'She was the pretty one, and she loved me. You don't love me. You don't even like me.'

'She didn't love you either,' I told him bitterly. 'She was your victim, Dad, that's all.'

'You think you know it all,' Dad said. 'But you don't understand anything.'

And in a way he was right about that. Because I did know it all. And I didn't understand any of it.

Does any of that excuse any of this? Clearly it doesn't, and that's not my purpose in telling you. But it maybe throws a little light of relativity, let's say, on the subject. Because some crimes are manifestly worse than others.

Anyway, I'm still that woman. I'm the woman who stole another's husband. And I don't suppose the fact that there are worse crimes, or the fact that I was unhappy, or even the fact that *she* was unhappy – I don't claim any of that changes anything.

But the idea had been to take Ant to the airport, spend an evening getting my head together, and then drive back to patch things up with my husband. I swear to you that was the plan.

What had happened had been a stupid drunken mistake, I told myself. It was something that should never have happened, and something that could never happen again.

The problem was that it hadn't been quite the spur-of-the-moment incident it appeared – more the culmination of months of longing.

I'd first met Anthony in February, at Red Nose Day at Ben's school. I remember the moment vividly, spotting him across the room, catching his eye; I remember the way he smiled at me.

He looked a bit like that Spanish footballer, Xabi Alonso, and I'd had a crush on Alonso for years. Both he and Ant were the kind of men I'd fantasised over ever since I was a teenager: smart, athletic, well-dressed men with a hint of meanness lurking behind the eyes.

I'd known it was dangerous in that very first instant, which was why I'd turned away and forced myself to tune into the conversation around me instead. It had been a sterile debate about whether we might be better raising money for the school rather than Comic Relief and it seemed pretty obvious to me that it was entirely possible to do both. I couldn't help but notice that those who systematically argued that money collected to help people 'over there' should be spent on people 'over here' instead were invariably the same people who gave absolutely nothing to either. It was always just an excuse to not help anyone at all.

The next time I spotted him, he was standing right next to Joe, and without even realising I was doing so, I compared them: Anthony's tall, muscular frame, his slick suit and crisp white shirt, against Joe's friendly stockiness, the rounded amiability of his face; his desert boots and faded jeans. I sighed, I think, at the realisation that I wished my husband looked more like Ant.

Now, I'm sure that everyone has these kinds of thoughts; at least, anyone who's been in a long-term relationship does. The main thing is simply not to act on them.

So I avoided being in the same space as Ant for the rest of the event, and did my best not to think of him again.

But that night, bang in the middle of having sex with my husband, the image of a man, half Ant, half Alonso, popped into my mind's eye. I tried, for a few thrusts, to push it away, but then I caved in. A friend of mine always said that 'it doesn't matter where you get your appetite, as long as you eat at home', and that had to be true, didn't it? Joe certainly looked pretty thrilled when I came.

Ant began dropping contracts and payments off at our house, rather than at Joe's workshop. It was more convenient than driving all the way out to Hoath, he claimed, and Joe would agree and hand him a beer from the refrigerator. I'd catch Ant's eye and see the desire lurking there, and then make an excuse and vanish.

Pretty soon he worked out the rhythm of Joe's schedule and took to dropping by when I was home alone. He always had an excuse – an envelope he'd leave on the countertop, or a question he hoped Joe could answer – but the real reason for his presence was pretty obvious. The tension in the air was unmissable and I'd be lying if I said that I didn't imagine kissing him. Sometimes I'd see Ant's car from an upstairs window and hide until he drove away. I'd mutter, 'God! Not him again!' and tell myself I was too busy for the interruption. But the truth, revealed by the flutter in my chest, was that I was merely avoiding temptation.

And yet until I saw Ant that day on the doorstep, I truly had no idea that he was Lucy's father or Heather's husband. Because why would he ever tell me *that*?

I'd mumbled something vague about needing to get going and bustled poor Ben down the drive. But from those few seconds of proximity on the doorstep, my heart was racing, which should give you some idea just how powerful the attraction felt.

I don't blame myself for any of this because the magic of attraction is precisely that – it's magical. We can't predict who will set our pulses racing and nor can we explain why it happens when it does. As to the archetypes of attraction – in my case: tall, muscular, suited, and yes, a bit mean-looking – they've been anchored in my subconscious for as long as I can remember. I expect a psychological archaeologist who went digging through my childhood could unearth the origins: the villain in a James Bond movie, perhaps, my father's attractive business colleague, or the uncle who sat me on his lap and bounced me up and down once too often. Everything has an origin, even if you can't work out what that is.

So no, I don't believe that any of that was my fault. My racing heart was simply not under my control.

Where my personal responsibility *did* come into play, because I do believe in free will – I'm not putting what happened down to destiny – was bringing them with us to Spain. I knew it was dangerous, I knew it was stupid, and, worst of all, I'm pretty sure I knew what would happen. But I did it anyway.

Part of me hoped that I'd hate him, I think. There was something unpolished about Ant, a scally lurking beneath the suit. He was what my mother would call a 'rough diamond' and I hoped that I'd simply get bored with his company. Perhaps I was just kidding myself, but I told myself that spending time with him was maybe the best antidote; that I'd be able to compare him to indisputably lovely Joe, who couldn't fail to come out on top.

But I'd underestimated the power of attraction even as I was succumbing to it. Ant set my pulse racing by simply walking past me, in a way that Joe never had. Being in the pool with him yet *not* touching him was so unbearable I took risks by brushing up against him. We both knew it was going to have to happen.

I convinced myself I was doing it in order to get him out of my system. The alcohol had worn down my defences – it had diluted my ability to say *no*. But as I followed him into the outhouse, I told myself I was doing it in order to save my marriage. I'd get this over and done with and forget it. Because how good could it possibly be?

The experience of having sex with Ant was ecstatic. He smelt amazing, his skin felt like velvet, and once he was inside me I came almost immediately. Joe was no lazy lover and he invariably managed to get me there in the end, but it had always been something of a marathon he was forced to run, long after he'd reached the end of his sprint. But with Ant . . . I don't know quite how to explain it, except to say that merely the concept of him had been enough to bring me to the brink.

The drive to the airport began in silence. I was feeling wretched about everything: about how upset Joe had been, about leaving Ben behind, about what I'd potentially done to our marriage and about crossing paths with poor Heather on my way back down to the house. But perhaps the hardest bit to own up to is that I was feeling distraught about Ant's imminent departure, too.

'I fucking hate this,' he said, about half an hour south of Granada. 'I hate all of this.'

I sighed and licked my lips. I tried to think of a reply.

'Are you happy with him?' Ant asked me a few minutes later. 'You aren't, are you? You can't be. Tell the truth.'

I drove on in silence and eventually he asked if I was giving him the 'cold shoulder'.

I smiled at him sadly. 'I'm just trying to think of an honest answer,' I told him. 'It's complicated.' The honest answer would have been, *I've never been happy with anything*, I guess, but how unattractive was that?

'I *thought* I was,' I finally told him.

'And now?' Ant asked.

'And now I'm not so sure.'

He turned to look out of the side window, and I forced myself to think of Joe and Ben, of the life we had built together. I forced myself to think of all the things Joe had done to try to make me happy.

'I've always believed that anything is possible,' Ant said. 'D'you know what I mean?'

'Go on,' I told him. 'I'm not sure I do.'

'I mean that if you want something bad enough, you can have it,' he said. 'You have to work hard for it and you have to believe in yourself, but basically, anything you want, you can have it.'

I nodded. I wondered if he'd read *The Secret*, as that was the book's basic premise: that the universe conspires to bring you what you want, as long as you believe that you deserve it. 'Yes, in a way, I believe that too,' I said.

'But here's the thing,' Ant said, resting his hand on my leg. 'I want *you*. I think we'd be amazing together. Sky's the limit.'

I laughed gently. 'Would we, though?' I asked. I could picture myself beside him with shocking ease. He was the kind of man I'd *always* pictured myself with, if truth be told.

'You know we would,' Ant said, and he pushed his hand down between my thighs.

I wanted him desperately, even then. We'd made love twice in the hotel in Orce, but still I wanted more. I stared out at the shimmering motorway and asked myself how it was possible to want sex with someone so badly.

'What about Heather?' I asked, hoping that saying her name would act like a spell to save me. 'What about the girls?'

'She doesn't want me,' Ant said. 'I think she hates me, if truth be told.'

'But she *needs* you,' I said. 'They all do.'

'I'm not so sure,' Ant said. 'And I'm not just saying that to . . . you know . . . convince you or whatever. Sometimes I think they'd all be happier without me.'

'I doubt that,' I said.

'I nearly left her once,' Ant said. 'I probably should have, really. I've regretted it ever since.'

'God, really?' I said. 'What happened?'

'It was right at the beginning. We'd been going out for a few months and I decided to call it a day,' he explained. 'But then she told me her mum had cancer. I couldn't tell her after that, could I? She'd just found out. She was all over the place. And then by the time that was over, she was pregnant . . . It was just one of those things.'

'God,' I said. 'That's terrible. Does she know? Did you ever tell her?'

'Of course not,' he said. 'I'm not a monster.'

'So you've been unhappy from the get-go,' I said, comparing his story with mine and Joe's. I'd never been particularly happy either, but I honestly wouldn't say that was Joe's fault. But what if it was? Not his fault, so much, but what if I'd just spent all these years with the wrong man?

Ant slid his hand a little deeper. 'I know I'd be happy with you,' he said.

'Happy,' I said, in a sarcastic tone of voice, even though I wasn't entirely sure why.

'Yes, happy,' Ant said. 'We get one life, you know, and then it's gone. And I'm halfway through mine. Don't you think we deserve to be happy?'

I nodded thoughtfully and sighed, because I did believe that. 'I have a husband,' I said, 'I have a son.'

'I know,' Ant said. 'But I think we need to find out what this thing is. We can try, can't we?'

'Try?' I repeated. 'Try what?'

'Try to see if this thing between us is real . . . I mean . . . if I can carry on feeling the way I feel right now, then it's worth it. If I can carry on feeling like this, then everything else is bullshit.'

I turned from the road and glanced at him. He was always so proud-looking, so upright, where Joe had always been such a sloucher.

'You're so beautiful,' he said. 'I just want to spend the rest of my life fucking you.'

Joe had told me that, back in the beginning. How beautiful I was. How much he wanted to make love to me. When had that stopped? I wondered. Five years ago? Ten?

'We could book a hotel in Malaga,' Ant said. 'And then I could fuck you to kingdom come.'

'I think I prefer to call it "making love",' I said, doing my best not to picture the scene, but failing. And was it even true that I preferred 'making love'? Wasn't Ant's touch of rough part of the attraction?

'Oh, I'll make love to you as well,' he said. 'But first I want to fuck you again. Come on. Spend the night with me in Malaga.'

'I don't think that would be reasonable,' I told him.

'Why not?' he said. 'Heather will think I'm back home. You can tell Joe you need a bit longer to sort out your thoughts or whatever.'

'But what then?' I asked. 'It's just putting off the inevitable, isn't it?'

Ant started rubbing his hand against my inner thigh. 'If we get sick of each other, then we go back to our boring little lives,' he said. 'And no one needs to know.'

'So there's no point,' I said. 'Not really.'

'But what if we don't, Amy? What if this is real?'

I shrugged. 'I don't know, Ant,' I said.

'Then maybe you don't feel the way I do,' he said, pulling his hand back.

The absence of his touch felt like grief. I wanted it back. I *needed* it back there, right now. I needed all of him.

'I don't know about you,' he said, 'but living the rest of my life feeling like this . . . well, that's not something I can just give up on.'

Until the very last moment, I maintained the fiction that I could resist him, that I'd simply go back to my life. But then, less than a mile from the airport, he pointed at a sign. 'There's a hotel there,' he said. 'Please, Amy?'

'What about your flight, though?' I asked, glancing at him quickly while trying to read all the signs.

'I don't give a shit about my flight,' he said.

I pulled into a bus siding so suddenly that a truck almost rear-ended me. 'I don't know,' I said, but my heart was racing again, and I'd admitted my hesitation, so in a way the decision had been made. It's not for no reason that people say *he who hesitates is lost.*

'What don't you know?' Ant asked. 'Talk to me.'

'I have a husband, Ant!' I said again. 'I have a son!'

'And they'll still exist,' he said. 'Neither of them are gonna vanish. But if you'd rather be with me, then what kind of life is that? What if you regret this for ever? That's no good to anyone, is it? That won't make anyone happy.'

'I don't know,' I said, glancing over my shoulder in case an airport bus should arrive.

'OK, listen: I'm not getting on that flight,' Ant said. 'You can drop me there.' He pointed at the entrance to the Holiday Inn car park. 'Then you can come inside, and we can talk this through without getting a Spanish bus up the arse. And if you decide to, you can still drive back tonight.'

'I told him tomorrow anyway,' I said. 'I already told Joe that I'd stay over somewhere to get my head straight.'

'Well, then!' Ant said. 'Come inside and get your head straight.'

We didn't talk so much, in the end. We drank the contents of the mini-bar and ordered a tapas platter from room service. And then Ant did exactly what he'd promised to do, and this time it was even better because afterwards we really did make love. By the time it was over, I was lost to him.

I woke the next morning to find him sleeping beside me. He had an angelic expression on his face that I'd never seen before, and I realised that it was a glint in his eyes that made him look hard. It was an exterior he projected rather than his innate nature, and sleeping, he was stunningly beautiful.

I propped myself up on a pillow so that I could look outside, just as the morning sun began to creep around the edge of the window. When I turned to study Ant's features more closely, a gentle strip of orange sunlight had fallen across his face, and I took this as a sign from the universe. I knew in that instant that I wasn't going back. I just had to work out how to do it causing the least harm to all concerned.

By the time Ant opened his eyes, my decision had been made, reflected on, and psychologically notarised. To his surprise, I climbed on top of him and smothered him with kisses.

'Hey, hey,' he said. 'What's going on with you?'

'Nothing,' I told him, straddling him and pulling him inside me. 'Nothing's going on with me except this.' I reached out and pinched his nipples, wondering if he'd enjoy it or, like Joe, complain like hell.

'Oh God, I love you,' he said, blindsiding me. 'I'm totally fucking in love with you, Amy.'

'I know,' I said. 'Me too.'

We stayed in that generic hotel room for three nights, only dragging ourselves out and into Malaga once for a total of maybe three hours.

It's not that there was anything wrong with Malaga – in fact, it was far prettier than I had expected. But everything we wanted was in that room; everything we wanted was in that *bed*. So we drank and ate snacks and made love, and when that was over we showered and started all over again.

On the morning of the final day, I borrowed Ant's laptop so that I could write Joe a proper thought-out email.

I'd toyed with the idea of driving back up there so that I could say what was needed to his face, but it was better this way, I decided.

Writing has always struck me as the purest expression of thought. You have the time to weigh up every word and you can rewrite bits and move them around. You can look out for things that could get misinterpreted and change them to make sure you're being clear. You don't get interrupted, and most importantly, you don't get angry and say things you don't mean.

Of course, you don't have to face the other person's emotional response to whatever it is that you're saying either, and that perhaps makes it all a bit cowardly. But by the time I'd written, edited and re-edited my mammoth email, I was satisfied that this was the least harmful solution.

'Are you sure you don't want to call Heather before I send this?' I asked. Ant had read my email and approved. He shook his head dismissively.

'You understand that Joe's going to tell her we're together, right?' I pointed out. 'Don't you think she at least deserves to hear it from you?'

'She won't care,' Ant said. 'It's not the same as you and Joe. I told you. She hates my guts. She'll be glad.'

I was pretty sure that this was untrue, but ultimately, how Ant dealt with Heather was for him to decide. It really was none of my business.

'You're sure?' I said. 'I'm about to click.'

Ant leaned over so that he could see the screen, and then he reached out and clicked *send*. 'Now put that bloody computer away and come back to bed,' he said.

Nine

Heather

Joe's taxi, driven by a Spaniard with a comic-book moustache, arrived just after four. He didn't work between twelve and four but there was no point leaving earlier anyway as the car-hire place opened even later.

Because Ben had pleaded to go with Joe, and because he'd ultimately caved in to Ben's demands, Lucy was spitting blood as we walked back to the house. 'I hate you!' she told me repeatedly. 'I hate you! And I want Daddy.'

Lucy's moods had never bothered me unduly. They were like violent storms that swept in from nowhere and vanished again just as unexpectedly. So I'd always treated them exactly like weather – I ignored them and waited for the sun to come out. Her 'I want Daddy', though, had felt like a stake through the heart. *We all want Daddy*, I thought at one point. But then I wondered, *Or do we? Do we want Daddy at all?*

Lucy's indoor sulk gave me some quiet time with Sarah in the pool, and as I swung her around, dragging her through the water, I thought about Amy and Ant and wondered what the attraction was. Because to my eye, at least, pop-star Amy was way out of Ant's league. Then again, she was out of Joe's league too, so perhaps she just liked slumming it.

Still, they were both physically attractive, I admitted. Hadn't I read somewhere that the couples that last the longest are those where both participants are equally good-looking? It crossed my mind that it was a wonder Ant and I had lasted this long, but then perhaps he liked slumming it too.

I tried to imagine life without him, but the void of it terrified me into numbness. I toyed with the idea of phoning Kerry again – she'd be reassuring, I was sure of it. But as I was looking after the girls, I couldn't really speak to her, even less cry – and cry, I would. Just the thought of her friendly voice was enough to bring tears to my eyes.

'Is Joe going to get Daddy?' Lucy asked, making me jump. Her sulk was apparently over.

'You know he isn't,' I said. 'I told you, Daddy's gone home. To England. To our house.'

Lucy glared at me as she thought about this. I could almost see her debating whether there was anything to be gained by having another hissy fit.

'Is Joe coming back?' she asked then, mirroring my unspoken fear that he might not, that we'd be abandoned here alone without food or transport. He'd insisted he would be back by seven, so in theory I didn't need to worry. But then I'd never expected Ant and Amy to vanish, had I? I'd never expected any of this.

'Of course he is,' I said, wondering if I still had the taxi number in my phone. I remembered that I did, so at least we'd not die of starvation. 'I told you, he's renting a car and buying food and then he's coming right back here.'

'With Ben?' Lucy asked.

'Yes, with Ben.'

'Then can we go to the pool with the fishes?'

224

'Yes,' I said. 'Tomorrow we can go back to the pool.'

'With Ben?' Lucy asked.

'Yes!' I said, struggling to keep calm. I took a deep breath and thought about the fact that it was no wonder she needed so much reassurance, then continued more calmly, 'It'll be you and me and Sarah plus Joe and Ben, and we can have a lovely day at the pool.'

'OK,' Lucy said. Then, 'I'm bored, Mummy.'

'I know,' I told her. 'I'm a bit bored too. Do you want to play cards?'

She shook her head. Cards was boring, she said, and without Ben the pool wasn't going to keep her happy for long, either. So in the end we went into the cool interior and ran around playing hide-and-seek, which at least killed the best part of an hour.

About five thirty a jeep came bumping down the track and for a moment I thought it was Joe returning early. But then I heard a dog barking and the sound of Spanish being spoken and realised that we had new neighbours.

They let themselves in two doors down, and suddenly the air was filled with noise. They seemed to communicate with each other exclusively through shouting, and the dog – a yappy Jack Russell – simply never paused for breath.

I felt sad at the loss of the silence, but also safer somehow. Lucy moved to the far end of the courtyard, all the better to watch the daughter, who was about the same age. I was pretty sure that within the hour they'd be friends, and I wasn't wrong. By six she was splashing in our pool.

As the girls were now entertained, I did my best to think in some structured way about my relationship with Ant: about our future, about the kids, about custody and access and possible scenarios for reconciliation. But I couldn't get to grips with any of it. There were so many unknowns, that was the thing – so many unknowns and so many mixed emotions. Of course, there were also three young girls shrieking in the pool, so I was literally unable to hear myself think.

Little Lola's mother came to collect her just before seven, and the dog, yapping at her heels, leaped quite spectacularly into the pool. This pleased Lucy and Sarah enormously.

Lola's mother didn't seem to speak much English, but she pointed at the pool and said, 'Thanks you,' and I nodded and smiled and replied, '*De nada*,' which I seemed to think I'd heard Amy say in lieu of 'you're welcome'.

Joe arrived just then, and the Spanish woman looked relieved, as if he was the answer to a puzzle that had been bothering her. 'You husband,' she said, pointing and smiling almost grotesquely.

'Oh, no,' I said. 'No, he isn't, actually. He's a friend.'

She frowned at me.

'*Amigo*,' I said. 'Not husband.'

She frowned even more deeply at this and then, with a tiny upward nod of the chin that I didn't really know how to interpret, she vanished, calling Lola and the dog, who was apparently called Nacho, to follow on.

'We have neighbours,' Joe said, as he walked towards me with two carrier bags of shopping.

'We do,' I replied. 'Extremely noisy neighbours. Is there more?'

'Yeah, loads,' Joe said, handing me the bags. 'Take these and I'll go back for the rest.'

'She looked grumpy,' he said when he returned, joining me in the kitchen. 'Everything OK?'

'Yes,' I said, pausing my fridge-stacking to consider the question. 'She thought you were my husband, I think, and she was a bit shocked when I said you were just a friend.'

'If only she knew,' Joe said, and for some reason – paranoia, no doubt – I thought he meant that we weren't *even* friends.

'If she knew what?' I asked, freezing with a carton of what looked like some kind of milk in one hand.

'If she knew what's been going on next door,' Joe said. 'Then she'd be *really* shocked.'

'Oh,' I said. 'Yes, of course. And you managed to rent a car then?'

'Yeah, it's only an Ibiza,' Joe said. 'It was all they had. I had the choice between black or white.'

'Is that no good?' I asked. I know absolutely nothing about cars.

Joe shrugged. 'Nah, it's fine,' he said. 'It's just a standard hatchback kind of thing. But it's got five seats and they threw in the boosters, so it's fine.'

'I was wondering, after you left,' I said, 'how come you actually rented a car? I mean, we could have just got a taxi to go shopping, couldn't we? And if she's bringing the other car back tomorrow . . .'

'I dunno,' Joe said, lifting another bag from the floor, plonking it on the counter and peering inside. 'Just a feeling, I guess.'

'A feeling?'

'Yeah, it makes me uncomfortable. Being without transport, it makes me nervous. If something happens to one of the kids, or . . . I don't know, really. I like to be able to get out if I need to, you know?'

'Yes, I can understand that,' I said. My feeling of being stranded here alone was one of the reasons I'd felt safer when the neighbours arrived, after all. I too now felt safer, knowing we had a car.

'I don't much like depending on other people,' Joe said.

'You mean the neighbours?' I asked. 'Or the taxi?'

'I was thinking more of Amy,' he said.

Promising ourselves we'd make healthier choices tomorrow, we took the lazy option of heating up and divvying out the four frozen pizzas Joe had purchased. They'd defrosted in the car anyway.

He was quiet and seemed preoccupied, which was understandable, and even the kids seemed more tired than usual. So by nine they were all in bed, and as it seemed clear that neither Joe nor I was feeling particularly chatty, we also retired to our rooms, to read.

As the next day was Saturday – I'd actually lost track until Joe reminded me – the public pool was crazily busy. There were so many people that it was all but impossible to swim.

The upside of this was that it felt totally safe to leave the kids to their own devices. There were children and adults a-go-go and there were even two muscular lifeguards on high chairs, even if they did seem to be chatting more than watching. They were smoking, too, which seemed shocking – passing back and forth, in plain view, something that looked suspiciously like a joint.

Joe and I had nabbed a shady spot to lay our towels and were both reading. I'd finally managed to lose myself in the story, which was both a break from my own miseries and, as it featured a divorced couple, an oblique way of thinking about them.

On arriving, Joe had tried repeatedly to phone Amy, wandering off into the distance each time to do so, but it seemed she wasn't picking up.

When his phone buzzed, I glanced at him and watched as he sat bolt upright. '*Ouch!*' he said, crossing his legs on his towel. He jabbed at his screen a few times, and I was just wondering if it would be intrusive to ask for news when he looked over at me and said, 'Apparently she's sent me an email.'

'An email?' I said. 'Amy?'

'Yeah, she sent me a text to tell me to check my mail.'

'Can you do that here, on your phone?' I asked.

Joe nodded. 'Yep,' he said. 'I'm just picking them up now.'

He rolled on to his side so that his back was towards me and read whatever she'd sent him. It must have been quite some email, because he was reading for a good ten minutes.

When he'd finished, he rolled on to his back, exhaled through pursed lips, and said, 'Wow! OK.'

I watched him with concern until he glanced over at me, whereupon I raised one eyebrow in an unspoken question. His reply was an almost indistinguishable shake of the head.

He closed his eyes for a bit and I tried to read, but I was distracted by the nervous tapping of his fingers against his phone. Unexpectedly, he leaped to his feet. 'I need . . . to walk or something,' he muttered. 'I'll be back.'

I tried once again to read, but my concentration was gone. I kept getting to the bottom of the page and realising that I hadn't taken in a single word. I thought about Joe's face before he'd left, how grey and sad and serious he'd looked, and I started to worry if he was OK.

I gave up on the book and dropped my Kindle into my bag, then stood to see if I could spot him. There were people everywhere, but no Joe. I checked in on the kids – they were playing with some Spanish locals, watched closely by two overweight mamas eating ice creams – and then I set off around the perimeter fence to look for him.

I found him in the scrubby car park, sitting on a tree stump. He had his head in his hands and though, as I approached, he wasn't making a sound, it was pretty obvious he was weeping.

I thought of leaving him alone, but an old woman was looking on concernedly, so deciding that he'd be less troubled by my intervention than by hers, I crouched down beside him. It wasn't until I rested my hand on his back that he even noticed I was there.

'Are you OK?' I asked. I knew it was a stupid question, but I couldn't think of anything else to say. He looked up at me and shook his head gently. His eyes were red and his cheeks were wet, and just the sight of him brought tears to my eyes.

'Is there anything I can do to help?' I asked.

'Later,' he croaked. 'Just . . . later. I need to be alone. I'm sorry.'

'Don't apologise,' I said, standing and reluctantly leaving him to it. I glanced at the old woman and smiled gently in an attempt at reassuring her. To calm myself, I walked twice around the perimeter of the pool before finally jumping in with the kids.

On the way home we stopped off in Orce for another batch of takeaway pizzas. It seemed silly when we had so much food back home, but neither of us could summon the energy to cook, and it was what the kids wanted anyway.

We managed to get them to bed by ten that evening, and it was only then that Joe seemed ready to talk. I poured us two glasses of wine from the fridge and carried them out to the courtyard.

'So, I expect you want to know what's going on?' Joe said as I handed him his glass.

I sat down. 'When you're ready, Joe,' I said. 'And only if it helps. Otherwise there's no reason you need to tell me anything.'

He nodded and sipped his wine. 'Actually, there is,' he said. 'A reason, that is. Because it kind of involves you as well. Actually, *involves* is a bit of an understatement.'

'Oh,' I said. My heart skipped a beat.

'So, I've had a think, and there are three ways we can do this,' Joe said, sounding like he was forcing himself to be efficient. 'I can show you Amy's email. Or you can call Ant and get him to tell you himself.'

I nodded and thought about the two options, neither of which really appealed. 'And the third?' I asked.

'I suppose I could tell you,' Joe said. 'I could, you know, give you a summary sort of thing. But to be honest, that's my least favourite option, so . . .'

I nodded again. I looked out over the pool and licked my lips and wished there was a way to freeze this moment. I wished I could remain *not knowing* in this sultry Spanish evening with my glass of chilled rosé by the pool. I wished I could choose to never know that everything had changed.

'The email then,' I finally said. The fact that Joe felt I needed to know told me everything really, didn't it? I had no desire to speak to Anthony, so what would even be the point? 'As long as you don't mind?'

'No,' Joe said. 'I don't care.'

He handed me his phone, and slowly, I started to read the email. Halfway through, he said something to me and stood, but I was in a daze and I wasn't really sure what it was that he'd said.

Dear Joe.

I'm sorry to do this through an email but I honestly feel it's better for both of us that I do it this way.

I said to you the other day that things haven't been right between us for a while. I know you looked surprised when I said that, but I'm pretty sure if you think about it you'll see it's true.

I know that you love me because, unlike me, loving is something you're incredibly good at. I've always known that you love me, and it's felt good, and that's all to your credit.

And I love you too, I really do. I love you like family. I love you like a brother. I love you like a friend. I love you as the father of our wonderful child, Ben.

But I'm not *in* love with you any more, in fact I don't think I have been for years. I'm really sorry to have to tell you that, but it's true.

Now, you know what a psychological mess I am, so it probably won't come as much of a surprise to know that I've never been that happy in our marriage. Right at the beginning, perhaps, when all those endorphins or whatever were rushing around . . . Because I <u>was</u> in love with you at the beginning, it's true. But since then, I've been trying to find a way to plug what feels like a big, dark pit inside me. Sometimes I think that pit is full of despair, and sometimes I think it's full of hate or even evil. Whatever it is, the core of me isn't that nice, I'm pretty sure of it. At times the call of that swirling pit has been so intense that I've had thoughts about killing myself to spare you all, but then something's generally come along to get me through. I know how much you hated Mungaro, but he really helped me through a difficult time. Pure Being therapy was great for a while, as well.

At other times, I've been able to cope so well that I kidded myself my black hole had vanished. But it never completely had.

Not until now, Joe, that's the thing – not until this chance meeting with Ant happened. Because he made it go away. It's gone! And I can't begin to explain what a relief that is. So I'm wondering if I wasn't in the wrong relationship all along. I'm wondering if that wasn't what kept this awful feeling going inside me.

I haven't told you much about my parents and there seems little point in doing so now. But know that my father in Toronto isn't the cuddly, lovely man I told you he is. He is, and always has been, a total and utter bastard. As for Mum, well, you worked that one out yourself: she's mentally ill (schizophrenia is the official diagnosis) and she spends about half of her time in the psych ward. Why have I never told you any of this? I think I've always feared that I'm mad like my mother, or a bastard like my father, or very possibly both. And I always worried that if you knew about them, you'd start looking for those character traits in me. And you'd very probably find them.

Perhaps this thing with Ant is all bull. Perhaps it's like *The Secret* and Mungaro and *The Power of Now* – a sort of sticking plaster that will help me feel better for a while and then fall away with time. But despite the horror of what I'm doing to our family, I feel so centred right now that I need to know; I just have to find out if it's real. I hope that with time you'll understand that.

I don't hate you, Joe, in fact I don't even have anything I could really criticise about you. And I don't hold you responsible for anything that has happened in ANY WAY. It's important that you know and accept that. This is all me. This is all my fault and my doing. I take full responsibility.

I love you still, Joe, though I've never been a very good wife, and I love our son too, though I've never been that good at being a mother.

So I'm hoping and praying to the universe that we can find a way to get through all this without hating each other. That we can find a way to be friends and be there for our son and avoid all the horror that divorcing couples tend to make for themselves.

Ant and I are flying back to England today, and by the time you get back home, I'll be gone. Though the house is mine, I want you to stay there for now, with Ben, at least until we're calm enough to work out what's best.

I'm not sure what you will want to tell Ben, but knowing you, you'll try to be truthful, and as long as you do your best not to paint me as a monster (even if that's how you think of me right now) I'm happy to go with whatever you decide.

I think it would be best if we waited a few days before we spoke, to let the dust settle, so to speak, but if you need to talk to me, call and I'll pick up.

I'm so sorry to do this to you, and I'm so grateful for everything we've lived through together, but I'm forty-six, Joe, and if there's a chance I can be truly happy, then I need to take it. I really hope you'll try to understand.

With all my love, and all my sorrow, Amy.

PS. On a practical note, I'm about to check the car back in, so you'll have to rent one locally. Of course, I'll cover any costs incurred (just stick it on the AMEX). Sorry about that but I can't think of any other practical solution.

PPS. Ant has declined to tell Heather any of this, which is another situation we've created that you'll have to deal with alone. I would suggest that you encourage her to phone him so that he's forced to tell her himself. He has promised to pick up if she does, too. But if you prefer to show her this email, then that's fine by me as well. Whatever you think is best. He's convinced that she'll feel nothing but relief, by the way. She hates his guts, apparently. But if you do let her see this, he wants her to know she can remain in the house with the girls. He doesn't want her worrying about anything material. Even if their marriage has fallen apart, he doesn't want her to suffer unnecessarily.

By the time I'd finished, Joe was gone, and I somehow managed to recall the words I thought I'd missed: that he was going to bed and that he wanted me to leave his phone in the kitchen.

I was glad to be alone. It struck me as extremely sensitive of him to have left me to live this moment in solitude.

I put the phone down, but Amy's email was still there filling the screen, lighting up the night, and I couldn't bear to see it any more, so I picked up the phone again and switched it off.

And then I began to weep, silently, much as Joe had that afternoon. I wept because Ant thought I hated him, and out of sadness that, in a way, he was right. I wept with relief that my life would now change, and with fear that I had no idea how. I wept for my daughters, who would have to live through our separation, and out of relief that perhaps they'd get to know a slightly better version of their mother. I cried for Joe, who was losing the woman he loved, and out of jealousy that at least he'd *known* that kind of love. I cried for Ben, who was losing the stability of two parents who loved each other, and for Amy, who really couldn't imagine what she was letting herself in for; for myself and all the wasted years, and then finally, and strangely most powerfully, I wept for my mother and my father.

I've no idea why they popped up at that moment, but there they were in front of me in all their misery of love and longing, and they were as present in their absence as they had ever been when alive.

The next morning, I woke up ridiculously early with an astonishing and unexpected sense of clarity. It was as if my brain had spent my sleeping hours processing everything and now it had jiggled everything around to make things clear.

I switched on the little bedside lamp and lay there revelling in the sensation even as I tried to identify and name it. Because this wasn't happiness exactly. It was more a peculiar feeling of being centred within my own body, as if, for the last nine years, I'd been just outside it, like a blurred stereoscopic projection with one half looking in on the other.

But here we were – Ant and I were separating. I'd almost certainly go back to nursing. We would live apart. Nothing had ever felt so logical. Perhaps my mother had said, *Go with the flow*, after all.

I got up just after six and cleared last night's mess from the garden table, and then quietly started to sort out the kitchen.

The children all woke up about seven thirty, so I set their breakfast outside in order that Joe could, for once, sleep in. By the time he surfaced, little Lola had returned with her yappy dog, and they were all splashing around in the jacuzzi.

'Coffee?' I asked, pointing the pot at him when he returned sleepy-headed from the bathroom.

'Yeah,' he said, more slouching than sitting at the kitchen table. 'Coffee would be good.'

I poured two mugs and sat down opposite him.

'You seem . . . I don't know . . .' he said, speaking through a yawn.

I looked at him enquiringly over the top of my mug.

'*Perky*, I suppose, is the word,' he continued.

I smiled vaguely at this. Joe's directness never failed to surprise me.

'It's a bit weird, actually,' I admitted. 'I cried my heart out last night, but this morning I did wake up feeling quite perky. It wasn't what I expected, but there it is.'

'Make the most of it,' Joe said. 'It doesn't last.'

'Oh,' I said. 'Right.'

'Though maybe yours will.'

'No, I'm sure you're right. I'm sure these are just phases.'

'But you're not devastated,' Joe said. 'That's good.'

'I was,' I told him. 'Last night I was totally devastated. This morning I'm not so sure.'

'Is . . .' Joe started, before interrupting himself. 'Look, you don't have to answer this, OK?'

I nodded, encouraging him to continue, but he sipped his coffee and instead said, 'Nah, maybe I shouldn't get into that.'

'Please, Joe,' I said. 'It's what I like about you the most – your honesty. Ask away.'

'Well, is Ant right? About you hating him? I couldn't help but wonder if that was true or if he was just telling Amy that to make himself feel better.'

I chewed my bottom lip as I tried to think how to answer the question honestly. 'It's complicated,' I said finally. 'But there's definitely some hatred in the mix. There's a bit of love, too, and if I'm honest, that's the bit I find most confusing. He's spent years bossing me around, telling me all the things I can and can't do, and yet in a weird way I think if that stopped, I might miss it. Which is a terrifying thought, really.'

'It sounds a bit like Stockholm syndrome,' Joe said. I frowned at him, so he expounded. 'You know – when people who've been held captive defend their abductors.'

'Oh, gosh,' I said. I reflected on this for a few seconds and nodded thoughtfully. 'Yes, in a way, I suppose that's exactly what it is.' I felt shocked that Joe had so easily handed me a key to thinking differently about my relationship with Ant. Having a label to hang on my conflicted feelings enabled me to feel a bit less confused almost immediately.

'Do you think it can work?' Joe asked. 'Between the two of them, I mean?'

'Ant and Amy?' I asked. I tried to imagine it for a moment and then shook my head gently.

'If that's too painful for you to think about . . .' Joe said.

'No, it's fine,' I told him. 'I'm just trying to visualise it. And I suppose I'd have to say that I doubt it. I really doubt it. Ant's an incredibly difficult person to live with.'

'You said that before,' Joe said. 'But how? How is he difficult?'

'Well, he's pretty aggressive,' I said. 'He's passive aggressive mainly, but sometimes just plain aggressive aggressive. He's controlling and obsessive; he's a bit of a narcissist, and quite perverse sometimes. He's pretty moody and unpredictable, too.'

'Wow,' Joe said. 'All that, huh? No wonder you're feeling perky.'

I surprised myself by laughing at that. 'I feel guilty about it, though.'

'Guilty?' Joe said. 'What do *you* have to feel guilty about?'

'About feeling perky, I suppose,' I said.

Joe stood then and crossed to the window to look out at the kids, and I suddenly panicked that I'd forgotten to watch them in the pool. But apparently everything was fine.

'They get on really well,' he said, and so I crossed to stand next to him, looking out.

'Yes, they're good kids, aren't they? Ben's great company for my two.'

Joe sighed deeply.

'And you?' I asked.

'I don't know,' Joe said. 'I thought my relationship was solid, so now I'm just confused.'

I nodded thoughtfully. 'I suppose sometimes you just have to look at what-is.'

'I'm not sure I follow.'

'I suspect we lie to ourselves about how things are,' I explained. 'But when something like this happens, it reveals how they *really* were all along. It's just that we didn't want to see.'

'Yes,' Joe said. 'Yes, I suppose. Gosh, that's quite wise.'

Because no one had ever called me wise, I laughed at this. All the same, the compliment felt good. Perhaps I did have useful things to say, I thought. Maybe the problem was simply that I hadn't had anyone to talk to who was interested.

'Anyway, I'm basically gutted,' Joe said. 'I'm not going to deny it. I'm all wiped out about it.'

I rested one hand on his shoulder and said, 'I'm sure.'

'I want to tell Ben the truth,' he said with another sigh. 'But I'm not sure how that fits in with your plans.'

'The truth?' I repeated. 'I suppose that depends which bit of the truth.'

'I thought I'd tell him that Mum—' His voice cracked then, and he shrugged and moved away to fill his coffee cup from the pot before sitting once again at the table. He cleared his throat and continued, 'I'm thinking of telling him that Mum's new best friend is Ant. And they've gone off to spend some time together because they get along so well.'

'Ah,' I said. 'I see.'

'That seems to me to be something he can understand. And something that isn't actually a lie.'

I stared out at the girls as I thought about this.

'Is that OK for you and your two?' Joe asked. 'Because they're bound to compare notes.'

'Best friends,' I said, trying the words for size. 'Best friends,' I whispered again. Then, 'I suppose it leaves it open for . . . whatever . . . evolution, or whatever you want to call it, happens.'

'As in *they're not best friends any more*. Or *they're . . .*' Joe coughed again, and then said, '. . . they're in love, or getting married, or whatever.'

'Getting married?' I said, with a laugh. 'That I doubt, somehow. But yes.' I dragged my eyes from the girls to look at him. 'Best friends. For now, let's go with that.'

'OK,' Joe said. 'I'm just going to wait until he asks me. If yours ask first, then you can say the same thing.'

I nodded. 'Is the flight home . . . it's not tomorrow, is it? I keep losing track of the days.'

'It is,' Joe said. 'Tomorrow's Monday. We'll need to leave just after lunch.'

'God,' I said. 'That's going to be quite something, going home to all of this.'

'I know,' Joe said. 'Tell me about it.'

'Whose car did you take to the airport?' I asked. It had suddenly dawned on me that without Ant we'd be stranded at Luton.

'Mine,' Joe said. 'Thank God.'

'So you can drive us home?'

He nodded. 'Of course,' he said. 'We won't have enough booster seats, but we'll just have to manage. For one trip, it'll be fine.'

Almost the second that we stepped back outside, Ben ran to Joe to ask him when his mother would be back. It was quite uncanny really, almost as if he'd been listening to our conversation.

'She's actually gone off with Ant for a bit,' Joe told him, sitting down cross-legged to explain. I was impressed by how unflustered he sounded. 'Ant is Mum's new best friend.'

'Oh,' Ben said, frowning as he thought about this. I was watching Lucy and Sarah and could see that they too had tuned in to this conversation and were struggling to listen over Lola's Spanish nattering.

'But is she coming back?' Ben asked.

'Not here,' Joe said. 'We'll see Mum when we get home.'

'Tomorrow?'

'Yes, we're going home tomorrow,' Joe told him. 'You know that.'

'But will Mum be at home tomorrow?' Ben asked.

'I'm not sure, champ,' Joe told him. 'It depends if she got bored spending time with Ant, I guess.'

Ben wrinkled his nose at this information. 'But what about us?' he asked, and I thought for a moment that maybe he was going to cry.

'We're good, aren't we?' Joe told him. 'We're having fun here in the sun with Lucy and Sarah.'

'I s'pose,' Ben said. 'It seems a bit funny, though.'

'You're right,' Joe said. 'It *is* a bit funny. But we're OK, aren't we?'

'I s'pose,' Ben said again. 'Can we go and find the pig later on?'

'I thought we might go back to that lake,' Joe said. 'If we go early, we could grab that shady spot under the tree and spend the whole day swimming.'

'But we could look for the pig on the way home,' Ben said.

'Sure,' Joe said. 'Why not?'

As we gathered our things together ready to leave, I thought about how well Joe had dealt with Ben. He hadn't wanted to lie to him, and so had managed to tell him the truth – or at least a version of it – without upsetting him. I found that combination not only clever, but rather touching.

Kids do love repeat performances, so the idea of returning to the lake pleased everyone. The only thing was that they wanted the day to happen exactly like before – they wanted to eat the funny tapas in the restaurant (rather than the picnic we'd prepared) and they wanted 'Macarena' on the radio. The picnic they finally came around to, but Sarah, particularly, was not happy at all when we explained that we didn't get to choose what songs played on the radio.

Lucy seemed a little quieter than usual, and I guessed that she was pondering what she'd overheard, trying to square the circle of it in her young mind. She was also no doubt picking up on my own mood, which swung violently and unpredictably between brief sensations of deliverance and longer periods of despair. Joe had been right – the feeling had not lasted.

It wasn't until I was showering her that evening, back at the house, that she dared to ask the question that had been troubling her. Perhaps she simply hadn't wanted to ask it in front of Joe and Ben.

'Mummy?' she said. 'Is it true that Amy is best friends with Daddy?'

'Yes,' I told her, as I rinsed her hair. 'Apparently that is the case.'

'So will *Daddy* be at home when we get there tomorrow?'

I swallowed. Here it was, the heart of the matter.

'No, dear,' I told her, inspired by Joe's strategy of simplified honesty. 'I'm not sure that he will be. He might be off spending time with Amy somewhere.'

'Oh,' Lucy said. 'So who's going to read us the bedtime story? Will it be Joe?'

I laughed drily at this. 'No,' I said. 'No, it won't be Joe. Joe will be in his house with Ben. You remember Joe's house, don't you?'

Lucy nodded.

'I expect *I'll* have to read you the story, won't I?'

Lucy looked into my eyes quite piercingly then, and I braced myself for a terrifying moment of from-the-mouths-of-babes honesty. But instead, she simply bopped me on the nose with her finger and said, 'Well, just make sure you do, Mummy. Or there'll be trouble.'

Joe had bought too much food – way too much food – plus, due to all of the pizza we'd been eating, we'd hardly consumed any of it. So that final evening, we loaded the excess into bags and took it next door to our neighbours.

The Spanish family were particularly strange about this, sifting through the bags and dividing the items into two piles: acceptable food items and rejects, which were essentially all of the vegan bits.

The French boys enthusiastically took all our offerings, hemp milk and tofu included, and insisted that we go round for a drink before we left, so once we'd eaten, that's what we did.

They had a tiny but incredibly loud wireless speaker with them, and though they sadly didn't have 'Macarena' for Sarah, they did have some eighties disco stuff that all three kids seemed to enjoy. So while we drank our beers outside, the kids strutted around like idiots to the Bee Gees.

Amy had been right, it transpired: they were a couple, albeit a rather long-distance kind of couple. The tall one, Valentin, ran a record shop in Paris, while his partner was a clothing designer from Montpellier. He showed us some photos of the jackets he made on his iPhone, and they were really quite amazing pieces of high-fashion art. I was impressed.

'So what about you?' Valentin asked eventually. 'How long have you been together?'

'Oh, we're not,' I explained. 'We're just friends on holiday.'

'Oh,' Valentin said. 'Sorry.'

'It's because you look like a couple,' said his friend, who had a much stronger accent. 'You look like family with the children and everything.'

'Yeah, well, we're not,' Joe said, and I wasn't sure if it was a trick of the fading daylight or whether he was actually blushing.

'There were more of you before, right?' Valentin asked, missing the vibe. He swigged at his beer. 'I talked with an American woman, I think. A blonde woman.'

'Amy,' Joe said. 'My wife.'

'She's nice,' Valentin said. 'She's really cool.'

'Yeah,' Joe said, looking uncomfortable. 'Yeah, she's great. But she had to go home early.'

'As did Anthony,' I said, getting the information in before he asked me. 'He had to go home early too.'

'And now, lovely as this is,' Joe said, gulping down the remains of his drink, 'I think we need to get the kids home to bed. We've got a really long day tomorrow.'

With the exception of checking Joe's car in at Malaga airport, which for some reason was incredibly complicated, the journey went by without a hitch. Ant and Amy's seats remained empty – they'd clearly booked new ones rather than changing their bookings – and their absence felt strange and upsetting.

Back in Luton, Joe managed to remember where he had parked his pickup – something he'd been worrying about, even though it was so big you could see it from a mile away.

As we drove along, the children chattered excitedly, happy to be going home or perhaps simply to have flown again, and by seven in the evening we were back in our cool, empty home, the English drizzle pattering gently on the roof.

Lucy held me to my promise about reading a story but fell asleep before I was even halfway through. She, at least, didn't seem overly perturbed by our arrival in this big, empty house.

I sat in the lounge and listened to the air around me and tried to think about how different it all seemed without Ant.

It was quiet, that was the most noticeable thing. Ant always switched on the TV the second he sat down. He never switched it off, either, leaving me to do that once he'd gone to bed. So yes, everything was much, much quieter. I could hear the whoosh of cars going past on the wet lane at the bottom of the drive, and the rain falling on the conservatory out back. I could even hear a cat somewhere, howling.

It felt calmer, and somehow safer too. If Ant was in the house, there was always a crackle in the air, a pregnancy in the silence, waiting to deliver its next batch of mayhem.

I wondered where Anthony was then. I wondered if he was still with Amy, and just as I decided he almost certainly was, my phone buzzed with a text message.

'Are you home yet?' it said. 'Are the girls OK?'

I thought about not replying. I was worried he was nearby and would appear to interrupt my moment of contemplation. But then I thought about him worrying about the girls and replied simply, 'Yes.'

'I'm in one of the Powell flats out in Marshside,' he replied. 'Do you want me to come round so we can talk?'

I'm, I thought, not *We*. Did that mean it was already over? It was perfectly possible that Amy had already had enough of him. And if he wanted forgiveness, would I give it?

'Tomorrow,' I replied. Then, 'Tomorrow evening, once the girls are in bed.' Whatever our discussion was going to hold, I needed more time to think.

Of course, it was silly of me to imagine that Ant would ever ask my opinion on anything and the conversation the next day was an exact repeat of the one we'd had in Spain. He said that things hadn't been right between us for ages. He said he wanted me to stay in the house with the girls and that he was happy to continue paying the bills. He said, once again, that this was an opportunity to move on in our lives, and that he thought I could probably be happier with someone else too.

The only difference this time, and it was quite a big difference, was that instead of listening in dumb silence, I agreed wholeheartedly with everything he said. And that made me feel surprisingly powerful.

Ten

Joe

It was weird and uncomfortable being home without Amy. I didn't do any more crying and I didn't feel quite as angry as I'd expected, either. I was struggling to feel anything, really. Things just seemed deflated, it all felt flat, as if someone had left the top off my life and all the fizz had gone out of it.

We arrived home on Monday evening, but it wasn't until Wednesday that I got news from her. I'd picked up my phone tens of times to call or text but hadn't had the nerve to actually do it. Sometimes I just needed to know how to remove the child lock on the new hob, or to ask for the recipe for one of Ben's favourite dishes. Other times I wanted to know how she was, if she was missing me, or if she was ever coming back. In the end, I found I could get by without her answering any of these questions.

Ben understood everything. Not on a conscious level, I don't think, but in some way of his own, he made sense of what was happening. I know this because he didn't mention Amy once, and that absence of Amy, even in *name*, struck me as one of the most awful aspects of it all. I sensed that I should prompt a discussion. I understood that as an adult, that was my role, not Ben's. But I feared I couldn't do so without falling apart. And having his father fall apart was the last thing my son needed right then.

Though I needed to go straight back to work, I took the Tuesday off, and Ben and I went food shopping. In an attempt at finding some fun for him in the midst of our dire situation, I let him choose whatever he wanted. I couldn't find it within me to give a damn about what we ate.

At the checkout, we unloaded the contents of our trolley on to the belt. We had microwavable veggie burgers, frozen chips, crisps and pizzas. We had potato cakes shaped like smileys, chocolate mousses, lollipops and Coke. I saw the elderly cashier raise an eyebrow and understood that, in her eyes, I'd become that man: the single dad who feeds his kid rubbish.

When Amy finally called, I was in the process of leaving for work with Ben in tow, worrying about how I was going to get anything done. The set-up wasn't ideal for either of us and her phone call came at the perfect time, so I asked her if she could look after him for the day and suggested we talk in the evening when I got home.

Amy said that sounded 'just great', and that she'd be round in fifteen minutes, so I could go, and as I got my stuff ready to leave, I thought about that word *great*, running it over and over in my mind and twisting it like a knife in a wound.

Just as I was leaving, it crossed my mind that she might be with Ant, and so I called her to make sure that wasn't the case. The idea of Ben spending the day with the two of them was unbearable to me.

'No, don't worry,' she reassured me. 'Ant's at work too. I thought I'd take Ben shopping in Canterbury.'

'Good,' I said. 'He'll like that. And if you see a shoe shop, he needs new trainers.'

I spent the day pulling down ugly units from a rich old lady's kitchen. It felt good to be destroying something, and once I'd finished, though there was no reason whatsoever to do so, I smashed the old cupboards with a sledgehammer.

When I got home at six, Amy's sports car was parked outside, and that seemed really weird. It was as if she was taking a liberty by parking it there – I can't really explain why.

I found her in the kitchen drinking herbal tea, and her ownership of the kitchen got to me even more. I reminded myself that the house was hers, but it didn't seem to help.

'Hello, Joe,' she said, when I reached the doorway.

I merely nodded by way of reply.

'Do you want tea or something?'

I shook my head and crossed to the kitchen sink, where I filled a glass with tap water.

'Have a Coke,' she said. 'There's loads and loads of Coke in the fridge. You've got gallons of the stuff.' Amy didn't approve of Coke. This much we knew.

'Water's fine,' I said, refusing to rise to the bait. I moved to the window and looked out at the garden. 'Where's Ben?' I asked, without looking back at her.

'In his room. I bought him this Atari thing and I think he's trying to set it up.'

'A games console?' I asked, addressing her reflection in the window. It was the same strategy I used during the gory bits on telly, where I'd squint at a reflection of the surgeon with the scalpel rather than looking directly at the screen.

'Yeah, they're back in fashion, apparently. It's all gone retro.'

I nodded and thought about the fact that Ben would almost certainly tire of *Space Invaders* within half an hour, but that I'd probably enjoy playing it myself. 'Cool,' I said, and then, mocking her without her knowing it, I added, 'That's just great.'

A silence fell and eventually I turned back to face the room. 'So?' I prompted.

'I'm not sure what I'm supposed to say,' Amy said.

'Me neither,' I told her.

'Do you have, you know, any questions?' she asked.

I snorted at this, then closed my eyes and attempted to cool my mounting anger. 'Just one, I guess. Are you still with him?'

'With Ant?' Amy asked obtusely.

I shrugged. 'Unless there are others? But maybe there are. How would I know?'

Amy took a deep breath and stared straight ahead, past my left shoulder. 'Yes, Joe, I'm still with Ant,' she said flatly.

I nodded slowly. 'So it's a goer, is it, your little love affair?'

Amy thought about this and I thought I saw her stifle a smirk. It made me want to slap her. 'Yeah,' she said. 'Yeah, it's a goer.'

'He is a tosser, you know. I hope you realise that.'

'Yes, I'm sure that's what you've been told,' Amy said. 'Exes do tend to say that kind of thing.'

'Is that what you've told him about me, then?' I asked.

'No, Joe. You know it isn't,' she said. 'Anyway . . .'

'Anyway . . .'

'Look, I don't know what you want me to say, Joe. I pretty much said all I have to say in the email.'

'And I don't know what you want *me* to say.'

'Maybe tell me how you *feel?*' she said. 'You could have answered the email, but you chose not to.'

I glared at her and wondered why she felt the need to witness my pain. But then I thought, *Fuck it! Let her own it.*

'I'm devastated, Amy,' I said. 'I'm angry and I feel betrayed and depressed. And a whole shitload of other stuff besides. Happy?'

'No, Joe,' she said. 'No, that doesn't make me happy at all. It makes me really sad, if you must know.'

'Good,' I told her. 'I'm glad you're sad. I just . . . I can't believe you've chucked our whole family down the drain, Ame. Do you even realise what you've done?'

'It was a mistake,' Amy said.

'No kidding,' I said.

'I mean, coming here, today . . . it's too soon.' She crossed to the sink and poured away her drink.

'If you want to see me all bright and breezy, I suggest you come back in a few years,' I said.

'So, Ben,' she said, with a sigh. 'I can take him any day you want. I'm not working until mid-September, and I know that you are, so . . .'

I covered my eyes with my hands and took a couple of deep breaths to calm myself. I was struggling to believe that this conversation was real – that this really was where my life had got to. 'That would be good,' I said finally. 'But I don't want him hanging around with that twat.'

'Ant was fine for him to hang around with in Spain,' Amy said.

'Yeah, well, he wasn't shagging my wife then,' I muttered.

Amy stared at me robotically and blinked a few times before saying, with forced calm, 'No, of course. I understand. So maybe I should take him on weekdays, while you're working, and you can have him at weekends when Ant's off. OK?'

'I guess. This week, at least. He's back to school on Monday, so . . .'

'I'll come and pick him up at eight forty, just after you've left for work,' Amy said.

'Can you spend your time with him here?' I asked. I'd just visualised Ben wherever Amy and Ant were living and hadn't liked the image. 'I think it would be better for him. Healthier, if you know what I mean.'

'Sure,' Amy said. 'Why not? The flat's small and a bit empty, anyway. He'd get bored.'

'It's Powell's, is it?' I asked.

Amy nodded. 'How did you know? From Heather?'

I shook my head. 'A guess. I know he's still got empty units out there.'

'We're in the show flat,' Amy told me, and I really wished she hadn't. I'd fitted the kitchen units and bedroom cupboards in the show flat, so I knew it well. Now I could imagine their living arrangements only too perfectly. I imagined Ant hanging his suits in the fitted wardrobe I'd built, right next to my wife's dresses. I shuddered as if I was cold.

'But you're right, it's better if he spends time here as usual,' Amy continued. 'It's why I want you and Ben to stay here for now, even though, technically, the house is mine.'

I nodded. 'OK,' I said. I was probably supposed to be thanking her for her largesse, but that wasn't happening, not today, and probably not ever.

'Is he OK?' she asked. 'I mean, he seems OK, but . . .'

'Yeah, he's fine,' I said. 'For a kid who's living through what he's living through, he's doing great.'

'You told him that we're best friends,' Amy said. When I frowned, she added, 'Me and Ant? You said *best friends*, apparently.'

I nodded vaguely.

'Thanks for that,' she said. 'It's classy. So I'm grateful.'

'Classy,' I repeated, thinking that it was a strange word to use, considering the situation. 'Whatever . . . Look, Amy, are we done here?'

'Sure,' Amy said, heading for the door. 'I'll just say goodbye to Ben, OK?'

The final days of August whizzed by – I was working like a madman.

Joe-the-younger was still on holiday, and where my usual day finished around eight, now I had to be home by six to look after Ben. Amy tried to be home by six thirty for Ant, she told me. He liked to eat quite early, she said. Just the thought of it made me feel sick.

She'd arrive to look after Ben just as I left the house, and because she generally jumped in her car the minute she saw me coming home in the evening, there was very little communication between us.

I was feeling dazed about it all – that was my overriding sensation. When I was working, I'd slog hard enough to drive the entire situation from my mind, but in the evenings, though I put on a brave face for Ben, the truth was that I just felt numb. There was a vague feeling of waiting for something, too, as if the status quo couldn't continue to exist. Sometimes I thought I was waiting for her to realise the folly of her ways and come back to us, and other times I was merely waiting to feel better about the fact that she was gone. But basically, those were the sensations: numbness and waiting.

The following Monday Ben started back at school, so Amy was no longer required to look after him during the day. I'd drop him at school in the morning, and he'd walk back with Heather and her kids in the afternoon, then stay at her place until I got home.

Though Heather and the girls were just down the road, and despite the fact that I did think of them often – wondering in particular how Heather was coping with her similar situation – the truth is that I avoided engaging with her. She was a part of this whole horror story and things seemed complicated enough without throwing her feelings into the mix.

But at the end of Ben's first week back, I got home to find her sitting on the wall at the end of our drive. I parked the truck and walked back down to greet her.

'Hi,' she said, once she'd hung up. 'Just chatting to my sister. Sorry.'

'Hello, Heather,' I said. 'How have you been?'

'Oh,' she said lightly, 'you know . . . Ben's in the back garden with Lucy and Sarah.' She nodded towards the rear of the house. 'He wanted to show Lucy something and they ended up playing with a football, so I thought I'd leave them to it for a bit. Sarah was chatting to your cat the last time I looked.'

'You *can* go back there and sit in a chair, you know,' I told her. 'You are allowed.'

'Thanks,' she said. 'But here's fine. And I need to get home soon anyway.'

'So, come on,' I said. 'How have you been? Are you OK?'

She looked at me soulfully and licked her lips. 'Do you know,' she said, 'I have no idea? I think I'm waiting for some profound realisation to come along, but nothing's popping up. I don't expect that makes any sense to you.'

'It does,' I told her. 'It totally does. Come inside. Have a drink. We can catch up.'

'Thanks,' she said, 'but not today. I really do need to be getting along. But maybe another time, OK?'

'Sure,' I said. 'Any time.'

'Have you heard . . . ?' she said. She cleared her throat and started again, saying, 'I don't suppose you've had any news, have you? About whether they're . . . you know . . . happy? I can't help but wonder how it's all going.'

'Sorry,' I said. 'Me and Amy aren't exactly chatty right now.'

'No,' Heather said. 'I can imagine. Ant doesn't tell me anything either.'

'But there are no signs of cracks that I know of. If that's what you're hoping for.'

'Oh, no, I'm not,' Heather said. 'I'm not hoping for anything at all.'

'No?' I said. 'Well, good for you.'

'But everything just feels so . . . temporary, I suppose,' she said. 'I mean, Ant's still living in that show flat. We have no real arrangement about anything, really. Not about the bills, or the house, or the future . . . It's all just ad hoc, day to day, you know . . . It's a very strange way to be living.'

'It's destabilising,' I said. 'I agree.'

'Yes, it is,' Heather said. '*Destabilising* is the word.'

At that moment, Ben came running around the corner of the house, followed by Lucy, who was brandishing a stick.

'Go and get your sister, will you?' Heather told her, pulling the stick from Lucy's grasp and throwing it into the bushes. 'We need to be getting home.'

Once Lucy had caught Sarah, we waved them goodbye and started to walk back towards the front door, only to be interrupted by the arrival of Amy's red Mazda.

Ben ran to greet his mother, giving her a hug when she stepped from the car. On being told she needed to talk to me, he climbed the stairs to his bedroom. I led Amy into the lounge and closed the door behind us, wondering what this was about.

'So,' Amy said. 'What's up?'

'Um, you're the one who just said you needed to talk,' I told her, feeling confused.

'You're right. And we do. We need to talk about when I can get to see Ben,' she said, sounding almost aggressive.

With Ben having started back at school, it was true that she hadn't seen him all week. So I'd guessed we would have to rejig things somehow.

'You're going to have to choose between weekends or week nights,' Amy continued. 'Because you simply can't have both, Joe. I do need *some* access to my son.'

I frowned. 'Right,' I said. 'Of course. No problem.'

'And if that frown's about Ben seeing Ant,' Amy said, 'then you're really going to have to get over it. Because there's no way around that one, I'm afraid.'

And I *was* worried about that, it was true. But I was also trying to imagine how Amy *could* have Ben to stay. The show flat at Powell's was a single-bedroom unit, after all.

'Are you still in that tiny flat?' I asked. I instantly regretted having said this, fearing I'd opened a path to a potential conversation about my tenancy in the house.

'We are,' Amy replied. 'But another one's come free – a three-bed unit on the second floor – so hopefully we'll be moving into that one.'

I nodded and tried not to imagine the scene, but failed, remembering the high-gloss kitchen units I'd screwed to the walls with my own hands, the cupboards I'd fitted in all three bedrooms.

'So, what do you think?' Amy prompted.

'I think we need to see what Ben thinks,' I told her.

'Sure,' Amy said. 'But I don't think we should put him in a position where he thinks he's responsible for what happens. We don't want him thinking he has to control all this, do we?'

I crossed to the sink and poured a glass of water to give myself time to think about this. 'Actually,' I said, on returning to the table, 'maybe we *should* let him feel he has some control. I mean, obviously he needs to see both of us, but we could at least let him choose when and where and how, couldn't we? He hasn't had any say in the rest of this, after all.'

Amy nodded and licked her lips. Her expression was impossible to read.

'What?' I asked.

'I'm scared,' she said.

'Scared?'

'I'm scared he'll choose you,' she said quietly, her voice gravelly with emotion. 'If we give him a choice, I'm scared he'll just choose you.'

'Oh, Amy,' I told her. 'You're his mother. He adores you.'

'Maybe,' she said. 'Maybe not. So do you want to talk to him about it, or shall I?'

'Both of us together might be best.'

Amy nodded and brushed a forming tear from the corner of her eye. 'OK,' she said. 'Let's get him down here and see.'

I poured a packet of Cheesy Wotsits into a bowl. I'd read somewhere that bad news is easier to accept while you're eating, though – like most of what we read these days on social media – I have no idea if it's true.

Amy spelled out the dilemma for her son. She was missing him, she said, and she needed to know when she could see him.

Ben shrugged and filled his mouth with Wotsits.

'Basically, your choices are weekends or school nights,' I explained.

'I don't care,' Ben said, in a weird unemotional voice that I hadn't heard before.

'OK, well, what works best for *me* is if I have you at weekends,' I told him. 'Because that's when I have time to actually *do* stuff with you.'

'OK,' Ben said.

'But that means staying with your mum on school nights.'

'OK,' he said again.

'Not here, though, yeah?' I explained. I suspected that he wasn't really getting the picture. 'In the flat.'

'In the flat?' Ben repeated. 'With Ant?'

I swivelled slowly to face Amy and indicated with a nod of the chin that she could continue the conversation. I couldn't bring myself to discuss Ant with my son.

'Yes, with me and Ant,' Amy said. 'You like Ant, though, don't you?'

'What about the girls?' Ben asked. 'What about Lucy and Sarah?'

Amy shook her head. 'Not yet, but hopefully soon, once we have a bigger place.'

Ben pulled a face.

'You told me you liked him the other day,' Amy said.

'He's OK,' Ben said. 'But it's boring there. There's nothing to do. And where would I sleep?'

'You can have our room,' Amy said. 'Ant and I can sleep on the sofa bed.'

'Eww,' Ben said. 'That's rubbish. I don't want to sleep in your stinky bed. I want my room.'

'I know,' Amy said. 'But it's all we have, because for the moment I want to let you and your dad live here.'

For the moment, I thought. I had a self-destructive urge to say, 'You know what? I'll just leave.' But I managed to restrain myself.

'Only you don't. You want me to live with you in that stupid flat,' Ben said.

'Yes, but at weekends, you'd be here with your dad. Do you understand?'

Ben nodded but looked utterly miserable. 'Are you with Ant now?' he asked her, surprising me, and, by the look on Amy's face, confusing her. 'Are you with him, like, for ever?'

Amy chewed her bottom lip and swallowed. 'I'm, um, not sure about *for ever*, darling,' she told him. 'But for now, yes, I'm with Ant.'

'Don't you love Dad any more, then?' Ben asked. 'Not at all?'

Amy rolled her eyes towards the ceiling and took a deep breath before replying, and I looked away out of the kitchen window and tried to think about something else – anything else. 'No, I do, Ben. I love your dad very much,' she said. 'But I don't want to live with him any more. I want to live with Ant.'

'I'll just stay here then, I think,' Ben said matter-of-factly, as if the subject was now closed.

I heard Amy stifle a gasp.

'The flat is a bit small for all three of you,' I suggested, turning back to face them, trying to help Amy out by making this about the flat rather than about her. I could see she was close to tears. 'Why don't you leave Ben with me this week and see if you can get the other place sorted? You can take him out on Saturday or Sunday instead until you get a bigger place.' I turned to Ben and asked, 'Would that work better for you?'

Ben shrugged, but deigned to nod vaguely at the same time.

'And then, once they've got a place where you have your own room, you can take some stuff over and make it your own, and stay there on school nights so that I can work late. OK?'

Ben took a fistful of Wotsits and stood without replying to the question. 'Can I go now?' he asked.

'Sure,' I said, reaching out to ruffle his hair, but failing because he flinched from my touch.

The cat jumped up to take Ben's warm seat the second he was gone, and as Ben left the room Amy stood. 'I need to go now, as well,' she said, giving Riley a brief stroke.

But as she moved towards the door, I jumped up and caught her by the sleeve. 'Amy,' I said. 'Are you sure about this?'

She paused and looked back at me. 'Am I sure?'

'Yeah, are you sure?'

'Well, it's not ideal, is it?' she said. 'But I don't really see that we have a choice.'

'I don't mean that,' I told her. 'I mean all of it. Are you sure this is what you want? Really?'

Amy shook her head. 'No, Joe,' she said, sounding sad. 'No, I'm not. I'm not sure about anything any more. But for now, this is where I'm at, so . . .'

Once she had gone, I grabbed a beer from the fridge and necked it straight from the bottle. I thought about the fact of her not being sure any more and wondered if that opened a window of hope for our future. I hated myself a little for still wanting it. If I had more pride, I thought, I'd have closed that window myself.

I went upstairs to Ben's room. He was playing *Pac-Man* on his new Atari console.

'You OK, champ?' I asked him.

He nodded, but didn't pull his eyes from the screen.

'Do you want to talk about all this, because I do get that it's all a bit messy and difficult to understand.'

He shook his head and carried on playing.

'I'm here for you, that's all I'm trying to say.'

He shrugged.

'I'm pretty good at *Pac-Man*, you know,' I said, trying to sound chipper. 'Do you want to challenge me?'

But again, my son just shook his head.

So that's how things stayed throughout September. Ben lived with me, meaning that I had to come home early, and on Saturdays, while he spent the day with Amy and Ant, I'd do my best to catch up on work.

I worried constantly about my living arrangements, wondering why there had been no news of Amy's move and expecting every crossing of our paths to be the one where she'd announce I had to leave.

I needed to knuckle down and find a place of my own to live in, I knew I did. But I was working like crazy, and my only day off – Sunday – was the day all the estate agents were closed.

The Internet, of course, remained open, and I did half-heartedly look at rentals on the laptop from time to time. But I couldn't imagine myself in any of them. Moving out would seem like driving the final nail into the coffin of our marriage. As long as I was living here with Ben, there was something for Amy to come back to. Once I moved, it would be well and truly over.

On the last Saturday in September, news arrived that they had moved. It was Ben who told me, while Amy was turning her car around in the driveway. He was angry, confused and tearful. He didn't want to stay there, he insisted.

I did my best to reason with him and I tried to get him to express why he was so upset. But the truth was that both were pointless because what Ben wanted was what I wanted: for everything to go back to the way it was before. And it simply wasn't within my power to make that happen.

Finally, as I put him to bed that night, I told him to try it for a week, and if he really hated it, I'd call a meeting with his mother to see what could be done.

'But I *will* hate it,' he told me.

'Then we'll have that meeting and talk it all through together,' I said. 'We'll come up with a different solution, but you have to try it for a week. Deal?'

'You promise?' he asked.

'I promise,' I told him solemnly.

In the end, not only did Ben not mind staying there, but I think he rather liked it. He never would have admitted that, though.

Ant and Amy spoiled him rotten, letting him buy pretty much anything he wanted for his room, and by the end of October this had become nothing more than routine: weekends with Dad and week nights with Mum and Ant. It never ceases to amaze me how resilient kids are about change – perhaps it's because their brains are still growing.

My own brain had long since lost all flexibility. I *hated* the new set-up with a vengeance. My lonely evenings stretched before me like deserts to be crossed, and the only way I could seem to get through them was to drink.

Sometimes this was 'social' drinking down the pub with Marius or Joe, but mainly it consisted of a lonely stream of beers from the fridge, consumed with lacklustre ready meals from the freezer. When I took the recycling out and saw the sheer number of empties, it scared me.

The alcohol wasn't helping, either. Sure, it made the evenings slip by in a blur, and that was preferable to minutes that felt like hours and hours that dragged by like weeks. And it certainly made the telly more entertaining, or, at the very least, less dull. But it did terrible things to my sleep patterns, and I started waking up to pee at three in the morning and not being able to get back to sleep. This lack of sleep, plus the inevitable hangovers, left me feeling tired and irritable by day, and ruined my concentration at work. Worst of all, as the weeks went by, the drinking left me feeling even more depressed than before.

My roll-with-it personality was gone, and I caught myself ranting about politics or Brexit or Boris Johnson – 'going off on one', as my dad would say, about pretty much anything. By mid-November, Joe and Marius had begun declining the invitations to my fun-filled evenings down the pub as well. Life had just got even lonelier.

I needed to get a grip on myself – this much I knew. It's just that I had no idea where to start.

Eleven

Heather

I felt happy and I felt surprised. In fact, feeling happy *was* the surprise. After all, you're not supposed to feel great about being dumped for a neighbour, are you?

But I did – in fact, sometimes I felt ecstatic. I'd wake up in a good mood, and snuggle against whichever of the girls had crawled into my bed. Downstairs in the kitchen, as I made breakfast, I'd notice that my body was tingling with joy, and occasionally I'd even dance around to whatever song was on the radio. It felt a bit like being in love, only it wasn't that. It was simply no longer being in hate.

I felt guilty, too, about feeling happy, so it was a complex set of emotions. I tried to temper my joy, preparing myself for an inevitable rebound, for the wave of misery and sadness that would submerge me once I came to my senses. It's just the rebound never came.

Or course, I had plenty of concerns about my situation. I was living in the house Ant had bought, and he was still paying for everything. I was only too aware how dependent I was on my ex, and so I started looking for work. But finding any kind of nursing job that fitted around the girls' out-of-school hours *and* the local bus schedule seemed to be impossible. If I was going to work full-time again, we'd have to move as well, and that was, by a long shot, more upheaval than I felt ready to face.

Ant surprised me with his generosity. He took his responsibilities as a father seriously, it transpired. Perhaps he felt he was paying off a debt incurred by his infidelity, or perhaps he thought he owed his daughters some stability because he'd broken up our family. Maybe the idea of our dependence on him soothed his fragile ego. Actually, it was probably all of those.

Whatever the reason, he made staying on in the house easy.

But as time went by, I couldn't help but suspect this was his way of continuing to control me. As long as I was entirely dependent upon him, I remained exactly that – dependent on him.

So when a postcard advert popped up asking for part-time help at the local farm shop, I jumped at the opportunity. The pay was only minimum wage, but the hours – 11 a.m. to 3 p.m. – fitted in perfectly with the girls' schooling, and the owner, who I already knew from having been a customer, was a ruddy-faced man who laughed a lot. He gave me the job straight away.

Now that Ben was living with Ant and Amy during the week, I crossed paths with Joe far less than before. I think he worked late most nights and certainly there was never any sign of him when I walked past the house with the girls. During the autumn term I only bumped into him twice, once at the school one Monday morning as he dropped Ben off, and once at the farm shop as I was arriving for work. But two momentary sightings were enough to see that he wasn't happy. With dry skin and bloodshot eyes, he looked so shocking that on both occasions I asked if he was OK – and he insisted that he was. I asked him if he was eating properly and even invited him round to dinner, but he declined both times. He was busy, he said. He was *fine*.

Working made me feel so much better about myself, it shocked me. I found myself chatting and joking with Peter, the farmer, and whistling as I washed and packed the veg. What I was doing was hardly earth-shattering, but it was indisputably useful and being useful felt good. People were happy when I handed them their boxes of veg, and Peter even more so when he emptied the till at the end of the shift. My days felt shorter and less pointless, and I found myself feeling saner, physically stronger, and more the way I'd always imagined 'normal' adults might feel. I even had to open my own bank account to receive my wages, and it was only when I received my debit card – with my own name on it, rather than Ant's – that I realised just how much of my identity had been erased over the years. I bought jeans and wore trainers for the first time in a decade. I got my hair cut shorter and cooked curries and Thai noodles instead of endless rounds of steak and chips. I found myself watching less TV and listening to more music. In a nutshell, I felt more like *myself* than I had done in years.

On Sundays Ant would collect the girls and take them out for the day, and these empty Sundays were the only times my new-found sense of well-being faltered. Most Sundays, especially if it was sunny, I'd be fine: I'd clean the house or do the washing, and then I'd go for a walk. Sometimes I'd stop somewhere and eat a burger, or down a glass of wine, and I'd tell myself how lucky I was. But a couple of times – and for some reason this only ever occurred when it was cold and rainy – I found myself overwhelmed by loneliness. And this wasn't any ordinary kind of loneliness either. This was an all-encompassing sense of void that left me feeling as if I'd been gutted with a fish knife.

It was as though, in the absence of anyone to see me or hear me, I was ceasing to exist – I felt like I was actually disappearing. I'd phone Kerry, in Rome, and if she answered, I'd be fine – the day was saved. But if she didn't, if she was busy, then I'd start to feel scared. I'd try to read, only to find myself skimming the page. I'd watch a film and be unable to concentrate on the complexities of the plot. Finally, I'd end up lying on my back on the sofa, my heart thumping in my ears. I'd stare at the ceiling, counting the minutes until my girls would be returned to me and life could pick up where it had left off.

On one of these terrible Sundays, I caught sight of myself in the mirror and was shocked to see how awful I looked. It was something about my eyes – there was a deadness in them that scared me. My soulless face reminded me of the way Joe had looked when I'd seen him at the farm shop.

In November, Christmas ads started appearing on TV, and the website where I ordered food began offering me baubles and tinsel as well. I started to worry about Christmas, specifically about who would have custody of the girls. Because the twenty-fifth without my girls seemed unimaginable.

I phoned Kerry to see what she was doing – I was hoping that she'd come and stay, just in case I ended up childless and alone. But she had to work on the twenty-fourth and the twenty-sixth, she said – there was no way she could get away before Easter. She was strangely detached from my problems these days and I knew that was entirely my fault. I'd spent too long pushing her away.

Eventually, one Sunday after he'd dropped the girls back home, I plucked up the courage to broach the subject with Ant.

'Dunno,' he replied, with a shrug. 'I suppose I just assumed we'd just spend Christmas together.'

'Together?' I repeated. 'You mean, you and me and the girls, *together*?'

'Well, yeah,' he said, with another shrug. 'Why not? It'll be weird for them otherwise, won't it?'

For some reason, out of shock mainly, I said, 'OK.' But even as I was saying it, I felt sick.

I didn't sleep a wink that night – instead, I lay staring at the wall, running a film of Ant and me pretending to still be a family across the cinema screen in my head. It was a horror film, and by around 3 a.m., it had upset me so much that I was finding it difficult to breathe. I was on the verge of a full-blown panic attack, and I seriously considered phoning for an ambulance.

The next morning, first thing, I texted Ant. 'Christmas together isn't going to work,' I typed. 'Couldn't you take them for NYE instead?'

'Not sure,' he replied almost immediately. 'I'll talk to Amy and get back to you.'

It was December by the time he replied. He had come to pick up the girls, and once he'd strapped them into their car seats, he returned to deliver the verdict quite casually, as if it was really no big deal.

'Oh, by the way, for Christmas, you're all right,' he said. 'You can have them.'

I was so relieved that I almost kissed him. I say *almost*, because clearly that was never going to happen again.

'But I'd like to take them for the New Year's Eve weekend if that's OK?' he continued. 'Amy's having Ben over too, so we're going to try to rent somewhere with a fireplace or something, or maybe even find somewhere with snow. Make it special, like.'

'Oh!' I said. 'Um, of course! When is New Year's Eve? I mean, what day does it fall on?'

'It's the Monday night,' Ant said. 'So I'd pick them up on Friday and bring them back on Tuesday the first.'

'But in exchange I can have them for the whole of Christmas week?' I asked. As far as my hours at the farm shop were concerned, Ant's timing was perfect. I felt like there had to be a catch.

'Yes, the *whole* of Christmas week,' Ant said, sounding sarcastic. 'Amy and me are going to Broadstairs to see Mum anyway, so . . .'

'Gosh,' I said. 'How lovely.' I hadn't been trying to sound facetious – it had just slipped out.

Ant merely raised an eyebrow. Nothing I said seemed to upset him these days, which was a constant source of surprise.

He must have explained the plan to the girls that day because in the evening, while I was getting Lucy ready for bed, she said, 'Mummy, you know how we're spending Christmas here . . . ?'

'Yes, sweetheart?' I replied, pulling her pyjama top over her head.

'Can Ben come too?'

I paused and smiled at my daughter. 'That's a lovely idea,' I told her. 'You can ask him tomorrow at school.'

Whether Lucy forgot to ask Ben, or whether Ben forgot to mention it to Joe, I'll never know, but the longer I waited for a reply to come, the more convinced I became that it was the best idea ever. It simply had to happen.

My mind was filled with strange – some would say not particularly healthy – images of Joe and I hosting Christmas like a makeshift replacement family. But though I told myself to stop it, I couldn't help but think that it would be absolutely lovely.

I had to phone Joe repeatedly to make it happen, but eventually he accepted my invitation. He'd been struggling to think what to cook anyway, he said.

They arrived on Christmas morning, about ten, their arms laden with packages.

Joe was wearing the same blue suit I'd seen at that dinner party way back when, and I was shocked when I calculated that way back when was only, in fact, six months ago. It felt so much longer, a whole lifetime ago, really, and he'd lost so much weight since then that his trousers bunched at the waist where he'd had to cinch them in with a belt.

As the girls had already opened their 'Father Christmas' presents, and Ben had done the same before coming to ours, we saved our fresh batch of gifts for after lunch. While the children played in the lounge with their new toys, Joe kept me company in the kitchen.

At first he just chatted shyly to me while I cooked, but after a few gin and tonics he relaxed and started to help.

In deference to Joe's sensibilities, I'd made, for the first time ever, a River Cottage recipe nut roast. It wasn't actually vegan, I explained, but at least it was vegetarian. This made Joe laugh because, he revealed, he hadn't been eating vegan, or even vegetarian, since Amy left.

'Oh God, you don't mind, do you?' I asked, wondering if there was any chicken still in the freezer. 'You weren't hoping for turkey or something, were you?'

'Not at all,' Joe said. 'Nut roast is fine. Nut roast is better than fine. I *should* be vegan. I should *totally* be vegan. But everything's hard enough, you know, without trying to source vegan food on top of everything else.'

I glanced over and saw that he was busy digging for ice cubes in my freezer, apparently making yet another round of gin and tonics. 'Not for me, Joe,' I told him. 'I think two's about my limit.'

'Two's not even my minimum,' he said.

'You want to watch that,' I said. 'Alcohol will destroy you if you let it.'

'Yeah,' Joe laughed. 'Right.'

'No, seriously, Joe,' I said. 'You're talking to the daughter of an alcoholic, here. It killed my father at fifty-three.'

'Oh,' Joe said. 'Sorry. I didn't realise. I don't usually drink that much . . . It's just things are a bit difficult at the moment.'

'Sure,' I said. Then, 'Are they? Really difficult, I mean?'

'I'll get a grip on it in the new year. I promise,' Joe said.

The gravy was ready, so I pulled the Yorkshire puddings from the oven and began to plate up. As I did so, I thought about the fact that he'd completely ignored my question and felt bad for having asked it. It was hardly a suitable subject for Christmas, after all. 'Can you get the roast and maybe try to tip it on to that plate?' I asked him, pointing, and he took a swig from his drink and moved to the oven.

But as, beside me, he did what I'd asked, he surprised me by saying, 'In answer to your question, though, yes. Yes, things have been difficult. This separation is the most difficult thing I've ever lived through.'

'I'm sorry,' I told him. 'I shouldn't have asked. Especially not today.'

'No, it's nice,' Joe said, smiling at me sadly. 'It's really bloody nice that you care.'

The dinner was lovely. My nut roast was excellent, even if I do say so myself, and the Yorkshire puddings were, Joe said, the best he'd ever tasted. With him having lived all those years with master-chef Amy, I kind of doubted that was true, but they were certainly the best I'd ever made.

After a shop-bought pudding, the kids opened another batch of presents, and while they played, Joe and I cleared the dining-room table.

Once this was done, we sat in the kitchen and chatted as we drank our coffee. I'd forgotten how honest and direct he was, and we found ourselves talking quite intimately about our feelings.

Joe admitted once again that things had never been quite right with Amy, but that he loved her all the same, in spite of her faults. He said that he was quite shocked at his own reaction to the separation, at how blindingly sad he felt about it all. He'd downed half a bottle of gin by then, plus at least three-quarters of a bottle of wine, so his eyes glistened as he spoke – his emotions were never far below the surface.

For the first time, I found myself expressing how I felt about things as well. I told Joe that I was fairly happy at the moment, though I was scared about what the future might bring. I admitted to enjoying my little job at the farm shop, and dancing around the kitchen with the girls. I told him about my solitary Sundays too and Joe said that he knew exactly how those felt.

I was surprised to find myself opening up in that way, and I wondered why it was so easy to talk to him. I decided it must be because his own heart was so definitively on his sleeve. Plus, it was a very long time since anyone had asked me to express how I was feeling – since anyone had even seemed genuinely interested, in fact.

Among the second set of presents, the ones that were officially from Ant and me rather than Father Christmas, was a half-sized guitar for Lucy. She'd been begging me for one ever since they'd started music lessons at school, and though I'd been loath to submit myself to that kind of sonic torture, I'd finally caved in.

'Bit of an own goal, that one,' Joe laughed, as Lucy ripped off the wrapping paper.

'I know,' I told him. 'I'm crazy.'

'Can you play?' he asked me.

I laughed and shook my head. 'But they're getting lessons at school next term, and she insists she wants to learn guitar, so maybe she'll teach me.'

'I want to be a singer,' Lucy informed us, striking a sassy pose with her new guitar, and strumming the strings tunelessly. 'I'm gonna be in a band, like The Aces.'

'The Aces?' Joe repeated, turning to me.

'A girl band . . . youngsters. They're OK, actually,' I explained. 'Quite rocky.'

'They're the best group ever, Mummy,' Lucy said, twanging the strings of the guitar again and starting to sing just as tunelessly.

'Could be worse,' Joe said. 'She could have started singing like Anne-Marie.'

'Oh, the 2002 girl?' I said. 'That song makes my ears bleed.'

'Mine too!' Joe said. 'I have to turn the radio off every time. Absolutely bloody unbearable.'

Lucy was still strumming the guitar tunelessly and Joe pulled a face as if he was in pain and reached out for it. 'That guitar needs tuning,' he said. 'Give it here.'

'Uh-uh,' Lucy said.

'Just for a minute,' he said. 'So I can tune it for you.'

'Do you really know how to tune a guitar?' I asked, as my daughter reluctantly handed it over.

'Sure,' Joe said. 'I used to play quite a lot. Nowadays, not so much.'

'He writes songs, too,' Ben announced proudly. 'Don't you, Dad?'

'Again,' Joe said, fingering a chord and strumming before starting to fiddle with the tuning keys. 'Nowadays, not so much.'

I was surprised by this. I'd always taken Joe at face value, accepting the quiet blokey exterior that he appeared so determined to project. But the more I spoke to him, the more hidden depths he seemed to reveal.

Sarah had just opened a package from Ant to find a battery-operated dog that performed tricks, and it seemed to be a hit with all three children. So while they were distracted with the trick-loving pup, Joe bent over the little guitar, forming chords and strumming and tuning until it sounded right.

'There you go,' he said, holding out the guitar once he'd finished, but Lucy was no longer interested. She was too busy playing with Sarah's puppy.

'That didn't last long,' I said. 'I knew it was a mistake. Quite an expensive one, too.'

'Oh, she'll come back to it,' Joe said, propping the guitar against the sofa. 'Great gift, by the way. Well done. I wish I'd thought of it for Ben.'

'Go on, play something then,' I urged him, laughing.

'Oh, it's too small for my big fat fingers,' he said, grinning.

'Go on, Dad,' Ben urged, looking up from one of his presents, a flashing hi-tech gyroscope.

Joe glanced at me and raised an eyebrow. 'Ben used to love it when I played,' he said. 'I don't really remember when I stopped.' He shrugged and reached for the guitar and then picked out a few bars of a tune before pausing.

'Oasis!' I said, impressed.

'Well spotted,' Joe said. 'But the guitar's too small. I can only really strum chords.'

'Then strum something,' I said.

He sighed deeply and stared into the middle distance for a moment, thinking.

'Oh, go on,' I begged. 'Please?'

He looked back at me, smiled sadly and shrugged, and then finally started to play.

When he started singing, the tears came from nowhere – they were a complete surprise even to me. Even now, I'm not quite sure why I cried so suddenly. It was almost certainly something to do with the lyrics. The song he'd chosen was 'Yesterday' by The Beatles, and the notion of a past without troubles was certainly a tear-jerker at this point in both our lives. But more than the words to the song, it was something about having another person sing to me, there in the intimacy of my lounge. Joe's voice was gorgeous – rounded and warm and soft – and it was a moment of such unexpected beauty, a moment that felt so shockingly personal, that it tapped into something that I'd completely forgotten existed. The beauty of life, perhaps. The beauty of other humans, maybe – the beauty of profound sadness, of life, of love, of all of it . . . As for the singer, I think it was at that moment that I saw him properly for the first time. And that, too, felt like a revelation.

Joe was concentrating so hard positioning his fingers on the tiny frets that he didn't even notice I was crying until he reached the second chorus and looked up, whereupon he stopped playing immediately. 'Shit,' he said, pulling a face. 'I'm sorry. Bad choice of song?'

I opened my mouth to reply, but nothing came out. I shook my head and swallowed and smiled, and then swiped away the tears with the back of my hand. 'That was just so . . .' I said. 'God, your voice!'

'Yeah, bad, huh?' he said.

'No, no, not at all. You sing beautifully, Joe. I'm in shock.'

The children had stopped playing and were staring at us. Ben was glancing back and forth between his father and me, wide-eyed. 'You made Heather *cry*, Dad,' he said.

'Yeah, I know,' Joe replied, frowning at me concernedly. 'I guess my playing really is that bad.'

Christmas had been a success. With it being the first one since Ant had left, it struck me that was no mean feat. So for a few days afterwards, as Sarah broke her expensive trick puppy by throwing it down the stairs and as Lucy discovered that playing the guitar was 'just too hard, Mummy', I continued to surf on the buzz of that success. Lurking on the edge of consciousness was the approaching New Year's Eve, but I was too scared to look it in the eye.

I've never much liked New Year, if truth be told. Oh, maybe once or twice when I was at nursing college, but then only because I was so drunk I couldn't even remember what naughtiness I'd got up to. It's something about all that expectation that gets me: the expectation that you're going to – or *must* – have fun; the expectation that the coming year actually merits celebration when all past experience suggests that's almost certainly wishful thinking. But this year, without the kids, the whole concept of New Year's Eve left me feeling terrified.

Ant had picked up the girls late Friday afternoon. He'd rented a cottage in Wales, he said, and snow was forecast. There would be an open fire and they had marshmallows to toast. The girls were excited and climbed into the car with an enthusiasm that pained me.

Catching sight of Amy in the passenger seat peering out at me, I waved them off and closed the front door. I stood for a moment, contemplating the silence of the house. I blew through pursed lips. 'You're OK,' I said out loud. 'You can do this.'

Friday evening was fine. Actually, if I'm honest, I'd even have to say it was nice. I heated up a frozen quiche and downed the best part of a bottle of wine. I watched a romantic comedy on Sky and ate a family-size bar of Fruit and Nut.

Saturday was OK, too. I hoovered and mopped, I stripped, washed and folded; I took pleasure in how clean my house looked.

But Sunday left me edgy, and by Monday I was feeling tearful. It was silly, I told myself. New Year's Eve was an evening like any other. It was better than spending it with Ant, after all! I could snuggle with a book. I could eat anything I wanted. I'd be fine!

By seven I was flailing, so I phoned Kerry in Rome. She was getting ready for a night on the town, she said. A friend of hers was DJing in a nightclub. She'd probably be out dancing until dawn.

I was shocked by the contrast between our lives. *How come lesbians get to have all the fun?* I wondered. I supposed it was the fact that Kerry didn't have kids that made the difference, but then my own children were away for the weekend, and *I* wasn't heading out clubbing, was I?

I told her about Christmas and she said the obvious thing: why didn't I invite Joe over? That was another idea I'd had floating on the edge of consciousness for days, another thing I'd been refusing to confront face on.

'I can't,' I said. 'It would be weird.'

'Why would it be any weirder than Christmas?' Kerry asked.

'Well, to start with, there'd be no kids,' I explained. 'So it would be just the two of us. It would be awkward.'

'Then go out,' Kerry said. 'Go to the pub. Have a drink.'

'I never really go to pubs. Or not in the evening, at any rate.'

'Well, try it,' she said. 'Make an effort, for Christ's sake. Or go to a restaurant. Take him for a nice meal out.'

'Then it would *really* feel like a date,' I said, finally spearing the elephant in the room.

'Oh,' Kerry said, and I could sense that I suddenly had her full attention. 'You don't *fancy* him, do you?'

'Of course I don't. No, absolutely not.'

'Well then,' Kerry said. 'Where's the problem?'

'I don't know,' I said. 'It just doesn't feel right, I suppose.'

'What's he like, anyway?' she asked then. 'This Joe . . . Tell me about him.'

'He's just a really nice bloke. He's ordinary.'

'Ordinary,' Kerry repeated. 'Ordinary, as in boring?'

'No, more in a good way,' I told her. 'He's quite clever, actually. He's one of those people who, if you talk to him, he knows what you mean immediately. You don't have to spell everything out. He's got that, you know, emotional intelligence, I think they call it. He reads people quite well. He likes to joke quite a lot, too. He's quite funny when he wants to be. He surprised me on Christmas day – I gave Lucy a guitar – and Joe picked it up and started playing. Just like that. He's really good, actually, and his voice is incredible. He's ever so honest, as well. Quite shockingly honest sometimes. But it's better to know where you stand with people, don't you think?' I suddenly realised how long I'd been talking about Joe and pulled a face. 'Anyway . . .' I added vaguely. It was an invitation to Kerry to change the subject.

Instead, she said, 'And physically?'

'Oh, he's really nothing special, Kes,' I said, trying to make up for my bout of overenthusiasm for all things Joe. But as I said it, I pictured his chunky body and, for the first time ever, imagined myself kissing him. The image my mind had created shocked me, and I felt lucky that Kerry wasn't there to see me blush.

'Tall, short?' Kerry said. 'I'm just trying to imagine him.'

'He's sort of average height and chunky,' I said. 'Thickset.'

'You mean fat?'

'No, no, he isn't fat at all. His job's pretty physical – he's a kitchen fitter. So no, he's quite muscular, but in a sort of rugby-man kind of way. Not like a runner or whatever.'

'Right,' Kerry said. 'So let me get this right. He's clever and funny and sings; he's fit and looks like a rugby-man . . . But you don't fancy him at all.'

'No,' I said. Then, 'Oh, I don't know, Kes! But there's nothing cooking there anyway, so . . .'

On hanging up, I poured a glass of wine to calm my nerves and thought about my phone call with Kerry. I reran the conversation in my head – hearing how I'd sounded like I had an adolescent crush on Joe – and I wondered if what I was feeling was real. And then I thought about what Kerry had said. Because her final attempt at persuading me had really hit the spot. 'He's probably alone and feeling miserable as well,' she'd said. 'Don't be so bloody selfish. Call him.'

Eventually, I poured a second glass of wine and then, muttering 'Oh, what the hell,' I reached for my phone. Joe answered immediately. 'Heather,' he said simply.

'Hi, Joe,' I said, trying to sound casual. 'I just thought I'd check in on you – see how you're doing?'

'Um, I'm good,' he said. 'Yeah, I'm fine.' He sounded a little slurry, and I suspected he was already drunk.

'So, what have you got planned for tonight?' I asked. 'You out painting the town, or what?'

But Joe's life was clearly not my own. He had actual friends to hang out with – of course he did. 'You can join us if you want,' he said, rather unconvincingly, I thought. 'But we're only going to The Gate.'

'Nah, you're all right,' I said. 'New Year's Eve isn't really my thing. I generally just watch a film and eat chocolate. I just wanted to check you're OK.'

'Yeah,' Joe said. 'I'm fine.'

'You have a lovely evening with your friends then, OK? And I'll talk to you in 2019!'

'Sure,' Joe said. 'You too. I mean, have a lovely evening with your chocolate.'

Outside, it had started to rain heavily. At least I wasn't out in *that*, I told myself.

I heated some leftover lasagne I'd frozen and ate it in front of a saved episode of *Doctor Who*. I watched *Terry and June* and *Absolutely Fabulous: The Movie*, neither of which managed to make me laugh. I watched *Jools' Annual Hootenanny*, and by the time midnight struck I was quite tipsy. The fake TV studio merriment made my teeth ache, so I clicked off the TV and sat for a moment listening to the rain outside. I thought about the girls and wondered if they had snow in Wales.

I switched off the lights and stumbled upstairs. As I slipped beneath the covers, I pictured Kerry dancing in a nightclub in Rome. She was such a manic dancer – just the thought of it made me smile. A smile! I'd finally managed it.

And then, even though the alarm clock still only read 12.22, I closed my eyes and slipped into the far less challenging world of sleep.

Twelve

Joe

Everything I'd told Heather was true. I really had planned a night in the local pub with Joe, his girlfriend, and his mates. But even as I was inviting Heather to join us, I suspected not only that she wouldn't come, but that I wasn't going to go either. Joe's crowd were all in their twenties and on New Year's Eve they'd be rioting. The more I thought about it, the more I realised that I simply couldn't face it.

So I stayed home alone, and I drank. I started off on gin and tonics, and when I ran out of tonic I drank gin on the rocks. And as I got ever more bladdered, my mood shifted through a number of phases. I felt happy briefly, and then lonely. I felt sad and then, thinking about how I'd been cheated out of New Year with my wife and son, jealous. I thought about the fact that Amy had chosen Anthony over me and got so angry that I punched a wall. It was the first time I'd ever done that, and it proved to be less satisfying and more painful than it looked in films. And then, as the TV screen became increasingly blurred, the alcohol finally did its job, taking me to a place where I felt nothing at all.

Dad sent me a text just after midnight, but though I tried, I was too drunk to read what it said, which should give you some idea of the damage.

I woke up at seven on the sofa, with Riley snuggled against me and the TV still playing to the room. On-screen, a couple of bright and breezy presenters were chatting on a colourful sofa. My head was throbbing and I needed to pee, so I switched off the happy couple and headed upstairs for an aspirin and bed. But when I got there, I couldn't get back to sleep. I tried for an hour, tossing and turning, before finally, feeling utterly, utterly awful, I got back up and said hello to the fabulous new year that had begun. Riley wanted feeding right *now* and the smell of cat food made me retch.

On the evening of the second, when Amy turned up on the doorstep with Ben, I was still feeling rough enough that I'd taken a rare day off work and been home all day.

'I want to talk to you,' she said.

I barely managed to stifle the groan.

Ben went off in search of Riley, so I led the way through to the lounge. I noted that Amy had closed the door behind her for privacy and wondered what this was going to be about.

'You look terrible, Joe,' she said, perching on the edge of the couch.

'Thanks,' I replied. ''s always good to hear.'

'You had a rocking New Year's Eve by the looks of it, then?'

I told her I really didn't want to talk about it.

'Fine,' she said. 'Well, we had a great time. The cottage was—'

'Amy,' I said, interrupting her. 'I don't want to hear about your New Year's Eve either, OK?'

'Oh. OK. I was only making conversation, but . . .'

'Yeah, well . . . don't,' I said. 'Was there something specific, or . . . ?'

Amy nodded, and looked uncomfortable. She shuffled back in her seat and laid one arm across the back of the sofa. She caressed the fabric gently with her hand. 'So, look . . .' she said, 'this is difficult . . .' She glanced around the room, taking in all that was hers, and I instantly knew what was coming.

'You want the house back,' I said, pre-empting her. 'The answer's *yes*, of course. You can have it. When do you need me out by?'

'Oh!' Amy said, visibly thrown by the fact that the spiel she'd so carefully prepared was no longer needed. 'It's just that the flat's been sold, and we can't go back to that tiny—'

'Amy,' I interrupted. 'I get it. OK? You don't need to justify yourself. You own this place.'

'I just don't want you to feel like you're being kicked out.'

Despite my best intentions, I laughed sourly. 'Only, I am,' I said. 'That's exactly what's happening. But it's fine. Really. Just tell me when, and I'll sort it.'

Amy chewed her lip and nodded. 'OK then. So, mid-February, say the fifteenth? Does that work for you?'

'Mid-February,' I repeated, as flatly as I could manage. I hadn't been expecting it to be so soon.

'I'll help you, financially,' she said. 'You've done so much to the place, and . . .'

'I don't need your help,' I told her. 'I don't want it.'

'But you've done so much here, Joe, and—'

'Look, if you ever sell it, split the profit with me, OK?' I said. 'Or my part of it, or whatever. I don't care.'

'Of course,' Amy said. 'That's very understanding of you, and I promise I won't let you down. Ant said he can help you find—'

'Fuck Ant,' I spat. I was surprised. I honestly hadn't intended to say that. The words had just erupted from within.

'He works in real estate, that's all. He said that the show flat's going to be—'

'Amy!' I said. 'Stop. I'm all grown up here. I can sort myself out, OK?'

'But the show flat, if you want it—'

'I don't. I really don't.'

'OK,' she said. 'OK, if that's . . . OK. Whatever.'

'Could you leave, do you think?' I asked. I was starting to feel angry, and I didn't, for some reason, want to lay a guilt trip on her. She was struggling enough here as it was.

'Sure.' She jumped to her feet. 'I'm sorry, Joe, I really am. It's just—'

'I know,' I told her, raising a hand in a stop sign. 'It's fine.'

'I haven't told Ben anything.'

'Good,' I replied. 'Let's leave that until I know where I'm going, OK?'

'Sure,' she said again. 'Sure, sorry, bye.'

Once she'd left, I sat staring at the fireplace I'd built. Then I looked around the room, taking in the gap where I'd knocked out the wall, and the shelves I'd built in the corner. I thought about the swimming pool out back and the new windows and the kitchen units I'd hand-made, and the shower room and the skylight and the conservatory . . . The list went on and on.

But I realised that I honestly didn't care about any of it – in fact I'd be glad, I decided, to see the back of it all. Because the only reason any of it had ever mattered was that it had all been a symbol of my love – it had all been done in devotion to my family. That was well and truly trampled on now, so that all it seemed to symbolise was pain.

◆ ◆ ◆

The following weekend I left Ben with Amy and drove up to Whitby to see Dad. I'd been avoiding visiting him ever since Spain, and hadn't once mentioned Amy on the phone. This had been less complicated than you might expect, for the simple reason that he'd been so tied up with his new lady-friend he hadn't asked. Not wanting to spoil his happiness with my misery had been part of the reason I'd not told him. But I'd also imagined, until recently, that it was possible we might get back together. I hadn't wanted to taint Dad's view of Amy until I was absolutely sure I wouldn't be bringing her back to his door. But the time had come: we weren't getting back together, that much was clear. I was about to move house, and I was even toying with the idea of moving back up north.

It was sunny when I left Chislet but lashing it down up in Whitby. I parked the car, hitched my jacket over my head, and ran to Dad's front door.

'A fine weekend you've chosen,' Dad said as he ushered me inside.

'Good northern weather, that,' I said, as I hung my jacket on a hook and followed him into the lounge. 'None of that poncy southern rubbish.'

The wind was blowing off the sea, making the rain lash against the windows so that it bubbled up around the edges of the frames. Dad had put rolled tea towels on the sills to catch the drips, a ritual I remembered from my childhood.

'Dry yourself off over there,' he said, gesturing at the open fire. 'Before you catch your death.'

I crossed to the fire and turned to look at Dad – specifically at his brand-new jet-black hairdo. 'Have you dyed your hair, Pops?' I asked, grinning lopsidedly.

'Hush thee,' he said, through a smirk. 'Of course I haven't.' When I raised one eyebrow, he laughed. 'OK, Emma did it for me – well, more for herself, really. She thinks it looks better this way.'

I nodded and tried not to smile too broadly.

'I'm assuming you don't agree,' Dad said.

'Maybe you could tone it down a bit,' I told him. 'Leave a bit of grey showing through. It looks a bit like a toupee otherwise, that's all.'

'From the mouths of babes . . .' Dad said. 'Well, you can tell the colourist herself later on.'

'I get to meet her, do I?'

'Of course,' Dad said. 'She's coming over to cook us all dinner.'

I told him I was looking forward to meeting her and he said he was sure that I'd like her.

'No Amy, then?' Dad asked. 'No Ben?'

I shook my head and swallowed with difficulty. 'No, I told you. It's just me.'

'Fair enough,' Dad said. 'Are they well?'

'Yeah, they're fine,' I told him, wondering if I was going to have to get into the whole thing straight away. I glanced around the room, noting various female touches to the decor, not least of which was an imposing dried-flower arrangement on the sideboard.

'Emma's work,' Dad said, following my gaze. 'Likes a dried flower or two, does our Emma.'

'Nice,' I said. 'And you look well.' Because, Dad's hair aside, he *was* looking well. He looked at least ten years younger than the last time I'd seen him.

'Thanks,' Dad said. 'You've lost a fair bit of weight, haven't you?'

'Yes,' I said. 'Yeah, I have a bit.'

'You not eating properly, or something?' Dad asked.

'No,' I replied. 'Not really.'

He nodded and then crossed the room to stand right in front of me. He grasped my forearms gently. 'How long's she been gone, son?' he asked.

I sighed. 'August,' I said. 'She's been gone since August, Dad.' But I couldn't speak any further. Because for the first time in months, I was crying.

'Oh, Joe,' Dad said, releasing my arms and then wrapping me in his. 'Oh, son!'

Eventually we sat down and I told him the full story, from our ill-fated holiday in Spain to my imminent eviction from the house. He listened in silence until I'd finished, then said that he'd suspected it for months. He'd simply been waiting for me to tell him.

'So you're toying with the idea of coming home,' he continued, and I was unsure if it was a question or a statement. He's always been able to read me like a book.

'Maybe,' I said. 'I don't know. There's the whole Ben situation to sort out, so that makes everything a bit complicated.'

'I think you should,' Dad said. 'Even if it's only for a while. The boy'll be OK with his mother. Sometimes a return to the source is the only thing that makes any sense.'

'A return to the source,' I repeated. 'I like that.'

'Your room's still upstairs,' Dad said. 'You'll probably be wanting to fix it up a bit, but it's still there, still waiting for you, with all your stuff.'

I laughed at the concept of 'my stuff'. These were things I'd last used over twenty-five years ago. 'Thanks,' I said.

'And if you need a room for Ben, you know there are plenty,' he said. 'You can take a whole floor if you want.'

'Thanks,' I said again. 'We'll see. Right now, I might go and lie down for a bit. The drive up was pretty hellish.'

'Of course,' Dad said. 'I'll call you for dinner if you don't wake up.'

With the exception of the bed, which they'd replaced at some point with a double, my room on the top floor hadn't changed much since my teens. The turquoise wallpaper was the same, if faded, and my old Akai ghetto blaster was still in the corner. I opened the drawer and rifled through a jumble of ancient cassettes, but only the rubbish ones remained. I must have taken all my favourites with me when I moved out.

I lay down on the bed and looked over at the window, at the raindrops dribbling down the pane. I listened to the familiar whistling of the wind around the chimney stack, and the distant sound of waves crashing on the beach.

There was a poster on the wall beside the headboard – the cover of *Moving Pictures*, an album by Rush, one of my favourite bands from adolescence. The image was a photo of a team of removal men in red overalls carrying paintings from a gallery, and just from looking at it I could hear the songs in my head – I could remember every detail of the guitar riffs. Staring at that poster made me feel weird, but in a good way, and I thought about all the hours I'd spent studying it.

A return to the source, I thought, and Dad was right – just being here felt healing. It was reminding me who I was, where I came from. I'd lost track of myself in all that madness, I realised. But here I was, Joe Stone, the kid who had mates, the lad who liked rock music, the adolescent learning to play the guitar. I was the son of Megan and Reg, and though I wasn't the best-looking guy on the block, I was solid, people liked me, people *trusted* me. Solid Joe. That's what my friends had called me, back then.

I'd had parents who were cool, who were clever, and who, more importantly than anything else, had always, indisputably, loved me. Another round of tears welled up, and I let them happen, I let them rise and slide down my cheeks, and I felt glad, because they weren't tears of sadness, but tears of remembrance. I was remembering my warm, caring mother, Megan, and my spiritual seeker of a father downstairs; I was picturing my childhood: learning to play the guitar, smoking joints out of the window, kissing Tiffany Dennis on the bed – and whatever happened to her?

This was Joe, this was where I came from, and for the first time in ages I knew I was going to be OK.

I liked Emma instantly. She was a bit of a cliché Buddhist, but I mean that in a good way. She seemed calm and friendly and kind. She listened more than she spoke, too, and I liked that. She reminded me of Dad's friends when I'd been growing up, so I felt instantly at ease.

She'd made a vegetable hotpot with dumplings, good hearty nosh for a cold winter's day, and we chatted comfortably as we ate.

Dad told Emma quite matter-of-factly about the breakdown of my marriage, and it was peculiar to hear it told second-hand, like a story. Emma nodded and reached for my wrist. 'I'm so sorry,' she said, scrunching up her nose. 'It's one of the hardest things that can happen, that is. But I somehow sense that you'll be fine.'

'Of course he'll be fine,' Dad said. 'He's a Stone! Nothing's tougher than stone.'

'Erm, I think diamonds might be tougher,' I offered cheekily.

'Yep, and a diamond would be . . . ?' Dad asked. 'Come on, boy. A diamond is a . . .'

'OK, it's a *stone*,' I said. 'You win.'

'A proper little diamond, this one . . .' Dad said, winking at Emma.

She squeezed my wrist and let go. 'I can see that,' she said. 'Like father, like son. I can tell.'

I awoke the next morning to sunshine and shrieking seagulls, and momentarily I couldn't work out what decade I was in. But as I came to, I remembered, and everything seemed clear. The change in the weather mirrored the shift in my mindset, and though this was a kind of clarity I had little faith in, a state of mind that I knew from experience owed more to desperation than to wisdom, I was happy for now to cling to it. It left me feeling decisive, and optimistic, and strong.

After a long, leisurely breakfast with Emma and Dad, followed by a brief blustery walk along the seafront, I climbed in the car to head home.

As I drove, I worked out the details in my mind. Any future jobs that we hadn't yet started – the kitchens we'd planned to fit from March onwards – I'd just cancel. If Joe and Marius wanted to take those on then, as long as they could convince our clients, they could have them. That would be my parting gift.

I'd talk to Amy and Ben to negotiate a new deal whereby he'd either come to me in school holidays or during term time. If I was living with or even nearby Dad, then either of those solutions would work fine. All Ben had to do was to choose.

The furniture? Amy could have it. The house? I didn't want to see it ever again.

During the three remaining weekends in January, I'd start moving my stuff up to Dad's, and by February, it would all be done. I'd have a fresh life waiting for me in Whitby – I was taking control, and that felt good.

Back in Chislet, I found Amy and Ben watching *Star Trek* while they waited for me. The scene was so domestic, so familiar, that the sight of the two of them together gave me a physical pain in my chest.

I pinched Ben's shoulder affectionately, *Star Trek* style, and then, catching Amy's eye, I nodded towards the door.

'Good visit, then?' she asked, on entering the kitchen.

'Sure,' I said. 'It was fine.'

'Are you moving back up there?'

I nodded. 'Yeah,' I replied. 'I think I might be. How did you know?'

Amy shrugged. 'It just came to me when you drove off yesterday,' she said. 'I don't know why, but it did.'

'It makes sense,' I said. 'I need a proper fresh start somewhere new.'

'Only Whitby isn't new, is it?' Amy said. 'It's more like going backwards.'

'Maybe,' I said.

'Wouldn't you rather start over somewhere fresh?' Amy asked.

I looked at her in consternation, and she got the message. 'Sorry,' she said. 'That's, of course, *entirely* up to you.'

'Yes,' I said. 'Yes, it is, kind of.'

'I suppose you'll be taking Ben in the holidays?' Amy said. 'So that he doesn't need to swap schools?'

'Hopefully. That would seem to make most sense. Do you think he'll mind?'

She shook her head. 'No, I honestly don't think so. As long as he can live in his beloved bedroom here, he'll be fine.'

'When he's eleven, he'll have to change schools anyway,' I said. 'So he can decide then where he wants to be.'

'Maybe. We'll see. You look happier, anyway.'

'I am,' I told her. 'I needed to make a change. And now I've worked out this is it.'

'I get that,' Amy said. 'I'm the same.'

On Monday, I took Joe and Marius for a pub lunch. It was the gentlest way I could find to break the news. Neither of them seemed unduly worried or even particularly surprised when I told them. If anything, young Joe looked positively stoked about it all. 'So we can set up our own company, and just take over all the new jobs?' he asked, bright-eyed. 'Is that what you're saying?'

I nodded. 'That's pretty much it. Yeah.'

'You up for that, then, Marius?' he asked. 'Just me and you?'

Marius wobbled his head from side to side. 'We'll see,' he said. 'I have to deal with this, how you call it? This *leave to remain*. When I deal with that, we'll see.' *Leave to remain* was the new legal status for EU citizens who wanted to stay in the UK post-Brexit, and the press had been full of horror stories about people being unexpectedly refused.

'You'll be OK, won't you?' I asked. 'You've been living here for years.'

'Of course he will,' Joe said. 'He's almost as English as I am.'

'We'll see,' Marius said again.

Telling Ben wasn't much more challenging when it came to it. At nine, he was in a phase where his most frequent reaction to things was *Whatever*. Though that had frequently annoyed me in the past, and though I suspected he was using this fake nonchalance to hide his pain about everything that was happening, I'll admit that it suited me right then. So I restrained myself from digging any deeper. Life almost certainly wasn't panning out the way Ben would have liked, but nor was mine . . . *Whatever* seemed as good a reaction as any.

I spent January deconstructing everything I'd built: cancelling jobs, closing bank accounts and, back at the house – a house I now thought of as 'Amy's' – pulling pictures from the walls. As my stuff was withdrawn from her carefully constructed love nest, the place started to look threadbare and sad. It was surprising how little I needed to remove – revealing a stain where a picture had once hung, or a closet containing nothing but mouse droppings – before the whole place began to look as if it had been abandoned. As this new shabby status seemed to match the reality of our lives so much better than the catalogue-perfect interior we'd been living in, it didn't feel so much like destruction, more a kind of reveal of an innate shabbiness we'd been masking all along. Pulling it apart felt *honest*, somehow, like ripping a plaster from a wound so that it could heal.

January went by so fast that I didn't find time to drink, or even notice that I *wasn't* drinking. And that was a very good thing.

I was working twelve-hour days, from eight to eight basically, and then collapsing in exhaustion once I got home. We were running late on two out of four jobs, and I needed them finished before I moved.

On weekends, I'd load the pickup with my stuff – select items of furniture or hi-fi, CDs that were indisputably mine, plus books and clothes and lots and lots of tools – which I would then drive up to Dad's.

For most of these trips, Ben came with me, and I have great memories of the conversations we had during those long hours spent side by side in the car. Because once we'd exhausted Ben's favourite subjects – namely school, video games and space exploration – we found ourselves talking about ourselves in more depth than ever before. Gradually the conversation shifted towards a discussion about everything that had happened, and more importantly, where we were going from here.

I was so impressed by how mature he was, and I found myself telling him the truth. He'd suddenly grown up and I hadn't noticed, but now here he was, someone I could really talk to. Answering his questions, which were many, I explained how his mum had never been that happy being married to me, and that I was glad to see that she finally was. I admitted that I'd been hurt by the idea that she could choose Ant over me, but that I was starting to find it easier to accept. At one point, Ben asked me if I thought I'd ever get married again, and I told him honestly that I hoped I would. 'Well, maybe not married,' I said, 'but I certainly hope I'll find another girlfriend.'

'So that you can have sex?' he asked, making me burst out laughing.

'Yeah, sex is nice,' I admitted. 'I sure *hope* that my sex life isn't over. Forty-two is a bit early for that.'

'Eww,' Ben said, and I laughed some more. He was at the precise age where sex intrigued and embarrassed him in equal measure.

'So, what do you think of Ant?' I asked him. 'And tell me the truth. It's totally OK for you to like him, you know.'

'He's a dork,' Ben said. 'But he's OK.'

'How can he be a dork *and* be OK?' I asked.

Ben shrugged. 'He tries too hard,' he explained. 'He wants everyone to like him, but he doesn't know how. He buys me loads of stuff, though, so I suppose he's OK really.'

'Right,' I said. 'I see.'

On the first weekend in February, I took the trip to Whitby alone. Heather was hosting a birthday party for Sarah, and because Amy and Ant were on a romantic weekender to Bath, she invited Ben to sleep over. As I was intending to spray-paint the walls of our future bedrooms, not having Ben along suited me fine.

On Sunday I got back later than intended, flecks of paint still lodged in my hair.

Ben was eating in Heather's kitchen with the girls, and while I waited for him to finish, she and I chatted for the first time since Christmas. She'd heard, via Ben, about my imminent relocation, and she wanted to know all the details.

So, I told her about Dad's house, and how they had run it as a bed and breakfast. I described the sea views and the gulls, and the storms lashing against the windows.

'That sounds gorgeous,' she said. 'I love the coast. I always wanted to live by the sea.'

'I didn't know that,' I said.

'Well, it's just so beautiful, isn't it?' Heather said. 'I love the way that every time you look it changes. Even in bad weather, the sea looks amazing. And the light on the coast is so different, isn't it? It always makes everything look brighter, more vibrant. I always thought my life would be more vibrant in a way, if I could just live overlooking the sea.'

'It is pretty nice,' I said, thinking about the way that every now and then Heather seemed to open up, seemed to allow herself to express her thoughts. And when she did, her eyes sparkled and her voice changed. It was like there was this whole different person hiding inside her that she rarely let out to play. I remember wondering if it was Ant's fault that she had shut down, and what she would have been like if she'd never met him.

'You're so lucky to have grown up there,' Heather said. 'It must have been amazing.'

'Yeah, it was pretty cool,' I said. 'You'll have to come and visit.' Addressing Ben, I added, 'Won't she, Ben?'

Heather blushed and laughed and said, 'Oh, of *course!*' in a peculiar mocking voice.

'No, seriously, Heather,' I insisted. 'You should. Come in the school holidays, and the kids can go to the beach. It's not like there's a lack of space or anything.'

'Well, that's very kind of you,' she said. 'But I'm sure your dad doesn't want us running around under his feet.'

'That's only because you don't know him,' I told her. 'Dad's very much a *more's the merrier* kind of guy.'

'Are you taking Riley with you?' Lucy asked. 'Or is she going to live with Dad and Amy?'

I gritted my teeth and turned to face Heather. 'Ah,' I said. 'Riley . . .'

She looked at me quizzically.

'So, Heather,' I began, with a nervous cough. 'I have a confession to make to you about Riley.'

'It *is* Dandy!' she said, wide-eyed. 'I knew it!'

I nodded and grimaced as if my teeth hurt. 'I'm so sorry. I was going to tell you the truth,' I said. 'That first time you recognised him, I wanted to say. But Amy came up with that stuff about us having him from a kitten, and I felt kind of stuck in the middle.'

'God, I knew it!' Heather said again. 'You naughty, evil cat-thief, you!'

'But he honestly came to us of his own accord. We had no idea he was anyone's, I swear.'

'Oh, I'm sure,' Heather said. 'You know what cats are like. No loyalty at all! At least he landed on his feet.'

'But seriously, do you want him back?' I asked. 'Because now's the perfect moment. Ant won't have him, apparently, and my dad's already got a cat. I'm not sure Boris and Riley would get on, so . . .'

'Dad!' Ben protested. 'You can't just give Riley *away*. He's my cat!'

'Yeah, only Riley is actually *Heather's* cat, champ,' I explained. 'You remember how he just started coming in our kitchen window, don't you? Right back in the beginning?'

Ben shook his head.

'OK, well, you were little. But he just started coming in through the window, and he was hungry, so we fed him. But he was Heather's cat all along. He'd just got lost. That's how he ended up at ours.'

'Yeah, but now he's *mine*,' Ben said.

'But if he's Dandy, he *has* to come home,' Lucy said.

My phone buzzed then, and as it was Joe-the-younger, and as it was also the third time he'd called, I made my excuses to Heather and stepped out into the conservatory to take it.

'Joe!' he said as soon as I picked up. 'Thank Christ. I've been trying to call you for hours.'

'Yeah, I can see that,' I told him. 'I was driving. What's up?'

'It's Marius,' he said. 'He's only fucked off.'

'You what?' I said.

Marius, Joe explained, had unexpectedly gone home to Romania. He'd been renting a small flat from the owner of a local pub, and it was the barman who'd given Joe the news.

At first, I found the story hard to believe. After all, I'd worked with Marius all day Friday, and he hadn't said a word. I was even pretty certain he'd said, 'See you Monday,' on leaving the job at five, though perhaps that had been me. But Joe insisted it was true and when, on hanging up, I called Marius, his phone went straight to voicemail. As I'd paid him in full just before the weekend, it wasn't beyond the realms of possibility.

'So is it true? Can we really have Dandy back?' Heather asked, when I finally stepped back into the kitchen. 'I've told Ben he can visit any time he wants, and he says that's OK.'

'He'll probably just come back to ours anyway,' Ben said. 'The gardens all join up.'

'Um?' I said, still thinking about Marius and all the jobs we needed to finish. 'Oh, yeah, if you're willing, that would be great.'

'Are you OK?' Heather asked. 'You look, I don't know . . . strange.'

'Yes, strange news,' I said. 'Kind of bad news, I suppose, if it's true.'

'Nothing serious, I hope?' she said. 'Everyone's OK, aren't they?'

'I don't know,' I said. 'One of my employees has gone AWOL.' I moved across the room to squeeze Ben's shoulder. 'Can we go, champ?' I asked him. 'I need to go round to Marius's place and see what's up.'

Shocking as it was, it was true: Marius had done an overnight flit. His flat had been completely cleared out.

I went to the pub and spoke to the landlord. He said Marius had paid him till the end of the month, and that he'd already found a new tenant.

I phoned Marius about twenty times during the next few days, but my calls always went straight to voicemail. Later on, at the end of the month, that number would cease to work entirely.

As we were working on site, I didn't call into the workshop until later in the week. I'd cleared out most of the tools anyway by then, so other than to pick up the mail, I had no real reason to go there. But on Thursday afternoon when I dropped in, a letter from Marius was waiting for me on the workbench.

Despite the fact that his written English was pretty approximative, he managed to make himself clear. In a nutshell, it seemed that his request to remain had been refused, and he hadn't had the stomach to fight the decision. That refusal, in the form of a letter from immigration, which he'd enclosed, was the 'small log that overturns the big cart', he said. Which I can only assume is the Romanian equivalent of the straw that breaks the camel's back. The letter informed him, pretty abruptly it has to be said, that he had twenty-eight days to leave the country. In his handwritten letter to me, he explained that he'd been thinking of going home since the Brexit vote, but had stayed on out of a sense of duty to me. *But now you are go home, Marius go home too. Goodbye, my friend.*

While I could understand the man's anger completely – I was feeling pretty angry about how he'd been treated myself – I just wished he'd given *me* twenty-eight days' notice. Because without him there was no way we could finish the jobs we had underway, and certainly not by the fourteenth of February.

If Marius's departure threw a spanner in the works for me, things were even more complicated for Joe-the-younger. He'd signed contracts with two new clients to do their kitchens, it transpired, and had already ordered flat-pack units for the first.

'You've gotta help me out, Joe,' he pleaded. 'Because otherwise, I'm screwed.'

And I'd worked with the guy for years. What else was I going to do?

Thirteen

Heather

It was the girls who first told me about Joe's change of plans. It was a cold, grey, drizzly Sunday morning and we were waiting for Ant to arrive. He was due to take them out for the day, though Lord knows what he was intending to do with them in such dreadful weather.

Sarah was busy throwing those sticky jelly-men at the big conservatory window, leaving stains that would be a bugger to clean, when a neighbour's long-haired cat nonchalantly crossed our lawn. This prompted her to ask when Dandy was coming home.

'Soon,' I told her, looking up from a magazine I was absent-mindedly leafing through. 'In about a week or two, I expect. Why? Are you looking forward to giving him lots of cuddles?'

She nodded. 'I want him to sleep on my bed like before. Do you think he will?'

'I'm *sure* he will,' I said.

'What day will he be coming?'

'I don't know, sweetheart,' I said. 'It depends what day Joe's moving house. I'll give him a call later on if you want.'

'I hope it's tomorrow.'

'It won't be,' I told her. 'But maybe at the weekend if you're lucky.'

Lucy, who was playing with Lego, looked up. 'Joe's not moving any more,' she announced.

I laughed. 'I think you'll find that he is.'

'OK, only he *isn't*.'

My daughter suddenly had my full attention. 'Why do you say that, Luce?' I asked, putting the magazine to one side and leaning forward.

'Well,' she said, taking a deep breath. 'He was *going* to move, but then Marius – that's the man he works with who makes all the cupboards – went back to live in . . . *somewhere*. Some foreign place, where he lived before, I think. Anyway, now Joe has to stay here so that he can do all the kitchens in everybody's houses.'

Lucy had always spoken in long, breathless monologues, but recently they'd come to at least be coherent, and occasionally, like now, they were even interesting.

'So Joe and Joe, that's the other man he works with – they're both called Joe, which is really funny if you think about it – they have to do all the jobs that Marius was s'posed to do, only Joe doesn't have anywhere to live any more because Daddy and Amy are moving back into the house down the road that Joe lives in, so who *knows* where he'll go now or what will happen to Dandy.'

She stretched out her arms, palms up, Shiva-style, and shrugged theatrically.

'Gosh!' I said. 'I didn't know that.'

'No, you didn't,' Lucy said proudly. 'Ben tells *me* everything.'

About ten minutes later, Ant rang the doorbell, so, on the doorstep, I checked to see if what Lucy had said was true. We'd reached the point in our separation where we could just about have a normal conversation.

Ant confirmed that Joe was staying on to finish some jobs, but said he didn't know anything about his living arrangements, or how long he was intending to stay. 'He's a twat, though,' he told me. 'I offered him the show flat and he said *no*. And it's too late now, because it's sold.'

Once they'd gone, I felt a bit funny, so I sat in the lounge and tried to work out why. I had a strange feeling of butterflies in my chest – the physical sensation preceding the idea itself. But then it came to me.

I thought about it all morning. The house was empty, and the rain continued outside, but instead of being depressed and lonely, I was feeling vaguely excited. And the more I thought about my idea, the more excited I felt.

I tried to temper the sensation by forcibly telling myself that my enthusiasm was inappropriate. But it didn't seem to work, and at two, after lunch, I caved and called Joe. When he failed to pick up, I grabbed an umbrella and walked round there instead. I found him in the garage, sorting through a pile of toolboxes.

'Hey, Heather,' he said, as I stepped beneath the shelter of the opened garage door and folded my umbrella. The rain was pattering on the wet drive, splashing my feet and drumming on the metal above my head. 'I was just about to call you,' he continued. 'I wanted to finish up here first. What's up?' He looked better than when I'd last seen him. Less haggard, somehow.

'Nothing much,' I said, sounding, even to myself, as if I was lying. 'I heard about you delaying your move, that's all.'

'Oh, that,' Joe said, peering into a box, rifling around, and pulling some kind of wrench from the depths, which he then set aside. 'Did Ant tell you?'

I shook my head. 'Ben told Lucy, I think. And then Lucy told me.'

'No secrets *at all*,' Joe said, grabbing a rag and wiping the grease from his hands.

'Did you find somewhere to stay?' I asked, doing my best to sound completely casual. 'Lucy seemed to think that was something of a problem.'

'Really?' Joe said. 'She told you that? Kids! Wow! I hope Ben's not worrying about it.'

'I'm not sure,' I said. 'But maybe. So did you find anywhere?'

'Yeah, kind of,' Joe said. 'They've got rooms at that B&B next to the pub. It's a bit flaky, but for a couple of weeks, it'll do.'

'Right,' I said. I took a deep breath and tried to choose the perfect tone of voice for what I was about to say. 'So, I was thinking . . . Why don't you just stay at ours?'

Joe looked up from the toolbox. He smiled and frowned simultaneously. '*Yours?*' he said.

I shrugged. 'We've got two spare rooms. You're out all day anyway . . . Why not?'

'What, like a lodger?' Joe asked.

'Yes,' I said. 'Yes, exactly like a lodger.'

'I'm not sure,' he said, and it looked to me like he was trying not to smile. 'Would it . . . ? I don't know . . . Wouldn't that feel weird or something?'

'Weird?' I said. 'I don't see why. No weirder than knowing that you're staying in some dodgy B&B while I've got empty rooms at mine.'

'Right,' Joe said. 'Yeah, I don't know . . . And Ant? What about him?'

I shrugged. 'What about him?' I said. 'I don't consult Ant on anything these days. I'm not sure if you heard, but we separated.'

We stared at each other for a moment, and then Joe averted his gaze and said, 'Look . . .'

I knew in that instant that he was about to say *no*. So though I was loath to say it, specifically because it was entirely untrue, I decided to use my trump card. 'Maybe you could chip in a bit for bills or something,' I said. 'Not much, of course. But I could do with a little extra cash, if that works for you.'

'Look, I . . .' Joe said again. But then what I'd said registered, and he paused once again and looked back up at me. 'Oh,' he said. 'Are things a bit tight, then?'

'A bit,' I lied. 'Not really, but . . . you know . . . I'm only working part-time and kids are expensive, so . . .'

Joe nodded thoughtfully. 'It would only be for a couple of weeks, though.'

'I know,' I said. 'A couple of weeks would be great. It would be a sort of test, wouldn't it? To see if having a lodger is a good idea after all.'

Joe nodded. 'I'm not any old lodger,' he said. 'You know I'll drive you crazy, right?'

'Well, if you do, then I'll just have to poison you with my cooking.'

He nodded slowly and then sighed. 'Sure,' he said casually. 'Why not?'

'*Really?*' I grimaced internally. I'd sounded far more enthusiastic than I'd meant to. I cleared my throat and forced myself to look suitably dour.

'I guess I'd rather pay you than that scummy B&B owner,' Joe said. 'Are you really gonna cook for me?'

I laughed. 'Don't expect the food to be up to Amy's standards,' I said. 'But yes, I'm happy to cook.'

Joe snorted. 'That would be amazeballs,' he said. 'I'm knackered by the time I get home, and I'm sick to death of eating bloody ready meals.'

'Well,' I said, 'it'll be a pleasure.'

'And what about Ben?' Joe asked. 'You know he stays with me at the weekends, right?'

'He can have the other room,' I said. 'It's a bit bare, but there's a bed, so he can have that if it suits you. And if he wants to bring some stuff and leave it, then that's OK too. The girls will be thrilled to bits.'

'If you're sure you don't mind, that would be great. Because Ben was my big worry as far as the B&B was concerned.'

'And what about half-term?' I asked. 'Will he be staying with you – I mean, with *us* – at half-term?'

'Half-term?' Joe repeated. 'Shit, when *is* that?'

'Next week. All week.'

'Jesus,' Joe said. 'Totally slipped my mind, that one. He was meant to be spending the week in Whitby with me, but of course I'm not going now.'

'Well, he can always hang around at mine with the girls, if he wants.'

'Thanks,' Joe said. 'That's kind. I'll, um, check in with him and see what he says. And you're sure about all this?'

'I'm sure,' I said. I was feeling a bit trembly, so I decided it was best if I left. But as I turned to go, Joe spoke again, making me pause.

'Would Thursday be OK?' he asked. 'For me, I mean. *This* Thursday?'

'Sure. Thursday's fine. Any day's fine.'

'Right then. And if you change your mind—'

'I'm not going to,' I told him.

'Right,' Joe said. 'But if you do, then that's OK.'

'I'm *really* not going to.'

Joe nodded. 'OK, then. Cool.'

I gave him a little wave, put up my umbrella and started to walk away, but once again he called me back.

'Heather?'

'Yes?' I'd stepped beyond the shelter of the garage door, and the rain was pattering on my umbrella.

'That's . . .' he said, and as he sighed, his face looked strange – sort of swollen.

'Yes?' I prompted again.

'That's really fucking nice of you,' he said. His voice sounded like sandpaper.

I smiled at him and then, just as he turned to resume sorting through his boxes, I thought I saw the glint of a tear in his eye.

As I walked away, the image of kissing him that I'd first imagined while talking to Kerry popped up again, only this time I let the image linger. I allowed myself to luxuriate in that thought, and it felt illicit but shockingly appealing. I wondered if there was any possibility such a thing could ever come to pass.

Joe moved in, exactly as planned, late on Thursday evening. He arrived with a simple backpack that he carried straight up to his room, before returning downstairs for supper.

As it was after nine thirty, the girls and I had already eaten, so to keep Joe company while he ate his reheated dish of pasta, I sat and sipped a glass of wine.

He thanked me a couple of times for letting him stay, and I insisted that it wasn't a problem. He apologised for not having got any cash out to give me yet, which embarrassed me. I wished that I could own up to the fact that I didn't need his money at all, but it seemed to me that this would just embarrass us both, so I told him that for the moment I was fine, and that there really wasn't any hurry.

'It was weird locking up the house for the last time,' he said. 'Even weirder thinking about Ant moving in.'

'I'm sure,' I replied. I was having quite a complex mixture of feelings about the situation myself, so I could only imagine how difficult it must be for him.

'But not weird the way you'd think,' he added once he'd swallowed another mouthful of food. 'Weird because I don't seem to care as much as I should.'

'Maybe it just hasn't hit you yet,' I said. 'Sometimes these things take time to digest.'

'Yeah, maybe,' Joe said. 'I thought that. But maybe not. Maybe it's just the right time for this, you know? Kind of like the end of a holiday?'

I frowned. 'The end of a holiday? I'm not sure I follow.'

'Yeah, you know how at the end of a holiday . . .' Joe said, '. . . how you're sad to have to leave, but also, kind of accepting of the fact you have to go? Because you just know that it's . . . well, it's just time, really, and this is what needs to happen next.'

'Um, OK . . .' I said vaguely. 'I think I get what you mean.'

'It's a bit like what you said in Spain, actually,' Joe said.

I shook my head questioningly, so he continued.

'About how we lie to ourselves, but how at some point you just have to look at what-really-is. And I've looked at what-is and sort of . . . *assimilated* . . . the new status quo, if that makes any sense? And now I'm ready to take on the next phase.'

'I suppose the main thing is that you feel OK about it all,' I said, thinking about the fact that he had remembered that conversation since Spain. I'd spent so much of my life being ignored, it came as a shock to realise that not only had Joe been listening, but he'd actually valued what I'd had to say.

A noise from the hallway caught my attention, so I stood and crept to the kitchen door. Seated on the stairs were Lucy and Sarah, their little faces peering between the banisters.

'And what are you two doing out of bed?' I asked softly.

Lucy looked up at Sarah and said, 'Well, go on, tell her.'

'We want to see Joe,' Sarah said, on cue.

'Hmm, all right, but not for long,' I told them. 'Tomorrow's still a school day.' I scooped Sarah up from the bottom stair and we followed Lucy into the kitchen. By the time we got there, she was already nattering away at Joe about how she'd helped me prepare his room.

Sarah's interest turned out to be in Joe's story-telling capabilities, which she remembered, apparently, from Spain. But it was much too late for story-telling, and Joe was tired as well, and so, promising them stories at the weekend, I ushered them back upstairs to their bedrooms.

By ten thirty, Joe had retired to his room as well, and if I'm honest, I was both disappointed and relieved by this – disappointed, because I'd been enjoying having some company, and relieved, because it made his presence in the house feel like that of a proper lodger. I'd been doing a pretty good job of convincing myself that this was all that was happening here, and so was happy he was adhering to the script.

On Friday and Saturday Joe worked, meaning that the routine of that first night remained unchanged. He'd come home late from work, eat his dinner and then go to his room to read, while in the mornings he'd simply grab a cup of coffee before bolting out of the front door.

On Sunday, though, Ben joined us, and this forced us together for the day. We shyly prepared and ate lunch together, and in the afternoon Joe drove us out to West Blean Woods for a walk. Not being able to drive, and with Ant no longer living with us, I hadn't been anywhere for months. So it felt wonderful to get away from Chislet, and as the kids buzzed around us like wasps, we wandered along the footpaths and chatted, talking about Joe's work and my past career as a nurse; about his father's house up in Whitby and a dog he'd had as a kid.

Out of the blue, Joe commented how strange it was that he and Ant had ended up swapping houses.

'I suppose it *is* strange,' I told him. 'I mean, no matter how you look at it, it clearly *is*. But it actually *feels* perfectly reasonable.'

'Really?' Joe said, whacking some bushes we were passing with a stick. 'Explain.'

I thought for a moment, trying to work out what I meant, because I wasn't that sure myself. 'I suppose I just mean that it feels nice to have someone in the house,' I said. 'I'm sleeping better, for some reason, knowing you're under the same roof.'

'You miss having Ant around, I suppose,' Joe said.

'No, no, it's not that,' I told him honestly. 'Things actually felt pretty stressful whenever Ant was in the house. His moods were so unpredictable . . . But with you, things just feel, I don't know . . . *easy*, I suppose. You're the perfect lodger, really, aren't you?'

'Yeah, I'm just such a great guy,' Joe said sarcastically. 'Perfect everything, me.'

'Well, you may joke,' I told him, 'but I actually think that's quite true.'

'Right,' Joe said. 'Well, thanks for the vote of confidence.' And then, as if the awkwardness of the moment, the sheer embarrassment of receiving a compliment, was too much for him, he chased off after Ben with his stick.

As I watched them racing through the trees, I thought about the truth of my statement, and felt frustration at the sensation that Joe hadn't really heard, or at any rate, hadn't *believed* me. Because the more I knew him, the more I was realising just what an amazing man he was. He was gentle and funny and kind. He was strong and nurturing and capable. And as far as I could see so far, he had no real faults at all. I wondered if Amy had any understanding of the gem of a man she was letting go.

Half-term came and went. Because the Whitby trip had been cancelled, Ben was now officially spending the week with Amy and Ant, but he kept turning up at ours instead. Amy and Ant were on a cleaning frenzy, by all accounts, and all he wanted to do was escape. Ben reported that Amy was 'furious' at how dirty Joe had left the place, something I rather doubted was true.

Dandy/Riley's preferences were seemingly the opposite – Ant kept dropping him off at ours, but as soon as Dandy could escape, he'd return to theirs, picking his way through the gardens. My suspicion was that he simply enjoyed annoying Ant.

Joe worked all week and continued to turn in pretty early, so I only really saw him at suppertime. But my glass of wine while he ate became a ritual, and our conversations became less stilted by the day.

The weather the following weekend was simply stunning. Though the air temperature was low enough to require big coats and scarves, the sky was an almost Mediterranean blue. A gentle wind chased wispy clouds across the sky.

On Sunday, Joe drove us all to Whitstable for fish and chips, stopping off on the way at a cashpoint. When he climbed back into the car, he handed me four hundred pounds in cash. I told him it was too much, and for a minute or so we fought. But he insisted it was still cheaper than the B&B he'd been intending to stay in, and as I could see he was never going to give in, I sighed and put the money in my purse.

As he drove to the seafront, I told him that he must tell me if there were any special foods he'd like me to cook.

'Not really,' he said. 'Your cooking's great.'

I laughed. 'Well, no one has ever said *that* before.'

'No?' Joe said. 'Why not? Your cooking's lovely.'

'Well, thank you, sir,' I said jokingly.

'But – and I don't want you to take this the wrong way . . .' Joe started.

'Oh God,' I said. 'I knew there had to be a *but*.'

'It's just, do you think you could cook a bit more?' Joe asked. 'I do know that I eat like a horse.'

'Not a horse,' Ben shouted from the rear. 'A *pig*. Mum always says you eat like a pig.'

'That's, um, a different thing,' Joe said, glancing at me and pulling a funny face.

I felt so embarrassed. I'd been serving him double the amount I ate myself, and it truly hadn't crossed my mind that might not be enough. 'God, Joe,' I said. 'I'm so sorry. Of course! Why didn't you say?'

'It's just the job's really physical,' he said. 'So I burn through a lot of calories.'

'Please, you don't have to justify yourself,' I said. 'I'm just shocked I didn't realise.'

'It's honestly not a problem,' Joe said. 'I've been filling up on bread and cheese, so it's fine. But if you could up the portion size a bit, that would be great.'

'Of course,' I said. 'No problem.' I was thinking about the quantity of bread and cheese we'd been getting through and felt annoyed at myself for not having guessed the reason. 'How did you manage on those ready meals?' I asked, after a moment. 'There's never enough in those even for me.'

'I was eating two.'

'*Three*,' Ben chipped in. 'He used to cook three for him and one for me.'

'Yeah,' Joe said, glancing at me and grinning lopsidedly. 'Sometimes it might have been three.'

'I'm so embarrassed,' I said, and it was true. My teeth were hurting just at the thought of how I'd watched him wiping his plate with bread every night. I turned to look out of the side window and pulled a face at my own reflection in the glass.

'Don't be.' Joe reached across and squeezed my knee, and this surprised me so much that I physically jumped.

'Oops,' Joe said. 'Sorry!'

'No, it's . . .' I said. *Fine?* I thought. *Nice? Lovely?* Because I couldn't think of anything appropriate, the sentence remained unfinished for a few long seconds. '. . . just me,' I said finally. 'I'm jumpy.'

That evening, we all watched a film on Netflix. It was a teen movie called *Lady Bird* that Lucy had been nagging me to watch.

Joe and Ben shared the big armchair, while I snuggled on the sofa with the girls. Though the film was surprisingly good, my attention strayed about halfway through. For ten minutes I thought not about the film, but about a series of images running through my mind's eye. In them, Ben and the girls were seated on the sofa, while Joe and I snuggled in the armchair together. The visualisation was surprisingly powerful, and I could imagine the feel of his body wrapped around me, picture the scent of his breath mingling with mine. By the time I snapped back into the room, I had beads of sweat pearling on my top lip.

'. . . actually cried a bit, there,' Joe said, once it was over.

I was surprised. Ant had never cried during a film, as far as I could recall, and if he had, he had certainly never owned up to it.

'Me too,' I said. 'It was lovely, wasn't it? Good choice, Lucy.'

Ben, who had dozed off on Joe's lap, stretched and linked his arms around his father's neck. 'I wish you could stay here for ever,' he said, through a yawn.

'I'm sorry, champ?' Joe said.

'Instead of going to live at Grandpa's,' Ben said. 'I wish you could just stay here.'

Joe cleared his throat and stood, scooping sleepy Ben up in his arms. 'The way the job's going, I might well just be here for ever,' he said. 'Come on. Time to get you back to the house of horrors.'

From the corner of my eye, I watched them exit the room, and a few minutes later I heard them leave by the front door.

I was feeling strangely emotional as I put Sarah to bed, but I couldn't work out why. The film had been quite moving in parts, so for a while I convinced myself that was the cause. How good we are at lying to ourselves! Well, I certainly am, at any rate.

Joe returned ten minutes later, while I was in the bathroom with Lucy. Getting her to brush her teeth was always something of a trial because she could never stop talking long enough to do it properly.

When I got downstairs, Joe was back in the armchair, watching a news channel.

'Are you really behind on your job?' I asked, and as I said it, I was hit by another wave of emotion and I suddenly understood that it came from my fear that he really would leave us in a week's time, mixed with hope that he might yet stay a bit longer.

'Yeah,' Joe said, turning his attention from the TV. 'This job we're doing out in Hersden's a real bitch. Half the wall came away with the cupboards, so we're having to rebuild all that first.'

'You know you can stay on longer,' I said. 'You can stay as long as you like.'

'I was gonna ask you about that, actually,' Joe said. 'You don't have another lodger lined up yet, do you?'

I shook my head. 'I've no plans to line one up, either,' I said.

'Having me has put you off for good, has it? I get that.'

I laughed. 'No, I really like having you here.' And there they were again, my almost-tears.

'Good,' Joe said. 'Ben seems to like me being here, anyway.'

'Well, it's convenient. It's almost next door.'

'Yeah, I guess,' Joe said. 'But I think it's more just the atmosphere, really.'

'The atmosphere?'

'Yeah, you run a very relaxed household, don't you?' Joe said. 'You're really easy-going.'

I laughed. 'That's like my supposed good cooking. No one's ever said that before, either.'

'Really?' Joe said. 'That surprises me. Maybe you've just been hanging out with the wrong people.'

Joe's deadline came and went. He handed me another four hundred pounds, and I increased the quantity of food that I cooked day by day until he seemed satisfied. He really did eat like a horse.

My moods were very up and down about it all. Some days – most of the time, in fact – I could convince myself that nothing was happening here. He was just a lodger, I told myself, and if other thoughts began to manifest, I'd arm-wrestle my mind back under control. Those thoughts – such *dangerous* thoughts – were still there, of course, lingering in the periphery of consciousness. But by staring steadfastly straight ahead, I could almost pretend they didn't exist.

From time to time, though, specifically if I'd had a drink, I'd lose my steely sense of self-control and let myself think about what it was like living with Joe. Because the truth of the matter was that it was wonderful. After years of living with someone who never understood – or even cared to understand – anything I tried to say, Joe, it turned out, 'got me'. He was interested in my views. He liked my cooking, he laughed at my jokes, and I at his. We both liked the seaside and walking in the forest. We both loved nineties Britpop and arty films but hated trashy TV. Joe encouraged me, almost daily, to think more deeply and to laugh louder, and in his company I couldn't help but do so. When I was with him, I could hear myself being funnier and sexier and more interesting, even to myself.

The fact of the matter was that Joe was heavenly. I could barely believe it had taken me so long to notice.

But Joe's qualities, Joe's beauty, too, weren't classical, I suppose. He wasn't flashily generous in the way Ant had been, and he didn't have chiselled features or perfect skin. His clothes weren't the elegant suits that made Ant stand out in a crowd, but faded jeans with ripped knees and dusty builders' boots. So, in a way, everything that was good about Joe fell outside my frame of reference. It was as if I'd been trained to look for the wrong things, and so had needed to learn how to think differently before I could see him. But here he was, grinning at me lopsidedly and scratching at the bristle of his beard. Here he was, hitching up his jeans unselfconsciously, and making me laugh by taking the mickey out of himself.

I began to imagine him staying for ever, though I couldn't come up with any scenario that could possibly make that happen. His wife was just down the road with my ex – that was the only thing that linked us. His things and his family were waiting for him in Whitby, after all, while at mine he was living out of a backpack. Every clue indicated that this was temporary, and yet, and yet . . . I just couldn't quite convince myself that's all it was.

Time and again, I'd push all of this from my mind, and, for a day or two, I'd be fine. But then I'd come into the lounge and see his son seated on the sofa with my girls as they waited for tonight's film to begin. Joe would be crouching down to light the fire, his builder's bum peeping over the top of his jeans, and he'd look up at me and give me that lopsided smile and say, 'I thought I'd light a fire. Make it cosy, like,' and my heart would start to ache all over again. Because not only would it have been hard for us to look more like a family, we didn't look like *any old* family, either. We looked like the family I'd always dreamed of. We looked like the family I'd never had.

Ben lived at ours almost all of the time. In fact, the only days he went with his mother were the days when Ant took the girls. If they were all doing something together – and quite often, it was something expensive that Ant had organised – Ben was happy to tag along.

I asked Joe one day why he thought Ben spent so little time with Amy. It seemed strange to me that he could get by without seeing more of his mother, and even stranger that she could accept it.

Joe shrugged, and smiled vaguely. 'I think he just prefers it here,' he said. 'I think we *all* just prefer it here.'

By the end of March, I was feeling quite febrile about it all. On every other two-week anniversary, Joe had asked if he could stay on well before he was due to leave. This time we'd reached the thirty-first of March, and he still hadn't said a word.

But the job he'd been working on was finished, this I knew – he'd gone over to pack up his tools that morning. So I was worried. Actually, I was more than worried, I was *terrified*.

I sat at the kitchen table all day, biting my nails and trying to imagine what might come next. Perhaps I should have said something, I thought. Maybe I should have given him some inkling about my feelings, and now I'd surely left it too late. But how can you tell your lodger you're . . .

I couldn't finish the sentence, even for myself. And was I? Was that really it? And if I named it, wouldn't I be simply opening myself up to a fresh new world of pain?

Perhaps Joe had merely been the first man to come along after Ant, I thought, trying to reason myself into a calmer state of mind. And that was indisputably true. Joe had *absolutely* been the first man to come along after Ant.

But then I thought of Joe's face, of his chunky body, and his thick hair, and the smile lines around his eyes, and couldn't help but smile myself. Because no, that wasn't it.

It was that Joe made me want to be a better version of myself. He noticed me, that was the thing. He really *saw* me. And that attention – something that had been missing my entire life – made me want to be wittier and kinder and cleverer. In a nutshell, being with Joe made me feel *alive*.

He got home extra early that day. It must have been about three, because I hadn't even left to meet the girls from school.

'All done?' I asked, on entering the kitchen. He was washing his hands at the sink.

'All done,' he said, shooting me a sideways smile. 'I thought I'd never finish. Jesus, that was a shitty job. Pardon my French.'

'You've got . . .' I said, raising a finger to my forehead and rubbing it, imagining how it would feel to be stroking Joe's hair instead. 'You've got paint, here . . .' I said. 'In your hair.'

'Oh,' he said, turning back to the sink, and washing his face with gusto.

'So what now?' I asked, as he dried his face on a tea towel.

'Um?' he asked, sounding fake, sounding as if he was pretending the subject was unexpected.

'What now?' I asked again. 'Have you decided on your next move yet?'

Joe dried his hands and threw the tea towel on to the countertop, and then picked it back up again to hang it from the rail. Finally, he turned his back to the sink and frowned at the floor for a moment before looking up at me. 'Yeah, I need to talk to you about that,' he said.

His partner, Joe-the-younger, had found more work, he explained. He'd been begging Joe to stay on.

'I see,' I said. 'And what have you decided?'

'Well, it's up to you, really,' Joe said. 'I, um, totally get it if you want me out.'

'I totally *don't* want you out,' I said. 'I love you being here, Joe. Really I do.' It was the closest I'd ever got to saying how I felt, but even though I'd managed to slip the word *love* in there, it was still so far from the truth.

Joe shrugged. 'I'm loving being here,' he said. 'And it's great for Ben, too. And the work just keeps coming in . . . So it would seem silly to walk away, you know?'

'It would,' I told him. 'It makes perfect sense.'

'But that's not it, really,' Joe said. 'I'm . . . um . . . I don't know how to say it, really. But I'm happy at the moment. I didn't expect that, not now, not with, you know, everything that's happened. But I am. This . . .' He gestured vaguely around the kitchen. 'It just works for me, you know?'

I nodded and blinked back tears. 'I do,' I said. 'I know exactly what you mean.'

'So I thought maybe we could . . . you know . . .' Joe stammered.

'Yes?' I asked. I gripped one hand with the other to stop it trembling.

'Maybe we could plan a bit longer term,' Joe said.

'That might be nice,' I told him. I winced at myself. Nice sounded so mealy-mouthed, after all.

'So . . . I thought . . . maybe, end of April. Or even May?' Joe said. 'See how it goes?'

'That would be lovely,' I said, both thrilled that he was staying and distraught that, even as he was announcing it, he was maintaining the temporary nature of his stay.

'Um, another thing is Easter,' Joe said.

'Easter?'

'Yeah. I have to go up to Dad's.'

'Oh,' I said. 'No problem. Do you want me to look after Ben or something?'

'No,' Joe said. 'No, that's not it. Ben's coming with me. He loves to see his grandad and everything, so . . .'

'Of course,' I said.

'No, it's just . . . well . . . I was wondering if, maybe . . . I mean, only if you fancy it . . . but I thought perhaps you might want to tag along?'

'Me?' I said.

Joe shrugged. 'Yeah. And the girls, of course. We could make it into a holiday kind of thing. Well, a break, anyway. What d'ya think?'

I chewed my bottom lip for a second and swallowed with difficulty. And then I made myself be brave. 'That would be lovely,' I said. 'I'd really, really like that.'

Even though I hadn't seen Kerry for years, and had been incredibly excited about the Easter trip she had tentatively planned, I phoned her that evening to reschedule.

'It suits me better, to be honest,' she said. 'I've been invited to a massive party on Lake Como by my DJ friend. It's going to be absolutely amazing and there are rumours that Clooney's going to be there.'

My sister's lack of disappointment made me laugh, and I strongly suspected that she would have cancelled me in favour of the party anyway.

◆ ◆ ◆

The run-up to Easter was such a strange, emotional no-man's-land, I really didn't know what to think.

In a way, of course, nothing had changed. Joe was still a paying lodger, vanishing to his room at ten thirty and still planning, in theory, his move north. But in another way, everything *had* changed as well, because he'd told me something quintessential: he was happy here; he *preferred* living here. And so did his son. I ran that conversation over and over in my head and wondered if it was unreasonable to let myself dream.

My moods swung back and forth, depending on whether I chose to concentrate on Joe-the-lodger, or Joe, the object of my desire. Suffice to say, I was terribly excited about the upcoming trip to Whitby.

Ant and Amy were living down the road by then, so when I passed their house I would see their two cars parked side by side and invariably imagine them indoors together. Sometimes, particularly when I was walking home after having taken the girls to school, I would take time to try to work out how I felt about it, but the only real conclusion I ever came to was that, like Joe, I didn't seem to care as much as I probably should.

Funnily enough, it was thinking about how Amy had treated Joe and Ben that gave rise to the strongest emotion – anger on their behalf. But if I wanted to temper it and calm myself down, I found that I could do so simply by remembering the fact that poor Amy was now living with Ant. *Because how could anyone ever choose that?* I wondered, even though, of course, I'd chosen exactly that myself.

Back home, I could analyse my feelings rather better, and I came to realise just how lonely I'd been. And I don't mean lonely after Ant left, either; I mean before, when we were still together. Because though being alone hadn't been easy, there is truly nothing that makes you feel more lonely, I now saw, than living with someone, spending your weekends and evenings with someone, who simply doesn't relate to you at all. Spending your time with a partner who doesn't even *like* you that much – a partner you don't have any respect for either – that, my friends, is what *real* loneliness feels like.

Ben was now at ours five nights a week. Only on Saturday nights and Sundays did he and the girls stay at *number 12*, as we now called it. It was Joe who'd started referring to it as *number 12*, no doubt because it was less painful than calling his old house *Amy's place*, or even worse, *Amy and Ant's*.

Once I'd managed to lure Dandy back home – by switching to an inordinately expensive brand of cat food – our house felt like a proper family nest. I'd sit in the middle of it all with the cat on my lap, knowing that Joe was reading in the conservatory and the three kids were playing upstairs, and I'd feel ecstatic about the benevolent buzz of it all. I'd imagine how sterile and awful things must seem down at number 12, and allow myself to feel smug.

On Easter weekend we changed our routine, and the children went to number 12 for Friday and Saturday, so that we could leave for Whitby on Easter Sunday morning.

In order to avoid Ant's wrath, I'd got into the habit of getting everyone ready with military precision, so I had to keep reminding myself that Joe was *not* Ant. 'We'll leave when we leave,' he told me, and I wandered through the house gathering stuff together, murmuring, 'We leave when we leave, we leave when we leave,' while still expecting to be told off.

'Can we stop on the way if we get hungry?' I asked him, when our paths crossed in the hallway.

'Of course,' Joe replied. 'I'm not gonna drive for five hours without a break, am I? We can stop any time you want.'

It was half past eleven by the time we'd bundled everyone out of the house, and it was after six when we got to Whitby. The journey had been entirely stress-free, had been fun even, with Joe and I chatting easily up front and the kids in the rear pulling faces at the occupants of other cars.

Joe's dad's place was pretty amazing. It was a four-storey Regency terrace, with three bedrooms on each of the upper floors. A faded plaque on the door said it had once been called The Waves, and an even more faded sign in the window still read *No Vacancies*.

While Joe's dad made a pot of tea, Emma showed us around the house.

The ground floor was quirky and comfortable, if a little shabby with wear, while on the first floor were Joe's dad's bedroom, study and junk room.

The second-floor bedrooms, which included my room, needed a coat of paint, but were otherwise perfectly functional.

As Joe had decorated Ben's top-floor room with a huge Spider-Man mural, that's where all three kids wanted to sleep, so we moved some mattresses around and left them there to play.

It was a surprisingly warm, sunny evening – *warmer than Corfu*, they'd said on the radio – so once we'd drunk our tea, we went for a walk along the seafront and then down to the beach so that the kids could run off all their excess energy. As Amy had once described Whitby as 'gritty', I was surprised just how nice it all was. It looked more like *pretty* to me.

On the way back we bought fish and chips for everyone from a takeaway, and these we ate in the kitchen, straight from the paper.

I loved the absence of fuss or formality – it really made me feel welcome.

Once the kids were in their top-floor bedroom – and I say *bedroom* rather than *beds* for a reason – Reg broke out the wine, Joe lit a not-really-necessary fire, and the four of us settled in the lounge.

Reg's manner was warm but detached – he somehow managed the perfect balance of being attentive but not overbearing – and just from having met him, I felt as if I knew Joe better than before. Reg seemed to be the key to understanding why Joe was the way he was.

Emma was talkative enough to fill in any awkward gaps, chatting about a food bank she volunteered at, the unlikely characters she met there, and a trip she'd once taken to Japan.

Eventually the conversation turned in my direction, and Reg asked how I *spent my days*. I thought that was such a lovely way to ask the question, so much less guilt-inducing than the usual 'What do you do?' or, even worse, 'What do you do *for a living*?' questions that had always given me so much trouble when I'd not been working.

I told him about my job at the farm shop, and said I liked to walk and read quite a lot, so we chatted for a while about books.

We were interrupted by a banging noise from upstairs, so Joe went off to see what the trouble was. 'They've discovered how bouncy those old sprung mattresses are,' he announced, on returning. 'The little buggers are using them as trampolines.'

'Like father, like son,' Reg commented wryly.

Joe pulled a face.

'Did you do that as well, you naughty boy?' I asked him, grinning.

'Guilty as charged,' he said. 'It's actually really good fun. You can try it tomorrow, if you want. They're only old beds, anyway.'

'So what's your philosophy on life, Heather?' Reg asked me out of the blue.

I sipped at my wine, stalling for time, and frowned. 'Oh,' I said. 'Gosh. I don't know.'

'Give her a break, Pops,' Joe said. 'She only just got here.'

'Oh, I don't mind,' I told him honestly. 'I'm just not sure that I have a philosophy.'

'Everybody's got one,' Reg said, 'for good or bad. It's just that some people never bother to put theirs into words.'

'So what's mine, then?' Joe asked his father.

'Be helpful to everyone,' Reg replied, without hesitation. 'That way, if you ever need their help, they'll be there for you. You believe in a kind of instant karma.'

'Oh!' Joe said, grinning. 'Yeah, OK. I don't mind that one too much.'

'And mine?' Emma asked.

'Yours is, *always tell the truth*,' Reg said. 'You're the truth teller, aren't you? You believe everyone needs to hear the truth. And you're right, by the way. They do.'

Emma laughed. 'That's actually pretty accurate,' she said.

'And Amy's?' Joe asked.

'Amy's?' Reg said. 'Really?'

'Yeah, I'm just wondering what you thought of her. We never talked about it, so . . .'

'I'm not sure that's really appropriate any more.'

'Oh, come on,' Emma told him. 'If the lad's asking, it's appropriate. I mean, I never met her, but I can't say I'm not intrigued. I've heard so many stories about her.'

'You see, *the truth teller*!' Reg said, pointing at Emma. 'You want everyone to tell the truth, all the time.'

'So?' Joe prompted. 'Go on. I'm genuinely interested.'

'OK, if you insist. I'd say it was something like, *if I keep busy enough, I won't realise how unhappy I am.*'

'Wow,' Joe said. 'Talk about hitting the nail on the head. Cheers, Dad.'

'Sorry, son,' Reg said. 'It's never easy being cuckolded, but you're well out of that particular relationship, believe me. Such a messed-up psyche . . . I'm not sure she'll ever sort herself out, that one.'

'Now he tells me . . .' Joe said.

But I wasn't really listening, because my attention was elsewhere. That word, I'd heard it before – I'd heard it *in a dream*. 'Sorry, what does that mean?' I asked. '*Cuckolded?*'

'I beg your pardon?' Reg said.

'It's just that word,' I said. 'I don't know it. I think I've heard it before, but I don't really know what it means.'

'*Cuckolded* is a very old-fashioned word for being cheated on,' Emma explained. 'My mother used to say it – I shan't tell you why . . . But I don't think anyone uses it much any more.'

'Cuckolded,' I repeated. 'So it's a verb?'

'Or an adjective. Or a noun. A person can be *a cuckold*,' Emma said.

'So am *I* a cuckold?' I asked, still trying to grasp the exact meaning of the word.

'Kind of,' Joe said. 'It's usually just used for guys, though. I became a cuckold over in Spain.'

'For women, it's *cuckquean*, I think,' Emma said.

'But it might be cool if we could change the subject?' Joe said.

'It was you that brought Amy up,' Emma pointed out.

But I wasn't listening any more. All I could think was, *Go with the cuckold*, over and over. Because I was sure that's what my mother had said. *Go with the cuckold.* All the hairs were standing up on my neck and beads of sweat were breaking out on my forehead. I could see the dream in my mind's eye with such clarity, it was if my mother was here with me now, standing in front of the fireplace. But of course her words couldn't have made any sense back then, because she'd spoken them long before my husband and Amy had made cuckolds of Joe and me.

'Me?' Reg was saying, when I eventually managed to tune back into the conversation.

'Yes, you,' Emma said. 'You're so good at analysing everyone else, but what about you? What's *your* philosophy?'

'Oh, trying to explain stuff, I suppose.'

'Trying to explain what, though?' Emma asked. 'Life? People? The universe?'

'Everything,' Reg replied, matter-of-factly. 'But people mainly, I suppose. People are far less upsetting if you try to work out the *whys*.'

'Example?' Joe asked.

'Well, the extreme example would have to be the serial killer,' Reg said.

'The serial killer?' I asked, a little horrified.

'There's a reason for everything,' Reg said. 'And there's even a reason why the serial killer kills. Or Hitler. Hitler's a good example, too. The extremes are helpful when thinking about these matters. You'd probably have to dig through every tiny detail of Hitler's childhood, or his genes, or his parents' upbringing, but there's a reason in there somewhere. Nothing happens without a cause.'

'Um, I'm not that sure I want to excuse Hitler, Dad,' Joe said.

'Ah, but no one's talking about excusing him, are they?' Reg said. 'Nothing could ever excuse the Third Reich. But understanding *why* things happen – well, that's useful. Because it means you can stop them happening all over again.'

By the time we decided to retire, my mind and body were buzzing. I was more than a little tipsy, it's true, but the revelation about my dream had left me electrified. After all, had my dream mother *really* predicted a relationship with Joe, years before I'd even met him? How could that even be possible? And if it was, what if she had been right? What if Joe really was my destiny?

On top of all of this, the conversation with Reg and Emma had been the most stimulating I'd had in years – *ever*, in fact. How wonderful it must have been to grow up in the midst of that kind of debate, I thought. Just throwing ideas out there and arguing about them for the fun of it. No wonder Joe was so thoughtful and wise and open.

We'd reached the second floor – my floor – and so Joe wished me goodnight. I hesitated for a moment, wondering if there was some way I could now tell him about the dream, if there was a way I could use that story to move things in the right direction. But even drunk, I couldn't bring myself to attempt it. So I just gave him a fingertip wave, wished him goodnight, and opened my bedroom door.

When I switched on the light, I gasped. The bed was covered with plaster where a chunk had fallen from the ceiling. I called Joe back down and he joined me in the doorway to survey the damage.

'Shit,' Joe whispered. 'Must have been the kids bouncing around upstairs.'

'Maybe I can just shake it off?' I said doubtfully. 'But is it safe, do you think? Or might the rest fall on me while I'm sleeping?'

We both peered up at the damaged ceiling. 'It might do, actually,' Joe said. 'I think we need to move you to another room.'

He crossed the landing and opened a door, but though the room's ceiling was intact there was no mattress on the bed. It was also icy cold in there.

'If you can—' I started.

Joe shushed me. 'Dad'll be mortified if he finds out,' he whispered. 'We'll tell him tomorrow, OK?'

I nodded. 'If you can just help me carry the mattress through?' I asked, speaking more quietly. 'I'll sleep in here.'

'Sure,' Joe said, glancing back towards my room. 'Unless you want . . .' He nodded his head sideways, strangely, as if perhaps stretching his neck. 'Never mind.'

'I'm sorry?'

'Nothing. Just being silly . . . too much of the old vino, I think.'

He started to move back towards my room then, clearly intending to begin moving the mattress, but I grabbed his arm and pulled him back. 'Unless what, Joe?' I asked. 'Please say what you were going to say.'

He scratched his chin. 'Nah,' he said. 'Better not. Let's just get this mattress moved.'

'But I do, Joe,' I said, risking everything. 'I *do* want to.'

He froze and squinted at me. 'Really?'

I nodded, and as I looked up at him, I could feel that I had tears forming. 'I really do,' I croaked.

He leaned in, pecked me on the cheek and then grabbed my hand to pull me up the stairs. 'Yay! Bedding situation sorted!' he said happily.

Other than that kiss, nothing actually happened that night. We really did simply share the bed. The situation had taken us both by surprise, I think, and by the time we got to Joe's room we were already feeling as embarrassed as we were excited. I was also hyperconscious that our three children were sleeping next door, and I don't doubt that Joe was too.

But when I woke up in the morning, Joe's heavy, hairy arm was draped across me, and I was able to bask in the sensation of being held for almost an hour before he woke up. I'd forgotten just how wonderful that could feel.

Eventually Joe stirred. He opened his eyes, yawned and said, 'Oh! Hello, you.' He then pecked me on the cheek again and surprised me by scrambling from the bed. I watched, bemused, as he hopped into his jeans and then, with no more than a wink, vanished from the room.

I luxuriated in the warm bed for a while, but then doubts began to gather, spoiling the moment. Because why *had* nothing happened? Sure, we hadn't wanted to make a noise, but we could have kissed. We could have cuddled . . . And why had Joe jumped from the bed and all but run from the room if it wasn't simply that he was embarrassed about the drunken mistake of having shared a bed?

We were crazily busy all day, and that busyness was useful as a distraction from my worries about Joe.

We cleared the fallen rubble and dust from the bedroom and then Joe went off in search of plaster, while I helped Emma cook a big brunch for everyone. As the DIY store was closed, Joe was back within ten minutes, but instead of helping us in the kitchen, he vanished upstairs to strum on his old guitar, which struck me as a bit out of character.

'So are you and Joe together?' Emma asked me, at one point.

I was in the process of chopping mushrooms, and as we'd been discussing what Whitby was like in summer, her question rather flummoxed me.

'You don't have to answer that,' she laughed, when I hesitated. 'I'm always getting into trouble for being too direct. It's just that there's a vibe about you two.'

'No . . . it's . . . um . . .' I stumbled. 'It's just that I don't know really,' I finally managed. 'I don't think so. Not in any proper way, anyway. We just share a house for the moment, that's all.'

'For the moment,' Emma repeated.

'Yes,' I said. I could feel myself blushing. 'I don't know.'

'But you'd like to?' Emma said.

It was my turn to laugh. 'Gosh, you are a bit direct, aren't you?'

'Well, you're right to be interested, anyway. That's all I wanted to say. From everything I've heard, he's quite the catch. That Amy doesn't know what she's given up.'

'Yes,' I said. 'That's the impression I'm getting, too.'

Emma crossed to the sink behind me, but as she passed by she paused and rested one hand on my shoulder. 'And don't worry,' she said. 'I won't say a word.'

'Good,' I said. 'Thank you.'

'Not even to Reg.'

'Especially not to Reg.'

She gave my shoulder a squeeze then, and saying, 'It can be our little secret,' continued on to the sink.

Eventually, once the table was set and everything was ready, Emma sent me to call everyone to the table. I found Reg in the lounge, reading, and the kids playing cricket in the back garden.

I called to Joe a few times, but when he didn't hear me, I trudged up the stairs to the top floor.

The door to his bedroom was closed, but behind it, I could hear him strumming a tune, stopping and starting as he corrected himself.

I stood for a while listening, until he managed a full verse without a mistake. His voice, as ever, was beautiful, but I didn't recognise the song:

If you could just see me / if you could just feel me / if you could just understand / all I am / for you.
We are really miracles / we are made of star-dust / and if you'd just touch my skin / feel me here / loving you.

A wave of warmth for him washed over me, but this quickly morphed to a sad realisation that he was probably thinking about Amy as he sang, and then embarrassment for having listened in to such a private moment. So I crept down a few stairs and approached once again, only more noisily this time. I rapped on the door until Joe invited me in.

He smiled up at me weakly, and I could see instantly that he was tearful.

'Nice song,' I said, sounding fake, even to myself. 'Who's that by, then?'

'Oh, no one,' Joe said. 'It's just a ditty.'

'One of yours?' I asked, and he nodded vaguely.

'It sounded good,' I said. Then before my emotions gave me away, I added, 'Um, brunch is ready. So I'd get your arse downstairs before it's all gone, if I were you.'

Throughout the meal I fixed a gentle smile on my face and tried, but failed, not to think about Joe writing songs for Amy. His feelings for her were doubtless the reason there hadn't been so much as a proper kiss, as well. If anything was ever going to happen between Joe and me, it certainly wasn't going to be for a very, very long time.

We arrived back home late on Monday evening, and by the time I got the girls to bed, both Joe and Ben had gone to their rooms.

The trip had officially been a success: we'd picnicked on the beach, played the slot machines, and visited Whitby Abbey. We'd eaten dribbling ice creams in Robin Hood's Bay and overall had been made so welcome that I'd actually felt quite tearful when we'd wished Emma and Reg goodbye.

But I'd had to hide my devastation about the fact that Joe was still visibly pining for Amy, so I felt quite relieved that he'd vanished so quickly to bed.

The next morning I was awoken by the children's shrieks but, because I could hear Joe was up, I let myself lie in. Due to the fact I'd been thinking about Joe all night long – specifically about the various bad omens from our trip north – I'd slept pretty badly.

I must have fallen asleep again, because suddenly the alarm clock read 11.32, and the house around me was silent. I got up, pulled on a dressing gown, and checked the kids' bedrooms. I peered out at the empty back garden.

Dandy wanted food, so I fed him, and then took my mug of tea out to the conservatory. I'd been there only a few minutes when Joe returned.

'Hello, you,' I said, looking up at him in the doorway. 'I was wondering where everyone was.'

'Good morning,' he said, smiling vaguely, either with pleasure at seeing me, or perhaps with embarrassment. 'I walked them round to number 12. I thought we could use a little space, so that we can have a chat.'

'Oh, of course,' I said, wondering what kind of chat this was going to be. 'Good idea.'

'Weird atmosphere round there, though,' Joe continued. 'I suspect there may be trouble in paradise.'

'Really? The kids are OK, though, aren't they?'

Joe shrugged and nodded. 'Amy's gone AWOL, apparently. But I left them in the garden with Ant. He seemed fine about it.'

'Right,' I said. 'OK, then.'

'Just let me make a brew, and we can talk,' Joe said. 'You want one?'

I raised my steaming mug and shook my head, then turned to look out at the sunlit back garden, while I listened to the sounds of Joe in the kitchen. He was whistling, so perhaps that was a good sign. Then again, don't people whistle when they're nervous, too?

I heard him fill the kettle and switch it on.

I needed to make the most of this moment, I decided. I could see myself being too shy to tell him how I really felt and regretting it for ever more. So I had to make sure that didn't happen.

Then again, hadn't I just learned that he still had strong feelings for Amy? So, in the light of my half-hearted declaration in Whitby, wasn't it more likely that he was going to say something awful like, 'I really like you a lot, but I'm still in love with my wife'?

And if he did say that, what option would I have but to say, 'Of course. That's fine'?

I realised that the kettle had boiled some time ago, but that I hadn't heard a sound after that. I put down my now empty mug and stood. I frowned and entered the kitchen. Steam was rising from the kettle. The room looked, for some reason, like a stage set. I crossed to the closed kitchen door, and as I reached for the handle, I felt a sense of unease. We didn't often close the kitchen door, and I wondered why it was shut now.

I opened it an inch, enough to hear that there were voices coming from the front door. Joe was talking quietly – discreetly, I suppose you could say – to someone on the doorstep. I moved silently along the hallway, and then peered around the corner to see who was there.

Fourteen

Amy

I'm sure you've worked this out – in fact, I'm sure *everyone* knew this from the get-go – but Ant was not the answer. I'm not even sure what the question was, but whatever it was, Ant was not the answer.

I'd suspected it almost as soon as we'd got back to England, I guess. Because to say that Ant was *difficult to live with* would be a whole new crazy kind of understatement.

He complained, constantly, about everything. He'd kick off about my shoes in the middle of the room, or my handbag on the table. He'd complain about a coat on a chair back or a saucepan in the sink. He liked his dinner between six thirty and seven, and serving up at seven fifteen was enough to put him into a sulk for the entire evening.

My coping strategy, to begin with, had been to lie to myself. The flat was much too small, I admitted. We were, it was true, on top of each other.

I'd invested so much in the relationship already that, like an old car you just keep throwing money at, I continued to invest everything in Ant.

Just like a car, I would fix him, I decided. Hadn't it been Ant himself who had said anything is possible, as long as you're determined enough?

So, for a while, fixing Ant became my project. I've always been a bit obsessive, throwing myself into this thing or that, and now my obsession was making Ant whole again.

I managed to avoid getting angry when he was being difficult (read: being an asshole) by telling myself I was gathering data for my project. I needed to work out what had made him the way he was, and then I'd study it and find a cure. But staying calm was getting harder as time went by.

I didn't like the way he treated me, and I didn't much like the way he treated Ben. He was always pretty good with the girls, it has to be said, and when he was with them I'd kid myself that I'd got him all wrong. But then we'd go to a restaurant and he'd be rude to the waiter, or we'd be shopping and he'd insult the cashier. Of all of Ant's quirks and foibles, which were many, I think that kind of embarrassment on his behalf, in public, was probably the hardest to bear.

After all, if someone's rude to you personally, there's a discussion to be had about just whose fault that might be. Maybe, just maybe, you're the one at fault. And if you witness your partner being rude to a friend or a colleague, then there's always the question of history. Because who knows what that person did to your beloved, a few days or even years ago? Who knows why your boyfriend has chosen to get his own back now?

But when you witness someone being mean to an absolute stranger, well, it's really hard to ignore. Because the only thing that kind of behaviour reveals is the nature of the person being mean. And as I'm not Heather – as, unlike Heather, I've never been anybody's doormat – we began to argue. And once we started arguing, we also stopped having sex.

Even then, I'd convince myself that our biggest problem was living in that flat. If we just had more space, then everything, just maybe, would be different.

But things got no better once we moved into the three-bedroom unit – in fact, if anything, they got worse. The flat needed to be sold soon, Ant reminded me. Not only was the place not ours, but it needed to be kept spotless for its new owners, who would only too soon be moving in.

When I looked around for the causes of Ant's personality disorder, my gaze settled quite naturally on his mother. Because a sadder character I have never met. Just a few minutes in Marge's presence was enough to make anyone feel depressed, and I couldn't even begin to imagine how he'd coped growing up.

If you've ever seen the cult movie *Barbarella*, you may remember that, in it, the city is built on an evil sea of green slime called the Matmos. The defining characteristic of the Matmos, as I recall, is that it absorbs positive thoughts and replaces them with negative ones.

When I told Marge that I was a yoga teacher, she said, 'Gosh, that's got to be a hard job to do as you get older, hasn't it? Do you think you'll be able to carry on?' If you pointed to a cute kid while you were out with her, she'd say, 'It's such a shame we ladies have the menopause, isn't it? Otherwise you and Ant could still have kids.' If you made Marge a lemon meringue pie, she'd say, 'Now, my mother used to make an incredible lemon meringue pie. Far better than anything I've ever tasted since. People really used to know how to cook in the old days.'

So in my mind, I started calling her *The Matmos*. Because if there was one thing Marge knew how to do, it was to replace positive thoughts with negative ones. And if The Matmos had damaged my boyfriend, and she indisputably had, then all I had to do was find an antidote.

But Ant did not want to be saved. As utterly broken as he was, what saved him – the defining characteristic that enabled him to continue to function in life – was his belief that he wasn't broken at all.

Actually, Ant's armour was even thicker than that. He didn't just think that he wasn't broken, he believed that he was the *only* person who wasn't. Ant knew best about everything; he was perfect in every way. And anyone who disagreed with him, about anything, ever, was just plain wrong.

Once I'd worked this out, I didn't hate him so much. If anything, I felt compassion. I could see, suddenly, how fragile his ego was. I totally got how merely admitting that others could teach him something new – admitting he didn't know best about everything – would bring the whole edifice crumbling to the ground. And I could imagine, in my more empathetic moments, just how terrifying that might feel for him.

As the months went by, it became clear that there was no pathway by which I could help him. He was impermeable to spirituality, religion and philosophy. Meditation, he said, was 'bullshit', and therapy was for 'fucked-up New York Jews'. Yoga he could just about cope with, but only because he saw it as a type of keep-fit. Actually, sometimes, when I headed off to a class, he'd ask me what time I'd be back from 'keep-fit'. I pretty soon gave up correcting him.

Even discussions about what effects Marge's single parenting might have had on him were shut down with anger or reproach. Because, of course, if Ant was perfect, then his upbringing must, by extrapolation, have been utterly perfect too.

By the time we moved back to the house in Chislet, I was pretty sure that our relationship was over. Sure, I wanted to give him one last chance – wanted to see how things might evolve in more comfortable and familiar surroundings. But mainly I just wanted to be in my own home so that I'd have the power to tell him to leave.

Back home, things were even worse.

Joe hadn't exactly left the place spotless, so for days Ant and I cleaned.

But there were stains on the walls that wouldn't go, and there were dents in the carpet where a table had once stood. There was mould deep in the joints around the bath, and the door of one of the kitchen units was wonky. This lopsided door demonstrated, Ant claimed, everything one needed to know about Joe.

For months, I'd forbidden myself from letting my thoughts reach their natural conclusion, but on that Easter Tuesday, everything changed.

Ant was busy hand-washing all of the plates from one of the cupboards, ranting freely about how rubbish 'Joe's' dishwasher was. Anything Ant didn't like about the house he defined as being 'Joe's'. Anything that didn't work properly was 'Joe's fault', too.

'I don't know how you ever put up with him,' he commented, and it was the final tug that made the veil slip.

I'd been in the process of cleaning the oven, but I now paused and looked up at him. I let myself hear what he was saying. I let myself see this stranger in my kitchen and accepted that I no longer found him attractive in any way.

I thought about Joe then, about how easy he'd been to live with, about how wonderful he'd always been with Ben. I thought about how clever and thoughtful and generous he was, how self-mocking, and modest, and open.

Without Ant even noticing, I walked to the hallway, grabbed my keys from the hall table and let myself out of the house.

I drove to Herne Bay seafront, where, feeling numb, I walked the full length of the beach.

It was a sunny day, but windy, and though the air temperature was low, there were mad British families with windbreaks doing their determined best to sunbathe.

At the far end of the beach, I sat down on the pebbles and rested my back against one of the wooden breakwaters.

Thinking about the situation I found myself in, I started to gently cry.

After a few minutes, I admitted to myself that I hadn't really *found myself* in this situation at all. I'd quite knowingly made it happen, and so, feeling angry at myself, I began to cry more freely.

Finally, I listed everything I'd lost – no, everything I'd *thrown away* – and the tears began to roll down my cheeks in snotty waves of misery.

Eventually, I pulled myself together and made my way back along the beach to the car. A couple of people looked at me strangely, and I wondered if my make-up had run, or whether I was simply exuding angst.

Back at the car, I understood, from looking in the mirror, that it was the former. I had horrific panda eyes. So I wiped off what I could of my excess, blurry eyeshadow and then started to drive home. I needed to tell Ant that it was over, and I needed to tell him right now.

But as I drove into Chislet, I realised that Ant could wait. There was something else far more urgent that I needed to do, someone else I desperately needed to see first: my husband – the father of my son.

Fifteen

Heather

Amy was sobbing so hard that it was impossible to hear what she was saying.

It seems ridiculous, looking back on it, but the first thought, my very first thought, was that she had killed him. I've watched too much American TV, perhaps, but I imagined her having smashed a vase across Ant's head – his body crumpled across the kitchen floor, blood leaking on to the tiles. It was a crazy idea, of course, and Joe didn't react like someone might on hearing news of a murder. Instead, he wrapped Amy in his arms.

I was still frozen, peering around the corner, a voyeur struggling to hear. But Joe's reassuring murmurs were too quiet and the only words I caught from Amy were '. . . all my fault'.

It crossed my mind that the kids were still at number 12 and I started to panic that one of them was hurt. Stepping into view, I asked what had happened. I thought, as I spoke, of Amy's parents, and wondered if one of them had died.

Joe turned to look back at me. He frowned and gestured with one hand that I should leave them alone, and I started to withdraw, but then paused. 'Just tell me,' I said. 'The kids. Are they OK?'

Joe glanced at me again, this time looking confused or maybe irritated. 'Uh?' he said, then, 'Yes, yes. The kids are fine, Heather. They're with Ant. But just . . . we need a minute here, OK?'

I returned to the kitchen and closed the door lazily. If you didn't push it hard it always popped back open half an inch, and today that seemed like a good thing.

I sat at the table and strained my ears, but all I could hear was the reassuring tone of Joe's voice over a series of incomprehensible whimpers from Amy.

They'd probably just had a row, I decided. But then why would she come running to Joe?

I raised a finger to my lips. I noticed that my heart was pounding in my ears. I stood, silently, and crept back towards the door so that I could eavesdrop more efficiently, but just as I got there I heard footsteps and had to scoot back to the other side of the kitchen.

Joe burst through the door and froze for a second, glaring at me. I tried to lean against the counter nonchalantly but felt sure I looked as guilty as a child. He lowered his gaze and stared at the floor for an instant, as if frowning at a stain, and then turned to swipe his keys from the worktop. 'I, um, need to go and have a talk with Amy,' he said. 'There's a bit of a crisis at number 12.'

'What sort of crisis?' I asked.

'Just . . . you know . . .' Joe said, turning and heading for the door.

'Joe!' I insisted. 'What sort of crisis?'

'Your ex,' he said, pausing but not looking back. 'Being a bit of a knob, apparently. You know.'

'Is that where you're going, then?' I asked. 'To number 12, to get the kids?'

'No,' he said, as he left the kitchen. From the hallway he called back, 'I'm taking her to the pub for a drink. I'll be back in a bit.'

I walked to the front room and watched as his pickup pulled out on to the lane. I stood for a few minutes staring unfocusedly at the front garden as I waited for my thoughts to crystallise. So, Ant was being a 'knob' and Amy had walked out, had she? Maybe she just wanted Joe's advice. Or *maybe* she just wanted Joe.

I covered my mouth with one hand and took a deep, juddering breath. We'd been so close this morning . . . We'd been about to declare our love for each other, hadn't we?

But maybe we hadn't. Perhaps I had got that completely wrong. Because, what if Joe had already been speaking to Amy? What if they'd already decided to get back together, to give things another try? Perhaps *that* was why nothing had happened in Whitby. Perhaps that was why he'd wanted to talk to me.

I snorted sourly and shook my head. After all, wouldn't that just be typical? Wasn't life always exactly that way, letting you glimpse what you wanted only to systematically rip it away?

Tears were forming, but I pinched the bridge of my nose and willed them to stay put. I walked through to the kitchen and switched the kettle on. I stroked Dandy, who, unaware of all the angst, rolled over so that I could tickle his tummy, and I disliked him quite intensely in that moment for not understanding me better.

I moved to the conservatory and picked up an unidentifiable object that Sarah had made out of Lego and then put it down again.

I stared out at the back garden. It was a sunny day and it looked pretty out there. It crossed my mind that if Amy and Joe got back together, then Ant would be homeless. Perhaps I'd have to take *him* in as a lodger. The house was in his name, after all, so maybe I wouldn't even have a choice. And if that happened, perhaps I'd find myself right back in my old life.

I laughed manically at the idea that we could all find ourselves back exactly the way things were before, as if we'd just swapped husbands 'on loan' for a while. As if the nightmare I believed I'd woken up from had turned out, in fact, to be reality, while the time I'd spent with Joe was the dream. I thought about dreams and about my mother. I thought about how strange the word *cuckold* was.

I shook my head vigorously to dispel this latest idea. I would *not* go back. I would not be powerless in all of this. And if Ant did move back in, then I'd simply have to move out. I didn't know where I could go, but I'd leave, and I'd take the girls with me. I pictured the three of us walking down a dark street, dragging our suitcases behind us, like some dreadful image from the Blitz.

I returned to the kitchen and made coffee. I sat at the table nursing my mug, tapping my fingernails against the china and picturing Joe gesturing at me to leave him alone with his wife. I imagined him in the pub with Amy and thought, *How cosy!* and started to feel properly angry.

So, they'd gone off to decide their future, had they? Only in doing so, they were also deciding mine. I shook my head and sighed again. I bit my lip and scrunched up my face to prevent another bout of tears. I tapped one foot nervously on the floor. The tension of just sitting here was almost unbearable. And then suddenly, it really *was* unbearable, so I stood, almost knocking the chair over in the process. I pulled on some clothes, grabbed a coat from the peg and strode decisively to the front door.

Amy's car was still parked in our driveway and I childishly imagined keying it as I left. There was very little traffic on the lane, and as I passed by number 12 I could hear playful shrieks coming from the garden. I considered grabbing the girls and simply returning home, but, *no*, if Joe and Amy were talking about their options, then he at least needed to know how I felt.

Who was I kidding? I thought, as I marched on towards the pub. *As if I could somehow win out against Amy!* I thought of Amy's figure, her long blonde hair, and decided I hated her.

It took me ten minutes to get to The Gate. The car park was busy, but I spotted Joe's pickup parked down a side street.

I weaved my way through the cars and the beer garden to the pub. Once inside, I scanned the room, but there was no sign of them, so I made my way to the lounge bar, only to find that they weren't in there, either.

I stepped back outside and checked out the garden again. Happy families smiling and laughing in the sunshine. But still no sign of Amy and Joe.

I was just considering giving up when I heard a woman's voice – Amy's voice say, 'Of course I can change, Joe. Anyone can change if they really want to.'

I moved to the edge of the building, towards the direction the sound was coming from, and peered around the corner. They were seated side by side on the ground, their backs to the wall. Joe was smoking a cigarette, which surprised me. I had never once seen him smoke.

I ducked back out of sight and waited to find out if they had spotted me, but they simply continued to talk. Though I was out of sight, I could hear every word. I could even hear the sound of Joe taking a drag on his cigarette.

I almost walked away at that point. Listening in seemed unreasonable, and I had no idea what I wanted to say to them anyway. But then I heard Amy say, 'Look, I know I've been stupid, Joe. I know I've fucked up big time. And I'm admitting it all. That's got to count for something, hasn't it?'

I suddenly couldn't leave until I'd heard Joe's reply.

'Sure,' Joe said. 'Of course it does.'

'We're a *family*, Joe,' Amy said. 'We have a son. Surely you don't want to destroy that?'

'*Me* destroy it?' he said. 'Jesus, Amy.'

'No, no, that's not what I mean,' she said, sounding manic, sounding excited almost. 'I know it's all my fault. I've said that. I've admitted it. But I've come to my senses, Joe. I see everything clearly now, and I love you. You know I do. I want my family back, Joe. I want *you* back.'

I started to cry at that point – silent tears streaming down my cheeks. I fumbled in my pocket for a tissue.

'I get that, Amy,' Joe said. 'I do.'

'And don't tell me you don't love me,' Amy said. 'Because if you do, I won't believe you. I *know* you love me, Joe.'

'I . . .' Joe said.

'I've been hell to live with, Joe, I get that,' Amy said. 'It's . . . it's . . . like, almost a kind of mental illness with me. But I'll heal. I promise you, I'll sort myself out this time. I'll get some therapy. I'll get *proper* therapy, too, not the new-age stuff you hate. I'll be better this time around. We can make this work, I know we can.'

'Yeah . . .' Joe said. 'I hear you . . .'

'Please, Joe,' Amy said. 'Just say *yes*. You have to say *yes*. For me, for us, for *Ben*.'

There was a pause then – a long few seconds during which I held my breath.

'Amy, I love you,' Joe said finally. 'I do.'

'Oh, thank God,' Amy said, and I heard her kiss him.

A fresh round of tears started to cascade down my cheeks. I steadied myself with one hand against the wall.

'I love you,' Joe said. 'I always have, and I always will, Ame.'

I remembered the song he'd written for her then, and understood that I'd been right. I'd been dreaming to think that there was some kind of magic between Joe and me. Of course I had!

Just the idea that someone as ordinary as myself could snag a man like Joe – even the idea seemed absurd. I felt worthless and idiotic for ever having imagined otherwise.

I turned to leave, but just as I did so, Joe spoke again.

'It's just too late, Amy,' he said. 'That's the thing. It's done. That's what you're not getting.'

I gasped and leaned back against the wall for support.

'What do you mean, it's *too late*? What does that even mean?' Amy asked.

'It means there was a time,' Joe explained calmly, 'when I would have said *yes*. But not now. Not any more.'

'But why not?' Amy asked. 'I mean, you say you love me, so why not? I don't get it. Why not let yourself be happy?'

'But I *am* happy,' Joe said. 'That's the thing.'

'You're happy,' Amy repeated flatly. Then, 'How can you be happy, Joe?'

'I don't know, but I am.'

'And when did it suddenly become too late, anyway? You don't spend fifteen years with someone and decide overnight that it's too late to save the relationship. That doesn't make any sense.'

'Only it does to me.'

'But since when, Joe? Explain it to me.'

'Since I realised that I don't want all that drama in my life any more.'

'*Drama*,' Amy repeated.

'Yes, *drama*. It was hell living with you, Ame. And I didn't realise it for ages. But since I moved out, I see it all much more clearly.'

'Since you started living alone, you mean? You seriously want me to believe that you're happier alone than when we were a family?'

'No, since I moved in with Heather,' he said.

'With *Heather*?' Amy repeated.

'Yes. I think I'm falling in love with her, actually.'

'With *Heather*?' Amy said again.

'Yeah. She's the person I want to be with,' Joe said. 'I'm sorry, but . . . I don't know what to say. That's just the way it is. It's a surprise to me, too.'

'You cannot be serious,' Amy said, laughing bitterly.

'She's amazing,' Joe said softly. 'I know how . . . unassuming she seems, and everything. But she's one of – no, actually, she's *the* kindest soul I've ever met.'

Tears were still rolling down my cheeks and there was a physical pain in my heart as well. I wondered if I was going to maybe have a heart attack and die before I even got a chance at living this thing I'd barely let myself dream of.

'I don't believe you,' Amy said. She'd pulled herself together and sounded incredulous instead of upset. 'Do you have any idea how crazy that sounds?'

'Maybe it is,' Joe said. 'Maybe I am. Time will tell, I guess.'

'You'll never have what we had,' Amy said. 'Not with her. You know that, right?'

'Yeah,' Joe said. 'Yeah, I do. But that's kind of the whole point, isn't it? I don't *want* what we had, Ame. Living with Heather is so easy, and fun, and drama-free. It's kind. We're kind to each other. All the time. And that changes everything. It's made me realise just how miserable what *we* had was.'

'We were together for nearly fifteen years, Joe. How can you even compare?'

'It's just, this thing,' Joe said. 'This thing with Heather. These last few months . . . Well, they're the closest thing I've ever found to whatever it is that I want.'

I heard movement then, the sound of Amy standing – heels on tarmac. 'I'm trying really hard, here, but I just don't believe you,' she said.

'That's OK,' Joe told her calmly. 'I don't need you to believe me. Actually, I don't really care if you believe me or not, Amy. What you think makes no difference to me any more.'

'This isn't you, Joe,' Amy said. 'I don't even recognise you.'

'It's like you said in your email, Ame. I love you as a friend. I love you like family. But there's no *way* I want to live with you again. All that Mungaro and Pure Being bollocks, all the crystals and laying on of hands and . . . whatever . . . There was so much bullshit that I can't even remember it all. And you were *never* happy, despite any of it. Actually, you were a pain in the arse to live with, Ame, and if you must know, the truth is that I feel lucky to have got out when I did.'

'Lucky to have gotten out?!' Amy gasped.

'Well, yeah. I'm sorry, but that's how it feels to me. In retrospect, living with you was a horror story. It took all my energy just to put up with all your shit. You're a nightmare, Amy – a bloody nightmare!'

There was the sound of a slap, then. The short, sharp snap of skin on skin. 'Just . . . fuck you, Joe!' Amy spat. 'I mean, *really.* Fuck you!'

As she marched by, I turned to face the other way, and she didn't glance in my direction. I was feeling faint and my knees had gone weak, so I perched on the edge of a windowsill.

It was about a minute before Joe stepped into view, and I cried the whole time. He'd taken the time to finish his cigarette, I think, and as he walked past me he was scrunching the butt up between his fingers with one hand and caressing his reddening cheek with the other.

When I called his name, he spun on one foot and stared at me, his expression shifting from shock, to recognition, then finally to that beautiful, gentle smile of his. 'Heather,' he said simply.

I began to weep again, which surprised me. I'd thought I was all out of tears.

'Did you hear?' he asked, stepping towards me. 'Did you hear *all* of that?' He wrapped me in his arms and I pressed my face into his thick jumper, taking in the musky scent of him.

'Did you?' he asked again, while rubbing my back. I nodded in silent reply.

'Good,' he said. 'I'm glad. I've been struggling to tell you, but now you know.'

We stood like that for a few minutes, until a waiter passed by with a tray of empty glasses, prompting Joe to release me from his embrace.

It was then that he took my hand, and it was the first time we'd ever held hands. 'Let's go home, shall we?' he said.

'Home?' I repeated, because I liked the sound of that word.

'Yeah, *home*,' he said. 'Come on.'

When we got back, Amy's car was still in the drive, so I braced myself for a face-to-face confrontation. Instead, we found Ant indoors. He'd walked the three kids back to ours and let himself in with his key.

'I made myself a cuppa while I was waiting,' he called out, from the kitchen. 'I hope you don't mind?' As an afterthought, he muttered, 'Huh . . . not sure why I'm apologising.'

'It's fine,' I told him from the staircase. I climbed a few steps so that he wouldn't see what a mess I looked. I wondered why on earth he was here. Could this be him moving back in, already?

'Hey, Joe,' Ant said, as he entered the kitchen. 'I had to bring them back, I'm afraid. They're in the garden. Sorry about that, mate, but Amy wants to talk or something. She seems to be in a bit of a state, so I'm gonna drive her car back and I'll, um, let you know if I can have them later.'

'No, it's OK,' Joe said. 'Just leave them here with us. We're fine now, aren't we, Heather?'

'Totally fine,' I said, still speaking from the staircase. 'But you should probably get back home to Amy. I'd like to be alone with Joe, if you don't mind.'

'Women!' Ant said to Joe. 'Must be a full moon or something. Good luck.'

Once he'd left, I continued to the bathroom to wash my face.

When I got back downstairs, Joe was seated in the conservatory, watching the kids through the open door. Outside, in the sunshine, Ben was playing with a paper plane, while Lucy was dragging Dandy around.

'Gently with him,' I called out. 'He's old!'

'So how are you doing?' Joe asked, looking up at me.

I turned back to face him and smiled gently. 'I'm OK,' I said.

'OK?' he repeated. 'I was hoping for a bit more than OK. Unless you don't feel the same way?'

I swallowed with difficulty. 'It's just that I have a question for you,' I said. 'There's something I need to know. Something that's been eating away at me.'

Joe frowned at me and straightened in his seat. 'Go on,' he said.

'That song you wrote,' I said. 'For Amy. How long ago did you write it?'

Still frowning, Joe asked, 'I don't . . . which song?'

'The one you were playing in Whitby. *If you could just feel me / If you could just touch me.* That one.'

'Oh,' Joe said. 'Oh, right. You heard that then, did you?'

I nodded. 'Sorry,' I said. 'But yes, I kind of did. So, when did you write it?'

Joe shrugged. 'This is kind of embarrassing,' he said.

349

'I'm sure,' I said. 'Tell me anyway. I think I need to know.'

'Well, the thing is, I actually . . . um . . . Well, I wrote it there and then. I came up with it that morning. Like I said, it was just a ditty.'

'I see,' I said, my heart sinking. 'So the feelings, they were fresh. Even that recently.'

'But the thing is, I didn't write it for Amy,' he said. 'I didn't write it for anyone, really.'

'You didn't?'

'Actually, that's a lie,' Joe said. 'If I was thinking about anyone, well . . . that would have been you.'

'Me?'

Joe laughed then. 'Oh, come on, Heather!' he said. 'We'd just shared a bed for the first time ever. Of course it was about you.'

I started to cry, then – silly, happy tears – because once again, I'd been stupid and got it all wrong, only this time, that was *good* news.

Joe stood and wrapped me in his arms. 'I can't believe you thought that was about Amy,' he said softly. 'Jesus.'

I allowed myself to be hugged for a few minutes, and then unexpectedly, even to me, I said, 'Is this real, Joe?' The words came from nowhere.

He leaned back far enough to focus on me and looked confused, so I added, 'I'm scared. I need to hear you tell me that this, you, *us*, that it's real?'

He grinned broadly and laughed. 'Yeah, it's real,' he said. 'Can't you tell?'

'No,' I said. 'I don't think I can.'

'Well, it is,' he said. 'It is for me, anyway.'

'It is for me, too,' I said.

'It's a shame the kids are here, though.'

'Why's it a shame?' I asked. His comment had confused me.

He grinned at me lasciviously and winked. 'Let's just say that if they weren't here, I could show you just how real it is.'

'Oh!' I said, breaking into a silly grin and, I suspect, blushing. 'Oh, of course.' I let myself imagine the scene and wished that the kids were elsewhere too.

Joe shrugged. 'Oh well,' he said. 'I guess there's a time and a place for everything.'

'I think they might need an early night tonight,' I said softly.

Joe winked at me. 'Yeah,' he said. 'I think I might too. Way too much excitement for one day.'

Epilogue
Heather

It's a beautiful July morning in Whitby, and we are busy painting the hall. I always hated saying 'we' when I was with Ant. The concept of 'we' always made me feel a bit nauseous, but these days, I revel in it.

Now Reg has moved out to live at Emma's place – a seafront bungalow on the far side of town – we're on a frantic drive to renovate. In our more optimistic moments, we discuss reopening to paying guests by August. Running The Waves is going to be my new career, and I'm as excited about it as I've ever been about anything. Encouraged by Joe, I've even started driving lessons again, and as they're going pretty well I'll soon be able to drive out for supplies and pick people up at the station and what have you. Imagine that!

At the top of a ladder, above me, Joe is whistling while he paints. My job is to sand the skirting boards, a task Joe insists he can't bear.

From upstairs I can hear the sound of gunfire, so no doubt Ben and Lucy are waging war on the PlayStation. I'll kick them off it pretty soon and force them outdoors into the sunshine.

A drip of paint lands on my arm, so I look up at Joe and shout, 'Oi, you!'

'Sorry,' he says. 'But if you will insist on working right beneath me . . .'

'This is the last bit,' I tell him. 'I can't work anywhere else.' Then, naughtily, I add, 'Anyway, maybe I like being beneath you.'

'Yeah,' Joe says, with a snort. 'Sounds about right.'

I'm so happy here, sanding away – so happy, here in this house, with my man above me sloshing paint around. I remember all those dark days living with Ant and think that they would have been so much easier to bear if I'd just known that so much happiness was coming my way.

'I'm pretty much done here, actually,' I tell Joe. I give a final, frantic rub at a bump in the old paintwork, and then edge back and stand to admire our handiwork. 'It's so much brighter,' I declare. 'It's going to look bloody gorgeous.'

'Hello!' a voice says, and I turn to see Amy standing in the porch. We've left the front door open because of the fumes, so we've not had a second of warning.

'Christ!' Joe says, from above. 'She lives!'

'Indeed,' Amy says, stepping forward. 'Of course, I could say, "Christ! You've moved!"'

'I, um, just need to finish this last tiny bit,' Joe tells her, brandishing the paint roller. 'And then I'll be with you, OK?'

'Come through,' I tell Amy. 'I'll make you a cup of tea.'

As I lead the way through to the kitchen, I'm feeling stressed. I wish Joe would hurry up and join us. Amy's mental health hasn't been all that good since her split with Ant, and if she wants to discuss the rights and wrongs of our move north, then I'd really prefer she did that with Joe.

'So, normal tea, or something herbal?' I ask her, peering into a cupboard.

'Herbal would be better if you have it,' Amy says. 'Or green tea, maybe?'

'I've got this,' I say, showing her a box of vervain. It's supposed to calm people down.

'That'd be great,' she says. She's moving around the kitchen behind me, and it's making me a bit nervous. I'm scared, I think, that she's going to launch a surprise attack. 'So, you've moved,' she says again. 'Ant says it's permanent, too. I had no idea.'

'Well, we had to really,' I tell her, avoiding eye contact by fiddling with the kettle. 'Ant wanted the house back, so . . .'

'He didn't kick you out, did he?' Amy asks. 'Because I wouldn't have thought he had the right.'

'No, we did more of a deal, really,' I tell her. 'He sort of bought me out – well, a bit. We needed some money to do this place up, so . . .'

'And he's OK about the girls living so far away, is he?' Amy asks, and I realise we're going to discuss Ben being so far away from Amy through the proxy of Ant and the girls.

'Well, they have to live somewhere, and it was part of the deal,' I tell her. 'He couldn't have them during term time anyway. Not with working and everything, so this makes sense. He's going to take them from time to time during school holidays. He's taking them next week, actually. Joe and I are going to Rome. He was taking all three, but now you—'

'To visit your sister?' Amy asks, interrupting me. 'She lives there, right?'

'That's it,' I tell her. 'I've never been before, so that's really quite exciting.'

'He *is* here, isn't he?' Amy asks, suddenly, urgently.

'Ben?' I say. 'Yes, of course. He's upstairs playing video games with Lucy. Do you want me to get him?'

'In a bit,' Amy says. 'I'd like to take him out for lunch, if I can.'

'Of course,' I say. 'He's your son.'

'Yes!' Amy says pointedly. 'Yes, he is!'

I'm just about to launch into a defence of the fact that we have Ben here with us – perhaps even to point out that, having checked herself into a psychiatric ward, it's a damn good job we *do* have him with us – when, thankfully, Joe appears.

He crosses to the sink and starts washing his roller. 'Well, that's done,' he tells me. Then, turning to Amy, he adds, 'I didn't know you were coming. You're lucky we were here. We're off to Rome next week. Another few days and you would have missed us.'

'Yes,' Amy says. 'Heather just said.'

'You could have called,' Joe says. 'My number's still the same.'

'Yeah, so's mine,' Amy says. 'You could have called to tell me you were taking my son to the other end of the country.'

'*Our* son,' Joe says.

'I'll, um, leave you two to have a chat,' I murmur, handing Amy her drink and heading towards the door.

But Joe frowns at me and says, 'No, stay. Please.' So I swallow and return to the kitchen table, where I tuck myself into the corner, hoping they'll simply forget that I'm there.

'So, look, Ame,' Joe says. 'We *had* to move, OK? Ant wanted the house back. We didn't have anywhere to live.'

'No, I get that, Joe,' Amy says, sounding more reasonable. 'But, you know, maybe a phone call or something? It was a bit of a shock to come home to an empty house.'

'You were in a . . .' Joe says, and I suspect from the fact that he interrupts himself that he was about to say something unfortunate like *mental hospital* or even *loony bin*.

'You were in that clinic,' I interject, hoping to help him out.

'Exactly,' Joe says. 'It hardly seemed appropriate to worry you about all of this, not when you were in the middle of having a breakdown. As for coming home to an empty house, what were we supposed to do? Leave Ben there, alone, waiting for you?'

'It didn't seem *appropriate*?' Amy says. 'Christ, Joe! He's my son.'

'Our son,' Joe says again. 'And you're not listening, Amy. I *had no choice*. Neither I nor Ben had anywhere to live.'

'You could have lived at mine,' Amy says. 'You know full well you could have lived at mine.'

'Yours,' Joe says.

'Ours, the house, whatever.'

'Yeah, but you said *yours*,' Joe says. 'Which, if you think about it for a bit, is exactly why I couldn't stay there.'

'Oh, now you're just being argumentative,' Amy says.

'I'm not,' Joe tells her. 'I'm really not. I'm just explaining how things were. You can't just fuck off to Switzerland for six weeks and expect everything to stay in stasis.'

'I didn't *fuck off* to Switzerland,' Amy says.

'Only you kind of did.'

'I was *in hospital*, Joe.'

'Yes, you were. And if you try really hard, I think you can understand that it didn't seem a good idea to burden you with the fact that neither Ben, nor I, nor Heather had anywhere to live.'

'I . . .'

'Please, just take a breath and try to understand,' Joe says.

And surprisingly, Amy does just that. She stares into the middle distance for a moment, takes a deep breath, and finally sighs and sips at her drink. 'OK,' she says. 'OK, look, I get that. I do. But what happens now, Joe? I want my son back.'

'Our son,' Joe says, for the third time.

'Christ, OK, *our* son!'

'I'm not sparring with you,' Joe says. 'He is our son. And we both need time with him. And he needs time with both of us. And I guess what needs to happen is that we talk about it like adults and decide. But you know . . . you didn't give me a great deal of choice, Ame. I just want you to understand. We did the best we could.'

'We really did,' I add. 'There weren't a whole lot of other options.'

Amy nods at me. 'OK,' she says. 'OK. Fine.'

The sound of hammering footsteps descending the stairs reaches our ears, and then Ben appears in the kitchen doorway. 'Mum!' he says. 'You're out!' He runs to Amy and lets her sweep him up in her arms.

'I am!' she tells him. 'They finally agreed to let me loose on the world.'

'Are you better?' he asks. 'Or are you still mad?' And because he's only nine his bluntness just sounds like honesty.

'I am much better,' Amy says. Then, 'Mad, indeed . . . Huh!'

'Not from me,' Joe says, raising his palms.

'No, that didn't come from me, either,' I say.

They head out just before twelve, leaving Joe and me alone with the girls.

'So what now, Batman?' I ask him. 'Do you have a plan?'

Joe, who is perched on the garden wall just beyond the open kitchen door, replies, 'Well, I need to go and get some paint for in here.'

'You know exactly what I mean,' I say, smiling at him. 'A plan about *Ben*.'

He runs one hand across his face like a flannel and sighs. 'Well, I guess it has to be the same deal as with Ant,' he says. 'School holidays. As much access as she wants. But school holidays only.'

'As much access as Ben wants, too,' I point out.

'Yeah,' Joe says. 'Yes, it's going to have to be a sort of multilateral peace deal, isn't it?'

'And if she says *no*?' I ask. 'If she wants him in term time?'

Joe's eyebrow twitches. 'Do you think she might?'

'No, no, I don't,' I tell him. 'But if she does, then I think we need a plan.'

'Then we let Ben choose, I guess,' he says. 'He's nine. He's old enough to say what he wants.'

We call the girls downstairs and eat sandwiches in the garden.

'Is Amy going to take Ben for good?' Lucy asks, once I've explained why he isn't present.

'No,' I tell her. 'No, she's definitely not going to do that.'

'Is he still coming with us to Daddy's next week?' Sarah asks.

'No, I expect he'll go and stay with his mum,' Joe tells her. 'But it's just down the road from your dad's, isn't it? So maybe you'll still get to see each other.'

'I hope we can still use the pool,' Lucy says.

'Are *you* going to go and live with Amy again?' Sarah asks Joe, channelling my most irrational fear. In a way, I'm glad she's asked the question, not because I don't know the answer, but because hearing him answer it reassures me.

'No,' Joe says, sounding definitive. 'No, we're a family now, aren't we?'

'Good,' Sarah replies cutely. 'I like playing families with you.'

'We're not *playing* families,' I tell her. 'We really *are* a family.' Just saying it makes me feel a glow inside and I glance at Joe, hoping to catch his eye, but he's busy tossing the salad.

'Oh, OK,' Sarah says with a shrug. 'Even better.'

Amy

It was my mother's death that did it. That's what sent me over the edge.

I'd been doing fine, following Ant's departure. Well, I say *fine*, but that's probably overstating things somewhat. I was, I'll admit, feeling angry, sad, lonely, and from time to time quite severely depressed. But I was still functioning, just about. I was eating and cooking and working. All things considered, that didn't seem too bad.

Ant had left without argument, and though that had clearly been what I wanted, his easy acceptance, his, 'Oh, really? OK. Fine,' had also been a fresh source of trauma. Because how could I ever have let myself believe in *that* relationship? I wondered. How on earth could I have got things so very wrong? When you fuck up *that* badly in life, it makes you doubt your judgement about everything else as well.

On the third of May, I got the call. Mum had died in her sleep, the warden informed me. She'd slipped 'peacefully from this world'.

Even then, I managed to hold it together. I emailed Dad to tell him. I arranged the death certificate and drove out to Ashford to book a funeral.

Only three people attended: myself, my friend Wanda, and an old lady called Clare.

Afterwards, as we were leaving, she came up to speak to me. 'She's in a better place,' she said. 'Such a troubled soul, your mother.'

'Yes,' I agreed. 'She was.'

'You're OK, though, are you?' she asked, rather intensely.

I frowned and leaned towards her, unsure if I'd understood her meaning correctly.

'It's just . . . these things do tend to run in the family,' she said.

'You know that's not true,' Wanda told me, as I was driving her back to her flat.

'What isn't?' I asked. I'd been thinking about the cavernous silence of the house back in Chislet, and was wondering if I could stay at Wanda's for the night.

'That it runs in families,' she said. 'You are fine. You know that, right?'

But neither of those things was true. That was what I knew. These things *do* tend to run in families. And I definitely wasn't *fine*.

Back home, I went to see my GP. He prescribed benzos and put me on a waiting list to talk to a counsellor. But as the first available appointment was in September, I could barely see the point.

By the end of May I was falling apart. I felt broken, but, worse, believed that I now understood that I had *always* been broken. And from my fresh viewpoint of broken-ness, it struck me as inevitable that I would finish my days like my mother. Unless, that was, I got proper help. But I was terrified that returning to my GP would lead to my waking up in *One Flew Over the Cuckoo's Nest* – with Nurse Ratched dishing out the pills.

Wanda suggested a clinic in Switzerland she'd heard of, but though it looked to be as far from the Cuckoo's Nest as a clinic could possibly be, the prices were absolutely astronomical. It was impossible, I told myself: selling my house would barely cover the cost of a course of treatment. But though I tried to resist, I kept being drawn to the dreamy images on their website, photos of smiling, happy people who looked somehow like better versions of me.

My father coughed up the cash without argument. He was old, I guess, not to mention obscenely rich. Plus, I can only suppose that, having been the cause of so much of my trauma, paying to 'fix me' seemed only fair to him. 'It's your inheritance anyway,' he told me. 'And if this is what you want to spend it on, then who am I to argue?'

The clinic, near Zurich, was incredible. It was like staying in a five-star hotel.

In morning therapy, I admitted just how traumatic my sister's death had been, and during EMDR I remembered having told her that I hated her just a few days before she died. After a particularly traumatic hypnotherapy session, I recalled feeling jealous, of all things, that Dad had chosen my sister, not to mention guilty about that jealousy. There were layers and layers of trauma left from my childhood that none of the new-age therapies I'd messed around with had even begun to touch. But suddenly, here they were, submerging me, and I was thankful to be surrounded by smiling, well-trained staff ready to hose me down with high-pressure jets afterwards, so that I could inhabit my body once again rather than remaining lost in the horrors of my mind.

By the time I got back to England it was late July, and Joe, Heather and the kids had vanished.

It was Ant who gave me the news on the doorstep when I popped in to see my son, and the fact that I managed to cope with even that just goes to show how much better I was feeling.

Ant was back in his old house and I spotted a young woman wafting around in the background, who I could only assume was my replacement.

I wondered, for a moment, what she was like, but then decided that was really of no importance to me. What was important was seeing Ben.

That was only yesterday, but it feels like about a week ago. Time flows strangely since I cracked my mind open on the edge of Lake Zurich. There's so much for me to think about – so much more perspective framing the present, now that all those repressed memories are back.

Right now, I'm walking along the beach with him. We've just eaten falafel wraps while sitting on a bench.

'Are you happy, Ben?' I ask him.

'Yeah,' he says. 'Of course.'

'Are you really, though?' I insist. 'You have to think about it and tell me the truth. It's important.'

'Um . . . OK . . .' Ben says, frowning and kicking the sand. 'Yeah, I am,' he says. 'My room's really cool and we go to the beach every day and I do PlayStation with Lucy and on Fridays we have pizza.'

'And Heather?' I ask. 'Is she nice to you?'

He nods. 'Yeah, she is, Mum,' he says. 'She's really nice.'

'Good,' I tell him, trying to ignore the pinching sensation in my heart. 'That's great. Because, you know, we're going to have to decide where you live and when.'

'Here,' he says, without hesitation. 'I want to live here.'

I glance out at the horizon and take a deep breath. I tell myself I can do this. I tell myself that I am strong. I will not cry. I absolutely will not cry today.

'OK, but when do *I* get to see you?' I finally ask him. He has picked up a lump of driftwood and is dragging it along the beach behind him. 'I love you, and I need to see you sometimes, too.'

'I could come to yours next week,' Ben says, as if this is obvious, as if he's already thought about how best to solve this. 'I was supposed to be going to Ant's with the girls, but I don't really want to. He's such a knob.'

'Right,' I say. 'OK, that works for me. Does that mean you wouldn't mind coming to me for at least part of *every* school holiday?'

'Sure,' Ben says, with a shrug. 'Why not?'

'In which case, you'd have to go to school up here during term time?'

Ben looks up at me and nods again.

'You don't mind changing schools, then?'

He shakes his head. 'I'll be in the same school as Lucy anyway,' he says.

'Right,' I say. 'OK, then. That's the way we'll do it.'

I reach out and ruffle my son's hair. I'm proud of myself. I have not cried. These tears? They're just from the wind in my eyes.

When we get back to the house, Joe has gone out, purportedly to do some shopping.

'He's avoiding me, right?' I ask Heather.

She wrinkles her nose. '*Yeah* . . .' she says. 'Yeah, he probably is, a bit.'

She offers me another cup of herbal tea and then sends Ben off to play with the girls so we can talk.

'I feel that I need to thank you, Amy,' she says earnestly.

'Thank me?' I say. Of all the things I expected from Heather, thanks were not at the top of the list.

She nods. 'You might not want to hear this, but Joe and me and the kids . . . Well, we're just so happy, Amy . . . We have to keep on pinching ourselves. Being together, being here in this house . . . It's all just so unexpected. And none of it would have happened without you.'

'Without me sleeping with your man, you mean?' I ask, subconsciously trying, I suspect, to provoke her.

But Heather just nods. 'Yes,' she says. 'That's exactly what I mean.'

I swallow with difficulty and have to blink another pair of tears into submission. I look out at the back garden and see Riley and then remember that Riley is now called Dandy. She's even got my cat. Talk about winner takes all.

'I'm sorry,' Heather says, reaching for my wrist. 'I'm being insensitive, aren't I?'

'No, it's fine,' I say. 'It's really fine.'

'I'm trying to be more honest about things,' she says. 'But I don't always get the balance right.'

I brush away the wetness with the tip of one finger and manage to smile at her weakly. 'At least you're not angry with me,' I say.

'No,' Heather says. 'No, I'm really not.'

'Look, I'm happy for you,' I tell her, and for the most part it's true. I also hate her quite intensely, but I decide not to say that bit. Far better to appear magnanimous, after all. 'I'd much rather Joe was happy,' I say. 'Even if it's not with me.'

I start to cry, then, and there's nothing I can do to stop it. The tears roll down my cheeks.

Heather squints at me as if she has toothache and waits for me to speak.

'I miss him,' I tell her when finally I'm able to do so.

'Joe?' she asks. 'Or Ben?'

'Oh, both of them,' I admit. 'But Joe, well, that ship has sailed, hasn't it?'

By way of reply, Heather merely sighs.

'As for Ben . . . I don't know how I'm going to cope without him,' I say. 'I love him so much. But then you get that, don't you. You're a mother.'

'I do,' Heather says. 'But I don't think anyone's expecting you to cope without him, are they?'

'He wants to live here,' I admit. 'He wants to live here with you and go to school up here with the girls. I was devastated when he told me, but I don't think he noticed.'

Heather nods and looks like someone who's trying not to look relieved.

'So, you'll get to see him in the holidays, then. That's almost as long. And it's probably better quality time than when he's out at school all day anyway.'

I sniff and nod. 'I know that,' I tell her. 'But it's going to be so hard.'

'Of course it is,' she says. 'But you know you can visit any time you want, right? We've got lots of spare rooms here at The Waves.'

I laugh.

'Pricing will be jolly reasonable too,' Heather jokes, with a wink.

'I'm not sure how Joe would feel about that,' I say.

'No,' Heather agrees. 'Well, maybe not just yet. But one day soon. We'll get there, won't we? To being friends, I mean?'

'Sure,' I say. 'We can try, at any rate.'

'Do you have somewhere to stay tonight?' she asks, and I'm touched by her concern.

'I do,' I tell her. 'I'm at the Bay Royal.'

'Oh, good,' she says. 'It's supposed to be nice there.'

'Could I borrow Ben again, do you think? For dinner? It's just that tomorrow, I'm going to head home, so . . .'

'Oh, of course,' Heather says. 'Take them all!'

I laugh. 'Nice try, but I'll just have Ben, if it's all the same to you.'

She nods and smiles. 'He's your son,' she says. 'Don't worry. We're not going to forget that. We're never going to forget that.'

'Actually, Ben said – you know, for next week? He said he'd rather come to mine.'

'Of course,' Heather says. 'I don't blame him. If I had to make that choice, I'd rather go to yours too.'

She reaches out for my wrist again, but I snatch it away. 'Don't,' I say. 'Please don't be too nice, otherwise I'll cry again.'

'Sorry,' she says. 'People being nice always makes me cry too.'

'Is Ant doing the same thing?' I ask. 'Taking the girls in the school holidays?'

She nods. 'Not that much, to tell the truth. Not as much as I would have thought. But it kind of suits me that way, if I'm being honest.'

'Yes,' I say. 'I'm sure.'

'Maybe later on,' Heather says. 'Perhaps he'll take them more once things settle. Or maybe not.'

'Did you know—?' I start to ask, but Heather is speaking at the same time.

'He's got a girlfriend, now,' she says. Then, 'Oh, you know, do you?'

'Yes, I saw her,' I tell her. 'She was there.'

'What's she like?' Heather asks.

'Skinny,' I say, with a shrug. 'Young. Very young.'

'You don't care then?'

I shake my head. 'No,' I say honestly. 'No, I really don't.'

'No. Me neither. You know, Amy, just so you know, I always liked you.'

'Why, thank you!' I say, embarrassed at the unexpected compliment.

'I just . . . I don't know. I needed to say that for some reason. Because it's true, I suppose. And I never said it.'

'Oh, I just remembered,' I say, standing. 'I have something for you in the car.'

Heather follows me outside to the Mazda and I pop open the trunk. The sun is shining and gulls are screeching and swooping overhead, surfing the sea breeze.

'Oh,' Heather says, not sounding particularly thrilled as she peers at the contents. 'The Buddha!'

'I thought I should bring it back,' I say. 'It was a wedding gift from Reg. He brought it back from Thailand, I think. You said you liked it once, didn't you?'

'I liked it at *yours*,' Heather says. 'But it's very big, isn't it?'

366

I laugh. 'You don't want it at all, do you?'

'It's just so big,' Heather says. 'And so green.'

'I can take it back home if you want,' I tell her.

Heather stares at the Buddha for a moment and gently taps a finger against her lips. 'Would you mind?' she says finally, while brushing her hair from her eyes. 'It's just . . . I really . . . I don't know . . .'

'You're right,' I say, finally understanding. 'It doesn't belong here, does it?'

'No,' Heather says. 'Not really. I mean, we could ask Joe, but . . . well . . . especially as it was a wedding present.'

I close the trunk just as Joe's pickup arrives. He climbs out and comes to join us. 'So, how are my favourite two ladies?' he asks, gently resting a hand on each of our backs.

'Um, I doubt that I'm still among your favourites,' I say. 'But that's OK. I deserve it.'

Joe frowns, visibly considering the matter. 'No,' he says. 'No, you're definitely still up there, in the top two.'

I pop the trunk open, revealing, once again, the Buddha.

'Ooh!' Joe says. 'The Buddha in the boot.'

'Yes, we're just discussing what to do with it,' I explain. 'Do you think Reg wants it back?'

Joe shakes his head. 'He'd be mortified,' he says. 'It was a wedding present.'

'It was supposed to bring us good luck,' I remind him.

'Yes,' Joe says. 'Exactly. Like I say, he'd be mortified. Just flog it, maybe, if you can? It's got to be worth a bob or two. I don't want it any more, that's for sure.' And with that, he slams the trunk shut. 'I bought the paint,' he tells Heather, 'for the dining room.'

'Ooh!' Heather says, 'Let's see.' She follows him to the rear of the pickup truck and exclaims, 'Christ, Joe! What the hell is that?'

'It's paint,' he says. 'It's called *Crimson Night*.'

'We said *teal*, Joe,' Heather laughs. 'That's about as far from teal as you could find. In fact, if you had one of those colour charts, that would be right on the opposite side of the wheel.'

'That may be true,' Joe says, scratching his ear. 'But I think it'll look cool, don't you?'

'A boudoir is what it'll look like!' Heather says.

'Maybe a boudoir is what I'm aiming for.'

'You're so naughty!' Heather says, reaching out to poke him in the ribs.

'Yeah, but not as naughty as you,' Joe says, fighting back.

I stand there in a daze, watching them. They look so right together that it hurts. They look as if they have never been apart. They seem young, for some reason, too, as if they're just starting out in life. Which, in a way, I suppose they are.

'I'm off,' I shout, giving them a fingertip wave. 'I'll pick Ben up about seven, OK?'

'But we need to talk, don't we?' Joe says. 'We need to talk about Ben.'

'No, it's sorted,' I tell him. 'Everyone's agreed.'

'It's OK,' Heather reassures Joe, slipping one arm around his waist. 'Everything's OK.'

'Oh, OK,' Joe says. 'I'll, um, see you later then, Ame. Seven, you say?'

'That's right,' I tell him. 'I'll be back at seven.'

Joe

We watch Amy drive away, and then I turn to Heather and frown. 'Have you negotiated a peace deal in my absence, clever clogs?'

She grabs one of the pots of paint from the truck and I lift the other one and begin to follow her across the main road. 'I have,' she says. 'Though, actually, I didn't have to negotiate anything at all.'

We enter the house and stack the pots of paint against the wall. 'Well?' I ask.

She turns towards me and pecks me on the lips. 'Only everything we wanted,' she says.

'Term times here?' I ask, and Heather nods. 'School holidays with Amy?' Another nod. 'You're a genius,' I tell her, kissing her back.

She takes my hand and leads me through to the kitchen. 'It really *wasn't* me at all,' she says. 'It was just what Ben wanted. All I did was reassure her that we'll never get in the way of her seeing him.'

'That's still amazing,' I say. Things have been so messy for so long and suddenly the last cloud on my horizon has vanished. I wish I'd bought champagne instead of paint.

'What?' Heather asks.

'What, *what*?' I say.

'What, *what*?' she repeats comically. 'I mean, what are you grinning about?'

'I just can't believe everything's sorted,' I tell her. 'Just like that.'

'I know,' she says. 'It's like a dream, isn't it? This house, the kids, the two of us . . . Who ever thought any of that could happen?'

At that moment, Sarah enters the kitchen. 'Mummy,' she says. 'I can't find the Lego.'

'That's Lego,' Heather says, releasing my hand and crouching down to indicate the object in Sarah's hand.

'I mean the *rest* of the Lego,' she says. 'I want to make a plane. Ben's got a proper one, and if I find the box of Lego then I can make one, too.'

'What's this, though?' Heather asks, examining the wheeled monstrosity in Sarah's hand.

'It's a bus,' Sarah says, holding it up. 'Like the one at the airport in Spain. But now I want to make the plane.'

'Well, I'm sorry, honey, but I don't know where it is,' Heather says. 'You'll just have to look.'

'But I *need* it!' Sarah says. 'Can you look, *please?*'

'Not right now, sweetheart,' Heather insists. 'I'm afraid you'll just have to make do for now. But I'll look for it later, I promise.'

'But I need to build a plane!' Sarah says again.

'Hey, why don't you use those pieces to make a plane?' I suggest, crouching down to join them both at floor level.

'You can't use a bus as a plane,' Sarah says. 'Silly!'

'If you pull it apart, you can,' I tell her. 'Pull it to pieces and use the bricks to make a plane.'

'But I don't want to pull it apart,' she says.

'Well,' I say, looking up at Heather and winking. 'Sometimes, in order to build something new, you first have to break something old into pieces.'

Heather frowns at me for a moment before she understands what I'm saying, and then slips into a smile instead. 'That's true, actually, Sarah,' she says. 'Just make sure whatever you decide to build is much better than the thing you're pulling apart and you'll be fine. That way you'll have no regrets.'

Sarah grimaces. She looks unconvinced.

'I'm sorry, honey,' Heather says. 'But for now that's your only choice. But later on, I'll help you find the box, OK?'

Sarah rolls her eyes and tuts, making us both laugh, and then flounces her way out of the kitchen.

We straighten and I spin Heather around so that I can slip my hands around her waist.

'So, is *that* what we've done?' she asks as I nuzzle her neck. 'I was wondering.'

'What's that?' I say.

'Have we pulled something apart to build something new?'

I laugh and kiss her neck. 'We have,' I tell her. 'That's exactly what we've done.'

'Well, I hope the new relationship *is* a bit better than the old one,' she says cheekily.

'It had better be,' I tell her, tickling her waist. 'Otherwise, there'll be trouble.'

ACKNOWLEDGMENTS

Thanks to Rosemary for the original idea from which this novel hatched and for being my writer's touchstone since this whole adventure began. Thanks to Lolo for being there day to day as I slog out those words. And thanks to Victoria, Celine, Jenni, Sarah and everyone else at Lake Union for all their hard work on this novel.

ABOUT THE AUTHOR

Photo © 2017 Rosie Aston-Snow

Nick Alexander was born in 1964 in the UK. He has travelled widely and has lived and worked in the UK, the USA and France, where he resides today. *From Something Old* is his sixteenth novel. Nick is the author of multiple international bestsellers, including *Things We Never Said*, *The Photographer's Wife* and *The Other Son*. Nick's novels have been translated into French, German, Italian, Spanish, Norwegian, Turkish and Croatian. Nick lives in the southern French Alps with his partner, four cats and three trout.